SWEPT AWAY

"No," Arienne whispered. She must end this crazy thing between them before it got out of hand. But how to stop it when her own body was awakening to desires she had never before experienced?

"Stop, please stop," she begged.

"You don't want me to stop, Arienne Dauphina Lloyd," he said. "You've never been kissed before, have you?"

"I've had lots of kisses."

Joshua's hold tightened on the back of her neck until her lips were poised a hairsbreadth above his. "Were any of them like this?" he asked huskily.

Sapphire

VENITA HELTON

HarperPaperbacks
A Division of HarperCollinsPublishers

HarperPaperbacks *A Division of* HarperCollins*Publishers*
10 East 53rd Street, New York, N.Y. 10022

Cover illustration by Renato Aimee

First printing: June 1993

Printed in the United States of America

HarperPaperbacks, HarperMonogram, and colophon are
trademarks of HarperCollins*Publishers*

❖ 10 9 8 7 6 5 4 3 2 1

To S. J. H. ,
my knight in slightly dented armor,
for inspiration.

V. H.

Prologue

July 21, 1861

Only the insane would have chosen Bull Run for a picnic on this particular day, yet on the hills surrounding the battlefield, Washingtonians lunched on cold fried chicken and lemonade. Major Joshua Langdon wondered how they had the stomach for it.

Through a wall of artillery smoke nearly as black as his hair, Langdon squinted at a Confederate battery crouched on the crest of a hill near a stone farmhouse. Beauregard had chosen his position well. His damned rebels were blasting the amateurish Union army to hell and back.

Langdon drew on a thin black cheroot clenched between his teeth to raise a glowing ash, then extended the cigar toward the fuse of the twelve-pound cannon he commanded. His crew winced in expectation of the earsplitting blast, but at that moment a clay-colored horse carrying a man in blue dashed out of the Federal lines toward the Confederate battery, straight across Langdon's line of fire.

The artillery commander reacted instinctively, crushing the burning fuse with his bare hand, his steel-gray eyes narrowing as he recognized the feckless rider he had nearly killed. The first sergeant thought he was going to swear, but Langdon only said, "Looks like Brigadier General Hunter intends to commit suicide."

"Murder, too," the sergeant said, angrily watching a brigade of Union infantrymen dodging up the slope on the heels of Hunter's bay.

Moments later there was a crackle of musket fire, and the general's horse screamed before crashing sideways onto its rider. The Federal troops broke and ran for cover.

"You're in command, Sergeant!" Joshua Langdon vaulted over the tree limbs his artillery crew had hastily thrown up in front of the battery at the commencement of the battle. At top speed he zigzagged toward his commander. Around his feet minié balls raised puffs of dust. Shots rang in his ears.

Two yards to go. He hurled himself through the air at the downed horse. Out of the corner of his eye he saw a Confederate rise up over a fallen tree, his carbine throwing a fiery kiss.

He hit the ground hard and rolled to a stop against the general. His left leg was numb from the hip down. It was a moment before he realized blood was pumping from a bullet wound in his thigh.

"What the hell are you doing here, Major Langdon?" General Hunter's legs were pinned beneath the horse. His scalp bore a long red crease.

"Thought you might like to get out from under the horse, sir," Joshua said in an eastern Tennessee accent. A cannonball thundered into the dirt nearby, bounced once, then rolled into the Federal lines. Bullets thumped into the horse. "Figured you could use some help."

"You figured wrong, Major! I'll get myself out. How the hell can I win this engagement if my artillerists abandon their posts? Get back to your gun!"

"Yes, sir!" The first pains lanced his muscular thigh. He rolled onto his back, braced his boots against the horse's backbone, and pushed upward with all his might, ignoring the blood streaming down his leg. Hunter dragged himself free and lay panting, facedown, behind the sheltering bulk of the horse.

"Are your legs broken, sir?"

"We'll soon learn." The older man's words were swallowed by a cannon fusillade. A dense cloud of black-and-yellow smoke rolled across the field, temporarily hiding the pair from the enemy.

"No time like the present to find out, General." Langdon yanked Hunter to his feet and half carried him across the cratered field to the Federal lines. Moments later an exploding shell obliterated the general's horse.

Safely deposited behind a hillock near Bull Run Creek, Hunter waited impatiently while an orderly tore open his trousers legs and inspected his injuries. A short distance away Joshua Langdon passed out from loss of blood.

1

August 2, 1861

Sir James Lloyd stared out of the library window at the formal gardens of Lloyd on the Downs. Little had changed since his boyhood. The boxwoods and trees planted in his great-grandfather's day remained lush and green, carefully pruned into fanciful shapes by the old gardener. Water streamed from urns poised on the bronze-green shoulders of sylphs, replenishing a host of ornamental fountains. On the Thames boys in small boats tacked back and forth, just as he had done sixty years ago. He could almost believe he was still a small boy in knee breeches.

A flash of red from the trees beyond the gardens brought the old man back to the present. A slim girl in a scarlet coat and a tall silk top hat, her ebony hair streaming behind her like the tail of the bay hunter mare she rode sidesaddle, galloped out of the woods.

As Sir James watched, the girl leaned over the mare's neck and urged her toward the four-foot privet hedge bordering the gardens. Great clods of dirt peppered the air behind the flying hooves, and then the mare launched herself into space and soared over the hedge like Pegasus.

Sir James went white and clutched his chest, screwing his eyes shut against the sight of his only child falling from the saddle. But when he ventured to open them again, he saw that she had landed safely and was cantering toward the far end of the garden. He exhaled.

"James! Have you been paying attention?" said a thick voice behind him.

Nervously adjusting the cravat knotted at his skinny throat with one hand, he combed his fringe of thin gray hair with the other and turned to look into the florid face of Lord Wendell Stuart Lloyd III, the British ambassador to the United States.

At sixty-eight, James's older brother had lost the good looks that, coupled with his great wealth, had won him the respect of men and women on two continents. All that remained of his former self were the polished opal eyes and the perpetual sneer, as if he detected a bad odor in the room. He lolled on the cushions of a tapestried love seat, one gouty foot straining the legs of a small embroidered stool.

"I heard what you said, Wendell Stuart," Sir James

said, returning his gaze to the more pleasant view in the garden.

The girl was jumping the mare over garden benches and boxwoods in a game of steeplechase. James fervently hoped that Wendell Stuart was deaf to the drumming hooves and the delighted shouts. Although he had allowed Sir James to live at Lloyd on the Downs for the past eight years as the caretaker, while he himself lived in Washington, Wendell Stuart would be sure to take a dim view of his niece's antics.

"Well, what do you think?" The ambassador picked a thread from one of the cushions.

James fingered his cravat, wishing he could turn back the clock to last night, before his brother's unannounced arrival from Washington. "I don't think that the Liverpool cartel ought to involve itself in the scheme you're proposing," he said. "This business of my escorting that murderous Louis DeCoeur to Pensacola to build torpedoes . . . and trying to get the plans for the Confederacy's underwater death ship . . . it's too heinous. History would judge us harshly if we were to accomplish such misdeeds, I should imagine."

Lord Wendell Stuart's color deepened to that of a ripe plum. "Your blasted opinion matters this much!" Heaving himself off the love seat, he slammed the heavy silver knob of his walking stick down on a Queen Anne writing desk, following up with a blow to the globe stand that sent the miniature world hurtling against a bookcase.

James retreated several steps. His faded blue

eyes flicked back and forth like those of a trapped rabbit.

"You're the cartel's attorney," Wendell Stuart said. "Or have you forgotten that fact, coddled here in the lap of luxury as you are, living off me like some bleeding sort of leech?"

Sir James drew himself up to his full five-foot, seven-inch height, choked down his fear, and wrapped his dignity around himself like a cloak. "I earn my keep, and I haven't forgotten my obligation to the cartel. Still, this scheme you propose is monstrous and I'll have no part of it."

Wendell Stuart's rage left him abruptly. Breathing stertorously through his mouth, he fell into his chair and unbuttoned the waistcoat straining across his vast abdomen. He mopped his wide brow with a silk handkerchief. "You don't have any choice."

"I can resign," Sir James said. His own temerity amazed him.

The ambassador's opaline eyes narrowed. "Aye, you can always do that. However, I'll no longer allow you to live at Lloyd on the Downs. I'll hire another caretaker."

"You may do so with my blessing. I should like to retire, anyway."

Wendell Stuart sucked air noisily into his lungs, taken aback by his brother's cool rejoinder. "You should, eh? And how will you keep young Arienne in the manner to which she's grown accustomed?"

Sir James looked around the library, his brother's

inheritance from their father. "My daughter and I will move to a town house in London. My years spent working in New Orleans left me nicely fixed. I'm not a poor relation, you know."

Wendell Stuart's lips parted in a vicious smile. "Oh? Perhaps you should call on your banker."

Sir James suddenly felt like he'd swallowed a pincushion. "What . . . what do you mean?"

"I mean that foreseeing your gutless reaction to what is clearly your duty, the company has seized your assets—"

"You can't do that!"

"—until such time as you strike a lucrative bargain with the Confederates," Wendell Stuart finished, levering his right foot onto the stool.

"Why don't you strike the bargain yourself? It was your idea in the first place!"

"My position as the British ambassador precludes any attempt on my part to deal with the Confederacy. Queen Victoria wouldn't want another American war." He leaned toward the end table, splashed some bourbon into a thick crystal tumbler, downed it in a gulp, and poured himself another.

Sir James turned to the window. His daughter had left the garden to gallop pell-mell for the stable. As the bay mare gathered herself to leap the brick wall, the rider skillfully shifted her weight to accommodate the animal's changing center of gravity. Clearing the wall by a hand, the pair landed easily in the yard.

A groom strode out of the harness house to help the girl dismount. James could see them exchange a few words as she untied the scarf securing the hat to her black hair. She flung the topper carelessly aside and then shoved her hand into the pocket of her long woolen skirt. After a brief search, she found a lump of sugar for the mare, gave her a final pat, and stalked regally from the yard.

Sir James became aware of his brother's harsh breathing. He turned to find him leaning on his tall cane, his eyes burning brightly as he gazed through the leaded panes of glass.

"By all that's holy, James, is that Arienne?"

"Of course."

"I had expected a child."

"Children have a habit of growing up. She's seventeen now."

Lord Wendell Stuart laughed. "Seventeen, the age of coming out. How will Arienne Dauphina Lloyd look coming out into London society dressed in rags because her father was too slack-witted to do his duty?"

James's world caved in. Since his wife's untimely death in New Orleans eight years ago, his only joy was Arienne, his only expectation to secure her future.

"Think about it, Jamesy-boy," Wendell Stuart said. Turning on his heel, he paced like an emperor from the library, his progress through the house marked by the heavy rap of his cane until a door slammed in the distance.

James's heart spasmed again. Dropping limply into an armchair, he fumbled in his pocket for his vial of digitalis.

* * *

Arienne paused on the threshold of the dining room to let her deep sapphire-blue eyes adjust to the dim glow of candles. Her uncle was seated in her father's customary place at the head of the table, his elbows resting on either side of a half-empty bottle of whiskey and a plateful of tea cakes, his expression thoughtful. He looked much older, much heavier than she'd remembered, but a warm rush of love filled her at the sight of him.

Holding her green taffeta hoopskirts behind her, she tiptoed up behind him and kissed his cheek, jumping back with a chuckle when he bellowed with fright and came halfway out of his seat.

"I caught you napping, Uncle!" Her voice was musical, with a French-Creole lilt.

"You nearly frightened me to death, young woman, appearing like that out of the dark night!" he said, collapsing back into his chair.

"As you richly deserved after not visiting us in nearly five years!" With her taffeta rustling, she hurried around his chair and planted a kiss on his forehead.

For a moment the smell of violets and rosewater filled the old man's nostrils, and he got a brief, close-up look at the ivory cameo brooch on the velvet choker around her throat. He quickly averted his eyes from her breasts, which swelled above her low-cut bodice.

"What sort of landlord are you, anyway?" she asked as she straightened.

For the first time in his long years of statesmanship, Wendell Stuart Lloyd couldn't think of a reply. The glimpse of his niece on horseback that morning had not prepared him for this glorious creature in hoopskirts tonight.

Arienne laughed at his expression. "Has it really been five whole years since we've seen each other?"

"It's been an eternity." Wendell Stuart clambered to his feet, grimacing when his gouty foot struck the leg of his chair.

"Are you all right?" Arienne wondered if she'd startled him into fits.

"Quite, my dear," he replied, regaining his ambassadorial dignity. Wishing he were years younger, yet knowing he still possessed a rather compelling masculinity, he took her hand and looked down into her huge eyes. "It's good to see you again."

"Thank you, Uncle. I hope you'll stay a long while." She glanced at the tea cakes on the table, then at a tall grandfather clock by the French doors. She looked at her uncle uncertainly. "I was planning to ring for dinner, but if you'd rather wait, why, I suppose Papa won't mind."

"There's no need to wait," he said. He patted his paunch, chuckling. "I've saved a bit of room."

"Good. Papa likes dinner by eight o'clock. I'm surprised he's not already at the table, fretting over the time." She crossed the room to tug a bellpull on the wall beside an elegant Queen Anne console. "I hope living in Washington hasn't

spoiled your taste for artichoke soup and leg of
lamb."

"Not in the least. Here, let me seat you," he said as
she returned to the table.

Taking her elbow in his hand, he settled her onto a
stool to the right of his chair, catching sight of her
ankles just before the hem of her skirt dropped like a
bell to the floor. Reclaiming his seat at the head of
the table, he began to sip his whiskey. The clock
ticked loudly in the corner.

Arienne cast about for something to say, dis-
mayed when she couldn't think of a single thing. It
used to be easy to talk to Uncle Wen, years ago in
New Orleans. He'd visited her parents and her at
their tall white house on Carondolet, told funny
stories, bounced her on his knee. He'd filled her
pockets with shiny picayunes and sent her to the
French Market to spend them on candy sticks and
pralines.

It was difficult to accept that their relationship
had changed over the years since she'd seen him.
It had to change, of course. She was a grown
woman now, and Uncle Wen an elder statesman.
Still, there ought to be some familiarity between
them.

She watched him covertly as he sipped his
whiskey. He seemed preoccupied, distant. She
wished her father would come. Unnerved by the long
silence, she fumbled with the pearl comb clasping her
heavy coil of hair at the nape of her neck. The room
was suddenly stifling.

Wendell Stuart, unaware of her discomfort, leaned

back in his chair and rested his whiskey tumbler on his abdomen. He smiled absently at his niece, admiring her honeyed skin tones, her cheeks and lips of desert rose. Her eyes were wide and blue, fringed with long, sooty lashes. She looked very like her Irish mother.

"You've some freckles on your nose," he said abruptly. "Odd. I don't remember your mother having them."

"I'm my father's daughter, too, remember," she said, relieved that they'd found a topic, even one as trivial as freckles. She dropped her hand from her hair. "You Englishmen have your fair share of brownie kisses. They go away when I stay out of the sun, which is seldom."

"I find them utterly charming," said Wendell Stuart, raising his whiskey to toast her.

Arienne acknowledged his accolade with a smile. "You are very kind, Uncle Wen. Do you remember that time when—"

"Excuse my tardiness," Sir James said, entering through the French doors. "Trouble with one of the carriage horses." He pecked Arienne on the cheek and sat down across from her. If he was perturbed that Wendell Stuart had taken his seat, he gave no sign, nor did he seem to remember their argument.

"Nothing serious, I hope?" Arienne said.

"A touch of colic. Tim let him eat too many windfall plums yesterday. He'll soon be right."

"Tim ought to be horsewhipped for incompetence," Wendell Stuart said, his chins quivering with anger.

"He's only ten years old," James replied.

"He won't see eleven if he damages any more of my horseflesh!"

Arienne touched her uncle's sleeve. "I'll speak to him, Uncle Wen," she said quietly. "He's normally very good with the stock."

Wendell Stuart drew a ragged breath, controlling his anger. "Just see that he keeps his eyes open in the future. I don't have money to throw around, you know."

"I know."

"You won't have horses to ride if he continues this sort of carelessness."

"I understand." She looked across the table at her father and noticed his face growing red. Afraid of an explosion, she went on, "I'd like you to know, Uncle, how much I appreciate being allowed to ride your horses. You are very generous."

Wendell, swelling at the compliment, forgot his irritation. "I saw you this morning, my dear. You looked part of the animal."

"I love to ride. Papa will tell you that I abandon my studies in favor of it."

"I can see why. You've an excellent form."

Sir James shifted in his chair. "She spends all day riding," he said testily. "How she intends to get a beau I haven't the foggiest."

"I haven't met anyone, yet, that I like that much, Papa." She paused when a servant entered the room holding a porcelain soup tureen shaped like a swan.

"Perhaps I can introduce you to the sons of the more prominent men in the district," Wendell Stuart said, watching the servant fill his bowl. He stuffed a corner of his dinner napkin into his high, stiff collar and adjusted the bib over his waistcoat. "Had I known that you'd grown into such a charming young lady in my absence, I would have paid a visit much sooner and fulfilled my avuncular duties."

"How long do you intend to stay?" Sir James asked.

Wendell Stuart slurped up most of his soup before answering. "Long enough to see you on your way to Florida, James."

"Florida!" Arienne's eyes glistened.

"Don't get excited—you're not going," her father said.

"But of course I will! You've been promising me a trip to America for a long time."

"Their blasted war makes traveling far too hazardous for a young girl," the ambassador said. He patted her hand.

Arienne jerked her arm away. "Is it any safer for an old man with heart trouble?"

"It's safe enough," James said, not looking at her.

"Nonsense!" Arienne jumped up and ran around the table to throw her arms around her father's thin shoulders. "I've lost Mother—what if you die, too?"

Wendell Stuart forced a smile. "Your father isn't going to die. He has some company business to transact. He will be quite safe, I assure you."

"Then there's no reason why I should stay here!"

James pushed her away gently. "You've got your

studies at the conservatory to think of. Besides, the horses would miss you. I'll be back before you know I've even gone."

Arienne looked from her father to her uncle. How different the brothers were! Yet they stood united against her. She turned and fled the room.

Wendell Stuart tapped his cheek with his soup spoon. He thought he'd had James where he wanted him. Might this girl ruin their understanding? His brother was just weak enough to give in if Arienne pressed him hard enough. Women could be too damned persuasive.

An hour later Arienne, clad in pantaloons and a thin camisole, bent over a porcelain washbasin in her room. Her eyes were red and her throat was raw, but her tears had finally stopped. Unlike her mother, Arienne tended to cry easily, to her everlasting disgust.

Soaping a rag, she began to scrub her face vigorously. She was determined to talk her father out of his mysterious trip. Knowing him as she did, it was obvious that he had no stomach for the business he was supposed to contract. Uncle Wen was trying to coerce him into doing something that violated his principles, but what was it? Rinsing the soap out of her eyes, she groped blindly for the towel.

"Oh, excuse me, Arienne. I hadn't realized you were preparing for bed."

She spun around to find Wendell Stuart standing

behind her, holding the towel. Backlit by a kerosene lamp, he was a dark, gigantic silhouette.

"Unc-Uncle Wen." She retreated against the washstand, gripping the polished wooden edge behind her. "What do you want?"

The ambassador took a step toward her, holding out the towel. She plucked it from his hand and covered her breasts, knowing that her wet camisole hid nothing from his eyes.

"I just wanted to reassure you that no harm will come to your father."

"He's not well. He'll not make the trip if I have anything to say about it. And I do, I assure you!"

"I've come to talk to you about just that. Sometimes we must do things we don't wish to do," he said. "Your father is a very important man. I need him."

"For what? What is so important that you cannot send someone else?"

Wendell Stuart touched her bare arm with his fingertips, his eyes holding hers. "Would you trust the fate of queen and country to someone else, my dear?"

Arienne could scarcely believe what she was hearing. "The fate of England rests in Papa's hands? Aren't you being a bit dramatic, Uncle?"

"I wish I could say yes, but I'm afraid I cannot." He encircled her wrist with his hand and pulled her closer. His bright eyes bored into hers. "You mustn't try to stop your father. It's very noble of you to feel responsible for him, but you're taking too much on yourself."

Arienne controlled a prick of fear at his nearness.

"Does this mean he's changed his mind about going?"

"No, he hasn't changed his mind. He sees his duty and will do it as an Englishman should. My concern is that your objections will hinder his success."

"That makes no sense."

"It does. A statesman cannot perform well if his mind is elsewhere."

"He can't perform at all if he is dead!"

"Now who is being dramatic?"

"I think you'd better leave, Uncle. Right now."

He chuckled softly and reached up to touch her hair. "There was a day when you'd beg me not to go. Your mother would have to threaten you with a switch to make you let go of my trouser leg."

Arienne tried to step away from him, but the wash-stand blocked her path. "I was five years old, Uncle. Our relationship then has nothing to do with this. Now get out of my room before I start screaming!"

His face hardened. Dropping his hand, he stepped back a pace. "Your father is going to Florida, whether you like it or not."

Arienne felt tears welling up again. "You are heartless. I don't know why Mama or I ever cared for you!"

Anger snapped in his eyes, but he made no move to touch her again. "Your father sails aboard the *Magna Carta* in three days. If you can be reasonable and refrain from upsetting him anymore, I'll let you go with him. Otherwise he goes alone. But go he shall. He doesn't have a choice."

"If he gets sicker, the blame will be yours!"

"It will be yours if you continue to upset him."

She glared at him. "When do we leave?"

"In the morning. My carriage will take you to Liverpool to meet the clipper. Were I you, I'd start packing. And remember, no more outbursts."

2

September 17, 1861

Arienne Lloyd sat on the afterdeck of the *Magna Carta,* her back braced against the bulkhead, her feet leaning on the rail. On her lap she held a wooden paintbox with a half-finished watercolor pinned to the surface. The lacy white frock she wore was spattered with indigo, and a streak of the same bisected her left cheek.

Black storm clouds rolled toward the clipper out of the northeast. To the west the clear sky afforded the artist a breathtaking view of the sunset. As though touched by King Midas, the Gulf of Mexico was changing slowly to gold.

Arienne glanced at her father, who was sitting hunched like an old eagle on a coil of rope a few feet away. He had grown extraordinarily thin during the six-week voyage from Liverpool. His shaky, blue-veined hands trembled as he tried to light his pipe. "Dash it!" he exclaimed as the rising wind spiraled hot ash into his face. "Blast and dash it to hell!"

Arienne smiled. She swished a wet brush through a small cake of watercolor, waited until the ship rode to the crest of a wave, then quickly painted in a cloud before the clipper glided down the other side.

"I don't see how you can paint with the infernal ship bucking up and down like a bloody carnival horse," Sir James said, stuffing his pipe into the pocket of his waistcoat. He centered the knot in his cravat over his prominent Adam's apple. "The picture won't be recognizable."

"It's not meant to be a Boudin, Papa. I'm painting that," she said, pointing her brush at the ragged clouds, "though I shall probably be obliged to finish it in my cabin."

Sir James watched the approaching storm for a moment and then eyed the crew working in the rigging. "I pity those poor blokes, toiling up there in all weathers."

"I envy them. I'd give anything to be a sailor."

"You're just a touch mad, Arienne."

"I prefer to think of myself as imaginative. I can picture myself oscillating a hundred feet up with the wind in my hair, nothing but a tiny rolling ship far below my feet. I'd feel like a bird."

"Until you tried to fly and ended up crushed and mangled on the deck, or prey to some monstrous fish. You couldn't get me up there for the scepter of England!"

"Well, I'd *give* the scepter of England to sit in the tops for even an hour." She frowned at her stained skirts. "Perhaps if I borrowed a pair of trousers . . ."

Sir James recoiled. "Trousers! It's bad enough that you abandoned your hoopskirts the day after we embarked. But trousers! Your . . . your . . . derrière would be exposed to the world!"

Arienne blushed. "It would be covered."

"It would be indecent!" He got up and staggered to the rail. "These waves make me sick."

"Then don't stare down at them," she said. "You'll get worse."

"I couldn't possibly get any worse." Moaning, he loosened his cravat. "I've been sick ever since we shipped out of Liverpool. I haven't eaten anything but broth in weeks."

"Poor thing. You've never been a sailor, have you?" Her heart ached as she noticed his bent back. How could he have grown so old?

She remembered him as he'd looked eight short years ago, just before her mother's death. Although nearly thirty years his wife's senior, he had looked young, a quality he'd attributed to marital happiness. Sara Lloyd's death after delivering a stillborn son had aged him overnight.

This other business had aged him, too, she knew. In all their time aboard ship, he had stubbornly refused to reveal his mission. He spent long hours in his stateroom, emerging pale and worried, meeting her attempts to discover his secret with a shake of the head.

"As I live and breathe, I'll never get used to this dashed bobbing about!" Sir James said with a groan.

"Can I get you something, Papa? Some tea, perhaps?"

"Just throw me overboard." He buried his face in his hands.

"I wouldn't dream of it. You'd hardly be wet before those chaps got you."

"What are you talking about?" He peered through his fingers. He could see nothing below his feet but the nauseating roll of green waves. Then a black triangle broke the surface and knifed toward the ship, veering away at the last instant.

Sir James jumped away from the rail as spryly as a man half his age. "Good heavens, girl! Why didn't you tell me there was a bloody shark in there? It might have bitten my head off!"

"Your friend Mr. DeCoeur says sharks can't jump that high. Look, there goes another one!"

"Another one! How many are down there?"

"Dozens. They've been following us for days."

"Following us? Why?"

"DeCoeur feeds them. You should watch—it's great sport."

"The cook feeds the sharks?"

"Mmm-hmm. The crew nets snapper for dinner, and Mr. DeCoeur throws the heads and entrails overboard." She neglected to mention that most of the time the cook just handed her the bucket and let her do the feeding. "Sometimes we—they manage to harpoon a shark that way. Maybe we'll have one for dinner tonight."

"Arienne."

"Yes, Papa?"

"The thought of a cold, dead shark eye staring up at me from a plate makes me ill. Kindly stop talking about it."

"As you wish. Come, sit down and watch me paint."

Sir James sighed and slumped down beside her, focusing on the raging seascape she was painting. His taste in art was rigidly traditional, but there was no doubt that Arienne Dauphina was good. "You should have stayed at Lloyd on the Downs and continued your studies instead of coming to Pensacola with me."

"You know I couldn't let you go off alone," Arienne said, streaking a long yellow sun ray through a gap in the clouds.

Sir James sighed again. "But you could have stayed and married Conrad Ashbury. His father is the richest man in London."

Arienne shoved her brush into the paintbox. "If Lord Ashbury were the richest man in the entire world, I wouldn't marry his son! Conrad's a simpleton."

"But he worships you. I've seen him at it."

"Pah! I don't want a man to worship me. I should detest him if he did."

"I worshiped your mother."

"That was different, Papa. You were never beetle-headed about Mama. But Conrad, heavens! Don't you recall him sitting in the drawing room staring at me out of those big moist eyes of his, never saying a word? I believe he would have let me saw his head off with a dull knife if I had wanted to."

Sir James chuckled. "He might have at that."

"A girl wouldn't be happy married to a weakling like Conrad."

"I'm sure you're correct—"

"A girl needs someone she can admire."

"I couldn't agree with you more."

"Someone clever, never at a loss for words. A poet, perhaps."

"Quite."

"Or a soldier. A dashing one, and a fine hand with horses."

"Absolutely."

"Someone whose every gesture sets a girl's heart afire—"

Sir James began to fidget with his cravat. "Where did you, ah, pick up that sort of information?"

"From Mama."

"*Sara* told you about men?"

Arienne smiled sweetly. "She told me a lot of things, Papa. She said it's a mother's duty to teach her daughter about love. I don't suppose you'd want to know what she told me."

Sir James shook his head. "I blush to think of it. Sara was rather, um, uninhibited." He was silent for a moment, struggling with emotions he usually managed to repress. "God, I miss her."

Arienne's eyes clouded over. "I do, too." She remembered the carpenter constructing two coffins in the blacksmith's shop behind Jasmine Cottage, their house in New Orleans. One had been very small. There was nothing anyone could have done, the midwife had said.

A vivid flash of lightning stabbed the sea, followed by a crack of thunder. Great drops of rain began to fall. The wind slapped the ship hard, hurling waves over the rail.

Arienne shoved her painting into the box and reached for her father's hand. "Come on, Papa. I'll help you to your cabin. Try not to think about Mama anymore tonight."

Standing on the bridge of the U.S.S. *Sheboygan* late the next morning, Major Joshua Langdon narrowed his eyes and stared ahead intently, as if through willpower alone he could burn holes through the thick fog and unmask the phantom ship the lookout had glimpsed twenty minutes ago.

Had he found the object of his search at last? Since sailing from Key West a fortnight ago, the *Sheboygan* had intercepted two English and three French blockade runners, none of which had yielded his quarry.

Langdon's heroism at Manassas had won him a position with Mr. Lincoln's secret service. Alerted by contacts in Liverpool of Louis DeCoeur's mission, Langdon had, on orders from Secretary of State William Seward, commandeered the *Sheboygan*. DeCoeur was thought to be traveling aboard the *Magna Carta*. The ship's destination was unknown, save that it was making for a Southern port, probably in the Gulf. Langdon guessed Mobile, but if he were to go there and his guess prove wrong, DeCoeur would disappear. His only chance was to track down the French inventor en route.

Deep in thought, Langdon absently rubbed the half-healed bullet wound in his left thigh. He ran a lean hand through his thick black hair, flicked the spotless white tails of his shipboard uniform over the rail, and leaned back, breaking open the chamber of his Model 1860 Colt revolver for the third time.

"Is she still loaded, Major?" Captain Ezra Pratt asked.

Langdon glanced up at the blue-coated skipper, taking in the straw boater's cap angled jauntily over his kelp-green eyes, the bony hands clasped tightly behind his back. "She's loaded all right, sir, and hot for another bit of action like yesterday's."

Pratt raised his hand to his thin cheek, wincing as his fingers traced the furrow made by a French privateer's musket ball during a brief but furious battle the day before.

"I'd hate to think where I'd be now if you hadn't shot the fellow that did this, Major," Pratt said. "He was lining up for a second try at sending me to hell."

Langdon holstered his gun and reached into the inner pocket of his frock coat for a black cheroot. He bit off the tip, lit the cigar, and passed it to Pratt. "Forget it, sir."

"Forget it? I'm the one that should be giving *you* cigars."

The major carelessly flicked a speck of ash from his shoulder bar, grinning boyishly. "You'd ruin my wind—I'm trying to give the damn things up, now that I don't need them to touch off cannons anymore."

The lookout in the main topgallant cut short Pratt's rejoinder. "She's spotted us, Cap'n. She's turning starboard. Fog's too thick to read her name, but she's British, all right."

The two officers exchanged glances. "Flag her down," Pratt ordered. Langdon waited in silence for the signalman in the rigging to flag the message.

"She ain't stopping, sir," he shouted after a minute. "She says to bugger off."

Pratt laughed softly, enjoying the game, and gnawed the cigar. "We'll just put ourselves astern to blanket her wind as she comes 'round, Mr. Greer," he said to the helmsman.

"We need more speed, Cap'n," Greer said, spinning the wheel hard aport.

Pratt barked into the speaking tube, "Engine room! Throw resin to the furnaces and open the valves."

There was a pause, and then the *Sheboygan* shuddered and leaped forward like a racehorse, a filthy jet of smoke spewing from her stack, her masts groaning under a full spread of canvas. The fog parted just long enough for Langdon to catch his first glimpse of a sleek Baltimore clipper almost a mile ahead. She was racing along on a broad reach, her crew raising every bit of canvas they could squeeze onto the yardarms.

Pratt rubbed his hands with anticipation. "This should be an interesting contest, Major. A clipper carrying that much sail is a hell of a bird to catch, and unless my nose deceives me, last night's gale has doubled back on us."

Langdon cursed and rubbed his jaw with the barrel of the revolver that had magically reappeared in his hand. "If that's the *Magna Carta* and she gets away, you can kiss the Union good-bye."

Pratt looked at the major. "That bad, eh?"

"Worse," Langdon said, narrowing his eyes against a sudden burst of rain. The fog was slowly dissipating on the freshening wind, revealing the widening distance between the two ships. "I told you that Louis DeCoeur intends to build self-propelled torpedoes for the Confederacy. What I didn't tell you is that William Seward believes the Rebs are building themselves a nasty little ironclad that sails underwater—"

"Like Robert Fulton's *Nautilus?*"

"Yes, sir. I might've known you'd read about his submarine."

"No one took Fulton seriously, Langdon."

"We'd better take the Rebs seriously, sir. Imagine what would happen if they were to build a submersible ship equipped with DeCoeur's torpedoes."

The two men stared at each other for a few seconds while Pratt made up his mind. "Clear the decks!" he commanded abruptly. "Battle stations!"

A midshipman piped three shrill blasts. Instantly the deck erupted with men—gunners' mates staggering out of the companionway with kegs of black powder under each arm, gunners running out big Dahlgrens, carpenters stowing furniture belowdecks, and seamen stretching nets beneath the masts to catch falling rigging. An artillery officer climbed into the topgallant and sighted on the fleeing clipper, calling the coordinates to the bow gunner. Within four minutes the *Sheboygan* was battle ready, her crew standing silently at their posts. It was eerie, preparing to fight a ship they could only see intermittently.

"Where'd she go?" Pratt said as the clipper disappeared into a rolling blanket of fog.

"Two points to starboard and a mile distant, sir," the watchman shouted. From his lofty height he could discern his English counterpart watching him through a spyglass.

"Flag her once more," Pratt ordered. "Tell her to heave to or be fired upon."

Joshua Langdon stood tensely. He reached into his coat for a cigar, then withdrew his hand empty. "Stop, damn you," he told the invisible ship.

"She's not responding, sir."

"Send her a bow chaser," Pratt said.

"Aye, sir!" The bow gunner waited until the *Sheboygan*'s bow pitched upward before touching off the charge. The big gun belched, and a thirty-pound ball tore through the fog like a locomotive.

Arienne left her cabin shortly before noon. With her bare feet gripping the wet deck, she made her way through the thick fog to the mainmast.

The captain brushed by her, excused himself, and continued his rounds. Sailors bustled here and there, appearing suddenly out of the fog like ghosts.

When she judged herself to be alone, she knotted her skirts at her left thigh, feeling almost naked when her pantaloons fluttered around her legs. Quickly, before anyone saw her, she began to climb the ratlines. Higher and higher she climbed, over the main course and topsail to the topgallant yardarm. Her hair whipped around her like a silken banner, and she had to keep pushing it out of her eyes, but the climb was surprisingly easy and left her only slightly breathless.

"Crikey! What the devil are ye doing up here, Miss Lloyd?" a young lookout said, staring down at her.

"I'm coming up to help you stand watch, Enos," she said, climbing onto the royal yardarm. The mast oscillated heavily between them. "This is everything and more than I'd imagined it would be!"

"Yer out of yer mind, crawling up here! Supposing ye was to fall?"

"I won't. This is easier than riding a horse."

Enos shook his head and raised a spyglass to his eye, muttering under his breath.

"Let me borrow your spyglass for just a minute," Arienne said after a while.

"Can't see nothing but bleeding fog."

"Let me look, anyway."

The youth reluctantly handed her the long brass

instrument. "Awright. But if ye drop the bleeding thing, Cap'n will have me knackers."

"Not if I drop it on his head," Arienne said, chuckling.

"Then he'd want me brain into the bargain! 'Course, he'd strike a poor trade. Me mam says I never had no brain."

Arienne peered through the glass at the small green patches of sea appearing through the swirling white fog.

"See anything? Pirate ships or suchlike?" Enos inquired. He leaned against the mast and closed his eyes. If the crazy girl wanted to stand watch for him, let her.

"Pirates? This isn't the eighteenth century, you know," Arienne said. Suddenly she squinted hard through the glass. No, it was gone. For a moment she had almost believed in pirates. The fog played funny tricks with a person's eyes. She started to lower the glass, then swung it to the right excitedly. There it was again! This time there could be no mistake. "Enos! Wake up and look—there's your pirate ship!"

"Right," Enos said with a sigh, retrieving the glass. He polished the lens with his sleeve, then peered out to sea. "I don't see nothing but fog. Ye're having me on, miss."

"I'm not—it's right there!" She wrenched the spy-glass around.

"Ow! Watch me eye, ye barmy girl! I can't see anything in the bloody fog—crikey! We been found out! Warship a mile off the port beam, Cap'n!" He jumped to his feet and pointed.

Arienne stood up and balanced precariously on the yardarm, one arm around the mast, then reclaimed the spyglass. She could see a big screw frigate closing on the clipper, its belching smokestack dirtying the fog for yards around. "She's flying the Stars and Stripes! It's a Union cruiser!"

"Ye'd better get below, miss!" In answer to the bosun's whistle, sailors were already scurrying spider-like into the rigging. "Them Yanks is bound to start firing."

"They wouldn't dare fire on a British ship!"

"Har!" Enos reclaimed his spyglass. "Cap'n's just piped to battle stations, Miss Priss. We're in for a helluva lot more than a Sunday-school outing, so ye'd best get yer pretty backside below-decks."

Arienne sat down. "I'd rather be shot to pieces than cower in the hold like a rat, so you can just consider me part of the rigging."

"Have it yer way, lady."

"I always do."

But thirty minutes later, when the *Sheboygan* unleashed a bow chaser that crashed into the water a hundred feet shy of the stern, Arienne remembered her father. How could she have forgotten him? She must get him into the hold at once.

Recklessly she launched herself into the ratlines, her fear for Sir James outweighing any thought of her own safety. A second cannonball shredded the heavy clouds and tunneled into the Gulf fifty feet off the port bow, followed by a third that struck the water close to the hull, drenching her with gallons of water.

Nearly drowned under the deluge, Arienne tumbled the last five feet to the deck, landing on hands and knees. As she struggled to her feet three sailors hustling aft with kegs of powder spun her toward the rail.

"Arienne!" Sir James cried, hard on their heels. "Where have you been? I've been out of my mind with worry!" He scooped her up and half carried her down the companionway steps to the hold. There he dropped her onto a crate and slumped down beside her, searching his pockets for digitalis.

"Are you all right?" Arienne wiped her cheeks on her skirt. She hadn't realized she had been crying. Her eyes widened as she noticed her father's heaving chest, his dusky skin tones. "You shouldn't have carried me like that!"

"Get me some water." He took a few panting breaths. "There's a dipper on that keg over there."

Arienne hurried to the keg, her hands shaking so badly that she spilled most of the water on the way back. Sir James tipped in three drops of heart tonic and downed it quickly.

The ship yawed, sending Arienne down in a heap. "I can't believe this is happening! How dare those Yanks fire on us? Why doesn't Captain Hughes shoot back?"

"If he does, we're all dead. I think the Yank just wants him to stop. There, I was right, we're heaving to." He buried his face in his hands and mumbled to himself, "I'm finished when they board us."

Louis DeCoeur, a red-headed, bearlike man wearing a greasy shirt and breeches, crept cautiously aft along the leeward side of the ship, the cabins hiding him from the *Sheboygan*. The Federal screw frigate lay less than fifty yards to windward, her guns trained on the clipper. Rain struck DeCoeur's face and trickled icily down the back of his neck as he squatted on his heels to listen.

"What is the meaning of this outrageous conduct?" Captain Hughes was shouting at the Yankee skipper. "You're violating maritime law!"

"No, sir, we're not!" Pratt shouted back. "Consider this action official notice of a blockade. Your ship is transporting contraband to a hostile port."

"We're transporting nothing of the kind! I protest this utter disregard for the law. The *Magna Carta* is a merchant ship of a neutral power. Stand aside!"

"Captain!" Major Joshua Langdon joined Pratt at the rail. "Flag Officer Goldsborough has ordered any ship making for a blockaded port seized. You are carrying contraband. I also have proof of hostile intent against the United States of America by one of your passengers. I demand permission to come aboard to arrest one Louis DeCoeur, a French national."

"I've no passenger answering that name, Major," Hughes said haughtily. "If you do not allow me steerage within the next two minutes, I will lodge a formal complaint against you with Parliament."

"You won't be able to, sir," Langdon said, "from the bottom of the sea. This ship is under orders to use deadly force to secure the arrest of DeCoeur."

Goaded beyond endurance, Hughes swore at him in ripe quarterdeck language.

Langdon waited until the Englishman finally spluttered into apoplectic silence. "Now that you've cleared the air, Captain," he said, "perhaps you'd be good enough to comply."

Hughes turned tomato red. "Give me an hour to confer with my officers."

"You may have thirty minutes, Captain," Langdon said, opening his pocket watch. "But nothing is changed. We will confiscate your cargo, and I mean to get that Frenchman."

Behind the cabins, Louis DeCoeur smiled as he passed a rope around his ample middle and tied the other end to a stanchion. He eased his legs over the rail and then dropped into the turbulent water.

Down he sank, two fathoms or more, staring upward at the cigar-shaped hull until the rope brought him up short. Agile as a porpoise, he propelled himself toward the stern and surfaced on the leeward side, kicking himself away from the barnacled hull. Waves rose higher than his head.

Taking a deep breath, DeCoeur plunged

beneath the hull. His fingers touched a copper canister approximately three feet long mounted to a swivel near the keel. Fins protruded at right angles from the sides. Inside was a small, lead-enclosed glass vial of sulfuric acid. The dead space was filled with a mixture of ground glass, sugar, and chlorate of potassium. This chemical fuse would ignite the forty pounds of gunpowder housed in the canister.

DeCoeur pivoted the torpedo to face the *Sheboygan*, cocked the fuse hammer, and swam to the surface, uncoiling a long copper wire from his fist. Two minutes later he was safely crouched on deck, crimping the wire to a stanchion. When the time was ripe, he would yank the wire, breaking the vial of acid and initiating the chain reaction that would end the enemy ship's life.

Satisfied that his movements had gone unobserved, he let down a lifeboat until it hung just above the waves. If the *Sheboygan* didn't blow up when the torpedo struck her, she would surely retaliate with a lethal broadside. Louis DeCoeur was in the business of killing people, not dying with them.

As he reached the hold Arienne came around a stack of crates. "What happened to you, Mr. DeCoeur?"

"I took a swim," he answered in French, watching Sir James.

The older man came to his feet. "Keep your mouth shut, DeCoeur," he said, "and maybe we'll get through this alive."

"Perhaps, perhaps."

"What's he got to do with us being stopped, Papa?"

"Nothing, nothing at all." Sir James fumbled with his cravat. "Why would anyone stop us for a cook?"

"They wouldn't," Arienne said, eyeing DeCoeur, "if that were all he was."

"And what would I be, little lady?" DeCoeur smiled at her.

"I'm not sure, but perhaps the rifles in these crates have something to do with it."

DeCoeur stopped smiling when Arienne strode around the stack of crates and pried open the lid of a long, flat box. She rummaged through the straw and then lifted out an Enfield rifle.

"You ought not to play with such dangerous things, lady," the Frenchman said.

Sir James sank down, winding his cravat around his fingers. "How did you find out about those?"

"I opened the crate a little while ago, looking for a blanket for you. I found guns instead."

"Oh, God."

"Those rifles are the reason for our trip to Pensacola, aren't they, Papa? Uncle Wen's making you run guns to the Confederacy." She pointed an accusing finger at DeCoeur. "And you're in league with him."

DeCoeur laughed heartily, raking her with his eyes. "A smart little girl you are, but you're just short of the mark."

"Shut up, DeCoeur!" James Lloyd said. "And the less you know, the better, young lady. Don't admit anything if those damned Yanks come aboard. You're a passenger, an English citizen. You know nothing of guns or a Frenchman. All the blame is mine."

Tears sprang into Arienne's eyes. "You're mad if you think I'll stand idly by while they arrest you! This is Uncle Wendell Stuart's doing, not yours!"

Sir James leaped to his feet and grabbed her by the arms so forcefully that she cried out in pain. "Don't forget that your uncle is the ambassador to the United States. Do you want us all hanged for sedition? Do you want to see England go to war with the Americans?"

She stared back at her father. "I don't give a brass farthing about politics—I just don't want anything to happen to you!"

"Then for God's sake, keep your mouth shut!"

Louis DeCoeur's booming laugh broke them apart. "It was a pretty scene and well played, Sir James, but Captain Hughes bids you come topside. No, not the girl. She's to stay safe down here. She can snoop to her heart's content—we'll only be gone a minute or two."

"I'm coming with you," Arienne said, bunching her wet skirts in her hand.

"You'll stay here." Sir James pushed her down on a crate.

"No!"

He cupped her chin tightly. "Never have I laid a hand on you in anger, but if you persist in this foolishness, I swear I'll beat you within an inch of your life!"

"That's ludicrous!"

Sir James slapped her cheek with his open hand. "I mean it!" he said, his pale eyes filling with tears. "Stay here until I get back. Lie down between the crates and cover up with something. Do it!"

Arienne looked at her father in anguish, as though she had never seen him before. Slowly she got up and made her way between the crates. She lay down, pulled a bit of old sail over her head, and shut her eyes tight against the tears.

"All right, DeCoeur," Sir James said, "let's go."

Arienne listened to them stomp up the companionway steps. When the small door slammed shut, she jumped up, tiptoed to the steps, and cautiously opened the door.

The unexpected sight stole her breath. Wreathed in gray fog against a backdrop of forbidding clouds, the Federal screw frigate had trained her monstrous Dahlgrens on the clipper. Her smokestack erupted an evil stream of black. Her engines were the angry, throbbing respirations of a dragon. Along the decks blue-uniformed sailors stood at parade rest, their muskets aimed skyward. On the bridge a group of officers conferred with bowed heads.

Suddenly one of the men raised his dark head and stared across the turbulent water at her. She involuntarily drew back, for even at a distance the officer's eyes seemed to flash steel sparks that penetrated her skin and burned her to the core. She could see his black brows slashing down like thunderclouds over his eyes as he strode to the rail and seized it with hands as brown and hard as the earth.

For a moment they stared at each other. Her gaze took in the broad shoulders straining the seams of his white uniform and the black hair showing in the open neck of his shirt. Then there was a sudden, terrific explosion, and his ship rolled to windward, exposing a gaping hole below the waterline.

3

Barely a second after the torpedo struck the *Sheboygan,* the concussion rolled back and smote the clipper, knocking men off their feet. Arienne was flung against the bulkhead. She saw stars, but by dint of will kept herself from blacking out. "Papa!" she shouted, scanning the deck. Where was he?

At that moment the wounded screw frigate retaliated with a lethal twenty-cannon broadside. Smoke boiled heavenward, and grape shot cut a bloody swath across the clipper's decks.

Arienne dove behind the bulkhead just as a round of chain shot brought down the *Magna Carta*'s standing rigging, crushing the hands like porcelain dolls. A ball glanced off the rail beside her, shearing off a huge splinter that pinned her skirts to the deck. She struggled to free herself, her nostrils and eyes burning from the acrid smoke, her ears deafened by the guns and bloodcurdling screams of the wounded.

Then the clipper's stern suddenly ripped away. She began to sink.

As the ship yawed, Arienne glimpsed her father. He was lying facedown in a lifeboat, with Louis DeCoeur at the oars. The old man struggled to his knees and waved frantically at his daughter, but the Frenchman caught him by the arm and dragged him down.

"Wait!" Arienne screamed. "Don't leave me!"

She tore her skirts away from the massive splinter, cast off the remnants of her gown, and clad in pantaloons and a camisole, dove over the rail and into the waves.

Seconds later a round of canister blasted away the rail. Underwater, the cannon fire reverberated until Arienne's ears threatened to burst. As she swam down by the stern the clipper created a tremendous undertow that sucked and snatched at her like a sea monster.

Her lungs screaming for oxygen, she struggled to the surface, only to be smashed down again by huge waves flying before the fast-appoaching gale. Mustering all her courage, she fought her way to the top of a swell and strained for a glimpse of the lifeboat. Nothing but black sea, rain, and fog came to view.

Keep your head, Arienne told herself, fighting panic. She must swim back to the *Magna Carta,* but where was it? And where was the screw frigate? Had she lost her sense of direction so completely that she couldn't find where she had come from? She spun around in a desperate attempt to catch sight of the lifeboat. Like its mother ship, the little boat was gone, leaving Arienne to the untender mercy of the sea.

She was tiring. Her arms and shoulders felt as if they were made of lead, and her kicks grew weak and uncoordinated. Not so much as a plank of wood could she find to rest upon. There was little hope of rescue. No doubt, all hands had gone down with the ship. She summoned her father's image to her mind, and that gave her enough hope to renew her efforts for a while.

Gradually his image was superseded by another face, a strong, vaguely familiar face with eyes as darkly gray as the sea. His mouth opened in a smile of unearthly beauty. Transfixed by the phantom's charm, Arienne nearly stopped swimming. Then his hand reached for her, and she swam eagerly toward it.

But before she could reach the phantom, the storm closed in and swallowed him up in a sea of blackness. Arienne screamed and dove after him into a mountainous wave. She came up empty-handed, choking on seawater but restored to reason. There was neither a ghostly rescuer nor one of flesh and blood to save her. If she were to live, she must keep her wits!

Yet wits alone could not save her from sixteen-foot waves and gale-strength winds, she realized as she clawed her way to the tops of watery battlements, only to tumble down their frothing slopes. She stopped struggling for a minute and floated underwater, but soon her lungs demanded air, and she was forced to resume the struggle.

Then the full fury of the gale struck, shearing off the tops of the waves until air and sea merged into a swirling white cacophony. Arienne was borne down into the vortex and tumbled like flotsam until pain commanded every part of her body and she knew that it was not life she felt, but its departing.

Joshua Langdon rammed his lifeboat's oars into the roiling water. He hardly understood his mission. What did he expect to find? Death, more than likely. Yet something more powerful than the ocean's rage drove him on.

Punctuated by thunder, rain slashed down in brilliantly electrified sheets. Like a bucking bronco, a wave lifted and swung him in a crazy circle, leaving man and boat hanging in midair for one terrifying moment until gravity yanked them into a deep trough with a force that nearly sundered them both.

Langdon pulled at the oars like a madman, scanning the void for survivors. There was nothing but foam boiling over curling walls of water. How could he have imagined anyone escaping the mangled Baltimore clipper? Now, unless he could find the *Sheboygan,* he was lost as well. Making a wild guess at where the screw frigate lay, he pivoted the boat and hunched his back in a Herculean effort to row against the towering water. Suddenly his eyes widened in shock.

A slender golden hand was protruding from the

waves near the boat—it needed only a sword to complete the Arthurian legend that sprang to his mind. He reached for the hand, but the voracious waves beat him to it and the Lady of the Lake disappeared.

Joshua immediately whipped a lifeline around his waist and leaped into the froth. He was instantly sucked deep underwater. Losing all sense of direction, he searched blindly for the victim until his bursting lungs forced him back to the living world for a snatch of air. He ducked underwater again, this time diving to the full extension of the rope.

Something soft brushed his fingers. He immediately entwined his hand in the hair and, pulling the slender figure to him, kicked up to the surface. With one muscular forearm around the survivor's waist and the other on the gunwale, Langdon heaved her into the boat, and then he hauled himself in after her.

The girl was as still as death when he took her in his arms, her face cold and pale. It was the girl he had glimpsed in the companionway moments before the world had exploded into flame and terror. The sapphire promise in her eyes had called him, shaken the very foundation of his being, carried him to her through the madding tempest until, against all odds, he had found her. Now he gathered her into his arms and cradled her to his breast.

Forgetful of the storm, he stroked the ivory cheeks, the full lips that should have been pink and laughing, the soft lids veiling the magnificent blue eyes.

Fearful agony at the twistings of fate boiled up in his mind until his body shook with wrath. His handsome features contorting, he crushed the limp body to his breast in an embrace that stole his breath. Again and again he contracted his powerful arms around the girl's rib cage, forcing water out of her lungs.

After a long time he became aware that she was struggling weakly against him, coughing up seawater, crying. Carefully now, lest a movement on his part cause them to capsize, he took her into his arms and cushioned her against the buffetings of the lifeboat.

Arienne opened her eyes, feeling as helpless as an hour-old kitten. She didn't care who or what had saved her, only that this hard body was her strength and refuge.

She drifted into sleep, awakening much later to find the sea calmer, the winds fresh. She lay on her back looking up into velvet-black skies resplendent with stars, a hunter's moon casting its reflection upon the mirrored surfaces of the waves.

She looked left and right at the white-clad thighs holding her body steady. Suddenly she realized that she was lying against a man's bare chest.

"Oh, my heavens!" She leaped up and scrambled to the opposite end of the boat, her eyes on the man reclining against the coaming.

He came instantly awake, his gray eyes scanning the sea for danger. Seeing only the girl, guessing the source of her discomfiture, he chuckled and leaned back again, bracing his knees against the gunwales. But when Arienne continued to stare at him, he said in an east Tennessee accent, "Don't fret your head about me, ma'am—I'm a man, not a sea monster."

"I know what you are." His every detail was visible in the moonlight.

His tattered shirt of white linen, open due to several missing buttons, disclosed a thick mat of black hair over chest muscles that would turn a stevedore green with envy. His white breeches fit snugly across his narrow hips and around his long legs.

When he smiled at her, a dimple appeared in his left cheek that accentuated his devilishly handsome features. His eyes glimmered like stars in the sky. He was the man she had seen before the explosion, and the phantom she had conjured while she struggled in the sea.

Langdon looked back at the lovely girl in perplexity, chafing a little under her scrutiny. What was she looking at? he wondered. He was impervious to his own attractiveness. It had never entered his head to see himself as anything other than a reasonably adequate man.

"Are you all right?" he finally asked.

"I think so. You pulled me out of the water, didn't you?"

"Yeah. I was lucky to come across you."

"So was I."

"Who are you?" he asked, his silvery eyes caressing her. In a moment she would realize her soaked undergarments were completely transparent and then, he supposed, she would be all atwitter to have his shirt and hide her voluptuous curves. A shame, he thought, to drape a Venus.

"Arienne Dauphina Lloyd." She couldn't take her eyes off him. Surely on planet Earth there couldn't be another man even approaching this one for sheer physical beauty.

Joshua repeated her name several times, liking the sound of it. Her speech, too, pleased him. He had never before heard upper-class English spoken with a Creole inflection.

"Does my rescuer have a name?"

"Langdon. Major Joshua Tobias Langdon, ma'am." He pillowed the back of his head on his muscular arms, his eyes slowly taking her measure.

"Major?" Arienne snapped out of her almost dreamlike state and recalled Langdon's immaculate shipboard whites, the gleam of gold on his shoulder. Although his uniform coat was gone, the authority of rank remained in his manner. She tossed her long, wet hair over her shoulder. "Now I see. I suppose I should thank you for pulling me out of the Gulf, Major, but in view of the circumstances, I feel more inclined to slap your face."

"What circumstances?" Langdon asked in surprise.

"What circumstances?" Her temperature rose a degree. "How about the ones resulting in my ship being blown out from under my feet and a very brave crew sent to the bottom of the sea! How are those for starters?"

Langdon's brows drew down stormily. "The *Magna Carta* reaped what she sowed, or have you conveniently forgotten that your captain fired on us first?"

"All I remember is that an American warship ran down a harmless merchant vessel from a neutral country and blasted her to pieces!"

"Harmless! Do you call a gunrunning, maniac-toting privateer *harmless?*"

"Are you calling my father a maniac?"

"If he had anything to do with the battle, I certainly am!"

"Well, he didn't, you idiot!" She looked away from him, out across the waves, wishing with all her soul that her father's boat would appear. Where was he? Had DeCoeur gotten him safely through the storm?

"Were you traveling with your father, Miss Lloyd?"

She preferred to ask a question of her own. "What are the chances of a rowboat reaching land during a gale like that?"

"You think your father escaped in a rowboat?"

"Yes."

"Did you fall overboard, fleeing with him?"

"No. I saw him from the ship."

"Hmm. Interesting."

"I don't think I like your tone."

"And I don't think I like your father, saving himself and leaving you to drown."

"It wasn't like that! He didn't have any choice in the matter."

"I see. The other survivors wouldn't let him come back to save you, is that it?"

"Something like that."

"How many escaped with him?"

Arienne was suddenly wary. Her father had warned her to reveal nothing about what she had learned. Why should this stranger care how many escaped the *Magna Carta?* Could he be more interested in *who* had escaped? If so, then the interdiction of the clipper was more than chance. Perhaps Wendell Stuart's plotting had not been a secret, after all.

"Your father must be awfully worried about you, Miss Lloyd. I imagine he's upset with his companions for deserting you." He looked at her for a while before saying offhandedly, "Do you happen to know if Louis DeCoeur was among them?"

Her heart bounded into her throat. How could he have known about the Frenchman? More importantly, what did he know about her father?

"I don't know anyone by that name," she said, staring straight into his eyes. Despite her bravado, she feared he knew she was lying. She fought a powerful urge to drop her gaze.

"Perhaps he was traveling under another name."

"In that case, I can be of no help at all, can I?"

The dimple appeared in his cheek. "DeCoeur would speak with a French accent. His hair, I believe, is bright red."

"Sorry." Unable to bear his steady gaze a moment longer, she leaned her head against the stern and looked up at the stars.

"It's very important that I find him."

"I can't help you."

"You can't, or you won't?"

"Are you accusing me of lying, Major Langdon?" she said, raising her head.

"Now, that would be ungentlemanly, wouldn't it?" Before she could retort, he said, "There's a chance that your memory is a little faulty, after what you've been through."

"My memory is perfectly intact, sir."

"Glad to hear it." He fell silent.

Arienne's nerves stretched tight as a bow-string, wondering what he was thinking. Who was this Southerner? Why was he in the Union army, and what reason did he have for wanting DeCoeur?

"What port was your ship making for, Miss Lloyd?"

There it was, then, the question she'd been dreading. "I'm not sure."

"You're not sure?" He made no attempt to disguise his incredulity. "I thought your memory was intact."

"Why don't you leave me alone?" She sat up, her eyes snapping angrily. "Don't you have something better to do than harass me, like rowing the boat, or something?"

He clasped his arms behind his head. "I would, if I hadn't lost the damned oars."

"Lost the oars! How are we going to get to land?"

"I hope the current will carry us. We're not far from Florida."

"What if we don't get there? We don't have

any food, no water, no shelter! We'll die out here!"

"We'll figure out something."

"How can you be so calm?" The thought of being lost at sea panicked her.

"No use getting worked up. We can pass the time talking."

"I don't want to talk to you."

"I'm afraid we're in for some mighty long silences, then."

"Look, can't we tear a plank off the gunwale and use it for an oar?"

He gave the heavy oak gunwale an experimental tug. It didn't budge. "We can probably manage to work it loose in a fortnight or so."

"You act as though this business were a joke! What's the matter with you?"

She rose angrily to her knees and yanked at the gunwale. Her soaked underthings left little to the imagination. Langdon sucked in his breath and stared at her taut breasts, her slender hips and thighs. He had seen many a woman wearing nothing but pantaloons and a camisole, but this one took the blue ribbon. Several blue ribbons. He released his breath in a low, reverent whistle.

Arienne snapped her head around to glare at him. Finding his gaze on her body, she looked down, discovering that her thin white camisole gave her no more coverage than a shredded cobweb. She screeched in shame and outrage.

Langdon grinned as she dropped into a fetal position, her hair shielding her body. "You don't have to cover up on my account," he said. "You're no strain on the eyes. I know scores of women who would kill to have what you've got."

"You—you voyeur!" The water sloshing in the bottom of the boat muffled her voice. She unleashed a string of invectives, most of which he failed to catch since she chose to remain in a ball.

"Would you mind repeating that last insult? It might prove useful next time I need to start a bar fight."

"If you want a fight, I'll give you one right now!" She launched herself at her rescuer, her small, hard fist aimed at his nose, her hair flying behind her like the wings of a hawk diving for the kill.

Langdon's breath rushed out as her knee ground into his belly, but he managed to block her punch by catching her wrist in his gun hand. While he struggled for breath, Arienne writhed in silent agony, unwilling to give him the satisfaction of seeing her cry. She began to fling herself about in an effort to break free, a movement that set the boat rocking dangerously over the heavy swells.

"Are you . . . are you out of your mind?" Langdon crushed her to his chest to hold her still. Her feet drummed against his shins, wringing a curse from him. "Stop it, you little banshee! You'll capsize us."

"Let go of my wrist!" She was surprised when he instantly did so. Dropping her head onto his chest, she cradled her wrist in her right hand.

The major's resonant voice rumbled against her ear. "Have I hurt you? Is it broken?"

"It's sprained, I think. You didn't do it."

"But I didn't help it, either. Sorry." He awkwardly patted her back.

"Let go of me!" She raised her head, recoiling as she found herself staring into his steely eyes from a distance of two inches. His warm breath touched her face, sending a wicked shiver down her spine. Pressed full-length against her, he was at least a head taller and twice as wide at the shoulder. She pushed against his chest. "Let me go this instant!"

Langdon, captivated by her wild beauty, found it difficult to loosen his arms. In all the world there could not exist another pair of eyes like hers, eyes that sparkled like iced sapphires in the moonlight. He wanted to rain kisses on those sulky pink lips, to wage war on them with his tongue.

He could take her, of course, and even make her enjoy it, but there would be hell to pay afterward. A gentleman didn't take a beautiful stranger and treat her like a whore. Besides, she'd been a passenger on the *Magna Carta* and, despite her reticence, might be able to provide information about DeCoeur. No matter what his baser urges, his mission came first.

Heaving a sigh, he opened his arms. She scrambled back to her place at the opposite end of the boat and tucked her knees up to her chest, glowering.

"I'll tear a piece off my shirt, if you like, and bandage your wrist to control the swelling."

"That won't be necessary, Major."

"Well, if you change your mind—"

"Just keep to your side of the boat."

"Fine." He bailed water with his cupped hands for several minutes. "I've never been struck by a torpedo before."

"What are you talking about now?"

"The explosion on my ship that started the battle. Unless I miss my guess, we were struck by a self-propelled torpedo."

Arienne had only a vague idea of what he meant. She'd read in the *London Times* that the Confederates had mined their rivers with barrels of gunpowder—a practice the Union decried as an ungentlemanly way to fight a war. A torpedo was probably something like that.

"Captain Hughes would have had no reason to attack you, Major. He was obviously outgunned. He wouldn't have compromised the safety of his ship."

"No, he wouldn't have, but Louis DeCoeur would."

There it was again. She looked quickly away before he could read the flash of recognition in her eyes. "I'm sure you're mistaken."

"Am I? What are you so afraid of, Arienne?"

"It's 'Miss Lloyd,' to you, sir." She couldn't keep a tremor out of her voice. What had her father said? *Do you want us all hanged for sedition?*

"You're frightened. I can see it. Why don't you just admit you know DeCoeur, and tell me his destination?"

"Why don't you drop dead?"

"I probably will after a few days, if the *Sheboygan* doesn't find us."

Arienne caught her breath. She'd assumed the Union cruiser had sunk along with the clipper. "You mean she might be looking for us?"

"She had better be. Pratt knew I was going after survivors."

In that case, it was doubly important that she keep her mouth shut about DeCoeur. No matter how much she desired to be rescued, she mustn't reveal what she knew.

"You've nothing to fear by telling the truth, Miss Lloyd."

"I've nothing to say." She curled up as best she could and closed her eyes, shivering.

"I wish I could give you a blanket," Joshua said. Arienne's eyelids flickered but she didn't reply. He settled back against the coaming to watch her. Eventually she would talk. By tomorrow evening, at the latest, he would know where DeCoeur was headed.

That DeCoeur had escaped in the lifeboat he had no doubt, just as he knew with absolute certainty that the inventor had torpedoed his ship. The only question in his mind was why this girl was covering for him. Was she in love with him? Was her father involved in the plot? His secret-service contact in Liverpool had been certain about some things, vague about others. Joshua needed more information.

"Tomorrow I'll get it," he said to himself, staring at the lovely girl in the stern.

Three hours passed in silence. Fighting sleep, he

continually scanned the Gulf for the *Sheboygan*. Was she searching for him, or had she already steamed to Key West for emergency repairs?

He was staring off the starboard beam when a swell raised the lifeboat. For a moment he thought he was seeing things. Had his imagination conjured the moon-washed sail he'd just seen?

Standing up, he braced his feet against the gunwales as the boat dipped into a trough. In an agony of suspense, he waited for the boat to climb another roller.

Ghostly in the moonlight, a full-rigged ship reached across the waves toward the little boat. It was not the *Sheboygan*.

4

Langdon's full-throated bellow awakened Arienne from sleep. He was standing in the boat, waving his shirt over his head.

"What is it? Your ship?"

"No, a China clipper," he said. He yelled again at the three-masted ship knifing silently toward them through the darkness.

"Have they seen us?"

"I hope so. Yes—hear those yells?"

Straining her ears, Arienne detected faint shouts. The ship drew nearer. Someone at the prow unshuttered a kerosene lantern and played its thin beam about the waves until it finally came to rest on Joshua's naked chest.

"Rescued, by gum!" He looked around at Arienne. "Whew, we'll be in a hell of a spot if they see you in that."

Arienne glanced down at her wet rags, knowing

she looked almost naked. "What do you suggest I do, Major Langdon? Find a dressmaker's shop?"

"Your gown, m'lady," he said, gallantly presenting her his ragged shirt.

Arienne wasted no time getting into the garment. The tail covered her to the knees. "Will this do?"

"Yeah. Now if we could make you ugly in the next five minutes, we just might manage."

"I should have thought I was ugly enough already." She tossed her unruly mop.

"Not by half." The ship was so close that he could see dozens of faces clustered at the bows, and here and there a musket aimed his way. "Try drooling and making vulgar noises."

"Major!"

Joshua sat down, screening the girl from the crew. "This is no time for vanity. We're about to be 'rescued' by a pirate ship."

"A pirate ship?"

"Well, a blockade runner, then. Same as."

"How can you tell?"

"The ship's painted white. They do that for reasons of invisibility. She's not showing her colors, either."

"What are we going to do?" she said uneasily, remembering the gruesome stories she'd heard of pirates.

"Get married."

"Ha! You must have struck your head, or swallowed too much water."

"I'm not mad. Pretending you're my wife is the best way I know to protect you. With luck, the captain will respect the laws of God. As far as matrimony is concerned, anyway."

"I see."

"Good, now listen carefully. I'm going to tell the captain I'm an officer in the Army of the Tennessee, coming back from leave." The clipper was forty yards away, moving at a crawl. He could clearly see pistols and knives in the hands of the crew, and a smooth-bore cannon looming over the bow. "We were making for Mobile when our ship was attacked and sunk by a Yankee cruiser."

"That part sounds familiar," she said acidly. It was this man's fault that her father was floating somewhere in the Gulf with Louis DeCoeur.

"You've got to back up everything I say, if you're asked. Do you understand, *Mrs. Langdon?*"

If her father had drowned, this man was to blame, and if he were alive, this man was a threat to him. "I understand that it was your blasted Yankee cruiser that sank the *Magna Carta,* Major U.S. Army Langdon."

Joshua's startled expression as he turned to look at her might, in other circumstances, have made her laugh, but now she only glared at him out of eyes as coldly blue as the sea.

"I thought we'd resolved that issue," he said angrily.

"Nothing's resolved until I find out if my father is alive or not!" Her venomous retort changed to a gasp of pain when he seized her arm.

"We can resolve that question later, you silly little schoolgirl. For now you'll do as you're told and play the part of a loving wife."

"And what part do you play—the scalawag who molests her in the bottom of a boat?"

"Molests her?" Joshua said in a low, furious tone. "You're the one who jumped on top of me, trying to beat my brains out, or were you hoping for a kiss?"

"You fatherless hound!"

"My pa would disagree with your judgment."

"A man like you doesn't have a pa!"

Pain flitted across the major's face and was gone, replaced by cold rage. "If you intend to keep your virtue, Your Highness, you'd best curl up to me and act chummy. I can't be responsible for the consequences otherwise."

Arienne ground her teeth in frustration and leaned stiffly against his back. "If I had a boat hook right now, it would be all over for you, Yankee."

"Thank God it got lost overboard."

"Too bad you didn't follow it in."

"Too bad, indeed. Then we could have both ended up shark bait."

"The only shark in these waters is already in the boat."

The clipper came about and stood off a short distance to windward. "Ye picked a right good evening for a sail," called a gruff voice from the quarterdeck. "Can ye row to us, lad?"

"No, sir. We've lost the oars."

"Awright. We'll throw ye a line. Stand by."

A halyard snaked through the air and struck the gunwale. Joshua seized it before it could slide into the water and made fast to the painter. Then he attached a second line to the stern and steadied

Arienne in his arms as the boat was hauled up the shadowy, barnacled hull of the ship.

Several rough hands grasped Arienne under the arms and deposited her on deck. Blinking under the assault of a kerosene lantern shoved close to her face, she stepped back against the rail.

"Gad, look at the wench!" said a sailor. He and his mates surged toward her, an almost palpable wall of stench from their unwashed bodies preceding them. Arienne shrank back, convinced she would have been better off with the sharks.

Joshua stepped aboard and pulled her close, gazing down at her with a calm strength that she found infinitely reassuring. He was a good ten inches taller than she, and formidable to look at. "My thanks, lads," he said in a resonant baritone, "for pulling a pair of drowned rats out of the sea."

Arienne fervently hoped that she did, indeed, look like a rat, though the crew might not care how she looked.

They had shifted their attention to Joshua, however, who stood half a head taller than the tallest among them. Arienne read a look of wary respect on the swarthy faces as they moved back several paces.

"Now then, lad, Cap'n Ames'll have a look at ye."

A short, rotund man of about sixty stomped through the crew. He planted himself in front of Langdon and tilted back his old-fashioned tricorn hat to better see him. "Who the hell are ye?"

"Name's Langdon. This is my wife," Joshua said, watching the crew out of the corner of his eye.

"Yer wife? She looks more like yer sister, laddie, with them dark locks." He stretched out a thick forefinger to flick a curl off her bosom. Arienne jerked her hair away. "Aye, yer baby sister."

Langdon laughed. "Now that would be illegal, wouldn't it?"

Ames chuckled. "Aye, and we wouldn't be having no lawless deeds aboard this ship, would we, laddies?" He winked at his crew, who chuckled.

Langdon grinned and stuck out his hard palm. "I can tell you're an honorable man. Thanks for picking us up, sir."

The captain ignored his hand. "Were ye shipwrecked, then, that we found ye abobbing about in the dark of night?"

Joshua squeezed Arienne's waist warningly. "You might say we were shipwrecked, sir. A Yankee cruiser sank us."

This announcement provoked uneasy murmurs from the crew. Many a filthy hand flicked the edge of a cutlass or checked the load of a musket.

Captain Ames narrowed his eyes and looked Joshua up and down. "How long past, lad?"

"Last evening."

"And ye've seen naught of the Yank since?"

"No, sir. She was taking on water from a hit below the waterline the last we saw of her."

The crew rumbled again, this time with satisfaction. Captain Ames removed his tricorn, placed it over his heart, and said in a tone of deep reverence, "May the fishies dine on Yankee flesh tonight, leaving naught but bones for the crabs, and may God in His heaven grant all Yanks the same end."

The crew roared "Amen." Captain Ames screwed one eye shut and told Langdon, "It'll cost ye a packet to sail on the *Scarlet Lady,* son. Have ye money?"

Joshua turned out his pockets. "Not on me. I've a banker in Mobile."

"It's New Orleans we're heading to. Ye'll have to think of some other payment." He smiled at Arienne, and his crew waited like wolves to spring.

Feeling Arienne shiver almost imperceptibly, Joshua gently pulled her closer. He was willing to fight to the death for her. If it came down to it, he decided, his last mortal act would be to carry her with him to the bottom of the sea rather than sacrifice her to the slavering pack.

"I've connections in New Orleans," Joshua said calmly. He detected a spark of avarice in Ames's eyes and quickly followed up his advantage. "Getting you a hefty purse of gold in return for our safe passage should pose no problem at all."

"Now yer speaking my language, laddie. I think two thousand in gold will do nicely. Think ye can raise the sum?"

Joshua pretended to consider. "I could buy a couple of prime field hands for that much, sir. Nope, make it fifteen hundred and you've got a deal."

Arienne dug her nails into his ribs. What was the crazy man thinking of, bargaining like a market woman at a time like this? She glared at the sailors' ugly, lust-crazed faces.

Ames only chuckled and fingered his bristly chin. "So ye value yerself and yer little sis less than a pair of bucks, do ye? Awright, eighteen hundred and not a penny less!"

"Eighteen hundred it is, sir, and your guarantee that we'll disembark no worse off than we are now."

"Done and done!" Captain Ames said, thrusting out his palm. "Welcome aboard the *Scarlet Lady.*"

Joshua clasped his hand firmly. "We need a private place to sleep, Captain."

"Ye can have first mate's cabin." He jerked his thumb at a scarred man standing close to Langdon. "Ye don't mind, do ye, Robert?"

The first mate showed his teeth in a horrible smile and winked at Arienne. "Nay, Cap'n. I'll be close by if the missus needs me."

"Just show us to our quarters," Langdon said in a coldly authoritative voice. Holding Arienne's hand tightly, he pushed his way through the crew.

Arienne noticed that he favored his left leg slightly as he walked. Had he hurt himself rescuing her?

Robert stared after the couple and then grabbed a lantern from a sailor and hurried to take the lead. Nearing the stern, he stopped to unlock the door of a tiny compartment. "Here's your quarters."

Joshua took the lantern and ushered Arienne into the cabin. "The key, mate," he said, holding out his hand.

Robert hesitated, but the major's steady gaze seemed to unnerve him. He handed him the key. "Anything else you'll be needing?"

"Food and water. Lots of it."

Muttering, the man shuffled off to the galley. Arienne examined the cabin. There wasn't much to see, just a bunk and an empty cask that served as a seat. Stale bits of food, broken bottles, and gouts of tobacco littered the floor.

Arienne picked her way carefully to the bunk, her nose wrinkling at the rank odor rising from the woolen blankets. She shoved open the porthole and drank in lungfuls of fresh sea air. Langdon stood in the doorway, looking out.

Soon Robert returned, bearing a trayful of hardtack and salt pork, a bottle of brown ale, and two cracked mugs.

Joshua shut the door after him and turned the key. He hung the lantern on a hook then squatted down to rake the food and broken glass into a pile, heaving the rubbish out of the porthole.

"Hungry?" he asked, sitting down on the opposite end of the bunk.

"Starving." She frowned at the bottle of ale. "I thought you asked for water."

"I did, but this stuff's safer than the scuttlebutt we would've gotten, I reckon." He popped the cork with his teeth and splashed a spoonful into each cup, swirled the nutty-brown liquid around for a minute, then dashed it to the deck. "That ought to make a few cockroaches happy." He filled the cups and passed one to Arienne.

"Oh, it's awful!"

"Drink it anyway. You're dry."

"I don't know how that can be. I drank half the Gulf of Mexico."

"Salt water dries you up inside." He placed his finger under the cup and tilted the ale into her mouth.

This time the brew didn't taste quite as bad, so she downed it quickly and refilled her cup. "I didn't realize I was so thirsty," she said after she'd refilled it for the third time.

Leaning back against the bulkhead, she crossed her legs like an Indian and washed down a hardtack biscuit with hearty swigs of ale. She tried to watch the stars sliding by the porthole, but her gaze was drawn to Joshua again and again.

He was reclining on one elbow, his left foot on the floor, his right knee bent. His untouched cup of ale rested on the flat plane of his belly. Even in repose, his dark torso rose smooth and granite hard from his torn breeches. Noticing her gaze, he ran his hand through his hair and grinned, deepening the dimple in his cheek.

Arienne looked away, blushing. Being closeted so privately with this man caused her pulse to throb. She had to try to focus on something else. "Where are you from, Major?"

"Sevierville, Tennessee."

"Then the accent isn't fake."

Joshua cocked a brow but said nothing.

"How is it that a Southerner ended up in the Union army?"

He thought about it a minute. "I couldn't stand to see the Union dissolved, I guess. I happen to believe in her, despite her problems."

"You don't believe states should have the right to decide their own fortunes?"

"We tried that after the War for Independence and almost lost it all to England again. Nope, the Union must stand together or we'll finish with nothing."

"Are there more who believe like you in Sevierville?"

"Quite a few. My father, unfortunately, isn't one of them."

"And your mother? Does she believe in what you're doing?"

"Don't mothers always believe in their sons?"

"I wouldn't know. How long since you've seen her?"

"Too long. I refused to turn in my uniform for Confederate gray when hostilities broke out. My father told me never to come back."

"You were in the army already?"

"You're awful full of questions," Langdon said testily.

"You're the one who said we might pass the time talking." She took another sip of ale. "People don't become majors overnight."

"They do in wartime, but I'll confess to prior service. I took an engineering degree from the University of Alabama, class of 1851, then went on to West Point for artillery training. I spent considerable time out west."

"Killing Indians, I suppose!"

"Only those who tried to kill me first."

She withdrew into huffy silence and took a long swallow of ale. Langdon split into two images as she glared at him over the top of the cup. She squinted hard at him until he merged into one.

"You look like an angry pirate princess," he said, his gray eyes twinkling in the light of the lantern. "By grannies, what a sight you are in those rags!"

She pulled his shirt closer around her, covering her knees. "Don't try to win me over with flattery, Major Langdon." She topped her cup for the fourth or fifth time. The ale had improved so much after the last few cupfuls that she couldn't see any point in going thirsty.

"Do you need to be won over?"

"No. Especially not by an Indian killer like you."

"What are you so damned mad about?" He dropped his fingers to her knee.

Arienne pushed his hand away and bit into another biscuit. She scowled at him while she chewed, and then drained her mug. "I'm not mad. I simply don't like you, that's all."

"Because you think I'm responsible for attacking your ship." Langdon was suddenly angry. "All right, then, I'll admit that I would have blasted her out of the water, myself, if I could have been assured of killing Louis DeCoeur in the process!"

"I was right about you—you're nothing but a conniving, murdering Yankee!" She seized the bottle and considered his frontal bone, wondering if she could get through his guard. Joshua gazed back at her, an unreadable expression in his eyes.

She finally sniffed in exasperation and, turning up the bottle, drained it to the last drop. "You're a thoroughly despicable human being, Major U.S. Army Langdon." Her speech was slurred.

"Don't call me that. I'm an officer in the Confederate army."

"You're a lying Yankee and you make me sick!" She gazed out of the porthole and hiccuped. "I can't stand being here with you!"

"Perhaps you'd rather bunk with Captain Ames, Mrs. Langdon."

"Why don't you go jump in the ocean?"

Joshua pillowed his head in his arms, his muscular chest rippling like a tiger's, his cup balanced on his hard abdomen.

In spite of her anger, Arienne had to battle a sudden urge to run her hands through the black mat of hair on his chest. Seeing her expression, Langdon said, "You don't want me to jump in the ocean. I think you like being locked in here with me."

"You puffed-up gamecock!" She drew her arm back to throw the empty bottle at his head.

Joshua pounced on her like a leopard, pinning her wrist to the wall. Warm ale from his cup splashed over her breasts. He dragged her beneath him, his mouth hungrily claiming her lips.

Arienne raked his naked back with her free hand

and bucked. Twisting her mouth away from his hard kiss, she shouted, "No! Get away from me, you Machiavellian roué!"

Joshua stiffened as though she'd flung a bucket of ice water over him. "Machiavellian roué? What are you talking about?"

"I'm talking about a man who tries to steal a girl's virtue and then . . . Oh, I'm going to be sick!"

Joshua's hallmark was his capacity to make lightning decisions. Whisking her to the porthole, he held her head while the ale forced its way out of her stomach into the Gulf of Mexico. She finally sagged back against him, exhausted.

"You poor kid," he said, smoothing damp tendrils of hair away from her clammy brow. He wiped her mouth and covered her with the blanket. "You're not used to drinking, are you?"

"I've never had anything more powerful than sherry, until tonight," she said, shuddering uncontrollably.

"I'll get you some water."

"No! Don't leave me!" She grabbed him by the seat of his trousers as he turned to go. "Those pirates might come in!"

Chuckling, he extricated his pants from her grip. "I'll lock the door behind me and I won't be gone but a minute. Be quiet now, lamb."

Arienne picked fretfully at the blankets. Five minutes passed, then ten, while she waited in growing alarm, marking the passage of time by the brightening day. She was just throwing off the covers to go look for him when the key scraped in the lock and he staggered in, slamming the door behind him.

He was covered with blood and someone had blacked his left eye. An ugly welt stretched from his shoulder to navel. He was holding a jug of water.

Arienne leaped out of bed and pushed him down in her place. "What happened to you?"

"I was attacked."

"They've cut you to bits—you're bleeding!"

"Not very much. Most of it belongs to the other chaps. Here, have a drink of water," he said, pouring her a cupful.

"I don't want any!"

Joshua contemplated her dolefully. "After all the trouble I went to to fetch it, now you don't want any?"

Arienne wordlessly snatched the cup from his hand and drained it. Then she yanked off the shirt he had lent her and, dipping it into the jug, began to wash off the blood. She gingerly placed a wet, folded piece of cloth over his black eye and pushed his head down on the pillow.

"All right," she said, "tell me what happened."

"I went down to the galley and had a pleasant little chat with the cook. When I started back up the companionway with the jug of water, three of Ames's best and brightest jumped me from behind."

"Why would they do that?"

Joshua sighed and gave her hand a pat. "I guess they wanted the key to our little stateroom, here."

She flushed and looked away. "There were three of them? That must have been some fight."

"I was lucky I had a nice, heavy pitcher. The cook was kind enough to refill it for me."

Arienne shook her head in amazement. He grinned up at her and winked his good eye. At least she thought it was a wink. It was difficult to be sure with the bandage over his other eye.

"Do you think we'll make it to New Orleans in one piece?" she asked.

"I don't know, but one thing's for sure."

"What's that?"

"I'm knocking three hundred dollars off for this black eye."

Arienne laughed and, dropping her head, planted a kiss over his eyebrow. She immediately drew back, her laughter gone, looking as though she had just touched a hot iron.

"Your eyes are as wide and blue as a Smoky Mountain mincral spring," he said softly, touching her cheek.

"Don't." She got up and stood with her back to him. In her agitation, she didn't consider how she looked in her flimsy underthings.

Joshua took the rag off his face to better behold her. His eyes traced a burning path over her buttocks and down the long line of her legs to her ankles, which showed beneath the hems of her pantaloons. She was a fetching sight, a spunky woman worth giving up anything in hoops and bonnets, if it weren't for the war.

He lay back with a sigh, his thoughts reverting to Louis DeCoeur. "Arienne, come and sit down."

Her back stiffened, then the fight seemed to go out

of her and she turned and sat at his feet. He spoke quickly before his fractious body could betray him into taking her into his arms.

"Was DeCoeur aboard the *Magna Carta?*"

"I answered that question before."

"I don't think you told me the truth."

"Why would I lie?"

"That's what I'd like to know. Are you in love with the Frenchman?"

"Certainly not! I mean, I don't even know him!"

"I see. Then you won't mind my telling you about him."

"Suit yourself." She stared out the porthole. Where was her father? Had he, too, been rescued? What if the Union cruiser had picked him up? The thought made her feel sick.

Joshua watched the emotions flitting over her face. If he could outrage her enough, he felt sure she would tell him what she knew.

"Eight weeks ago, William Seward of the secret service received intelligence that a madman by the name of Louis DeCoeur was hired by the Confederacy to build a self-propelled torpedo."

Arienne paled. So DeCoeur *had* started the conflict! And her father, sweet mercy, what horrible thing was he involved in?

Langdon continued, "This DeCoeur makes his living blowing up innocent people. He's killed scores of his own countrymen, not to mention countless enemies of the state."

"I don't know why you're telling me this," she said in a small voice.

"We were informed that he planned to sail from Liverpool on the *Magna Carta*."

Her father in league with a murderer? Dear God, no. This was all Wendell Stuart's doing. Her father surely didn't know the depth of his own involvement. It was up to her to protect him.

"I'm sure your information was wrong, Major. I met no one named DeCoeur aboard ship."

"I mentioned already that he might have used another name."

"If so, he certainly didn't confide in me or my father!"

So that was the connection. Arienne wasn't covering for the Frenchman, but for her father. "What is your father's involvement with DeCoeur, Arienne?"

"Leave him out of this!"

Langdon gripped her wrist and pulled her toward him until their eyes were three inchcs apart. "I don't intend to hurt your father. The man I want is that murdering DeCoeur."

Arienne tried to divert him. "Even if he was aboard, he would have been killed when your ship sank the *Magna Carta*."

"Not if he was the one who torpedoed my ship. He would have planned his escape before setting off the charge." His mind leaped to another possibility. "Is DeCoeur your father?"

"No! My father is an old man, the Frenchman can't be more than forty—" She broke off, appalled at herself. "You conniving spy! You tricked that out of me!"

Joshua released her, his face grim. "You're protecting a killer, Miss Lloyd."

"I'm not! My uncle forced my father into this. I only want to see that Papa comes to no harm, *if* he's still alive!"

"And you think he is alive, and DeCoeur with him," Joshua said flatly. "Damn it, woman, tell me where that maniac intended to go so I can stop him before he destroys the Union!"

"I don't know!"

" 'When my love swears that she is made of truth, I believe her, though I know she lies,' " Joshua said. His voice hardened. "Shakespeare may have been that foolish, but I'm not."

Arienne glared at him out of hot eyes. "If I tell you the truth, do you promise to leave my father alone?"

"Just tell me the truth, and we'll discuss the particulars later."

"You expect a lot for nothing, Major."

"I can't guarantee anything, except that my primary interest is in the Frenchman. Everything else is secondary. I'll try to be fair."

She could expect no more. Perhaps if she cooperated, he would overlook Sir James's part. "DeCoeur took my father away in the lifeboat," she said as calmly as she could. "They intended to reach Pensacola." She started to cry.

Joshua rolled his head back and stared thoughtfully at the grimy ceiling. Pensacola. So that's where the Rebels were building their nasty weapons. Could the *Sheboygan* have intercepted the lifeboat en route? There was no way to know. If DeCoeur had survived the gale and evaded the frigate, he might have reached land by now.

He reached down to pat Arienne's hair. "Come on, stop crying. A man like DeCoeur wouldn't let a little thing like a gale hamper his getting what he wanted. I'm sure your father is safe. I'll find him."

"And arrest him!" She slapped away his hand.

"I'm not in the habit of arresting old men."

Would he give her father a chance? "He's innocent. How can I convince you of that?"

"Swear that you are made of truth, and I will believe you," he said, this time without sarcasm.

"Then I swear. Papa can't possibly know these terrible things you've told me about DeCoeur. He'd never approve of murder."

"What is his connection with DeCoeur, then?"

"I'm not sure," she said miserably. "I think my uncle dreamed this whole thing up. Somehow he tricked Papa into going along with it. But I swear he doesn't know what sort of man DeCoeur is!"

"What makes you so certain?"

"I know him! He's a gentle man. He's taken very little interest in the world since my mother died."

"What sorts of things has he done?"

"A little legal work for my uncle's trust company from time to time. Other than that, he's tended Lloyd on the Downs. He just wanted to be left alone, but Uncle Wen said he had to come to the States as some sort of diplomat. He said the fate of England depended on his actions."

Langdon cursed softly. This thing went a lot deeper than the Confederacy's involvement. Was the British

Crown trying to use DeCoeur in order to obtain the submarine?

"Who is this Uncle Wen?"

"Wendell Stuart Lloyd, Papa's older brother. He's the British ambassador in Washington."

There it was, then. Seward was going to split a gut when he heard about *this.* The Confederacy had been trying for months to involve England. The submarine might be just the leverage the South needed to bring her in.

"What did your father tell you about his diplomatic duties?"

"Nothing."

"Tarnation, woman, now that's something I won't believe!"

Arienne jumped off the bunk. "I don't care what you do or don't believe, Major. Papa didn't tell me anything."

"That's because he's involved up to his neck!"

"No, he isn't!"

"The hell he's not! He's no innocent dupe, as you seem to believe. No one gets involved in a scheme this big without full knowledge of what he's doing. He's conspiring against the United States, and I'm going to stop him."

"You promised to leave him alone!"

"I didn't promise anything of the sort. I'll do what I have to do to carry out this mission."

"No matter if a poor old man gets hurt?"

"That's right. No matter."

"He's my father!"

"I don't care if he's the pope's father. He and

your uncle and Louis DeCoeur have got to be stopped."

"I'll stop *you*, Major Langdon! I won't let you hurt Papa. Now get out of my cabin and don't come back!"

5

Joshua didn't move. "You just simmer down, Miss Lloyd. If your father is guilty, which he obviously is, then he's got to pay the consequences. There's not a damned thing you can do to stop me from going to Pensacola."

"You'll have a hard time getting there from the brig of this ship!" She leaped at the door and twisted the key.

Joshua's fingers closed around her wrist. "You're not going out there."

She turned to rend his face with her free hand. "I'm going to tell the captain you're a Yankee spy!"

"Get hold of yourself, she-cat!"

"After I get hold of you and wring your neck, you lying fraud!"

Joshua tossed her onto the bunk and raised a warning hand when she sprang to her knees. "You'll stay."

Arienne sank back slowly, her eyes hot enough to burn holes through his head. "If I stay, you'll go. I detest the very sight of you!"

Langdon placed his hands on his hips. His bronzed, sweat-sheened chest rose and fell. To Arienne he was the very incarnation of a god of war. She glared up at him, her lovely eyes full of hate.

"I'll go, then," Joshua said. "You keep the key. Don't open the door to anyone but me."

"I'll open the door to anyone *but* you!"

Joshua was on her before she saw him move. His hands twisted her head so she had to look into his face. "Don't open the goddamned door to anyone but me."

Arienne struggled against him, but her efforts were as futile as those of a partridge in the jaws of a wolf.

"Will you obey me?"

"Let go!"

"Not until you promise to obey."

"I'm not your slave!"

"No, but you are my responsibility. Without my protection, those savages will line up to take you!"

Arienne twisted stubbornly in his grasp. She tried to ignore the pressure of his naked chest against her body.

"Do I have to stay here and hold you down, or would you prefer that I tie you to the bunk for safe-keeping?"

"You wouldn't dare!"

Joshua gave her a wicked smile. "I've dared worse things in my day, little girl."

"All right, blast you, I'll keep the door shut. Now get your greasy hands off me!"

Langdon released her and got off the bed, alert for further outbursts, but she only glared at him. He limped to the door and turned the key in the lock.

"Major Langdon!"

He turned quickly, expecting another attack. A wad of sodden fabric struck him in the face. He flung it into the corner and glared down at Arienne, who was perched demurely in the center of the bunk.

"I thought you might like to have your shirt back, Yankee."

Joshua drew a deep breath, walked out, and closed the door with unnecessary firmness. He heard the key rattle in the lock. Smiling grimly, he headed for the quarterdeck.

The sun had risen and now lit the sails peach and gold, throwing violet shadows across the rolling decks. Cumulus clouds hung like handpicked bolls of cotton in a soft blue sky, and the green waves of the Gulf replicated them a hundred times and more. Joshua dragged the tangy scent of the sea deep into his lungs.

"We're within reach of the delta, lad," Captain Ames said, spotting him. He made no comment on his passenger's black eye, or on the fact that three of his men were in the hold nursing their own injuries. "We'll take it slow the rest of the day, then heave to and wait till night to slip upriver."

"Good enough."

The captain's mouth widened in a lecherous grin. "I trust ye and the missus passed a restful night?"

"Restful enough," he replied, gazing into the rigging. The white sails billowed in the wind. Nothing in heaven or earth could equal for beauty a clipper under full sail. Except for Arienne, he amended silently. By Jove, she made his blood boil! It was a damned shame they were on opposite sides.

At lunchtime he knocked on her cabin door. She opened up just far enough to accept a bowl of watery stew and a pitcher of lukewarm tea before slamming the door in his face. He came back later with a sailor's shirt and a pair of dingy, calf-length breeches, which she accepted without comment before banging shut the door once again.

Late in the afternoon the sky clouded over, and it began to rain. Captain Ames rubbed his hands in satisfaction. Soon the fog would roll out of the Mississippi Delta, screening his movements from the Union warships patrolling the mouth of the river like a pack of guard dogs. They were so damned predictable, he'd never had much trouble getting by them before. His eyes glowed as he considered the money he'd make in beleaguered New Orleans off his load of French wines and silks.

Langdon, leaning against a bulwark to keep the crew where he could see them, noticed the captain's twitching fingers. He could almost see the phantom stacks of coins Ames was counting, but his smile faded when he remembered the eighteen hundred in gold he owed the old pirate. No, fifteen hundred, on account of his black eye. He could doubtless get himself off the *Scarlet Lady,* but Ames was sure to hold Arienne hostage. He'd have to get the ransom money from a Union sympathizer in New Orleans. If he couldn't get it, he'd grab the little hellion and blow up the ship.

By nightfall the obliging Louisiana fog had risen in a thick, muffling blanket. Three hours later, the ghostly clipper slipped past two Union warships guarding the main channel without being spotted.

Langdon paced slowly along the decks, enjoying the feel of the fog misting his skin. He wondered how Ames could see where he was going. Sailing up the Mississippi in this fog was like sailing through a snowbank. True, they were going at a snail's pace, but one false turn could land them on a shoal. The delta was a living thing, changing its form month by month with the deposit of thousands of tons of silt. It took a real smart pilot to stay in a safe channel.

"Fifteen fathoms, Captain," the hand in the mizzen chains said.

"How could he tell?"

The major swung around to find a small, fog-wreathed figure leaning against the rail. He had to look closely to make sure it was Arienne. She was dressed in boy's clothes, and she'd twisted her hair into a long braid.

Although she had disobeyed his directive, Joshua couldn't help but smile. Arienne only looked at him steadily and repeated her question. "How could he tell, in this fog?"

"The same way he would in daylight. By taking soundings."

"I want to see how it's done. I was a child the last time I sailed up this river." Declining to take his arm, she stepped past him.

Joshua followed in her wake, watching the womanly swing of her hips in the baggy sailor's breeches. She had found a length of rope somewhere and had wound it around her slender waist several times to hold up her pants.

The feel of his gaze made Arienne's spine prickle, but she continued all the way to the bow, determined to ignore the sensation. By straining her eyes, she could dimly make out a boyish form stretched along the spritsail yardarm, the Mississippi a bare two feet below him.

"What's he doing?"

"He's got a tallow-covered lump of lead attached to a rope. There's a man on the jib boom end, one on the main chains, and another in the mizzens, each holding a quantity of the line."

Joshua leaned forward and planted his hands on the rail on either side of her. He breathed in her scent, wondering even as he did so why the hell he was tormenting himself.

"Stop breathing down my neck."

"Excuse me, Your Highness," Langdon said in an amused tone as he moved to stand beside her.

"What are they doing now?"

"Listen and learn."

The first mate called hoarsely, "All ready forward for sounding?"

"Aye aye, sir!" said the boy on the spritsail yardarm.

"Heave!"

"Watch! Ho! Watch!" the boy said, dropping the lead into the water.

"Watch! Ho! Watch!" chanted the crewmen on the jib boom and main chains. The rope uncoiled from their hands.

"Fourteen fathoms!" called the hand in the mizzen chains, peering at the wet rope.

"Tallow's covered with black silt and crushed mussel shells, Cap'n," said the spritsail hand as he retrieved the lead.

"Ames'll compare the sounding to his navigational charts," Langdon explained to Arienne. "He'll have a pretty good idea where we are, but of course, there might be new sandbars."

"How will he know where they are?"

"He won't, until he goes aground."

"That's a reassuring thought!"

"It happens. Keep your fingers crossed that it won't this time."

"You keep your fingers crossed. I'm going back to bed."

Langdon followed her on noiseless feet, his eyes

alert for prowling sailors. The girl didn't realize how tantalizing she was for some hungry scamp. No one bothered her, though, and she was soon barricaded in her cabin. Joshua fancied he'd caught an icy flash of sapphire a moment before the door shut.

Morning found the *Scarlet Lady* far upriver, a bow wave the color of chocolate preceding her majestic passage. Yellow-and-green marshes stretched in the distance in all directions, dotted with *chênières*—oases of scraggly oak and cypress.

Vast flotillas of ducks and geese newly arrived from Canada blackened the still bayous. In the shallows, snowy egrets looked like balls of lace on black knitting needles, while alligators lay about with the animation of logs. Now and then, one of the logs came to life with thrashing tail and limbs, saw-toothed jaws snapping closed on an unwary waterfowl.

Kneeling on her narrow bunk, Arienne pushed open the porthole. A humid breeze trickled into the cabin, carrying the stench of decaying vegetation. She swung her long legs out of bed, quickly washed with the water remaining in the pitcher, threw on her sailor's togs, and hurried outside.

"Finally awake?"

Joshua Langdon was reclining on the roof of the cabin, his head pillowed on his arms. A fine sheen of dewdrops and mosquito bites adorned his bare chest, testifying to a night spent outdoors in the middle of a swamp.

"I would have awakened much earlier," she said sweetly, "had the cock perched on my roof crowed at daybreak."

"And ruffled the feathers of the little hen lying below him?"

At this, she stalked away on bare feet, her baggy trousers fluttering around her legs. Joshua whistled under his breath at her exposed calves. The fog last night had denied him a clear view of the curves that now winked at him with every step. He rolled over on his side, his attention shifting to the pert little twitch of her hips.

She placed her hands on the rail and tried to distract herself by studying a *chênière* sliding by the clipper. A bull alligator opened his tremendous jaws and roared before slithering into the murky water on a collision course with the ship.

"Damn, what a monster," Langdon said. He'd come up beside Arienne.

"Yes, you are," she said. Ignoring his chuckle, she bent her head to watch a water moccasin ribboning in and out of the cattails. The alligator flipped his tail and disappeared under the ship.

"I'd hate to be keel-hauled right now."

Arienne looked at him thoughtfully. Suddenly she slapped his chest with all her might.

Joshua recoiled. "What was that for?"

She pointed at a mosquito squashed on his chest. "I merely thought I'd save you from the bloodthirsty assault of that bug."

"Better its bloodthirsty assault than yours, ma'am."

Her eyes narrowed to brilliant slashes of blue. Then she strode rapidly up to the foremast and settled down against its base. Ignoring admiring looks from several sailors, she focused her attention on the wetlands.

The sight and smell of the delta aroused memories of her mother. Sara used to chafe in the heat and stench of crowded New Orleans and had often taken her to Plaquemines Parish, way down in the delta, where the reeds were high and the animals plentiful. There they had poled the marshes in a pirogue, searching for crawfish and ducks' eggs. They used to fish with bamboo poles they'd made and spend long hours talking and laughing.

Sir James had gone along a few times, but the heat and mosquitoes had nearly done him in. He'd been much happier staying in the city and working while Thomas, his freedman blacksmith, accompanied the women on their weeklong expeditions.

Arienne sighed and closed her eyes. She had missed the Edenic tranquillity of Louisiana, the warmth that enveloped her like the arms of a long-lost lover. And yet the very magic pierced her to the heart, for it thrust her back into the mind of the child she once was. And that child still ached.

Her mother had died on Shrove Tuesday—the madcap day that was the culmination of Mardi Gras. A servant had awakened Arienne just after daylight and rushed her into her pinafore and shoes, then walked her to the French Market for breakfast.

Today was special, the woman had told her. Miss Sara was going to have a baby.

Throughout the long day of feasting and merrymaking, of street parades and pony rides, Arienne thought about the baby. Would she have a brother or sister? Would the baby like her? Would she and her mother still have fun together?

She would never forget coming home to a house full of weeping servants that evening and finding her father nearly catatonic with grief. She'd gone crazy, fighting to get into the room where they'd laid out her mother and stillborn brother, screaming and biting and clawing until they'd summoned the doctor and he'd forced laudanum down her throat.

She'd awakened in her little room under the eaves. A servant told her that her precious mama had been placed in one of the crypts in the St. Louis Cemetery.

Arienne could forgive her father for a lot of things—for taking her away from her home and friends to a cold, lonesome estate outside London, for shucking the happy part of himself that she had loved, even for giving in to Wendell Stuart and becoming a party to Louis DeCoeur's scheme—but she'd never been able to forgive him for making her mother have that baby.

Perhaps if he'd recognized her grief, she could have forgiven him. Instead, he'd cloaked himself in silence for months, failing to acknowledge her. Wrapped in his own pain, he couldn't look outside himself enough to realize how difficult it was for her to lose the woman who had brought her into the world and loved her as no one else ever could.

In truth, Sir James would probably have died without Arienne. No sooner was Sara buried than he turned over the house and smithy to Thomas, packed up his attorney's office, and shipped himself and Arienne to Wendell Stuart's estate.

During the trip across the Atlantic, he had lain on his bunk as if dead. Arienne had been obliged to spoon-feed him broth twice a day, or he would have starved to death. She'd nursed him tenderly, waiting in vain for some sign that he noticed her.

After a while she was able to smile again and resume as normal a life as possible for a young lady left pretty much on her own. The pale English sun took some getting used to after Louisiana's bright mugginess, but she adapted well and began to spend most of her waking hours riding and caring for the horses at Lloyd on the Downs.

She watched her healthy, middle-aged father shrink into a wizened gnome despite her efforts to cheer him. Gradually she came to realize that much as she loved him, there wasn't much she could do to help him.

Where was he now? Had Louis DeCoeur gotten him to safety?

The Mississippi River curved sharply at English Turn, and for a while the sailors worked furiously in the rigging and at the halyards, resetting the luffing sails to catch the wind.

Arienne wondered if Captain Ames would mind her climbing into the tops for a better view. How delightful it would be to have brushes and paint, to render on paper a bird's-eye view of the marshes.

Lost in thought, she didn't move when Joshua Langdon squatted down in front of her. Would it be possible to paint the fathomless gray hues of his irises, the misty halo of sunshine in his black hair, the tones of bronze that defined his cheeks and lips?

"You!" she said, straightening abruptly. "What do you want?"

"Nothing. I thought you'd like breakfast." He offered her a tin plate of hardtack and molasses and a cup of steaming tea.

She was about to refuse, but then changed her mind and snatched the food out of his hands. She squealed as hot tea sloshed out of the cup onto her thigh.

Langdon immediately grabbed a bucket of salt water and poured it over the burn. Then he ripped the leg of her breeches open.

"What are you doing?" She tried to cover her thigh.

Joshua's hand arrested her movement. "Be still a minute." He poured more water over the reddened area. "Feel better?"

"Yes." The pain was almost gone. She should thank him and go back to her cabin. Instead, she caught her bottom lip between her teeth and, closing her eyes, leaned back against the mast, trembling at the touch of his hands on her naked thigh, shivers playing along her nerve endings.

Her eyes snapped open. Jerking her leg away from his hands, she said, "You've fixed the damage you caused, so go."

"I won't be dismissed that easily, Mrs. Langdon. I'm sticking to you like a burr on a dog's tail."

"Why?" Despising him as she did, it didn't seem fair that her heart threatened to leap out of her chest every time he looked at her.

"Why? Because every good-for-nothing roustabout on this ship has been making moo-cow eyes at you since you first came aboard, or haven't you noticed?"

"I've noticed *your* cow eyes, all right!"

"Ah, but I can keep mine in my head. The point is, you aren't safe without an escort."

"Oh? And I'm safe with you as an escort? A man who goes about tearing the breeches off girls—"

"You burned your leg!"

"—and making them drunk on nasty ale—"

"You act like I do it for a living."

"—and locking them up in suffocating, filthy old cabins for days on end—"

"You locked yourself in there!"

"Only because you ordered me to!" She began to rip a hardtack biscuit into tiny particles, dropping the crumbs on deck.

"You're going to get awfully thin that way, Mrs. Langdon."

"Stop calling me Mrs. Langdon!"

"Hush! Do you want somebody to hear you?"

"I won't hush! I wouldn't marry you if you were the last man on earth!"

"Good, then I don't have to worry about you taking this deception too seriously."

"Too seriously? You really have lost your mind if you think I want this 'marriage' to be anything but a silly game!"

Heaving a sigh, Langdon leaned against a bulkhead and folded his arms, feeling an unusual sense of defeat drain him of strength. Arienne began to nibble at the hard, tasteless biscuit. It was some time before either spoke again.

"That's a trumpeter swan," Joshua said, pointing at a huge white bird preening in the rushes.

Arienne had decided never to speak to him again, so it came as a surprise to hear herself saying, "She's beautiful. Her eyes and beak are as black as her plumage is white."

"They hatch out ugly little gray things. But I guess you've heard the story of the duckling."

"Everyone's heard it."

"The lowborn cygnet . . . drops her fledgling gray mantle . . . and uncloaks a queen."

"I hadn't heard that one. Did you make it up?"

"When I was a kid. It's a clumsy attempt at haiku."

"Japanese poetry?"

"You recognize it? I'm surprised."

"Evidently I'm not the ignorant bumpkin you took me for, Major."

"I didn't mean it that way. My apologies, ma'am."

She didn't answer. As long as they were arguing, she could keep her guard up. It wouldn't do to forget that Major Langdon was her father's enemy, and hers, too.

Langdon noticed a blush coloring her cheeks and throat. He suddenly wanted to lift her shirt to see if it extended to her breasts. From there he would inspect her firm abdomen, the angle of her thighs—

Stop it! he told himself. He had a job to do. It didn't matter that he wanted to take her in his arms, to run his tongue down her velvety throat to her delectable young breasts. Damn it to hell!

Arienne started like a fawn when he bolted to his feet and moved to stand facing the river, his muscular hands kneading the rail until the wood began to crack under the strain. The muscles of his back were tense under a sheen of sweat.

Arienne watched a rivulet of moisture trickle between his shoulder blades down his spine until it disappeared into the waistband of his trousers. She couldn't help gazing at the line of white skin showing just over the edge of his belt.

"What are you thinking, Joshua?" Her voice sounded strange to her ears.

His back stiffened, and he bowed his head. "You don't want to know."

Fire leaped inside her. She wondered how the hard muscles of his back would feel beneath her fingers.

"Tell me who you are, Arienne Lloyd."

The question surprised her. He was still facing the river, but he had raised his head to hear the answer.

"Who am I? Is there any reason you should know?"

Langdon turned slowly around, his gray eyes burning with something she could not interpret. She thought he was going to reach for her, but he did not move. "I have to know. Tell me about your family."

"Why? So you can use the information against my father?"

"No. If anything, it might help him."

"I'm not sure I believe that."

"What's it going to hurt?"

What, indeed? She didn't have to tell him anything important. "All right, I'll tell you about Mama. You'd better not yawn!"

"Was she that boring?"

"I didn't think so. She had a very interesting life—what there was of it. My grandparents died in Ireland when she was fourteen, so the Church sent her with a group of French orphan girls to New Orleans."

"Why?"

"To get married, of course."

"Oh. You mean like 'mail-order brides' out west."

"Yes. They called them 'cassette girls' in New Orleans because all they owned in the world was a small chest of belongings. The Ursuline nuns kept them at the convent."

"So your father found her there?"

"No. Mama apprenticed herself to a dressmaker shortly after arriving. She and Papa literally ran into each other on the street. He wasn't paying attention to where he was going, and she had her arms full of fabric. They collided. He got a tremendous goose egg on his forehead, so she took him back to the shop and nursed him."

"And he asked her to marry him."

"Not until two years later, as soon as she'd turned seventeen. He was almost thirty years older than she."

"They must have been quite a pair."

Arienne's hackles rose at his sarcasm. "They couldn't have loved each other more, despite their ages!"

"No offense meant. Tell me about your father. I don't even know his name."

Arienne clasped her arms around her knees and looked up at him. What could she say to make him understand what a harmless man her father was? "His name is James. He's an unlanded English knight. He used to have a law practice in the French Quarter. You already know that he's spent the last few years managing my uncle's estate."

"What happened to his law practice?"

"He sold it when Mama died. He hasn't been the same man since."

"In what way?"

"I think I've told you enough. Why don't you talk about yourself for a while? Isn't that what men do best?"

"Touché. All right, what do you want to know?"

"For starters, what do you plan to do after the North loses the war?"

"The North isn't going to lose the war."

"I suppose you saw that in a crystal ball."

"Maybe."

"Will you go back to Sevierville?"

"Probably not."

"Because of your father?"

"Yeah. He told me in no uncertain terms never to come back. I'm a traitor to the cause."

"Your mother's still alive?"

"As far as I know. She doesn't answer my letters."

"Then you'd best go and see about her. If my mother were alive, no one could keep me away!"

"It's more complicated than that."

"The only complicating factor is your pride!"

"No, my duty is plain."

Arienne stood up to face him. She could almost imagine the pain his poor mother must be feeling, knowing he put war before family. It made her mad.

"Who do you think you are, Joshua Langdon? God's gift to the army? Do you honestly think He demands the sacrifice of your family on the altar of a self-appointed mission that can only end in death for you and heartache for your mother?" She spoke much louder than she'd meant to.

Joshua grabbed her shoulders and glared down into her eyes. In a voice only she could hear, he said, "If this were a self-appointed mission, no power in heaven or earth could force such a sacrifice. I'm not after glory. It happens that I believe in the Union, and if I have to die defending her, then so be it. If you want to attribute that to selfish motives, then I can't stop you, but don't try to add to the burdens I already carry."

She stared back at him for a full minute before shrugging out of his grasp and turning to gaze at the marsh. "I'm sorry for you."

"And just why is that?"

"You're afraid."

"Of what?"

"Of your memories. Of going home and being rejected—"

"Rejected!"

"—of going home to ghosts, and finding out that when all is said and done, you'd wasted your life chasing dreams, because the people who really mattered are all gone."

"I'm afraid of nothing. No memories. No ghosts. No nothing."

Folding her arms across her breasts, she gazed at him coolly. "Aren't you?"

"Damn it, woman, who appointed you my conscience? Why do you plague me like this?"

"I've a right to. If it weren't for you, I wouldn't have to worry about my father being slapped into a Yankee prison."

"You think he should be allowed to peacefully carry out his scheme? This is *my* country being torn to bits."

"It will be my life torn to bits if you arrest my father. Can't you see, I don't have anyone else!"

"Your father should have thought of that before he left England. I can't give up a task that might mean life or death for the Union because of one man."

Arienne couldn't speak. Turning, she ran down

the long deck to her cabin. Peering through a flood of tears, she fitted the key into the lock and fell inside, shutting him out once and for all.

6

The Scarlet Lady docked in New Orleans shortly after one o'clock on a hot, muggy afternoon. The atmosphere compressed the smoke belching from the waterfront tanneries into an oppressive yellow blanket.

The clipper's lines had barely been secured to two huge posts driven deep into the Mississippi river mud when Joshua Langdon strode down the gangplank to the dock. He stopped to look at Captain Ames.

The seaman grinned down at him from the quarterdeck and gestured with his pipe. "Good luck, lad. Bring me back a hearty purse of gold, and a high yeller lass to help me spend it!"

"Just see that my wife comes to no harm, or I'll bind the gold to your ankles and drop you into the river." Naked to the waist, Langdon looked like a gladiator, the hard set of his muscles clearly indicating his ability to carry out the threat.

"There be worse ways of dying, lad." Sobering, he said, "The lass'll not be harmed. She's locked herself up tight and jammed a wedge under the door. Ye bring me the money, and Cap'n Ames'll hand her over."

"See that you do." Giving him a final, threatening glare, Joshua parted the crowds thronging the levee and stalked down Decatur Street to St. Philip, oblivious to the admiring stares of women promenading along the cobbled banquettes of the French Quarter.

Intent on finding the printing shop of a Union sympathizer he knew of, Joshua paid scant attention to the charming, old-world scene unfolding to his view.

Black slaves strutted by with baskets of vegetables balanced on their heads. Children of every size and color played in the gutters, ignoring the horse-drawn carriages clattering by.

The delicious smells of red beans and rice, of filé gumbo and jambalaya, of fried soft-shell crabs and *paín pâté* made war seem distant. Safe so far from Union incursions and reasonably supplied by blockade runners, New Orleans seemed destined to go on forever in idyllic isolation.

Pausing on the corner of St. Philip and Rue Chartres to get his bearings, Joshua studied a three-story mansion of pink stucco whose towering Doric columns and wide galleries attested to the wealth of its owner. A graceful wrought-iron gate protected a lush courtyard from interlopers. Peering through the bars, Langdon would have been pleased to know that the owner of this particular estate was looking through iron bars, too, having been caught in Washington smuggling secrets to the Confederates.

Eleven fifty-two Rue Royale was a tall, nondescript brick building sandwiched between two houses. A modest wooden sign hung askew from a rusty balustrade, its block letters advertising LITTLEBERRY'S PRINTING SHOPPE. The double doors giving onto the banquette were open, allowing air to flow through the shop to an overgrown garden in back. The rachety sound of a printing press issued from the dark, musty interior. Joshua ducked his head and went in.

A small, gray-haired man was feeding sheets of newsprint into the press as his foot powered the machine. Seeing the ragged stranger on his doorstep, he took his foot off the pedal and reached into the corner, bringing up a double-barrel shotgun.

"Wait a minute." Langdon raised his hands and took a step back. "I didn't come to rob you, Littleberry."

"Yeah? I suppose you've come in to order some fliers." The printer pushed his round spectacles up the bridge of his nose with a grimy paw. He inspected Langdon's tattered breeches before saying sarcastically, "We get millionaires like you in here all the time."

"Now just wait the hell a minute! Somebody we both know gave me your name and told me to come here if I was ever in New Orleans and needed help."

The gun barrel wavered slightly, then steadied as Littleberry's grip tightened on the twin triggers. "You read my name on the sign just now."

"I'm not denying that," Langdon said, watching the knuckles whitening on the triggers. "Bill Seward said to look for Littleberry's shop. According to him, you're on his team of secret-service operatives and would gladly help an agent in need."

The gun stock hit the wooden floor with a thump. "Why the devil didn't you say who you were to begin with?" He mopped his brow with a soiled rag.

"You didn't give me much chance to, waving that damned cannon in my face. Do you always greet potential customers like that?"

"I like to weed out the undesirables."

"Heaven help 'em, then!"

The small man nodded and returned the gun to the corner. His spectacles slid down his nose as he stared at Langdon. He pushed them up with an unconscious gesture and, making up his mind, jerked his thumb at the courtyard. "Have a seat out there. I'll close up shop."

Langdon walked out the back door into a jungle of weeds. With some difficulty he located a bench beneath the sweeping arms of a magnolia tree. He sat down, disturbing a slumbering vine snake coiled loosely around the arm of the bench. The little reptile puffed up and hissed like a rattler before sliding over Langdon's lap to the ground, changing course to avoid Littleberry's nearsighted shuffle through the tall grass.

It took Joshua a good twenty minutes of arguing

before the printer would consent to lend him the ransom money. The rest was easy. Joshua placed an order for a forged set of documents and a Confederate uniform to match the identity Littleberry would give him. Then, pocketing a leather pouch of gold the printer had grudgingly handed him, he set off for the *Scarlet Lady.* What he would do with the girl after ransoming her he didn't know, but he was damned if he'd leave her in the hands of a lusty old pirate.

Arienne paced from one end of the stifling little cabin to the other. He'd gone off and left her. She should have known he couldn't be trusted. He'd lied when he said he intended to get the ransom money. She stopped as a horrible thought struck her. "Maybe I'm the payment!"

Gooseflesh rose on her arms despite the heat. She wondered if they still sold slaves in New Orleans. With her black hair and golden coloring, it wouldn't take much to convince a potential buyer that she was a quadroon. She could end up on a sugar plantation!

She forced down the terrifying thought. If Joshua Langdon intended to use her as a sort of human sacrifice, he'd best find another victim. This was one game he was going to lose!

She kicked the wedge aside and unlocked the door, only to find Robert just outside. He contorted his features into a hideous grin.

"Coming out to play, girlie?"

As fast as she could, Arienne leaped back into the cabin and slammed the door, wedging it shut against the mate's determined attempts to break in. She turned the key and leaned against the door, panting.

A little while later Robert heard the key scrape in the lock. He unfolded himself from his seat on a coil of rope and waited, tingling with anticipation. He looked toward the starboard beam and saw that the crew was too busy unloading to pay attention to him. When he looked back, the door had opened on a sight he would never forget.

Arienne was posed against the doorpost with one arm curved seductively over her head. Her baggy trousers were gone. The striped shirt she wore barely covered her hips, giving him an unimpeded view of the most beautiful pair of legs he'd ever seen. As he watched in lustful fascination she slowly raised one leg and ran her bare foot up and down the doorpost.

"I've been waiting for you," she said throatily, fluttering her lashes.

With his eyes glued to her naked legs, Robert stumbled forward, arms outstretched. Then his eyes rolled up in his head and he crashed face-first onto the deck.

Arienne looked down in mild surprise at a broken ceramic handle in her fist. Fragments of a water pitcher littered the man's body. She dropped the handle and, grasping Robert under the armpits, dragged him into the cabin and slammed the door. The adrenaline that surged through her veins seemed to lighten the load.

Leaping into her trousers, she twisted her hair into a knot on top of her head and borrowed Robert's flat cap to hold her coiffure in place. Then she helped herself to a handful of lampblack from the kerosene lantern and smeared it over her face.

Blowing a kiss at Robert's sleeping form, she cracked the door. The sailors were rolling hogsheads down the steep gangplank, unaware of their prisoner's recent activities. Ames was nowhere in sight.

Arienne hurried to mingle with the crew. Keeping her face averted and her shoulders hunched to hide the swell of her breasts, she helped a pair of sweating young men wrestle a hogshead to the dock. She furtively inspected the crowd and spotted Ames a short distance away, haggling with a man in a white frock coat.

Quickly she ducked behind a mule piled high with mushmelons. The fruit vendor walked the mule down the levee toward the French Market, paying no attention to the ragged little sailor crouching along beside the animal. If the fellow wanted to jump ship, that was his business.

Once within the safety of the stalls, Arienne paused and placed a hand over her pounding heart. Then she dodged across the street to Jackson Square.

"Buy a trinket, sailor?" said a wrinkled old woman in the accent peculiar to New Orleans.

Arienne shook her head and began to walk faster, zigzagging between the hordes of vendors clogging the square. No one gave her a second glance. Passing the St. Louis Cathedral, she turned into Pirate's Alley and began to run, jumping over stagnant green puddles. At one point, a pack of starved mongrels shot out of a courtyard and chased her a short distance before giving up to root in a refuse can.

She slowed to a walk on Bourbon Street. The quarter didn't look much like she remembered it. Half the storefronts were boarded up, and other businesses seemed to be struggling to stay afloat. Their grossly inflated prices attested to the efficiency of the Union blockade. Still, the people seemed well fed. The lush fields and bayous continued to yield their plenty and would do so until early winter. Even then, alligator meat and crawfish would be easy to come by.

Arienne dodged the wagons and carriages that filled Canal Street to Carondelet. Fifteen minutes of steady running brought her to an alley behind a three-story house of white stucco. A small blacksmith shop leaned against the back of the house. The sounds of hammer and tongs rang through the open doors, and black smoke curled up from the chimney. Along a wooden fence framing the yard, freshly washed long johns and bloomers flapped in a remarkable imitation of a dance and frightened a cat that was tiptoeing around the smithy. Yowling with fright, the stray sprang up a wisteria vine and rocketed into a neighbor's garden.

Arienne gazed around the untidy yard, smelling the scents of jasmine and magnolia. This was the house, all right. She had entered the world seventeen years ago in that little room under the eaves. All she had to do now was go to the door and knock.

But what if no one recognized her? What if Thomas and his family had all died or moved away in the years since she'd been home?

Arienne wiped her palms on her breeches and forced her legs into motion. She walked past the smithy, climbed the stairs to the back porch of Jasmine Cottage, and hesitated for an agonizing moment before lifting her knuckles to the door.

"What the hell do you mean, my wife ran away?"

Captain Ames stepped back and glanced wildly around the levee for his men before he realized tardily that he'd released them to the taverns and whore-houses some time ago. A weak smile lifted the corners of his mouth. "She, er, tricked us, Mr. Langdon. Bashed Robert's noggin, she did, and slipped off like a wee ghostie."

"A ghostie, eh? *You'll* be a ghost if I don't find my wife!"

"We'll find her. I sent young Robert off to look for her when he waked up. He's a determined lad, is Robert."

Langdon could only imagine the mate's vengeful intentions toward Arienne. Cursing, he jerked Ames up by the scruff of the neck and shook him like a rat. "Which way?"

"I don't know, lad! He disappeared the minute I told him the chit was gone."

Langdon held Ames's collar in one hand and felt

in his pocket with the other. He smiled as he stuffed a five-dollar gold piece into the front of Ames's shirt. Then, striding to the edge of the levee, he dropped the privateer into the Mississippi. Without a backward glance, he turned and ran like one demented toward Jackson Square, shouting Arienne's name.

Thirteen hours later he made his way through the dark streets to Littleberry's shop and banged on the door.

"You look like hell." Littleberry scratched his belly through his nightshirt and pushed his spectacles up his nose. "Where's the girl?"

"She ran off. I looked for her all night." Langdon slumped into a chair and felt in his trousers for the pouchful of gold. Wearily, as though it cost him the last of his strength, he dropped the purse into Littleberry's hand. "I owe you five dollars. I won't be needing the rest, after all, damn it."

Littleberry gazed at him. He didn't like the big, pushy fellow, but he knew enough to keep his mouth shut for a respectful minute or two. Going to a battered cabinet, he lifted out a couple of printer's boxes and groped around at the back, surfacing with a bottle of whiskey. He wordlessly splashed the restorative into a glass and shoved it into Langdon's hand.

"Thanks." The major tossed it back with a flick of his wrist, grimacing as the liquid blazed a trail to his stomach. He poured himself a second shot.

Littleberry rescued the bottle and returned it to its

hiding place. "Sorry about the girl. I reckon she'll be all right, though."

"I hope so."

"Look, Langdon, you've got a job to do, and I don't want you hanging around here after daylight. I've got to protect myself, after all."

Langdon eyed him thoughtfully. Like it or not, he had to get to Pensacola. Arienne had made it abundantly clear that she never wanted to see him again, anyway. He'd just have to trust God to keep her safe in this wide-open river town. "Have you got the papers?"

"Come and see." Holding a lantern high, he led the major into a storage room and pulled aside a heavy tapestry hanging on the wall, revealing a low door. "Welcome to Aladdin's magical cave, my friend."

The room into which he showed Joshua would have done an army quartermaster proud. Neat stacks of Confederate uniforms were ranged alongside boxes of insignia and ammunition. Calf-length boots marched in ordered precision along one wall, while Enfield carbines stood to attention along another. On a polished wooden table lay a sheaf of papers.

Joshua strode forward, lifting a document from the top of the stack. "Bring that lantern over here."

"The paper you've got is a certificate of enlistment in the Army of the Tennessee."

"So, I'm Major Cyrus Enright, Artillerist."

"Right. And here"—Littleberry searched among the papers for a moment and grunted when he found the required document—"are your orders to report to Fort Barrancas to take up your duties as chief artillery officer."

The orders were signed by President Jefferson Davis in a strong, slanting hand. Langdon whistled reverently. "Whew, an excellent piece of forgery, Littleberry. That signature looks more like old Jeff's signature than his own does."

"What?"

"Just a little joke."

Littleberry shoved his spectacles back into position. "Save your humor for the sideshow, Langdon. I take pride in my work. You could hold Jeff Davis's genuine signature next to the one on your orders and not be able to tell them apart."

"Good. Let's just hope Braxton Bragg doesn't check my references when I show up on his doorstep."

"I thought of that, too, after you presented me with your harebrained scheme."

"I'm all ears."

"I keep a file on Confederate officers. Major Cyrus Enright was an artillerist who died in prison last month, a fact which we've kept from the rebels. According to the beat-up daguerreotype I've got of him, he bore you a passing resemblance. All you need to do is grow a mustache. That won't take long." He eyed Langdon's heavy growth of beard with distaste. "In short, Langdon, your references have already been established. One other thing, you've got a wife."

"What's her name?"

"Rachel Markwardt Enright."

"What's she look like?"

"I don't know. Make something up if anybody asks."

Langdon examined the last two documents on the table. One guaranteed him safe passage overland to Pensacola, and the other authorized him to use any horse in the livery stable down the street. Both bore Davis's signature.

"You've thought of everything, Littleberry."

"The day this secret agent forgets something is the day he gets buried."

"Keep that elephantine memory intact then," Joshua said, thumping his shoulder. "And send Uncle Bill the tab."

"I'd like to send Bill Seward more than a tab," Littleberry said, rubbing his shoulder. "That idiot's trying to convince Lincoln to start a foreign war to distract our lunatic countrymen from blowing each other up."

"Hell, they'd never cooperate with each other." He walked over to a bucket of water in the corner. "This for me?"

"Yes. You'll find a razor and mirror on that shelf. Remember to leave the mustache."

Langdon stripped off his pants and washed quickly. He inspected the red, puckered scar on his left thigh and was satisfied with the way the bullet wound was healing. Maybe the ball embedded in his femur would stop giving him pain, over time. He'd like to walk without that slight limp.

"What happened to your leg?"

"Nothing. Just a little souvenir from Bull Run. Don't let anybody tell you the Rebs can't shoot straight. They can knock the eye out of a squirrel at a thousand paces."

Finding the straight razor, he peered into a broken bit of mirror and began to scrape away the stubble on his cheeks and chin. He nicked himself twice, but managed to leave a fairly even line of hair above his lip.

"What do you think, Langdon? Will Seward get his foreign war?"

"I can't imagine trying to send a shipful of Yanks and Rebs anywhere together. Hell, they'd kill each other before their feet touched enemy soil."

"Damned fools." The printer extracted a pair of gray pants and a blouse from the stacks of uniforms and tossed them to Joshua. Then he affixed a gold star to the collar of a jacket and three black braids to the shoulder. He plunked a kepi bearing the crossed cannons insignia onto the table and squatted down to sort through the boots. When he turned around, Langdon had finished dressing and was standing in stockinged feet, inspecting the carbines.

"You don't want one of those." The printer slid open a drawer under the table and extracted a revolver. "This is the thing for you. It's a Leech and Rigdon thirty-six-caliber. They're made up in Greensboro. She's light on the trigger, as that hole in the ceiling attests, so try not to blow your fool head off."

"Thanks." Joshua helped himself to a box of ammunition. He loaded the gun and shoved it into his belt.

"Don't lose the damned thing. I'd like to have it back sometime."

"I'll return it." He pushed his feet into the tall boots and planted the kepi on his head. "Thanks, Littleberry. Watch your back."

"Yeah." Littleberry escorted him out of the room and carefully drew the tapestry over the entrance. He led him past the printing press and unbolted the street door.

Joshua tipped his hat and started outside, then stopped in his tracks. "Find her for me. Hire some urchins, post fliers with her description, do anything you can think of. I'll pay whatever it takes."

Littleberry didn't answer for fully a minute, his owlish gaze fastened on Langdon's face. "It'll be expensive, Major Enright. How do I know you can pay?"

"You have my word on it!"

"You might be poor," Littleberry said. He suddenly reached up to pull his pouchful of gold from Langdon's ear and ignored the major's incredulous expression. "However, I can see that you've a little gold tucked away. Keep it for now—I'll send you a bill after I've found the girl."

Joshua slowly tucked the pouch into his jacket, marveling at the printer's sleight of hand. He said nothing about the printer's generosity. Littleberry seemed to want it that way. Touching the peak of his hat, Langdon strode off down the street, a tall, upright figure in Confederate gray.

7

Three days later Arienne lay on a pile of quilts in the back of a lurching wagon. The wheels squished through the mud as she cradled her head on her arms and gazed into the velvety blackness of southern Mississippi.

As she had hoped, she'd found Thomas and his family living in a downstairs apartment of Jasmine Cottage. A black, six-foot Hercules, Thomas owned the smithy behind the house.

Sir James Lloyd had been the Negro's master for less than a day. Upon buying Jasmine Cottage nearly twenty years ago, he'd liberated the slaves and given the blacksmith half interest in the shop. He'd given him full title when Sara died.

Convincing Thomas to drive her to Pensacola had not been easy. Though he felt morally obligated to help find Sir James, he was reluctant to expose her to the perils of the road in wartime.

So far, their worst enemy had been the road itself.

From New Orleans the trail meandered eastward to Mississippi through treacherous, mosquito-infested swamps whose banks caved in without warning. Reptiles the color of tree bark slithered among the roots of cypress and waited in the branches for unwary prey, while bobcats and cougars prowled in the shadows.

There were always rivers and streams to cross. Sometimes there were ferrymen who would pole them across for ten cents. More often, they had to lead Thomas's old roan across fords in the sluggish brown creeks.

Of the hundreds of alligators they saw in the watercourses, only one nesting female bothered them. She erupted from the bank upstream with a roar that sent the roan plunging the last few yards to shore and Thomas and Arienne splashing after him.

Some of the deeper creeks and rivers were spanned by floating bridges made of logs lashed together and fastened to trees at either bank. Arienne found these uncertain structures more terrifying than the alligators. Holding on to rope handrails, she and Thomas had to walk ahead of the horse. The logs bounced and swayed from side to side, sinking lower and lower until, by the time the heavy wagon reached the center, the bridge was submerged half a foot below muddy, swirling water.

Worried about her father, Arienne insisted that they travel until late every night in order to get there as soon as possible. Sometimes they went until ten or eleven, sometimes just until they came to a river. Then Thomas would build a small fire so that Arienne could fry hotcakes and bacon on a flat, cast-iron griddle. She always cooked enough food for the next day's meal. Sometimes she boiled up a mess of grits in an old tin pot, and they ate them hot and plain, since they had no butter.

After the late meal Arienne would retreat, stiff and sore, into the quilts in the wagon bed. While she slept Thomas stood watch on the high wagon seat. They switched places after four hours.

Tonight, three days out of New Orleans, Thomas had chosen to travel well past eleven o'clock. He'd sent Arienne to the wagon bed, but sleep was impossible on the bumpy, rutted trail. She stifled a cry as the left rear wheel dropped into a hole and bounced her off the quilts.

Thomas flicked his whip over the horse's ears, but the churning hooves only buried the wheel to the axle and showered the riders with mud.

Snorting in disgust, Thomas climbed down from the seat. In the feeble light of the moon Arienne saw his white teeth glint in a wry smile.

"Damn thing's stuck again, Arienne. I'll push, you drive," he said in a deep bass voice. "And don't go to hollering at the hoss. Ain't no telling what in them woods."

Wiping her muddy face on the sleeve of the dress she'd borrowed from Thomas's wife, she climbed onto the seat, wrapped the reins firmly around her hand, and picked up the whip. "There's nothing but screech owls in there, Thomas."

"Screech owls and Yankees, more like."

"Then we don't have anything to worry about. It's not likely a Yankee will accuse you of being a runaway slave and haul you off."

"Ha! Yankees is the biggest pack of thieves and riverboat gamblers ever got up for a card game outside of hell." He slogged through the mud to the back of the wagon and put his great shoulder to the wheel. "Go!"

Arienne slapped the horse's rump with the reins. The roan surged against the traces and mud flew from his hooves.

At first the wagon stuck stubbornly in the mud, resisting the efforts of man and horse. Then, with a revolting, sucking noise, the wheels began to turn. Arienne cracked the whip, eliciting a fresh burst of power from the roan. The wagon broke free of the rut. She drove on a little ways before seesawing the reins to halt the horse.

"Who that dirty little scamp driving my wagon?" Wearing a mask of mud, Thomas was almost unrecognizable.

"You're a fine one to talk!" Arienne laughed and reached for his hand. Her fingers slipped off his muddy wrist. Shrieking, she fell backward off the seat.

"Lawd, she done broke her fool neck!" Thomas jumped onto the seat to peer over the other side.

Arienne lay on her back in the mud. Seeing her friend's worried look, she dissolved into giggles and flung a mud ball at him. He dodged the clod and hopped down beside her, chuckling with relief. Then he picked her up, and began to clean her face with the tail of his muddy shirt, smearing the muck around.

"Stop, oh please, stop!" Arienne leaned against the wagon, her shoulders shaking with laughter.

"Well, ain't this a chummy sight. A niggah and a white woman a-playing tag in the mud."

Thomas shoved Arienne behind his broad back, his eyes searching the darkness.

"Don't move, boy, or I'll spill yer black blood all ovah the road."

A shadow disengaged itself from the deeper shadows of the trees and became a skinny youth in overalls and a tattered flannel shirt. He wore a battered kepi with a brass CSA insignia on the front. A filthy bandage trailed from under the brim. He was pointing a musket at Thomas's middle.

Arienne stepped out from behind Thomas and swept the ill-fed youth contemptuously with her eyes. "Put that gun away, Private. My slave is driving me to Mobile."

Even slathered with mud, Arienne Lloyd was an impressive sight to the soldier. Her dress, plastered to her legs and bosom, was sure to please one who had known nothing but hardship and pain for months. His brain whirled with carnal thoughts, and he glanced at the giant standing next to her. It would be a simple matter to shoot the nigger and take the girl, but he wasn't sure his rusty old gun would fire.

"Y'all heading to Mobile, eh? Well, maybe y'all oughta rest for the night. They's a nice cozy fire over yonder, and lotsa fellers who'd take right good care of a fine lady like yerself, ma'am. Yep, yer niggah can sleep in the wagon. You just come on with me."

"You say there's lots of nice Southern boys over there?" she asked.

"Uh-huh. Back thataway."

"I don't see a campfire. Don't tell me they left you out here in the dark all alone!"

"Sure. I ain't a-scared. They's back in the woods about half a mile."

"I don't believe it. They wouldn't send a young fellow like you so far from camp."

The private spat out his plug of tobacco and twisted his head toward the woods. "They sure as heck would! They's way back yonder—"

Thomas's great black arm snaked out and locked around the youth's throat, cutting him off in midsentence, and Arienne wrenched his musket out of his hands. Thomas threw him into the wagon and held him down while she tore strips from her petticoat. They bound and gagged him, then covered him with quilts. In less than five minutes they were creaking down the road.

Arienne pulled the musket onto her lap and scanned the bushes on either side of the road. "Have you got a gun?"

"In my breeches. A Colt your pappy give me years ago."

"Shouldn't you get it out?"

"Nope. My money on the swindler sitting next to me. Your tongue's more dangerous than a gun. Ain't no Rebel stand a chance once you gets to talking."

"What are we going to do with him?"

"Drop him somewheres. Like in Mobile Bay."

"Thomas!"

"Just joking. We'll drop him someplace safe. Take him a day or two to work out of his bonds. By that time, we be gone."

"Won't his company be searching for him?"

"Yeah, but they ain't gonna look too far. They'll figger he done deserted to the swamps. Them boys do it all the time. They rather take a chance with 'gators and snakes than old Jeff Davis."

"Is it that bad? Are we losing the war?"

"Sound like you still got feelin's for the South, gal. London didn't wash 'em out of you?"

"No. I was born a Southerner. I'll die one."

"And the man you done tell me about, this here Yankee, he ain't change your mind?"

"Ha! Why should I let him change my mind?"

Thomas chuckled.

"What's that supposed to mean?"

"Mean you likes that man, that's what."

"Like him? He wants to arrest Papa!"

Thomas just smiled. Gritting her teeth, Arienne glared at the dark trees rolling slowly by the wagon. Her index finger caressed the musket trigger as she remembered Joshua Langdon's piratical tactics. If not for her cunning aboard the *Scarlet Lady*, she would probably be standing on a slave block right now, offered to a bunch of lustful old planters.

The ancient musket exploded like the crack of doom. Fire and smoke erupted over the roan's head. Hot petals bloomed from the barrel halfway back to the breech. Arienne yelped and dropped the weapon into the mud.

Terrified, the roan bolted, dragging the decrepit old wagon through the mud as though she were a champion harness racer pulling the lightest sulky.

With every bump and furrow, the wagon wheels left the road and spun in the air for a number of yards before landing with a jolt that nearly flung the riders off the seat. Thomas sawed at the reins to no avail. Arienne held on to the seat and yelled at the horse to stop. The Confederate prisoner bounced from one side of the wagon bed to the other, his screams muffled by the gag.

Then the road behind them filled with crackling lightning bugs. Arienne twisted around in the seat. Several dark shapes, some mounted on horses, emerged from the woods. The lightning bugs crackled again.

"Get down, gal! They shooting!" Thomas cracked the whip and shouted at the horse.

Arienne flung herself into the wagon bed and landed on top of the soldier. Bound and gagged, he could only glare his outrage as she rolled off him.

A volley of shots peppered the air around their heads. "Keep your head down, gal. Them's that boy's pals!"

"Give me your gun!"

"Hell no, you'd kill yourself with it!"

The wagon careened around a turn on two wheels. There was a moment when it seemed that the unwieldy conveyance would roll over, but Thomas flung himself to the left and the wheels thudded back into the ooze.

Seizing her chance, Arienne crawled along the jolting floor and reached over the seat. Thomas was too busy with the reins to prevent her from feeling in his belt for his gun, though he ranted and cursed. She crawled past the soldier to the tailgate.

Three mounted riders had left the rest of the patrol behind. Closing in on the wagon, they shot wildly at Thomas.

A bullet flattened into a hot pool of lead near Arienne's face. Shifting her position, she pushed the long barrel over the tailgate and waited until the wagon was rumbling along on a fairly even keel. She squeezed the trigger.

One of the Confederates cursed as his pistol dropped from his useless hand. The other two riders spurred their mounts to a fresh burst of speed. Flame spurted from a rifle barrel. Barely taking time to aim, Arienne fired at the rider. Whether she hit him or not she didn't know, for at that instant his horse stepped into a rut and went down, throwing him head over heels.

Finding himself shot at by an invisible marksman and his companions sprawled in the mud, the third rider wheeled his mount into the trees.

Arienne whooped and scuttled around her battered prisoner to Thomas. "They're gone!"

"Mebbe, mebbe not. I ain't stopping to find out. We wouldn't have got in this mess if you hadn't fooled with that damn musket."

"How was I to know it had a hair trigger?" She grabbed the seat as the wagon lurched around a bend. Mud flew from the wheels in a long, graceful rooster tail.

Thomas shook his head, his mind only half on his driving. Miss Arienne Lloyd hadn't changed much from the little rascal he'd known years ago. If her father had known about all the scrapes she'd gotten into, he'd have gone to an early grave.

"Thomas! Your arm's bleeding—you've been shot!"

"I ain't surprised." He eased the exhausted roan to a trot and tendered his arm for her inspection. It was grazed just above the elbow. "Am I gonna die?"

"This is no time for jokes!" It was her fault that he'd been wounded. If she'd kept her mind on watching out for Rebels instead of stewing over Joshua Langdon, she wouldn't have pulled the trigger and brought the whole Confederate army down on their heads.

She opened a small wooden trunk she'd brought from her mother's old room in Jasmine Cottage and rummaged around until she found a petticoat. It was the work of a moment to tear it into strips and bind up Thomas's wound. "Feel better?"

Thomas circled his arm and grunted. Arienne's

patch job would do. Jerking his head at the prisoner, he said, "No sense taking him to Mobile since we done give ourselves away. Take my knife and cut him loose."

"Sit up," she said. Cutting the fabric around his wrists, she backed away from him on her buttocks and picked up the Colt. "Untie your feet."

He yanked the gag out of his mouth. "Yer a sorry little niggah-loving bitch! I'm gonna kill that black bastard!"

"I don't like folks calling my friends ugly names," she said, raising the pistol. "Jump out before I lose my patience with you."

"I ain't untied my feet yet!"

Thomas turned a forbidding face to the Rebel. "You done heard the lady. Get your ass out of the wagon before I come back there and kick it out."

His ankles still bound, the soldier leaped overboard. He landed flat on his face in the mud.

Arienne laughed and climbed onto the seat beside her companion to reload the Colt.

"You didn't have no bullets in there."

"No, but the Rebel didn't know that. Besides, he was more afraid of you than a gun, you scary old thing."

"Mmmm, mmm. Same little rascal."

The wagon creaked into the coastal wetlands of Alabama the next day. A vast plain of saw grass dotted with islands of pine stretched as far as the eye could see. Storks and herons gobbled fish, small

snakes, shrimp. Cooled by a salty breeze, the air was
less humid.

There were plenty of people around, most of them
either too old or too young to go to war. Caribbean-
style cottages on stilts overlooked rice plantations.
Negroes poled the flats in pirogues, using hand
scythes to cut the stalks of grain.

The travelers spent the night in an abandoned barn
behind a burned-out plantation house. While Thomas
fished for the morning meal Arienne bathed in a
secluded stream and washed their muddy clothes.

Two more days of riding brought them to Florida.
Pines, scrub oak, prickly pear, cocklebur, and oleander
carpeted low hills of brick-red dust. Heat radiated
from the sandy shoulders of the road and distorted
the shapes of trees. An afternoon rainstorm turned
the air to steam.

Arienne endured each hardship without complaint.
It would all be worth it if she found her father in
Pensacola. She hoped she wouldn't also find Joshua
Langdon.

What should she do if he were there? Despite the
danger he posed to her father, she had begun to
believe she must let Joshua deal with DeCoeur. If the
Frenchman were really as bad as she'd heard, his
inventions would only bring more misery to the
world. Somehow she had to get her father out of this
morass of intrigue.

Early the next afternoon, the wagon trundled
down a gentle slope into Pensacola, a sparkling,
sun-washed gem on the shores of a sapphire-colored
bay. The architecture was distinctively Spanish,

with wrought-ironwork similar in style to that of New Orleans. Built of sandy brick, the houses had been polished almost white by sunshine and salt spray.

Thomas stopped at a hotel near the Seville Quarter for Arienne to take a bath and change her clothes. The freedman bathed in a horse trough behind the hotel. After donning a clean, patched shirt and breeches, he went looking for Sir James.

No one had heard of the Englishman. Perhaps he was at Fort Barrancas, the army post outside town. Thomas returned to the hotel for Arienne.

Two hours later the old wagon rattled up a steep, sandy road to the post of Fort Barrancas and halted before the barracks. Wild roses clambered over the walls of the white, three-story building. Other buildings were scattered among the live oaks crowning the hill.

Through a screen of trees on the ridge Arienne saw Pensacola Bay stretching wide and serene to the sugar-white shores of Santa Rosa Island. Union-held Fort Pickens squatted on the tip of the island, its guns guarding the channel. On the mainland opposite sat Fort McRee, and six hundred yards from Arienne's vantage point on the ridge, Fort Barrancas. The Confederates occupied the latter two forts.

A chorus of shouts drew the girl's attention away from the fortifications. A pack of Confederate soldiers was pouring from the barracks doors. They had seen the girl from the mess-hall windows.

"Take care of your hoss, ma'am?" A gangly young private fought his way clear of the pack to Arienne. Winded and slightly pop-eyed, he clasped his kepi to his breast and bowed clumsily. "Private Doug Barnes, at your disposal, ma'am."

Before Arienne could grace him with a reply, a surging tidal wave of young men engulfed him. Yelling desperately, he disappeared from sight. Thomas stood back and folded his arms across his chest as several soldiers fought for possession of the tired roan. The winners triumphantly led away horse and wagon, leaving the losers on the grass.

"Well!" Arienne said breathlessly, finding herself within a circle of admirers. "I had hardly expected such a warm reception!"

"Atten-shun!" A corporal on the fringes of the crowd came ramrod straight. The unruly mob instantly turned into wooden soldiers, eyes focused on the far distance.

A group of gray-uniformed men had come out of the officers' quarters east of the barracks, led by a tall individual in a gray-streaked beard. His square white teeth were clamped around the stump of a smoldering cigar. A plume of blue smoke trailed behind him into the eyes of his junior officers.

"Is that the general?" Arienne had to nudge one of the soldiers before he would whisper, "Yep." She shouldered her way through the men and marched boldly over to the officers.

"General Bragg?"

Braxton Bragg gazed down at the lovely young woman, his mind on the torpedo testing under way in the bayou. This must be one of the laundresses, judging by the faded blue dress she wore, but why would she approach him in such an unorthodox fashion?

Always a gentleman, he removed his hat and bowed stiffly from the waist. "How may I be of assistance, ma'am?"

"I'm Arienne Lloyd."

He raised his brows politely, waiting for enlightenment.

"Sir James Lloyd is my father." Her confidence flagged in the face of his continued silence. He acted as though he'd never heard the name before. That could only mean that her father had not reached the fort!

A laundress with a knight for a father? Bragg scratched his ear. He stared at her absently, considering the lovely set of her jaw, the way her eyes sparkled like the sunlit bay.

"Have you seen him, sir?"

Suddenly it clicked. "Of course!" Bragg swallowed a mouthful of cigar smoke and coughed and spluttered for a minute or so while his adjutant pounded him on the back. Regaining his breath, he gazed at her through tearing eyes. "Of course—Arienne Lloyd. Your father's been worried half out of his mind over you!"

Arienne grabbed his coat sleeve. "Is he all right? Where is he?"

"He's down at the bayou with the engineers. It's

that way." He gestured with his cigar. "Private Barnes! Escort Miss Lloyd to her father."

"Yes, sir, General, sir!"

Arienne didn't wait. Lifting her skirts, she bolted off in the direction Bragg was pointing his cigar with Thomas at her heels.

"Damn," said Bragg, "I didn't know a woman could run so fast. Go after her before a picket shoots her by mistake. Move!"

8

Sitting in the scanty shade of a palmetto, Sir James Lloyd pressed the heels of his hands against his throbbing temples and gave a groan calculated to melt the meanest heart. He squinted across an expanse of bayou at the huge, red-haired Louis DeCoeur, the author of his misery.

Clad in a filthy shirt and trousers, DeCoeur was standing on a dock that jutted into the bayou, directing the test-firing of his new torpedoes. The handful of Confederate engineers with him were apparently enjoying themselves, but the damned incessant booming beat on James's skull like Thor's hammer while the sun slowly baked what little brain he had left.

The old lawyer removed his shoes, rolled his trousers to his knees, and waded into the shallow water of the bayou. Several crabs and jellyfish immediately began to pinch, poke, and sting his unprotected legs. He hobbled out of the water and crossed the burning white sand to the palmetto, slapping at a buzzing cloud of mosquitoes.

In his absence, his shoes had somehow accumulated about a pound of sand apiece. As he wearily dumped out the grit his eyes fell upon a blue-tailed lizard clinging to a hollow reed.

Noticing his interest, the lizard leaped through the air and came to rest on his cravat, clinging there like a jeweled stickpin. A week ago, a reptile on his person would have sent James up the nearest tree, but now he only pushed his swollen feet into his shoes. If the lizard wanted to eat him, so be it. He was beyond caring.

"I should have died with you, Arienne," he said, resting his elbow on his raised knee. "There's nothing worth living for now."

"*Au contraire,* my friend," DeCoeur said. He had left the testing to the engineers. Kicking sand over the lawyer's feet, he flung himself on the ground beside him.

James Lloyd glared at him out of jaundiced eyes. "Why can't you leave me alone, you murdering blackguard?"

"And leave you thinking life isn't worthwhile? Bragg is pleased with the torpedo testing. It won't be long until he'll be able to use them against the Gulf-blockading squadron. And you say there's nothing worth living for!"

"My only child is dead."

"You can blame that on a trigger-happy Yankee battleship."

"I have my doubts about who's responsible. You jerked a wire as we rowed away from the *Magna*

Carta. The explosion followed immediately. I think you used one of your cursed torpedoes to start the battle!"

"I merely thought to get us away before that ill-begotten Yankee major uncovered our little scheme. I never dreamed of causing fair Arienne injury."

Sir James sank his head on his collar, too weary to argue. He had stopped taking his digitalis, hoping that every palpitation of his heart would be his last.

"I've got some news that will cheer you, *mon ami.*"

"Speak English, DeCoeur. I'm too sick to translate the garlic."

"All right, then. I've discovered a better way to propel that submarine your brother wants. All that remains is to convince Bragg's chief engineer that my method is better than his."

"You don't think Wilford Humes's idea of rowing his submarine about will work?"

"Har! It's folly of the first water to think a set of oars can propel a great iron ship like that. My aluminum propulsion method is the way to do it!"

Sir James tapped his chin, his interest piqued for the first time in days. The submarine project under way in the Pensacola Navy Yard was the best-kept secret of the war. Bragg had informed him that a team was working on a submersible ironclad in Mobile Bay as well, but that Humes's submarine promised better results. The only problem was Bragg's stubborn refusal to sell the plans to the

Liverpool cartel. He wanted to buy torpedoes, not give up a war machine that could eventually win him the world.

"Where would you get aluminum? There's a war on, and the stuff probably costs a hundred quid a pound."

DeCoeur's eyes twinkled. "There's a whole railroad car full of bauxite in the yard."

"So?"

"So, we'll reduce it with sodium, using the process Sainte-Claire Deville and I perfected ten years ago. I only need a small bit for the job."

"Perhaps we can work out a trade with these rebels, after all," Sir James said slowly. "Your propulsion system in exchange for the plans to the sub."

"The world will soon belong to the Liverpool cartel!"

"And to the Confederacy."

DeCoeur's smile froze for an instant, then broadened as he inserted his bare toe in an ant mound nearby. The mound erupted ants.

DeCoeur removed his toe and drew a slender glass vial from his breast pocket. Popping the cork, he trickled a few drops of clear liquid into the mound. Leaning over, he spat on the liquid. Nothing happened for a moment, then there was a muffled popping sound as a dense purple cloud belched out of the hole. The lava flow of ants trickled to a stop. "The world needs only one master."

Sir James wasn't listening. He had risen to his feet, his jaw slack, his eyes bulging. It couldn't be. No, no. He was seeing a ghost. That girl running down the shoreline toward him, her black hair flying in the breeze . . . it couldn't be . . .

"Arienne!"

"Papa!" Arienne's flying feet easily outdistanced Thomas and Private Barnes. With tears of joy streaming down her face, she threw herself into his arms. "I knew I'd find you!"

James Lloyd wept helplessly, his arms tight around her. It was a miracle, an outright miracle! Questions tumbled from his lips, but he was too dazed to listen to her answers. It was enough to hold his dear child against him, to feel life flowing into his tired veins.

"Do you remember Thomas, Papa?"

"My old friend? Is it really you?"

Thomas stepped forward and engulfed father and daughter in his huge arms.

"A touching scene," Louis DeCoeur said. He dabbed at his eyes.

"You!" As Arienne balled her fists to attack him Thomas scooped her off the ground.

"Let me go, Thomas! That—that creature abducted my father!"

Louis DeCoeur grinned up at the giant. "*Oui, mon ami,* I saved the little barrister's life."

Arienne emitted a strangled curse and drummed her heels against Thomas's shins. "He started the battle with a torpedo! Let me at him!"

"Stop it, Arienne!" Sir James said. "What's done is done. DeCoeur is no friend of mine, and the sooner we finish here, the sooner I'll be rid of him. All that matters is our being together again."

Thomas cautiously set the girl on her feet. She shook her fist at the scientist. "Stay away from my father!"

"Whatever the mademoiselle wishes, old Louis will endeavor to do."

"See that you do!" she said in French. She turned and nearly collided with Private Barnes. He was standing on one leg, twisting his kepi in his hands. Unnerved by her glare, he slid behind a live oak. "You are dismissed, Private!"

"Yes'm."

Throwing DeCoeur a hostile glare, Arienne took her father's arm and marched him away from the bayou. Thomas tagged along.

"That man is a murderer, Papa!"

"I'm afraid that's true."

"Then why are you helping him?"

"It's my job."

His words grated on her nerves like sand in a tight pair of pantaloons. Joshua had said that same thing, in exactly that same tone. Why did men have to be such fanatical dolts? It was a good thing she'd come. "Thomas and I are taking you away from here, aren't we, Thomas?"

"Is that so?"

"This the first time I done heard about it, sir."

"Well, we are!"

James waved his hands impatiently. "We'll talk about that later. Now tell me, what guardian angel scooped you out of the Gulf?"

"No guardian angel, Papa."

"But I saw the *Magna Carta* sink with my own

eyes! Are you real, or am I only imagining you again?" He gave her a pinch that was only half-playful, for anguish still lurked in his pale eyes.

"I was picked up by a blockade runner and taken to New Orleans." She frowned at Thomas's cluck of disapproval. She wasn't exactly telling a lie. She'd just neglected to tell her father the whole truth. He didn't need to know about Langdon . . . unless Langdon was at the fort.

"So you went to Jasmine Cottage?"

"Yes. At first Thomas didn't want to drive me here because of the danger, but we made it just fine. No problems." This time she didn't even frown when Thomas made a noise.

"You've just convinced me to start going to church again, Arienne. My prayers have been answered."

The trio walked along in silence for a few minutes. Arienne liked the feel of the tide rushing over her feet. "Papa, have any strangers shown up here in the last week or so?"

"Nooo. No civilians, anyway. Army men are constantly coming and going."

"Do Yankee soldiers come and go?"

"Bragg allows a few soldiers to come to the mainland from Fort Pickens twice a week to pick up their mail. They go into town under heavy guard, then sail back to the island before nightfall."

"Have any of them shown any interest in you?"

"No. I've only seen them from a distance. Why?"

"Oh, just curious."

They took a worn path up the hill to the barracks.

Thomas was housed with the servants, Arienne in the officers' quarters.

A canopy of ancient live oaks shaded the large whitewashed quarters from the late-September sun. The windows and doors had been left open to the sea breeze that flowed up the bluffs. The walls were quite thick, keeping the interior dark and cool.

The first floor consisted of a large dining hall with a kitchen at the back connected by means of a breezeway. A long mahogany table commanded much of the room, with floor space left for dancing near a grand piano. Airy ferns hung on hooks in front of the tall, narrow windows spaced along the front and rear walls. A staircase led to the second floor.

An orderly showed Arienne upstairs to a small room adjoining her father's. Someone had carried in the wooden chest she'd brought from Jasmine Cottage and filled a ceramic pitcher on the wash-stand with water. Half a cake of white soap lay in a cracked saucer by the basin, and a spray of pink roses trailed from a battered tin cup beside it. There was a cane-bottom chair in the corner, and the regulation army cot boasted a cheerful patch-work quilt.

Crossing to the cot, Arienne unpinned a tat-tered scrap of paper from the pillow. It said, *Hope everthang meats yur aproovul. We is hear to hep jest call out ifn yu needs us. P.S. yur the purtiest lady we ever seen.*

Arienne smiled and slipped the paper under the

pillow, wondering which of the boys had penned it. Then she frowned and bolted the door. The balcony doors were open, but there didn't seem to be any way to reach her room from the ground. Satisfied, she stripped to her underthings and lay down on the bunk to sleep away the remainder of the warm afternoon.

Dusk had fallen by the time she awakened. The room was dark and stuffy, reminding her a bit too much of the mate's cabin aboard the *Scarlet Lady*.

She sat on the side of the cot, thinking of Joshua Langdon. He hadn't come to Pensacola, after all. She tried to summon a sense of relief but found that she couldn't.

Where was he? Had he been captured on the road from New Orleans? She knew from experience that Confederates lurked in the woods. Perhaps he was in prison now.

She got up and fumbled for a match in a cast-iron box hanging on the wall by her bed. She lit the lamp and relaxed slightly as the glow drove the shadows away. She stripped off her underthings, remembering.

He'd given her the shirt off his back. He'd protected her from the pirates and gotten a black eye in the process. Had she judged him wrongly, thinking he'd left her on the *Scarlet Lady* to get rid of her?

Her thoughts had often strayed to Langdon during the long wagon ride to Pensacola. She'd tried to quell her memories of him, but all too often she had daydreamed of his arms around her in the lifeboat, his body warming hers. She remembered him looking at her with a fierce absorption that had shaken her to the core. She couldn't forget him holding her down on the bunk in the cabin, kissing her.

She looked at herself in the oval mirror mounted behind the washstand. She touched her lips, remembering the stolen kiss. Closing her eyes, she could almost feel his long fingers on her thigh, taking away the scalding pain of the tea she'd spilled.

She wanted him, hungered for him. No, she couldn't! He had such power—the power to hurt her father, to hurt her.

Gnawing her bottom lip, she poured water into the basin, lathered a rag, and began to wash. The breeze blowing in from the balcony chilled her. She hurriedly rinsed and dried, then misted herself with rosewater from a glass atomizer she'd retrieved from the wooden chest.

Next she slipped on one of her mother's silk petticoats, a pair of pantaloons, and a white camisole. Blessed with a tiny waist, she didn't need to wear the whalebone corset tucked among her mother's things.

The floorboards began to vibrate beneath her feet. She stood still, listening to the resonant chords of the grand piano downstairs. She supposed she was late for supper. Her father had told her that at Fort Barrancas, dinner was a nightly feast.

According to the custom of the day, each officer brought to his duty station a trunkful of china, silver, and crystal, his dress uniform, and his favorite wine and cigars. While the enlisted men queued up for army rations, the officers dined in grand style.

Arienne wasn't sure if the clothes she'd brought would do for a formal dining in. She chose a skirt of emerald silk and a black blouse her mother had bought in Paris years ago. The sleeves puffed at the shoulders and tapered at the wrists. The neckline was altogether too revealing. A double row of black pearls closed the bodice front.

She tried to pull the outdated blouse a little higher over her breasts. Drawing a deep breath was out of the question.

Folded into an extra petticoat she found black stockings and garters and a pair of eelskin slippers. The shoes fit well enough, though the stockings had holes in the heels. It was strange and rather sad to be wearing her mother's clothing.

She heard a rap at the door. "Arienne, are you ready for dinner?"

"Almost, Papa."

"Do you want me to wait?"

"No. I'll be down in a few minutes. You go ahead."

The sound of his feet shuffling away down the hallway brought a smile to her lips. She'd found him, thank heaven! They'd start for London as soon as they could find a ship. Wendell Stuart and Louis DeCoeur could go to blazes with their horrid plans.

She brushed her hair until it shone like a skein of ebony silk, then braided and coiled the heavy mass around her head. Then she leaned toward the mirror to admire her coiffure, catching sight of a light sprinkling of freckles on her nose. She'd gotten a tan the color of gold riding in the open wagon from New Orleans. Ah well, she had never pretended to be a proper English lady. It was much better to be a healthy country girl.

As she turned to leave, her eye fell on the battered tin cup with its spray of roses. It was the work of a moment to twine the flowers into her hair. Somehow their frágile pinkness made her tan glow seem pretty.

Pleased with her appearance, she walked into the hall past a gallery of hunting scenes to the wide staircase. She paused, one hand on the banister, listening to the opening chords of *The Marriage of Figaro*.

Whoever was playing the concert grand was doing a superlative job of it. Who would have expected such culture at a military camp in wartime?

Intrigued, she started down the staircase, feeling the vibrations in her hands and the soles of her feet. With every step the vibrations became stronger, the melody more powerful, as though a living entity were reaching into her depths. Breathless, she arrived at the bottom of the staircase.

Some twenty Confederate officers were standing around the room, the breeze flowing through the open windows ruffling their hair and flickering the flames of the candles on the long table. Sighting the beauty poised on the last step, they forgot their cocktails—and their manners—and gaped in admiration.

Arienne stepped onto the polished cypress floor-boards, her eyes glittering. Through the knots of men she could see the broad back of the pianist at the far end of the room. He was wearing a gray uniform. His dark head was tilted back slightly as if the music was almost too powerful to bear, yet his fingers ruled the ivory keys with the touch of a master.

Arienne passed swiftly through the officers. Enthralled by the music, she was deaf to the sudden whispers, the low whistles. She saw nothing but the tall soldier at the keys, heard nothing but the masterful lure of the overture that robbed her of agency. She stopped behind the man who, in that moment, owned her very being.

The music ended.

Arienne stumbled back, her mind in a whirl. The man sat perfectly still on the piano stool with his back to her. Without his even looking at her, she knew he possessed an uncanny awareness of who she was.

"Oh, my Lord," she said in a voice scarcely above a whisper. "It's you!"

9

General Braxton Bragg reached Arienne. "Come, my dear, we've waited supper for you."

No parched traveler sighting an oasis had ever reacted with such obvious relief as Arienne did at that moment. She wrenched her gaze away from the man at the piano, caught Bragg's arm in both hands, and spun him toward the table.

Bragg smiled at her hearty response, and his chest inflated until the brass buttons on his jacket threatened to burst their moorings.

"Don't I get an introduction, sir?" Rising from the piano stool, Joshua Langdon tugged the sleeves of his uniform jacket down over his wrists and turned around. He read terror in the glance Arienne threw over her shoulder at him. He smiled disarmingly.

Bragg about-faced, his beard jutting. "May I introduce Major Cyrus Enright, Miss Lloyd? Enright, this is

Miss Arienne Lloyd, daughter of our esteemed liaison from England."

"So happy to make your acquaintance, Miss Lloyd. Have you a dinner companion?"

She could only stare at him as her breasts rose and fell rapidly. Her father was in the corner, talking with Louis DeCoeur. What should she do?

She heard Bragg speaking as if through a roaring waterfall. "Yes, she has a dinner companion, Major Enright. Now, if you'll excuse us, I'll ring for dinner."

Langdon's white teeth gleamed under his trim new mustache. He bowed. "Certainly, sir. With your permission, and the lady's, I'll play the Allegro from Beethoven's 'Eroica' symphony."

"Play any damned tune you want." Bragg didn't like the devastating effect his new chief of artillery was having on the girl. Tucking Arienne's hand beneath his left elbow, he marched her to the table.

Feeling like a prisoner given a last-minute reprieve from the firing squad, Arienne allowed him to escort her to a chair.

Bragg's men stood behind their chairs, waiting for an introduction. Most had heard about Lloyd's daughter, but few had seen her arrive that afternoon. Certainly none had been prepared to receive an ebony-haired beauty who might have escaped from a sultan's harem. Many a hand was furtively raised to push down an errant cowlick or to whisk a pair of spectacles off a freckled nose.

"Miss Lloyd, these are my officers," Bragg said,

unaccountably irritated by their behavior. They reminded him of a pride of young lions stalking a gazelle. A gazelle ripe for the takedown, he added to himself, noticing the hunted looks she kept casting at that damned Enright, who was obliviously plinking away in the corner.

When Bragg pressed her hand firmly and cleared his throat, Arienne came out of her trance and curtsied, one small slipper peeking out from the hem of her emerald skirt. Her black hair reflected the candles' glow, and the pink roses set off her femininity to perfection.

"Gentlemen, this is Miss Arienne Lloyd, Sir James's daughter." By Montreal and Elinor Lee, how was he going to keep the lions off this supreme catch? She seemed to increase in beauty and grace from moment to moment, until it was questionable whether any male heart would remain unbroken, his own included. He cleared his throat again. "I'll trust you to tender her your greatest respect as becomes your rank."

He seated her next to him at the head of the table. To avert any flanking maneuvers by his officers, he ordered Sir James to the empty seat on her left. Then he sat down, with a warning glare at his men.

Arienne shook out her linen napkin and selected a fork from the array to the left of her bone-china plate. Her hands were still trembling after her encounter with Langdon.

Did he know who her father was? Would he try to arrest him? Surely he realized that if he tried anything, she would immediately inform Bragg that he was a Yankee spy. There, they had a truce!

She gazed at the white tablecloth embroidered with miniature wild roses like the ones in her hair. Bouquets of roses and ferns adorned the candlelit table. In the background, Langdon's long fingers caressed the black and white keys with a sensual warmth that brought a flush to her face.

Desperate to rid herself of his distressing influence, she lifted her gaze to the soldiers. She found them feasting on her face and décolletage rather than on the splendid supper being laid by a bevy of black slaves.

She raised her glass of sherry. "A toast, gentlemen, to the brave men charged with defending the honor of the South."

"Hear, hear!" Several glasses clinked enthusiastically.

"To the bonny blue flag!" Braxton Bragg said.

"Hear, hear!"

"To the flower of womanhood!"

"Hear, hear!"

"And to the bonniest lass ever to grace the halls of Fort Barrancas!"

The response fairly shook the rafters. Arienne smiled, and Bragg's heart gave a mighty lurch. He beckoned to a waiter and held out his glass. "Keep it filled."

Punctuated by innumerable toasts to Arienne's beauty, the dinner was a relaxed, festive affair. Traditional Southern food—boiled, fried, and heavily salted—was served from vast silver trays. Waiters were kept busy slicing sugar-cured hams hot out of the oven. Red-eye gravy arrived in boats to be poured over mountains of mashed potatoes.

Hopeful young officers continually replenished Arienne's plate. No sooner did she push it back than she would find it filled again with corn swimming in butter, sugary baked beans, panfried green tomatoes with milk gravy, fried okra, butter beans, and corn bread.

She finally signaled a waiter to take away her plate, much to the disappointment of a second lieutenant fighting his way to her chair with a whole lemon meringue pie. Tripped up by a glowering General Bragg, the unfortunate lad went down on his knees and caught the dessert inches from the floor. For a moment it seemed he would triumph, then one of his companions applied a hand to his shoulder blades and pushed his face into the pie.

Arienne leaned down to mop his face with her dinner napkin, her mirth betrayed only by the twinkle in her eyes. Through a mask of lemon and egg whites he beamed up at her, not caring that his friends were practically convulsing at his expense.

"I'll be your slave forever, ma'am!" he said.

Arienne laughed outright and, wiping a bit of meringue off his cheek with her finger, popped it into her mouth, much to the officers' delight.

"Why don't you go along and change your clothes, Lieutenant?" she said when he showed no sign of leaving his lapdog position by her chair. "We'll still be here when you get back."

Against her will, Arienne's eyes strayed to the pianist. What were his intentions? She looked over at her father and started to speak, then closed her mouth. Langdon couldn't harm him as long as he stayed on the army post. She'd keep quiet for a few days and see what happened.

She engaged General Bragg and a gray-haired lieutenant colonel in conversation. That an entire roomful of officers hung on her every word failed to unnerve her. Thanks to her untraditional upbringing, she was versed in a wide variety of subjects dear to the hearts of men.

Bragg was amazed. Poised, self-confident, his lovely guest was knowledgeable in areas that he had heretofore considered the province of men. It was obvious that Sir James Lloyd had had her educated, but who would have dreamed a female capable of mastering arithmetic, architecture, and the finer points of horse racing? She had more than a nodding acquaintance with firearms and woodlore as well. He wondered what other treasures she possessed.

A handsome young captain leaned across the table, his eyes dropping to the valley between Arienne's breasts. She casually plucked a spray of rosebuds from a vase and tucked them into her décolletage, effectively screening herself from further visual assaults. She grimaced slightly at the sharp prick of thorns but decided that the discomfort was worth it.

"An excellent tactical maneuver," Bragg said. His breath lifted the silken tendrils of hair that were escaping her braid. "You'd make a splendid general."

"I doubt it. I would abolish war. My troops would desert, having no one to fight."

"Ha! You think it's possible to abolish war?"

His patronizing tone annoyed her. "If a higher law prevailed instead of the rule of the jungle that men now obey, it might be possible, General. I am convinced we can govern ourselves without shedding blood."

"Pandora's box has been opened," Sir James said. "There's no shutting the lid, my dear."

"That's a fatalistic philosophy, Papa. It's nearly as bad as the concept of original sin."

"Maybe pride is the original sin."

"Do you speak of pride, or of honor?" Bragg asked.

"I'm speaking of the kind of pride that throws a nation's finest young men into senseless charges across open ground—"

"That's called honor, Sir James," Bragg said.

"Honor never stopped a round of grape, sir!"

Arienne looked from one man to the other. Her father's face had assumed an apoplectic hue, and Bragg's color was only slightly less so. The flow of conversation around the table had ceased.

"I know this woman."

Arienne paled. Langdon had taken over the young captain's seat and was helping himself to mashed potatoes and ham. His face and hands were very dark against the red collar and cuffs of his artillery uniform. His neat black mustache made him look like more of a devil than ever. He smiled at her, his gray eyes twinkling.

"Of course you know her, Enright," Bragg said, "I introduced you earlier."

"That was our second introduction, sir. The first was in an earlier time and place." He poured gravy over his food.

Was he trying to commit suicide? Arienne felt every drop of blood in her body drain into her toes.

"I met her in the pages of Homer's *Odyssey*. She's the siren who lures men from the safety of their ships into stormy seas. I'd know her anywhere."

Arienne reached for her sherry, wishing she could slide under the table. What did Langdon hope to accomplish?

Sir James chuckled, forgetting his quarrel with the general. He reached across the table to pour Langdon a glassful of port. "Ah, I should have known a pianist of your caliber would also love the classics, Major Enright. What do you think of Euripides?"

"I find his intellectual skepticism particularly apt for the theater of battle, sir. His depiction of man as a corrupt yet heroic figure rings true, as I'm sure any soldier here can attest."

Langdon gazed around at his fellow officers, most of whom were listening in silent envy. Bragg snorted and fished in his uniform pocket for a cigar.

"But don't you find some of his devices rather childish, Major? Take, for instance, the deus ex machina," Sir James said.

"Ah, the machine of the gods?"

"What the hell are you talking about?" Bragg demanded, chewing savagely on his cigar. Seeing the beautiful Miss Lloyd's attention diverted by a swaggering field-grade officer made his ulcer bleed.

"He's referring, for example, to the part of a tale, sir, in which the heroine is washed overboard during a storm and, losing the last bit of her strength—"

"—is located by the hero," James said excitedly, "who has overcome bloody great odds to save her!"

Arienne choked on her sherry. Her father thumped her on the back impatiently, anxious to continue his discussion with the learned Major Enright. It was rare, indeed, to find a soldier capable of talking about something other than war. "Try not to swill your drink, Arienne. You might choke yourself."

"Necessitating a deus ex machina, eh?" Joshua Langdon said.

Sir James chortled and refilled his new friend's glass. Arienne's eloquent look told Langdon where he could put his machine of the gods.

"If everybody's had their fill of ham," Bragg said, glaring at the major, "we'll get down to a little business."

While the slaves cleared the table and poured steaming cups of chicory, the men grudgingly pushed back their chairs and prepared to listen. Langdon helped himself to a second helping of potatoes and red-eye gravy, topping the mountain with a slab of ham. He clattered about with his knife and fork, oblivious to the general.

Arienne smiled, and Langdon glanced up at her. She immediately hid her smile behind her hand. By carefully stoking the fires of anger, she managed to burn away the tenderness she had lapsed into and give him the kind of glare he so richly deserved.

Langdon popped a forkful of ham into his mouth as the general began to speak on one of his favorite subjects: the submarine. Langdon appeared to show only polite interest, though Arienne knew he was listening intently.

This Confederate "machine of the gods" could spell disaster for the Union. Bragg could use the damned thing to pull the Confederacy out of the fires of defeat. He could win the war.

"I'm happy to report that Mr. DeCoeur has come up with a revolutionary method of propelling the submarine," Bragg said. Joshua took another heaping spoonful of mashed potatoes and pushed the empty bowl aside. "Making the necessary alterations will slow the completion date by a month. . . ."

That was something, anyway. So far he had been unable to get near the submarine. DeCoeur and Wilford Humes were keeping it under close wraps in the floating dry dock in the navy yard. Squads of soldiers guarded the thing day and night.

"His process involves rendering aluminum from the bauxite we've got in the railyard and suspending it in mercury before it solidifies. As many of you already know, we've detailed men to work on it around the clock. If all goes as planned, the sub will prowl the seas like a shark, launching DeCoeur's excellent torpedoes. Farewell, Yankee blockade!"

Langdon's gaze flickered to Arienne, who was staring pensively into her mugful of chicory. He had very nearly thrown himself into the grand piano and slammed the lid when he'd sensed her behind him earlier. What a surprise!

He'd been inspecting the cannons in the Spanish water battery that day and had not heard of her arrival. As glad as he was to know that she was alive and unharmed, he would have preferred her a thousand miles away. The last thing a secret agent cozily ensconced in an enemy camp needed was a blabbermouth woman showing up on his doorstep.

Sir James bolted upright and whispered excitedly across the table, "Plato was right! 'Either philosophers should become kings, or kings philosophers.'"

Langdon, his mind vacillating between the submarine and the exact color of Arienne's eyes, came out of his trance. "Eh?"

"How will these blokes end their war, short of wholesale destruction? If Davis and Lincoln would become philosophers, they might . . ." His voice trailed off as he noticed that his commentary had claimed more than the major's attention.

Bragg was gnawing his cigar, his brows compressing into one continuous line across his forehead. His staff sat poised on the edge of their seats. They had hardly expected such a diversion in the middle of their commander's speech. Arienne gripped her father's forearm and turned herself to screen him partially from Bragg's wrath.

Bragg looked over the girl's head. "Sir James, I was unaware that you had aspirations to the presidency."

"Me?" He heard snickers, covered immediately by coughs, as though the entire roomful of men had suddenly contracted a cold. "I'm sure your president is doing a, um, bloody good job."

"Then kindly keep quiet while we do ours."

"Um, quite."

Langdon's dark gaze shifted to Arienne. With her lips pressed into a thin line, she remained seated, stiff with rage. At any moment she might explode like a boiler iron, and he didn't want to be in the way of the shrapnel.

He stood up and bowed. "Excuse me, sir, but that was my fault. Sir James was simply answering a question I had posed earlier."

Bragg deflated like a bladder of air stepped on by a horse. What was there about Cyrus Enright that caught him flat-footed so often? The major had shown up on his doorstep last week with orders in hand. Although everything had seemed correct, something warned Bragg that all wasn't quite right.

"Let's get on with it, then, shall we?" he said. "I trust that no one has any more questions for our resident pair of philosophers? No? Good."

Sir James whispered across the table, "Dashed decent of you, Enright, taking the blame like that."

Langdon nodded at him but kept his attention on Bragg. Arienne seized the opportunity to study his classic profile. He looked the part of a Greek warrior—a hard, carnal man capable of heroism and tenderness.

He must have felt her scrutiny, for he turned his head and gazed into her eyes. She stared back hungrily, an uncontrollable impulse spreading from her belly to her breasts.

Joshua felt her heat from three feet away. No she-wolf had ever looked at her mate with such fierce longing, with such naked thirst. She could make a man forget his mission, forget that he had been born for any other purpose than to satisfy her need. Instinctively he knew that if he touched her again, he would never be able to let her go.

10

As soon as she could do so without being impolite, Arienne excused herself from the table and hurried upstairs, distressed by her desire for the Yankee. She stripped off her skirt and blouse and fell into bed.

She couldn't sleep. Every time she closed her eyes she saw his face. He was becoming an obsession. Although she loved her father dearly, she began to wonder if she'd really endured the trials on the road to Pensacola because she hoped to see Joshua again.

She mustn't allow herself to think that way. She was playing a dangerous game by not telling her father about the spy. In order to preserve the old man's safety, she had to maintain her objectivity and certainly should not engage in schoolgirl fantasies.

After tossing and turning for two hours, she got out of bed and stepped onto the dark balcony. The cool wind blowing off Pensacola Bay pasted her camisole to her breasts and fluttered her pantaloons. She paced up and down, scarcely aware of the chill.

A sliver of moon drifted out from behind a cloud, illuminating her in its pale light. In the darkness below the balcony, a pair of gray eyes glinted.

Joshua hadn't intended to take this path to the fort. Arienne's siren call had brought him to her like some besotted adolescent. He scowled as a familiar hunger grew in his loins—a hunger that had grown to madness since he had taken his leave of her on the *Scarlet Lady.*

She tormented him like a piece of a puzzle that wouldn't fit. There was no place for her in his life. Her arrival at the fort could only complicate his mission. Damn, was he falling in love?

He heard the whisper of her bare feet carrying her back inside. Released from her spell, he turned and ran down the path, his forehead damp despite the coolness of the night. He must think about the job at hand!

The days were passing with frightening swiftness, and he was no closer to nailing DeCoeur and his inventions than when he had first come to the fort. The torpedoes were guarded zealously, as was the submarine housed in the floating dry dock.

Reaching the northern counterscarp of the fort

recessed into the bluff, Joshua identified himself to the guard. Immediately the heavy drawbridge was lowered. Langdon glanced into the deep dry moat as he walked across to the fort. Just yesterday a soldier had fallen into it from the parade-ground terreplein and broken his neck.

Passing through a labyrinth of arched brick galleries beneath the parade ground, he inspected the cannons and powder magazines. Gunners snapped to attention at this early-morning visit by the chief artillery officer. Playing his role to the hilt, Langdon ordered a mock drill. It was going to be pure hell getting at the navy yard.

The inspection finished, he climbed to the terreplein, returning the salutes of the dozen or so men slouched around the cannons.

The sun had risen while he was in the casemates, turning Pensacola Bay violet pink. On the sugary sands of Santa Rosa Island two miles away, Fort Pickens loomed long and gray, its cannons an open-mouthed menace to any boat venturing into the channel. Still, Pickens's gun crews didn't hit everything they aimed at, as the two-masted schooner, the *Judah*, rocking at anchor in the navy yard below attested.

The blockade runner had slipped through the channel under the very noses of the Federals only a few nights ago, bringing ammunition and supplies. Langdon leaned his elbows on the parapet and raised a pair of field glasses to his eyes.

Through the lenses he saw a small sailboat jammed with Union soldiers tacking across the bay, totally unconcerned with the twenty-four-pound howitzers looming from the walls of Fort Barrancas.

"Here comes them Yanks after their mail, sir."

Joshua looked around at Private Doug Barnes's pimply face.

"After their mail, hell!" A beefy sergeant in tattered breeches and an undershirt punched Doug on the arm. "They coming over to git laid!"

Barnes blushed and scraped his big toe through the sand.

"Was that you I seen over at Seville House the other day, Barnes?" the sergeant asked, leering.

"Nope."

"You sure it wasn't you with Rita? She likes 'em young and kinda wet behind th' ears."

"It warn't me!"

"Naw? You ever been laid, Barnes?"

Barnes darkened to purple. "My ma'd skin me alive if I was to try it, Sarge!"

The sergeant jabbed the boy in the ribs with his thumb. "Hey, fellers! Barnes is a virgin!"

"Leave the kid alone, Sergeant," Langdon ordered, lowering his binoculars.

"Aw, c'mon, Major Enright. I was just having fun with the kid. Sort of encouraging him, like."

"Encouraging him, eh?"

"Yeah. If'n he don't start using that little thing, it's liable to fall off!"

The soldiers burst out laughing. Doug Barnes seemed to melt like a sliver of ice on a hot street. The sergeant staggered around, holding his enormous gut, convulsed by his own humor.

Langdon glared at him. He wanted to pound his face into the parade ground sand, yet reason whispered that he couldn't afford to get mixed up in something that might land him in the guardhouse. But he couldn't resist.

He struck the bully just under the breastbone with his rigid fingertips and snatched his hand back to rest alongside the other on the parapet.

The sergeant's breath rushed out, and he fell backward over a cannon and landed with his knees over his shoulders. The men guffawed.

Langdon licked his finger and held it up. "Wind's a mite stiff today, ain't it?"

Ignoring the hapless sergeant, he again raised his glasses to the Yankees. A plan was forming in his mind, one so simple that he should have thought of it before.

He watched the men beach their boat. They looked hot and scratchy in their heavy woolen uniforms. None was armed. A young Confederate lieutenant went down to the boat and painstakingly inscribed their names in a ledger, then motioned to six guards. The lieutenant led the way up the bluff toward the woods.

Joshua handed the field glasses to Doug Barnes and ran down the parapet steps. He hurried through a series of vaulted galleries and exited the beach-level sallyport. Then he took a shortcut up the wooded hillside and sat down to wait.

Ten minutes later the Yankees and their guards came up a trail, the group as boisterous as children at a Sunday-school picnic. The lieutenant was just getting to the best part of an off-color story when Langdon stepped out from behind a tree and yelled, "What the hell goes on here?"

The lieutenant stopped dead in his tracks, and two Yankees cannoned into him from the rear. He saluted Langdon, muttering, "Oh, my God!"

The rest of the guards shuffled their feet and looked to their commander for guidance. The Yankees waited for the explosion with undisguised glee.

"I asked you what goes on here, Lieutenant?"

"We're, um, escortin' these Yanks to town, Major Enright, sir. Gen'ral Bragg don't care, long as armed guards is with them."

"Is that so? Where's your carbine?"

The lieutenant looked down at his hands. Seeing nothing but his ledger, he twisted around to look behind. Of his six men, only a buck sergeant had a rifle. He looked back at Langdon and scratched his head. "Dunno, sir."

"You don't know?"

"No, sir. Had one a while ago. Musta set her down to write down these fellers' names. Forgot to pick her back up again, sir."

The guards shuffled their feet and looked imploringly toward heaven. Just a simple miracle would do, such as rifles raining out of the sky. Nothing happened.

"We're running a war, not a bloody school outing!" Seizing the ledger, Langdon jerked his head at the sergeant, who was now holding his rifle dramatically on the Yankees. "Sergeant, escort your buddies to the guardhouse and lock 'em up for dereliction of duty. I'll take these Yanks to Pensacola myself."

"Yes, sir!" He shouted unnecessarily as he hustled his friends off to jail.

"Gentlemen," said Joshua Langdon, turning to the amused Yankees, "Major Cyrus Enright, at your service. We'll just avail ourselves of a freight wagon and head into town. It happens that I know of an excellent brothel there. Shall we?"

Seville House, nestled in the heart of Pensacola, was a brothel that combined old-world charm with New World gratification.

Joshua Langdon saw his companions through a set of double doors into a lobby nearly as large as the halls of Congress. Plush red carpeting cushioned their footfalls, and an elegant crystal chandelier tinkled when Joshua inadvertently brushed it with his hat. A polished mahogany bar stretched from one side of the room to the other, and in front of it were round tables at which cardplayers sat in comfortable chairs.

Although it was only ten o'clock in the morning, the elbows of two dozen patrons rested on the bar. Ladies wearing little more than lace and feathers circulated through the crowd, occasionally disappearing upstairs with a customer.

Joshua grinned across the room at a fat lady in an organdy gown. The enthusiasm of her piano playing compensated for her lack of skill. Seeing the men reflected in the mirror over the piano, she hollered, "Come on in, boys!"

Langdon turned to the senior Union officer, a middle-aged man going gray at the temples, with a rim of prickly heat showing above the collar of his woolen uniform. "Captain Nance, why don't you turn your men loose for a while? You and your two lieutenants and I will have a nice game of cards."

Nance nodded at the half-dozen men who had accompanied him from Fort Pickens. Unleashing wild yells, they pushed through the crowd to the bar. No one seemed to mind rubbing elbows with Yankees. Nance glanced at his two lieutenants before turning inquisitive eyes on Langdon. "What's on your mind, Major?"

"I'll let you know in a minute."

A striking blonde in a tight red gown swayed toward the officers. She threw her arms around Joshua's neck and stretched up on tiptoe to kiss him, crushing her huge breasts against his chest. "Solomon Enright! Wherever have you been?"

"It's Cyrus." He gave her a dismissive pat on the behind.

"What's in a name, anyway, you big hunk of man?"

"Look to Shakespeare for the answer to that one, Rita."

"Do I know him?"

"I'll introduce you sometime. Now be a good girl and fetch Mrs. Walsh. These gentlemen want a quiet room for a game of cards."

"Cards? Oh, Solomon, whadya wanta waste time playing cards with a bunch of Yankees for, huh?"

"Go along and do what I said."

She soon returned with a plump, matronly woman in a blue gown fastened at the throat with a cameo, her gray hair under an old-fashioned white mobcap. The older woman took Joshua's elbow in a surprisingly strong grip. "Nice to see you again, Major Enright, and a warm welcome to your friends."

"Thanks, Mrs. Walsh." He introduced the men.

"Rita says you want a game of poker, gentlemen. Follow me."

A narrow loggia stretched along the rear of the house, its floor-to-ceiling windows curtained with French lace. White and purple wisteria crawled over the brick window frames, while the perfumed scent of roses drifted through several open panes from an untidy garden in the back. The floor was of white Alabama alabaster, dotted here and there with hooked rugs. A round table and four Queen Anne chairs decorated the room.

"This'll do nicely," Langdon said as he settled into a deep chair at the table.

Mrs. Walsh produced a pack of cards from her pocket. "Help yourself to the liquor cabinet, Major Enright. You can pay later, as usual." She bustled out of the room and closed the door behind her.

Langdon dealt the cards quickly and threw a nickel on the table.

"Now then, Major Langdon—" began Captain Nance in a loud voice.

"Why not go out, stand on the bar, and make a public announcement that a Union spy is playing cards in the loggia? It'll make it much easier for General Bragg to catch and hang me."

"Sorry. I'm not used to this cloak-and-dagger stuff. I nearly fell over when you told me who you were a while ago."

"Just keep your wits about you, Captain. Some bright girl might be listening outside." He went to the liquor cabinet and returned with four tumblers and a bottle of whiskey. "Might as well make this look real," he said, splashing the amber-colored fluid into the glasses. He pulled a face. "I never could stand this stuff."

"It's like nectar to us, sir," said Lieutenant Gleason, a lanky fellow of twenty-one. He tipped the contents of his glass down his throat, looked at his cards, and threw a dime into the pot. "All we get at Pickens is scummy water out of the cistern."

"Who's commanding Fort Pickens?"

"Colonel Harvey Brown," Lieutenant McMann said.

"The West Pointer?"

"Uh-huh." Nance raised him a quarter. Gleason consulted his cards and threw in a coin.

"How many men are garrisoned there?"

"Two thousand, give or take a couple hundred due to jungle fever and bad water. We're squeezed into that damned fort like lobsters in a basket. The men have to sleep on a parade ground paved with crushed oyster shells. They strow pine straw around to make it a little less hot and miserable."

"Which it don't," said McMann, picking a pimple on his chin. He ran his hand through his thatch of greasy yellow hair. "The worst part is that the colonel thinks wearing these damned uniforms night and day will make us better soldiers." He plucked at the sleeve of his quarter-inch-thick woolen uniform, wrinkling his nose at the odor. "Of course, we take them off and sleep naked at night. Couldn't survive otherwise."

"Sounds like hell." Joshua played a card. Gleason and McMann folded. "Think your men are up to mounting an assault on the navy yard?"

Nance nearly dropped his cards. "What on earth for?"

"To blow it up, of course."

"If that were possible, we woulda done it long ago. Bragg's troops outnumber ours three to one. We wouldn't stand a snowball's chance!"

"Yes, you would. Let me give you the bare bones of the plan I've been kicking around. We can flesh it out after I get your consent."

Langdon leaned forward and spoke for several minutes, outlining a daring plan. Nance's expression remained dubious.

"I don't know, Major, if the risk is worth it."

"Then let me sweeten the pot." Langdon threw a silver dollar onto the table. "Have you ever heard of a device called a submarine?"

"I've heard rumors."

"Bragg has got one near completion. He's also got self-propelled torpedoes."

"Balderdash!"

"Ask Captain Pratt of the U.S.S. *Sheboygan* if torpedoes are balderdash."

"You don't mean he was hit by one—"

"I do mean," Langdon said, throwing his cards on the table. He had a royal flush.

Nance's face whitened. "I'd better talk to the colonel."

"Make sure you're convincing, Nance. Tell him we'll hit the base tomorrow night." He raked in the small pile of money he'd won.

"I can't be sure of getting his permission, Major."

"You've got to get it. The outcome of the war may rest upon whether we destroy that sub or not."

"Your plan sounds like a surefire way to get our boys killed. I doubt if Brown will go along with it."

"He's got to, unless one of you has a better idea." He steepled his fingers and waited. No one ventured a suggestion. "All right, then, that's it. I'd like you, Captain, to meet me here at two o'clock tomorrow with Brown's decision. We can work out the details then."

Nance stood up and, reaching across the table, shook Langdon's hand. He didn't release it immediately, but stared hard into the major's eyes. "You know what they'll do to you if you're caught."

"I know."

"I've heard stories of the Rebs using Yankee skulls for soup bowls," McMann said, tossing back a final mouthful of whiskey.

"Union propaganda," Langdon said. "You hear horror stories all the time."

"All the same, you'd best write your wife a farewell note," Nance said. "I would, in your shoes."

"I haven't got a wife."

"Your sweetheart, then."

"I'll think about it. Get one of the Rebs out there to escort you back to the fort. I'm not ready to go back."

After the Yankees left, Langdon poured himself a whiskey, grimacing as the awful-tasting stuff burned a trail to his belly. Would Arienne care if he got himself shot? He'd made her mad enough to wish him dead, but if it actually came to that, would she be pleased?

No. She wasn't that vindictive. She was willful, yes, and stubborn in the extreme. But she was also fair, and forgiving, he hoped. She just wanted to protect her father.

He leaned back and trickled more whiskey down his throat. Maybe he should tell her that Sir James didn't interest him anymore. The little man was just what she'd thought he was—an innocent dupe. He didn't have any power over DeCoeur. Bragg, DeCoeur, and Wilford Humes had closed the submarine deal without his help.

"Solomon, you big hunka man, it's about time those Yankees left!"

He didn't move when Rita slipped up behind him and wrapped her arms around his neck. She leaned down and nipped his ear. Joshua sipped his whiskey, wishing Arienne would magically appear in Rita's place. How would her teeth feel on his ear?

"Ain'tcha gonna say nothing?"

"Don't have much to say."

Rita flounced around his chair and flung herself into the adjacent seat. She grabbed the bottle and sloshed whiskey into McMann's empty glass, tossing it back with an expert jerk of her elbow. "If I didn't know better, I'd swear you was a virgin, Solomon."

"And exactly how would you know better, Rita?"

"I can always tell. It's my job."

"And you're the best in the business, I'll bet."

"You win. Wanna collect?"

"Let's just call it a draw." He pushed the small pile of coins he'd won across the table to her. Rita scooped them into the deep cleft between her breasts. She looked up at him expectantly, but he only handed her the whiskey bottle and stood up.

"You ain't leaving already, are ya?" She clutched at his sleeve and looked up at him with her big blue eyes. "We was just getting acquainted."

Langdon was conscious of an odd mixture of lust and pity as he gazed down at her. It would be easy to forget himself for a while in her arms, forget about the submarine and the danger he faced, forget about the haunting Arienne Lloyd.

"I've got to get back to work," he said after a long moment, gently disengaging her fingers.

"See if I ever do anything for you, Solomon Enright!"

"I hope you'll never have to." He bowed with old-fashioned gallantry and left the loggia. Relief at his escape lent speed to his heels.

11

From her balcony, Arienne saw Joshua Langdon return from Pensacola late that afternoon. He walked along with head down, apparently deep in thought. He didn't so much as glance at her as he cut across the backyard into the woods on his way to the fort. Miffed, she stalked into her room to dress for dinner.

Maybe she'd see him downstairs. Bragg demanded that his higher-ranking officers be present for dinner, and Joshua, as chief artillery officer, would surely have to be there. She vowed not to speak to him.

She caught herself. What sort of game was she playing? She wanted to be with him, to feast on his every word and glance, yet he was her enemy. How cruel life was, that she should become obsessed with a Yankee spy!

Where had he been all day? How did he manage to keep up the pretense of being a loyal Confederate officer? That Bragg was foolish enough to give him free run of the fort confounded her imagination. Didn't they have papers, or something, to check? Could a soldier just walk into a fort and demand a job, and a prestigious one to boot? She didn't understand it at all.

She turned when she heard a knock on the door, her heart racing. Had he come to see her?

"Arienne, are you all right?"

It was only her father. "I'm fine, Papa. I was just about to dress for dinner."

"Take your time. I've got to lie down for a while. I'm not feeling too well."

Was it his heart again? She opened the door to find him standing on the mat, his face sunburned and puffy. "Papa, what's wrong? Do you need your medicine?"

"No, just a cool cloth for this burn, there's a good girl." He sat down in a chair as she hurried to the washbasin for a rag.

"How did you get into this state?"

"I got tired of hanging around the submarine, so Thomas and I went fishing."

"And you stayed out too long and didn't wear a hat." She patted his cheeks with the wet cloth.

"Right on both counts, my pet, but I had a jolly good time. Thomas caught a small shark, and I got a moray eel!" His sudden grin reminded her of the man he'd been before her mother's death.

"You surprise me. I thought you hated everything to do with water."

"I do, but there's something about a big ugly fish

on the line that makes the old juices flow! Bragg's ordered the cook to fry up our catch for supper."

"Then let's tame this sunburn so you'll feel better. I've got some lanolin in the trunk."

"That's Sara's trunk!"

"Yes, I brought it from Jasmine Cottage. I didn't think you'd mind."

Sir James's mouth trembled. Burying his face in his hands, he began to weep.

"Oh, Papa, I'm sorry." She cradled his head in her arms, her throat tight. Returning to the States had proven too much for him, just as she'd feared.

"We've got to go home, Papa."

"No. I can't. I've got to see this thing through."

"It's not worth the cost to you!"

"I'll gladly pay it to ensure your future."

"What are you talking about?"

"If I don't get the plans for the submarine, along with a hefty purse of gold for Louis DeCoeur's assistance, your uncle will ruin me financially. You'll be a pauper."

"Is that all?" She sank down on the cot and gazed at him.

"Is that all! We're talking about your future—your security! Your chances for marriage!"

"Do you think those things matter, next to my having you alive and well?"

"My life is almost over—"

"That's not true! You've a long life ahead of you, as long as you take your heart tonic and stay out of trouble. Please, please come away with me to London!"

"A few more days. Just give me a few more days to get what I need from Bragg."

"Will you last a few more days under this sort of stress? First Mama, and then you."

"Your mother's death has nothing to do with this."

"It has everything to do with this! You closed me out then, just like you're doing now. My concerns are no more important to you than a gnat's. I'm a person, Papa! I have feelings!"

"I know you do. Sit down and control yourself."

She lay down on the cot and stared at him forlornly, tears rolling down her cheeks. Sir James cupped her chin in his frail hand.

"I'm sorry, baby," he said. "But I can`t go home. Not yet."

"Why not?"

"If I do, I'll lose my last chance to make up for the past eight years. I've got to see this thing through. Please, won't you stay with me? Can't we begin again?"

Arienne looked up into the face she loved. It wasn't his fault that Sara had died. It wasn't his fault that he'd been unable to cope. She must try to forgive him. "We can begin again, Papa. Just you and me."

The day of Joshua Langdon's projected raid on the navy yard began like any other. Just after sunrise, Wilford Humes and Louis DeCoeur went down to the dry dock to check the submarine. Sir James Lloyd reluctantly dogged their heels.

Work on the submarine was going better than expected. The engineers predicted the vessel would be ready for launching within a week and a half, perhaps sooner.

At DeCoeur's insistence, security in the navy yard had been increased. Instinct warned him that some mischief was afoot, but as yet he'd been unable to detect its source.

General Bragg awakened later than usual and wished he hadn't awakened at all. His ulcer burned, probably due to the large quantity of wine he'd drunk last night. The early-morning sunlight slanting through his window exacerbated his headache.

Groaning, he closed his eyes. The submarine floated into his vision. He groaned again. Worrying over the cursed ship was making a wreck of him. He had other matters to occupy his time, among them the care and feeding of some seven thousand soldiers on the post. Money and supplies had grown scarce, with the Gulf blockading squadron's patrols of the coast. He could only hope the submarine project would be successful so he could get back to soldiering.

He staggered to the washstand, soused his head and neck, and then rang for an orderly to fetch him a glass of milk. Feeling somewhat better, he dressed and went down to breakfast. He was disappointed to hear that Arienne Lloyd had breakfasted at five and gone out.

* * *

Two miles from the barracks, on a deserted stretch of beach bordering Pensacola Bay, Arienne Lloyd tethered the brown mare she'd borrowed from the livery stable to a stunted tree. Stripping to the skin, she tossed her white frock onto a branch and ran down into the cool waters of the bay. After plunging in, she swam back and forth with lazy strokes.

Confronting her father last night had been a relief. She had needed to let him know exactly how she felt after so many years of pretending.

She flipped onto her back and studied the pink sky, letting her toes drift down to the grassy bottom. Then she waded to the shore, dried off with a linen towel, put on her clothes, and retrieved a crab net and wicker basket she'd tied to her horse's saddle.

Rolling her skirts into her waistband, she knotted the basket's strap around her hips and waded into the shallows. She watched the rhythmic sway of the sea grass until she detected a movement slightly out of sync. Deftly she scooped the net into the water and captured a pale blue crab. She shook him into her basket, caught two more, and closed the lid.

Had her father felt like a crab enclosed within the narrow existence of Lloyd on the Downs? Maybe his coming to Florida wasn't totally Wendell Stuart's fault. Perhaps he needed a bit of excitement, or maybe he hoped to get rich.

No, she couldn't blame her father's actions on selfish motives. He'd told her in the past of Wendell Stuart's lack of principle, and his tendency to trounce on everyone else to further his own ends.

She had to get her father out of Pensacola before Wendell Stuart's cankerous greed destroyed him. She'd ride back to the post and give her father an ultimatum. She'd make him listen, this time!

Suddenly she sensed that someone was watching her, and she whirled around in alarm.

A short distance away, inside the woods, Joshua Langdon quietly sat on a black hunter with the reins gathered loosely in his hand and his right fist propped on his thigh. His eyes glittered like live coals as he surveyed her from the crown of her head to the hem of her wet pantaloons.

Arienne yanked her hiked-up skirts down over her undergarment. "I know it's your job, Major Langdon, but aren't you carrying this spying business a bit far?"

Langdon's white teeth gleamed under his mustache in a pirate's smile. "I haven't carried it far enough, to my way of thinking. Besides, you obviously don't feel the need to keep secrets, swimming around in your, um, altogether the way you were."

"You *saw* me?"

Langdon swept his hat from his head and placed it over his heart. "The merest glimpse, only, before I averted my eyes in true gentlemanly fashion."

"I'll bet!"

"I wouldn't lie to you."

"Ha!"

Joshua gave her a wounded look before replacing his uniform hat on his head. His horse stamped impatiently and snorted. Patting the hunter's satiny neck, he said gravely, "I wasn't spying on you, Miss Lloyd. It so happens that you've found my favorite bathing spot. If I had shown up half an hour earlier, you would have come along and seen me *au naturel*. Then who would have been spying on whom?"

Arienne jerked her horse's reins free of the branch, vaulted into the saddle, and jabbed his flanks with her heels. He stood on his hind legs and pawed the air before bolting down the beach like a greyhound, with his ears back, his head down, and his hooves churning up great gouts of sand and water.

In the far distance Arienne heard Joshua shout, but she only kicked the horse and screamed at him to run, unwilling to let the man see the tears of rage streaming from her eyes. She hauled the horse around the point and splashed through a shallow inlet. Hearing hooves pounding behind her only made her angrier. Joshua was twenty yards behind, shouting at her to stop.

"I hate you!" she yelled over her shoulder, paying no attention to the path her horse had chosen. "Leave me alone!"

The beach ended in a cypress grove matted with vines and Spanish moss. Skidding down on his haunches, the horse flung his head sideways. Arienne hurtled out of the saddle into the hanging vines.

She writhed around in a vain attempt to get free, enmeshing herself still further. Her horse scrambled to his feet, snorted sand out of his nostrils, and then ambled off to munch a tuft of grass.

"Are you all right?" Joshua asked as he jumped off his horse.

"Just get me out of here! This place is probably full of snakes!"

He grabbed her under the arms and dragged her out. He began to dust her off and pull leaves from her hair, but she pushed him away and turned her back.

"This was all your fault, Major!"

"Naturally. Everything that happens to you is my fault, you spoiled little brat."

"Spoiled brat!"

"That's what I said."

"You're a fine one to talk about spoiled brats!"

"Yep. I'm gaining a heap of experience with them."

It was too much. With a cry of rage she rammed her fist into his belly. It was like colliding with a train. Pain shot all the way from her fist to her shoulder. She doubled over, holding her hand.

Joshua took her injured limb and fought her efforts to pull away. "Be still, you little she-cat."

"She-cat! I'm sick of your insults!"

He massaged the bones of her hand and wrist. "This is the wrist you injured escaping the *Magna Carta*."

"Yes."

"You're lucky you didn't break it just now, throwing a wild punch like that."

"I should have punched you in the nose, I guess."

Joshua pulled her to him and looked down at her, a passionate light in his eyes. "You don't mean half the things you say."

"I meant it when I said I hated you."

"No, you didn't. That was your temper talking."

"My temper tells you to get your hands off me!"

He pulled her closer, holding her hands against his chest. "I am not your enemy, Arienne Dauphina Lloyd. You must realize that."

She shivered and closed her eyes tightly, willing him to go away, but his warm breath on her face fanned into life a hot flame of desire. How could she continue to fight when her traitorous body wanted so badly to melt against him, to take his hard kiss on her lips?

"Your father will be worried about you. Let's go back to the fort."

She almost fell as he dropped his hands from her shoulders. He reached for her elbow to steady her, but she shrugged out of his grasp and stepped back. "Go away."

"Allow me to catch your horse first."

"Don't trouble yourself. I'll catch him." She walked away on trembling legs. Fortunately, her horse was too tired to do more than flick his tail when she approached him. She swung into the saddle with none of her usual grace, feeling more like a wooden doll than a horsewoman.

"I'll accompany you back to the fort, Miss Lloyd." Joshua mounted his black and spurred him forward.

"I don't need an escort."

Joshua cast a look back at the thicket where she'd tumbled. He fell in beside her. They rode for a mile in silence before she reined in and stared him in the face.

"Exactly what are your intentions, Major?"

"My intentions?"

"Toward my father. Do you mean him harm?"

"No."

"Does that mean you won't try to arrest him?"

"Probably."

Arienne's heart skipped a beat. "Then you know he's innocent."

"I didn't say he was innocent. He's doing all he can to get the plans to the submarine. I don't intend to let that happen."

"How do you plan to stop him?"

"Just what would you do with the information, were I to tell you?"

"It depends."

"Checkmate."

"Checkmate, my eye! This isn't a chess match— we're talking about my father's life. If you had enough brains to bait a fishhook, you'd know he's under duress. He's doing it for me!"

"Then perhaps you'd best talk him out of it."

"Why do you think my face is blue, you mush-headed Tennessee Yankee? Uncle Wendell Stuart has Papa's money. If he doesn't cooperate, he'll lose everything he's worked for."

"And you won't get to be a debutante."

Arienne's hand tightened on the reins as if she planned to lash him across the face. "You're a wretch,

JOIN THE
TIMELESS ROMANCE READER SERVICE AND GET FOUR OF TODAY'S MOST EXCITING HISTORICAL ROMANCES FREE, WITHOUT OBLIGATION!

Imagine getting today's very best historical romances sent directly to your home – at a total savings of at least $2.00 a month. Now you can be among the first to be swept away by the latest from Candace Camp, Constance O'Banyon, Patricia Hagan, Parris Afton Bonds or Susan Wiggs. You get all that – and that's just the beginning.

PREVIEW AT HOME WITHOUT OBLIGATION AND SAVE.

Each month, you'll receive four new romances to preview without obligation for 10 days. You'll pay the low subscriber price of just $4.00 per title – a total savings of at least $2.00 a month!

Postage and handling is absolutely free and there is no minimum number of books you must buy. You may cancel your subscription at any time with no obligation.

GET YOUR FOUR FREE BOOKS TODAY ($20.49 VALUE)

FILL IN THE ORDER FORM BELOW NOW!

YES! *I want to join the Timeless Romance Reader Service. Please send me my 4 FREE HarperMonogram historical romances. Then each month send me 4 new historical romances to preview without obligation for 10 days. I'll pay the low subscription price of $4.00 for every book I choose to keep — a total savings of at least $2.00 each month — and home delivery is free! I understand that I may return any title within 10 days without obligation and I may cancel this subscription at any time without obligation. There is no minimum number of books to purchase.*

NAME_____

ADDRESS _____

CITY_____STATE_____ZIP_____

TELEPHONE_____

SIGNATURE _____

(If under 18 parent or guardian must sign. Program, price, terms, and conditions subject to cancellation and change. Orders subject to acceptance by HarperMonogram.)

GET
4
FREE
BOOKS
(A $20.49
VALUE)

TIMELESS ROMANCE
READER SERVICE

120 Brighton Road
P.O. Box 5069
Clifton, NJ 07015-5069

Major, and I hate you. Leave Papa alone or I'll tell General Bragg everything I know about you. They shoot spies in the South."

He leaned across the space between the two horses and stared into her eyes. "I'm betting my life that you won't say a word."

"If it comes down to a choice between my father's life and yours, you'd best write out your will, Major Langdon."

With that, she slashed the reins across her horse's neck and galloped up the beach.

James Lloyd saw right away that something was wrong with his daughter when she returned from her ride. Remembering their discussion of last night, yet unable to come right out and ask her what was wrong, he suggested a shopping trip into Pensacola.

General Bragg offered them the use of his private carriage and matched pair of dapple grays. Thomas drove them into town and dropped them off at a dressmaker's shop. There, Arienne spent several hours having a gown fitted to her figure.

Made of white lace and linen, the gown had short, capped sleeves, a low neckline, and full hoopskirts. It had been fashioned for the wife of a Yankee officer, but when the Confederates captured Fort Barrancas, the lady had rushed home to New York. She'd neglected to pick up two other gowns as well, which the dressmaker was happy to offer Arienne at a reduced price. She also sold her a parasol, a bonnet, and a pair of shoes.

Sir James breathed a wistful sigh when Arienne stepped out of the dressing room garbed in white from the top of her fashionably small hat to the toes of her high-button shoes. Her shining black hair cascaded in ringlets to her shoulders.

"You look just like your mother, my dear."

Arienne kissed his cheek. "That's the sweetest compliment you've ever given me."

Blinking back tears, he extracted a handful of wrinkled notes from his money belt and handed them to the dressmaker. "Send the rest of the things up to the post, will you?"

Twenty minutes later he handed Arienne through the door of a small café in the Seville Quarter. A rotund little maître d' trotted out from behind the bar and escorted them to the nicest seat in the house, a corner table with a view of the quaint buildings across a tree-lined alley.

The men and women in the room stopped eating to stare at Arienne as though she had just dropped in from another planet. She nodded and smiled as she untied her bonnet and handed it to an elderly black waiter.

With a theatrical flourish, a second waiter presented her a menu card. "May we suggest the swordfish, ma'am?"

"Please. And the stuffed crab. What will you have, Papa?"

"The same, I guess." He waited until the man had gone off to the kitchen before saying, "I don't know if I can choke down another fish. Don't these people eat beef around here?"

"There's a war on. They can't get it."

Sir James fingered a pink primrose in a vase centered on the tablecloth. He didn't want to talk about the war. If it were up to him, he would do exactly what his daughter wanted and sail back to England. This was the last time he'd ever cooperate with Wendell Stuart. After this, he'd put his money in a place where the manipulating bastard couldn't get at it.

"This is a magical room, don't you think?" Arienne said, looking around.

Sunshine streamed through the narrow, open windows onto the cypress floor. Ancient oaken casks of Spanish vintage lined the worn brick walls, while from the smoke-darkened beams overhead hung massive sides of ham and bacon. Oil paintings hung crookedly from nails driven into the crumbling mortar, and on the brickwork surrounding a huge fireplace a childish hand had painted scenes from German fairy tales.

She tried to imagine the inn at dinnertime, with candles on the tables. What a romantic place it would be, with the right person. Sighing, she pulled a primrose out of the vase and plucked the petals one by one.

"He loves me, he loves me not?" Sir James asked.

Arienne dropped the flower on the table, blushing. "I don't know what you mean."

"I thought you might be thinking about someone. Perhaps one of the officers you met at the fort?"

"Don't be silly, Papa."

"I hardly think it's silly for a girl to be thinking

about courtship. Your mother was married by the time she was your age."

"That's because she found someone irresistible. You."

"You haven't met anyone irresistible? I'm no expert, but some of those young fellows over there aren't too hard on the eyes."

"I hadn't looked that closely."

"Oh? I seem to recall you and Cyrus Enright giving each other more than a casual glance the other night."

Arienne looked away. "He's . . . a good pianist."

"And smart as a whip. And a gentleman, I might add."

"Appearances can be deceiving. Just because he defended you to Bragg when you started on that philosophy lecture doesn't mean he's a gentleman. He might be perfectly horrible inside."

"Oh, come now. He didn't once try to look into your gown, like most of the others did."

"Papa!"

He raised his hand. "Sorry, but a father has to be alert for any sign of a wolf in his daughter's prospective suitor."

"That man is not my prospective suitor, for heaven's sake!"

"I wouldn't mind if he were. He's handsome, learned, and probably has a bit of money tucked away. I'm not getting any younger. I'd like to see a few grandchildren before I die."

"Would you stop talking about dying?"

"It won't make the reality go away, dear."

"You're upsetting me. I thought you brought me here to make me feel better after the terrible morning I had."

"Well, since you mentioned it, what happened? I haven't seen you that angry in years."

"Nothing. I fell off my horse, that's all."

"Good gracious, did you get hurt? Why didn't you mention it? Bragg's surgeon could have looked at you."

"I didn't need to be looked at. I'm fine. It just made me mad that I was so clumsy."

She looked around as a brigade of waiters marched out of the kitchen bearing covered trays, china, stemware, soup tureens, and a bewildering array of dusty old wine bottles.

"I think they're bringing enough food to feed everybody in Fort Barrancas," Sir James said. "I hope you're hungry."

"Famished."

The maître d' saw to it that everything was placed exactly as it should be. He shook out Arienne's napkin and placed it precisely upon her lap, then turned her plate to better show off the grilled swordfish on a bed of greens.

Sir James chose a white wine. The maître d' assured him that it had been hidden deep in the cellar for just such an occasion as this.

Arienne would have preferred water, but seeing the anxious look on the maître d's face, she took a sip and complimented him. He released a puff of air from his cheeks and bowed. The waiters applauded. Arienne mastered an impulse to giggle.

Sir James dismissed the waiters. "Give me one steak-and-kidney pie, Arienne, and I'll die a happy man!"

"Let me take you back to England, then, and I'll give you pie for breakfast, dinner, and supper."

"Still trying, are you?"

"Of course."

"I don't have the blueprints yet. I've got to have them, don't you see? Can you imagine what would happen if Bragg were to give them to DeCoeur?"

"Would it be much different than your giving them to Uncle Wendell Stuart? He's just as bad!"

"He hasn't DeCoeur's genius for destruction. With the plans in Wendell Stuart's hands, we can be assured that England will get the device and not some other country."

"Can we? Since when has Wendell Stuart been loyal to anyone but himself?"

"I do wish you'd stop, Arienne."

"And I wish *you'd* stop." She reached across the table and gripped his arm, her eyes sparkling. If she had to beg him, she'd beg. "Please, Papa, come away with me. Thomas said he'd take us to Mobile. We can board a blockade runner and slip out of port. Come away with me before it's too late. Something terrible will happen to you if you persist in this mad venture!"

"Nothing will happen to me. I know exactly what I'm doing. I've been an attorney for a great number of years now. You're worrying for nothing."

"I can't help being alarmed. Promise me that you'll bend every effort to getting those blueprints as soon as possible. Don't take no for an answer, all right?"

"I'll do my damnedest, that's all I can promise."

But the expression on her face told him that she wasn't satisfied.

They left the café after a dessert of cold lemon pie. "Now, what else did you want to buy before we meet Thomas?" he asked.

"Where do you think we can find some paper and paint?"

"There's a stationer's down the street."

On the way, Sir James stopped at a candle shop to buy her a bundle of beeswax tapers. Eager to indulge her, he bought her a bottle of rosewater at the next shop and, from a street vendor, a bouquet of roses, jasmine, and baby's breath. At the stationer's Arienne purchased a small box of watercolors and a few sheets of rag paper.

Thomas was to meet them at a park on Palafox. Arienne stopped to study a beautiful old building two blocks from the park, thinking she might come back to paint it tomorrow. Along the wrought-iron galleries women in colorful, revealing gowns promenaded, fluttering peacock fans. One of them waved to Sir James.

"Why, Papa, you're blushing. Do you know that woman?"

"Certainly not!" Turning vermilion, he fumbled with his cravat.

"Then why would she wave—" Arienne broke off in sudden understanding and playfully pinched his cheek. "I'm surprised at you—a man of your age!"

Before Sir James could protest his innocence, a group of Union soldiers came out the front door. Seconds later Joshua Langdon walked out with a giggling blonde on each arm. He gave each a chaste kiss on the forehead, then an ungentlemanly pat on the behind. As he threw back his head to laugh at their squeals of mock outrage, his eyes fell on Arienne standing frozen across the street.

Dropping the bouquet of roses into the gutter, she fled down the street to the park, her stupefied father trotting in her wake.

12

Arienne saw very little of the countryside on the return trip to Fort Barrancas. Instead, she sat in the corner, staring sightlessly at the bay. Try as she might, she couldn't get the image of Joshua and his whores out of her mind.

Sir James sat in the opposite corner, resting his chin on his palm, mystified by his daughter's sudden hysteria in town. He hadn't noticed Joshua in the crowd of people across the street. Perhaps seeing the Yankees had upset her, after what had happened to the *Magna Carta*. He ought to try to talk to her about it, but her brooding expression made him hesitate.

They were less than a mile from the post when Thomas turned around on the driver's seat and stared at her until she looked up. "You gonna say what'sa matter?"

"No."

"You mad at your daddy?"

She shook her head.

"What eating on you, then?"

"None of your business."

"You just go on and scowl, then. Make yourself ugly. Ain't none of them boys at the fort be looking at you, coming around with that face all pouted up."

"I don't want them coming around me. I wouldn't trust a man with so much as a buttonhook!"

"Why, Arienne!" her father said. "I've never given you a reason not to trust me, have I?"

"I'm not talking about you. I'm talking about your dear philosopher friend, that *gentleman,* as you called him."

"Young Cyrus Enright?"

"That's him."

"But we were just talking about him a little while ago. Whatever did he do to you?"

"She just jealous," Thomas said. "She finally done hear he married, I reckon."

"Married!" Arienne rose off the carriage seat to grab him by the back of the shirt. "What are you saying?"

"You ain't hear he got a wife?"

"Where did *you* hear it?"

"Bragg's nigger groom done told me all about it. He know everything the gen'ral know, I reckon. Keep his ears open. The gal's name Rachel Markwardt. German, he say."

Arienne sank back on the seat, white-faced. To think she'd been fantasizing about a married man, and one who played around with whores, at that! How could she have been so foolish?

Thomas drove the grays up the hill to the officers' quarters. Before anyone could help her, Arienne jumped out of the carriage and dashed upstairs with her paper and watercolors. In her room, she stripped to her petticoat and began to paint.

Long after nightfall, her eyes smarting from the strain of painting by sputtering lamplight, she placed the final stroke. She fanned the paint until it was dry and balanced the portrait on the washstand. "There, I've captured you, Yankee."

Joshua Langdon sat on the sable hunter he'd ridden that morning, only this time he was dressed in a Federal uniform, unbuttoned at the neck to show a twist of black hair. A silver saber hung by his left side, and he held a pistol in his hand. His hat was pulled low over a dispassionate pair of eyes. Beneath his horse's hooves lay a crushed bouquet of roses.

As Arienne cleaned her brush in a cup of water, she became aware that the floorboards under her feet had begun to vibrate. Langdon must be playing the grand piano. An image of his hands on the ivories flashed into her mind.

She felt betrayed. Despite the feelings of antagonism she'd held because of his threat to her father, she had begun to care about him. She had dared to believe he felt the same way about her. Hadn't he nearly kissed her this morning?

Yet by afternoon he'd gone to a brothel. And now he had a wife.

Men were slimy, underhanded snakes, and Joshua Langdon was the worst one of all. She ought to give his portrait to General Bragg, along with a full explanation of who he was and why he was here.

She went out on the balcony, leaned on the railing, and gazed at the dark trees. Beyond, the bay glinted like a thousand sapphires. She tried not to remember the night in the lifeboat, when the stars had come out after the storm and sparkled on the Gulf just as they were doing now.

Could she turn in the man who had saved her life? This morning he had nearly promised not to hurt her father. As long as he stuck to that, she would stand aside and let him deal as he wished with DeCoeur. But that didn't mean she had to be civil to him. A man of his moral turpitude had to be watched like a rattlesnake. If he threatened Sir James, she'd have no choice but to reveal his identity.

Back in her room, she stared at his picture. She was tempted to rip it into tiny pieces and throw it out the window. As it was, she could only gaze at his image through a distorting mist of tears.

Hearing her father's shuffling tread in the hall, she snatched the picture off the washstand and shoved it under her cot. She snuffed the lamp, got into bed, and pulled the sheet up to her chin, remembering belatedly that she'd forgotten to lock the door.

She didn't want to talk to him, so when the door opened and a ray of light fell across the cot, she kept her eyes closed.

"Arienne, are you all right?" he whispered. When she didn't respond, he closed the door gently and went away.

Just before she dropped off to sleep, her fingertips crept under the cot to rest on the portrait. The chords of the piano seemed to energize it with a throbbing life of its own.

At two o'clock in the morning, Joshua Langdon strolled onto the parade ground of Fort Barrancas, his way lit by the twinkling stars on the bay. Not a soul was in sight. Mrs. Walsh's timely delivery of five cases of black-market Scotch had seen to that. The gunners were in the casemates—the armored enclosures for cannons—drinking themselves into oblivion. Good old Mrs. Walsh. God bless patriotic madames.

And damn Josh Langdon for an ill-timed jackass.

He had agonized over Arienne all evening and half the night, remembering her stricken face as she'd stared across Palafox at him. Of course she had thought the obvious—she couldn't have helped but seen him bidding that featherbrained Rita and her friend good-bye. He'd only touched them that one time, damn it, but how could he tell her that? He had been trying to look like he'd gone there for sex, not to plan an act of sabotage.

He had to stop thinking about Arienne. The troops from Fort Pickens would be arriving in the navy yard at any moment, if all was going according to plan.

Counting on the Scotch to keep the soldiers busy, Langdon lifted a pot of melted lead from a small brazier he had prepared earlier. Quickly he poured lead down the touch holes of two mortars and three howitzers, then spiked ten other cannons bearing on the bay. He had already done the same to as many cannons in the casemates as he could get to, nearly getting caught by an old sergeant who had returned unexpectedly to his post.

If he could just target the floating dry dock with one of the cannons, he could call off the raid. One shell would do it. But the cannons were seated such that none could be brought to bear on the navy yard.

Twenty minutes dragged by before Joshua sighted a spark on the beach. A torch flared into life, then a dozen. A warehouse burst into flame with an unholy brightness that illuminated running figures in the navy yard.

Langdon almost smiled. "Good show, Nance. Now burn the dry dock and get the hell out!"

But the guards on the dock began to shoot at the running shadows. Soon shouts erupted from the galleries below Langdon's feet. Drunken soldiers surged out of the stairwells and began to shoot at anything that moved in the yard.

Joshua didn't wait but leaped down a dark staircase three steps at a time. He dodged Confederates carrying powder and ball to their posts. They'd be mad as hell when they discovered their guns had been spiked.

Joshua reached the Spanish water battery in front

of the fort in time to watch the *Judah* going down by the stern. She was one schooner that wouldn't run guns to the Confederacy anymore.

The floating dry dock lay dark and untouched, as the Confederates had massed their forces to protect the submarine inside.

Joshua had time to pound a railroad spike into one of the cannons before the gunners reached their posts. Minié balls whined around his head like angry hornets.

A rebel yell ripped from hundreds of throats. Leading an infantry charge, General Bragg ran around the eastern scarp and advanced on the navy yard.

Outnumbered four to one, the raiders fled for their small boats. They began to row frantically back to Fort Pickens.

Suddenly the gun beside Joshua erupted. A cannonball skipped across the water between two boats. Livid, he leaped at the gun crew. "Hold your fire! We've run 'em off, and I'm damned if I'll see you shoot 'em like fish in a barrel!"

Through clouds of black smoke he could see Bragg's men forming bucket brigades to douse the warehouses. There were several bodies on the ground and one in the water. Langdon couldn't tell whether the uniforms were blue or gray.

Five minutes later Louis DeCoeur and Wilford Humes wheeled into the yard in an open coach. They leaped out, stampeded down the pier to the floating dry dock, and disappeared into the warehouse.

Joshua smashed his fist into the palm of his left

hand and swore under his breath. Men had died that night, but the submarine slumbered in its watery cradle as safe as a baby.

General Bragg stalked into the officers' mess at a quarter to six in the morning and growled at the twenty officers springing to attention around a long table to sit down.

He gnawed on a thick black black cigar as his gaze slowly traveled from man to man. His eyes touched Langdon, went on, and then returned.

"Major Enright! What've you got to say about the spiked guns?"

Joshua Langdon steepled his fingers, his black brows joining in the middle. "I'd give my right arm to be able to tell you who sabotaged them."

"And I'd give mine for a competent chief artillery officer! Someone with the sense to make sure the guns were guarded from a cursed Yankee saboteur!" He dragged at his cigar, smoke trickling from the corners of his lips.

"Sorry," Langdon said.

"Sorry? Sorry!" He dashed his cigar to the floor and ground it beneath the heel of his boot. "I'll give you sorry! You've got twenty-four hours to get me the name of the man responsible for spiking those guns. And there's something else I want to know, Major Enright. What the hell happened to the lookouts? How in blazes did ten boats row unnoticed from Pickens and attack the navy yard?"

Joshua eased the collar of his uniform away from

his throat. His aspect radiated extreme discomfiture—
for which he could thank his drama teacher at the
University of Alabama.

"Well, sir, it seems that yesterday afternoon a
wagon load of Scotch arrived, compliments of
Seville House—you know that, er, place of business
downtown?"

"Yes, I know it! So the men decided to have a little
party, I suppose!"

"No, sir. They decided to have a big party."

"Are you trying to be funny, Enright?"

"No, sir. I don't feel much like laughing."

Bragg paused a moment, breathing heavily. "And
they got slop-faced drunk!"

"Precisely, sir."

"Were you aware that your men were drinking?"

"No, sir. I reported to the fort for duty at one
forty-five. I immediately went to the parade ground. I
wasn't feeling very well—blamed it on a bad crab at
dinner—so I failed to notice how quiet everything
was."

"Until all hell broke loose."

"Yes, sir. I learned that my men had been in the
casemates getting drunk. No wonder they couldn't
hit anything."

"No wonder," said Bragg in a strangled voice.
"Gentlemen, that will be all for now. See to the
repairs in the navy yard. Double the watch on the
submarine. I don't want any more balls-up in the
future."

Twenty chairs scraped back, and the men
jumped to their feet and saluted. Bragg, with a

disbelieving look around, exited the hall muttering to himself.

Overhearing himself compared to the backside of an ass, Joshua Langdon rolled his eyes with embarrassment. He hoped that word wouldn't get out to Phi Beta Kappa. They preferred their members a cut above the ordinary jackass.

From the tip of her pointed nose to the end of her huge vertical tail fin, the submarine in the navy yard was a wonder of modern technology.

She was shored up on props on the floor of the floating dry dock, the warehouse sheltering her from inquisitive eyes. At forty feet in length, she was proportioned like a giant iron shark with a five-foot conning tower. Long stabilizing fins angled away from her sides and belly. There was a hole six inches in diameter at the tail, from which gas generated by mixing air with the liquid aluminum in the tanks would exit and push the sub forward.

Sitting on an overturned crate a short distance away, sheets of newsprint littered around her feet, Arienne sketched a group of engineers going over every inch of the craft like remoras on a shark. Her slender hands were black with charcoal, and her nose and chin were smudged. She brushed a damp tendril of hair off her forehead, leaving a smear of charcoal on her skin, and blew out her cheeks, wishing someone would open the warehouse doors. The dry dock was stifling this morning and reeking with smoke.

Since the raid three nights ago, the Confederates had guarded the dry dock with fanatical zeal. Sir James had asked Arienne to sketch the sub, since Bragg had promised him a set of blueprints, anyway. The general had reluctantly agreed to let her in.

Arienne wasn't enjoying the task. The sub made her cold inside. It looked like a coffin. Surely no one could live inside its black hull. Too bad Joshua's raiders hadn't destroyed it.

That he had been responsible for the attack she knew perfectly well. What she couldn't understand was how he could go about so nonchalantly. Didn't he know what Bragg would do to him if he were found out?

Why should she care? She'd asked herself that question a million times, and a million times she'd shied away from the answer.

It angered her intensely that despite knowing him for what he was, she couldn't extinguish the fires he kindled in her breast. She hadn't said more than three words to him since that day in Pensacola, though he'd tried several times to speak to her privately. She had become her father's shadow, hardly ever leaving his side.

She vacillated between an urge to throw herself into Joshua's arms and an overwhelming desire to tear his whoremongering face with her nails. If she could only be cold toward him! If she could once rid herself of emotion when she glimpsed him striding about the fort, she might consider herself cured.

Hearing angry voices, she looked up from her sketch. Humes, the chief engineer, was waving his arms in DeCoeur's face. The big Frenchman stood motionless, his face wreathed in a smile. His sardonic comments had, as always, riled Wilford Humes to screaming frenzy.

Arienne had learned over the last three days that Humes couldn't bear having his submarine design changed by the upstart Frenchman, and that DeCoeur couldn't resist baiting him at every opportunity. It was a miracle that work on the sub was progressing so well. DeCoeur figured that the machine would be ready for testing ahead of schedule.

His arguments deteriorating into strangled curses, Wilford Humes stalked away. He kicked a long brass torpedo and then began to hop around on one foot, groaning. Arienne got up and helped him to her vacated seat. He huddled on the packing case like a buzzard on a tree limb.

"That damned Frenchie!" he said. "I'd like to get my hands around his ruddy neck and choke him to death!"

"He'd tear you apart," Arienne said, eyeing the skinny frame quivering in the black frock coat.

"Damn, damn, damn!" Humes massaged his injured toes through his black, high-button shoe. "If only there was some way to get back at him!"

Arienne squatted down and touched one of her charcoal renderings. "You'll always have the satisfaction of knowing you invented this ship, no matter what little changes they make."

Humes gave her a funny look. "I understand

that Bragg's planning to give your father a set of blueprints."

"In exchange for services rendered by DeCoeur, yes."

"Does your father understand engineering?"

"No. He'd be hard-pressed to tell you why a wheel turns, Mr. Humes. He knows law, and that's about it. Why?"

"Well, he's liable to find himself in deep trouble when he hands the blueprints to his clients. They'll string him up, I imagine, or tar and feather him. He'll be ruined."

"What are you talking about?"

"Simply this: Bragg intends to give your father a fake set of blueprints. Anything built from them will sink like a stone."

"Really? Then General Bragg is going to be a mighty sorry man when I've finished with him!"

"No! Don't let on you know about it. DeCoeur is a dangerous man. This double cross is his idea. He stands to make a quarter of a million in gold from the Confederacy."

"I told Papa not to trust him!"

"I've got an idea to pay back both DeCoeur and Bragg," Humes said as he stared at the newsprint. Arienne could almost hear the gears turning in his head. "You're a damned fine artist. Ever done any technical drawing?"

"Some. I can copy anything."

"Good, because at four o'clock this afternoon, I'm going to bring you the genuine blueprints."

"I thought Bragg kept them locked in his safe."

"I happen to know the combination, dear girl, so don't worry about that. I'll bring them to you, and you copy them down to the last detail. You'll have all of DeCoeur's calculations." He rubbed his bony hands in anticipation. "I'll have my revenge, and your father will have what he paid for."

Arienne sighed. She hated this business. She hated the submarine. The only reason she could agree to make the copies was to keep her father out of trouble. "I suppose I should thank you, Mr. Humes."

"Seeing DeCoeur facedown in a cesspool would be enough, if you could arrange it," Humes said.

Stripped to her underthings, Arienne sat on the cypress planks of her bedroom floor late that evening with the submarine blueprints scattered around her. She had bolted the door and pushed the cane-bottom chair against it as an added precaution, leaving the balcony doors open for the sea breeze.

As she reached over to dip her iron pen into a pot of India ink, she heard soft footsteps on the balcony.

Anger surged through her veins more than fear. That the prowler might mean to harm her she didn't consider. All that mattered were the blueprints and the engineer who had given them to her. Humes would be in terrible trouble if Bragg found out what he'd done. Well, he wasn't going to find out!

She jumped to her feet and seized the only weapon she could find—a ceramic water pitcher on the washstand. Then she tiptoed to the French doors, but she could see nothing but shadows. She'd have to go outside.

Her pupils dilated as she stepped onto the dark balcony, raising the pitcher threateningly. If the prowler attempted to grab her, he'd get nothing but a fractured skull!

The balcony was empty. She peered over the railing at the dark bushes below. The roses growing up the trellis to the right gave off a sweet smell, but she could see no indication that they had been disturbed.

"Nerves!" She lowered the pitcher and went back into the room. The delicate hands of her gold pocket watch stood at half-past ten. She was way behind schedule, because Wilford Humes had failed to show up with the blueprints until almost eight o'clock.

Pleading a headache, she had stayed in her room instead of coming downstairs to supper. Wilford Humes had finally come up to the room with a long canister containing ten sheets of plans. He had also provided blank blueprint paper.

"Couldn't get into Bragg's apartment until a few minutes ago, Miss Lloyd," he had said rapidly in a high voice. "I had to send the guard off on a wild-goose chase. Bragg's spending the night in town. Seems he got mighty angry when you didn't come down for supper. Be careful with the blueprints—I've got to get them back by morning. I'll call for them at four-thirty."

With six hours to go, Arienne had completed four

of the ten blueprints. The drawings were a nightmare, the scribbled chemical equations in the margins even worse. If she left out an equation or transposed a number, she might ruin everything for her father. Or cause somebody's death.

Biting her lip in renewed concentration, she laboriously began to transcribe the complexities of Wilford Humes's air filtration system.

Modeled somewhat after the gills of a fish, the system ran on bottled air. A thin membrane of oiled rice paper, bonded to a rubbery substance Humes had invented, would filter the air pumped into the crew compartment, recirculating it through the system. In this manner, a crew of six men could stay alive for twelve hours before having to surface and replenish the air tanks.

At 4:15, Arienne finished the last sheet. Her copies were nearly indistinguishable from the originals. Straightening up like an old woman, she eased the kinks from her spine and flexed her cramped fingers. Then she stacked the originals in order and rolled them carefully into the canister. Pulling back a rag rug near the cot, she laid her copies flat on the floor and covered them with the rug.

Twenty minutes later Wilford Humes tapped on the door. Arienne threw on a pink satin dressing gown and, shoving the chair away from the door, yanked the scientist into the room.

"You'd better be glad it was me, young lady! I might have been anyone."

"You might have been, but you weren't." As she handed him the canister she took in his haggard face, red-rimmed eyes, unkempt hair, and rumpled coat. "You look terrible."

"That's a kind description, considering how I feel. If a dozen men in hobnailed boots tromped over me, sprinkled salt into my wounds, and did a jig on my remains, I'd scarcely feel worse than I do right now. If anyone finds out I gave you the blueprints, I'm a dead man." He tucked the canister inside his coat.

"How will you get them back to the safe, Mr. Humes?"

"I doped the guard's chicory. When last seen, he was propped in his chair outside Bragg's room, snoring like a hog."

"Then you'd better go before he wakes up." She stood on her toes and kissed his gaunt cheek. "Be careful!"

"I will." He rolled his eyes to heaven. "If I live through this, I promise I'll never do anything like it again!"

"That's just as well, considering the wreck this business has made of you. Now go quickly." She pushed him into the dark hall, closed the door, and leaned against it wearily for a second before tottering off to bed. Her fingers instinctively groped around under the cot until they came to rest on Langdon's portrait. Strangely comforted, she fell asleep.

Wilford Humes stood indecisively outside her door for a minute or two, like a small boy afraid of the dark but too unsure of his parents' welcome to risk slipping into their room. Remembering the canister, he crept down the long hall, keeping one hand on the stuccoed wall. When he reached the end of the main hall, he turned right and tiptoed to the front of the building.

The guard was sleeping exactly as he'd left him. Humes paused with a hand on the porcelain doorknob. Slowly he turned it to the left, then pushed the door open with painstaking deliberation. The oiled hinges made no sound. Sighing with relief, he stepped into the pitch-dark bedroom.

Then the door slammed behind him, and he heard the key click decisively in the lock.

13

Wilford Humes turned with a hoarse cry. He flung his arms up defensively as a flash of light seared his face. He staggered back, his pupils constricting painfully. "Who—who's there?"

"Can't you guess, *mon ami?*"

Humes couldn't see anything but a huge, bearlike shadow in the gloom behind the lantern. He stepped back into a table. "DeCoeur!"

"What sort of business are you about this morning?"

"Nothing. No business. I must've gotten into the wrong room by mistake." Humes tried to laugh.

DeCoeur unshuttered the back of the lantern he held in his fist. "Lying doesn't become you, my little colleague. Remember the Lord's commandment: 'You shall not bear false witness. . . .'"

"What the hell do you know of the Lord's commandments, you thrice-cursed Sodomite?" Humes lunged forward and hooked his fingers at DeCoeur's eyes.

The giant sidestepped and drove a hammer fist into Humes's belly, dropping him to the floor. Humes writhed at his feet, gasping for air.

"Sodomite, is it? You've been spying on me, then. Mistake number one, *mon ami*. And this is mistake number two." He reached into Humes's frock coat for the canister and removed the blueprints. "Naughty boy! Naughty little Yankee spy. Who have you shown these to?"

Humes dragged in air with a rasping gulp.

"You don't want to answer, do you?" DeCoeur said in a deceptively soft voice. "Mistake number three." He kicked Humes hard in the ribs with his size-eleven boots.

The chief engineer cried out and dragged himself away from the Frenchman. "Please, I didn't show them to anybody! Don't hurt me!"

"Hurt you? Nay, I'll merely play with you a bit, my friend, until you tell the truth."

"Don't kick me again. I—I was jealous of you. I wanted to destroy the plans. I lost my nerve at the last moment and tried to return them to the safe."

"You feel better now, don't you? Telling the truth is always the best way." He squatted on his heels and smiled. Still smiling, he broke Humes's jaw with a vicious left hook.

Blinded by pain and engulfed by animal rage, Humes launched himself straight into DeCoeur's face. There was a horrible snap, and the Frenchman fell backward, clutching his smashed nose.

Humes scrambled to the door on his hands and knees. The key was gone, and the door locked. He glared over his shoulder.

DeCoeur was clambering to his feet, smiling through a welter of blood. As Humes watched he lifted the hot shade off the lantern with his bare hand and dropped it on the floor. Then he raised the wick until the flame shot several inches into the air. Humes clawed at the door with his fingernails, whimpering with terror.

But DeCoeur only reached for the blueprints. "You wanted to destroy these papers, my friend? All right. I'll do it for you. I've already written them in my mind where nothing can harm them." He shoved the papers into the flame and watched them ignite, then threw them into the dark fireplace.

Humes watched helplessly as the paper blackened and twisted until only a small pile of ash remained.

Then DeCoeur turned toward him. "This won't hurt for long."

Arienne awakened with a start, her heart thudding wildly. She heard papers rustling. Swinging her feet to the floor, she cried, "Who's there?"

A hand clamped down over her mouth. Blindly, she struck out with both fists, catching her assailant in the ribs. She screamed as his hand slipped from her mouth.

"Shut up!" He shoved her back onto the cot. Again she heard the papers shuffling. He was trying to steal her copies of the blueprints! With all her strength she lashed out with her feet, catching him in the head and chest as he squatted on the floor. As he went over backward she leaped on him, punching and scratching. The blueprints skated across the floor in all directions.

"Damn it to hell, Arienne, stop it!"

The intruder flipped her onto her back and pinned her wrists to the floor beside her head. She could barely see Joshua Langdon's face in the gloom. She started to scream.

His mouth came down on hers in a hard, savage kiss, choking off her cry. When she tried to kick him, he rolled on top of her. She twisted and lunged, but he applied pressure to her hips with his pelvis, his manly hardness pressing against her through his trousers.

"You will be quiet, Arienne," he said, lifting his head.

"No! Get off me!"

"Only if you promise to keep your mouth shut."

"But you're trying to steal my blueprints!"

"That's right."

"I won't let you!"

"You can't stop me."

She took a deep breath, but before she could scream, his mouth was on hers again, and his tongue slid between her teeth. He released her wrists and clasped her head in his hands, using his forearms to hold her fists down on the floor.

Arienne struggled to no avail. His arms, his hands, his thighs were made of iron. Red-hot iron of such burning intensity that she couldn't stop an answering fire in her loins. As the seconds passed she became aware that every muscle in her body was straining to its limit, craving release.

No, she wouldn't give in! This was a married man, a philanderer, and a spy! He'd come to steal from her. His kiss meant nothing. Reclaiming her rage, she arched her hips against him and tried to knock him off.

Langdon broke off the kiss and raised himself to his elbows, pressing hard on her hips with his own.

She was breathing too raggedly to scream. It was a moment before Joshua could control his own breathing enough to speak.

"I'm sorry I had to do that. I had hoped you wouldn't wake up."

"Thief! Spy!" she said in a strangled voice.

"So are you."

"I am not!"

"We both know you had no business copying those plans."

"I didn't copy them. Bragg gave them to me for my father."

"Right. I saw Wilford Humes leave your room half an hour ago. I didn't know what he'd been up to until he sneaked down the hall toward Bragg's room, hiding something under his coat. It wasn't difficult to guess what you two had been doing."

"Did you confront him?"

"No. I immediately went outside and climbed the trellis. It took me a while to find the plans."

"Brute!"

She tried to break free to slap him, but he only tightened his grip on her arms and said, "Do you want me to kiss you again, girl?"

"Certainly not! Get out of here!"

"I'm taking the blueprints with me."

"They're for my father!"

"Do you want to get yourself and the old man shot? If you try to leave the fort with those blueprints, the general will have you in front of a firing squad for espionage!"

"But he's trying to double-cross Papa! Mr. Humes said he intends to give him a fake set of plans. Uncle Wen will destroy him!"

Boots thundered in the hallway outside. Someone banged on the door and shouted, "Miss Lloyd! Are you all right? Is someone in the room with you?"

Joshua came to his feet and made a grab for the scattered blueprints just as a second voice shouted, "Break down the door!"

Arienne screamed as the door burst open. Shadowy figures leaped at Joshua and bore him to the ground before he could get to the balcony. Through the sickening crunch of knuckles on bone and flesh, Arienne heard triumphant shouts. Then someone struck a match and lit the lamp.

Langdon was prone on the rug, and the three soldiers on his back were holding him down. His violent attempts to get free won him jarring kidney punches and blows to the head.

"Stop it!" Arienne screamed. "Leave him alone!"

"Bastard was trying to rape you, ma'am!" one of

them said. He pushed Langdon's face into the rug with his knee.

"You're killing him! Get off!"

Sir James stumbled into the room in his nightshirt. He stared in outraged surprise at the pile of straining bodies and at his daughter's disheveled dressing gown. "What's happening here?"

Seeing him reminded Arienne of Joshua's warning. Would Bragg really have them shot because of what she had done? The blueprints were scattered everywhere. She rushed to gather them, knowing she had only seconds to hide them before the soldiers noticed.

"What the hell goes on here?"

General Bragg, with the perpetual cigar clenched in his teeth, stalked into the room with six or seven junior officers. He looked at his men grinding the prisoner's face into the rug and at the girl squatting on the floor, gathering several large sheets of paper into her arms.

"Who have you got there?" he demanded of a sergeant.

"Dunno, sir. A picket seen him a-climbing up Miss Lloyd's trellis. We come up here quick. Ain't had time to look at him."

"Get him on his feet!"

They grabbed their prisoner under the armpits and jerked him roughly to his feet. He sagged between them for a minute, chin on chest, before raising a pair of steely-gray eyes to Bragg.

"I'll be damned," said one soldier.

"You will if you don't get your hooks off me immediately."

The soldiers released him and stepped back warily. Langdon raised a hand to stanch the flow of blood from a cut lip. Fire lanced his kidneys when he moved.

"What the devil goes on here, Enright?" Bragg gnawed his cigar, his expression murderous.

Langdon looked from the blueprints to Arienne's white face. Before he could frame an answer, a guard pushed through the mob in the doorway. "General Bragg, I've just found Wilford Humes in your apartment. He's dead, sir. Beaten to a pulp. Your safe's open. The blueprints are gone."

Bragg scowled even more fiercely. He strode past Langdon to Arienne and grabbed the papers out of her hand.

"Did you and Enright murder my engineer and steal these blueprints, Miss Lloyd?"

"Murder? We didn't . . . those aren't . . ." Suddenly too weak to go on, she sagged against her father. He guided her onto a chair and turned to face Bragg.

Before he could speak, Joshua Langdon said, "Miss Lloyd is innocent. Someone else killed Humes."

"You?"

"No."

"Then who? Here are the blueprints!"

Joshua looked at Arienne's terrified face for a long moment. "If you'll examine those more closely, you'll see they are just copies."

"Copies!" Bragg snapped the top sheet open and glared at it. Arienne buried her face in her hands, knowing what would come next. Somehow she'd have to convince the general that her father had known nothing of what she'd done.

"Copies I made," Langdon said.

Arienne looked up at Langdon, her mouth opening in surprise. He shot her a warning glance and kept talking.

"Humes took the originals out of your safe for me to copy. He must have been putting them back when someone killed him. Find the originals, and you'll find the killer."

"I've found him already. Sergeant, arrest Major Enright on the charge of murder and espionage."

"I didn't kill him, General."

"Shut up! It all falls into place now. The attack on the navy yard, the spiked guns, the blueprints, all of it!" He looked from Langdon to Arienne. "You made a fatal mistake, Enright, when you stopped here to take advantage of Miss Lloyd."

Arienne bolted upright in her chair. "He didn't take advan—"

"You needn't lie for me, Miss Lloyd," Joshua said quickly. Damn it, how could he shield her if she kept opening her mouth?

"For two cents I'd shoot you now like the dog you are, Enright, but since you're an officer, I'll court-martial you first, then hand you over to the firing squad." Bragg rolled the blueprints up and shoved them into his jacket. "Take the murdering whoreson over to the fort and lock him up in the darkest hole you can find. Get a search party out for the missing originals. He's hidden them somewhere."

Joshua Langdon managed one last commanding glance at Arienne before the soldiers hustled him out of the room. Bragg didn't follow at once.

"I'm sorry that Enright dragged you into this unfortunate business, Miss Lloyd."

"He didn't kill that poor little man, General."

"Of course he didn't!" Sir James said. "Enright's a gentleman and a scholar."

"He's a Yankee spy," Bragg said. "I believe he's responsible for the attack on the navy yard and a dozen of my men being dead. It seems that he and Humes had some sort of understanding." He raised his hand to prevent Arienne from speaking. "They must have had a falling-out, and he murdered Humes. He came in here to have his way with you, Miss Lloyd. Now excuse me. I've things to attend to. Good morning."

He went out and slammed the door. Arienne seized her father's hands. "He didn't copy those plans, Papa. I did!"

Sir James paled. "What do you mean?"

Arienne explained. He sat down on the cot and plucked at the collar of his nightshirt. "I'm aghast that you could have done such a thing."

"I was trying to help you. Mr. Humes said they were plotting to cheat you—"

"I don't believe it!"

"You're so incredibly naive, Papa!" Then she remembered Joshua's battered face and began to cry. "Why did that—that *idiot* have to try to steal my copies?"

Sir James stared at the floor. "He had one of two

reasons. If he really is a Yankee spy as Bragg seems to think, the answer is obvious. If, on the other hand, he is innocent, then he was doing his duty as a Confederate officer in preventing you from making off with the plans."

Arienne dropped her head and stared at her hands. Though Joshua Langdon was willing to sacrifice himself to save her, she couldn't allow that to happen. She'd have to tell her father the truth about him and then go and tell Bragg a lie. "He was on that Yankee frigate that sank our ship. He rescued me and took me to New Orleans. He came here to stop DeCoeur. I guess I should have told you."

Sir James could only gape at her. In the stillness of the room, she could hear the ticking of her pocket watch. She looked around for it. It wasn't on the washstand where she had left it. One of the men had probably knocked it to the floor during the fight.

Unable to bear her father's look of betrayal a moment longer, she got down on hands and knees to peer under the cot. There was the watch, next to the painting of Joshua Langdon. She left the watch where it lay and brought out the portrait. She sat cross-legged on the floor, looking at it.

"Oh, God, it's true," the old lawyer whispered, staring at the picture. "I was hoping you were telling me a story. Enright *is* a Yankee."

"His real name is Joshua Langdon."

"You knew all about him, yet you didn't tell me! Don't you realize what you've done?" His voice rose to an agonized shriek. "Because of this, I might never get the plans! Your uncle will ruin us!"

"Is money all you can think about? Joshua has been arrested for a crime I committed—"

"Good Lord, you don't mean *you* killed Humes!" He clutched his heart and looked as though he would faint.

"I just copied the plans."

"And Enright has taken the blame. Let him, then! He's doubtless the murderer, anyway!"

"I don't believe that!" She wouldn't let herself believe it. "He wouldn't have done such a thing!"

"Oh no? But he would pose as a Confederate officer to try to get close to me and get the plans. He was probably planning to kill me, too."

"You're wrong! He had practically promised to leave you alone."

"Ha! This gets better and better! You left me in a position of danger based on the word of a spy! I hope they waste no time in shooting him."

A cold lump of terror settled in her breast. "Bragg intends to shoot him?"

"That's what they do to spies and murderers, or did you think everyone was like you—content to give them free rein?"

"He's not a murderer!"

"Don't disgrace yourself further by trying to defend him. He's everything Bragg said he is. He doesn't deserve to be shot, he deserves to be drawn and quartered." In an unusual outburst of violence, Sir James ripped the portrait into four pieces and flung it to the floor.

Sobbing, Arienne snatched up the remnants and held them against her bosom. "I'm going to Bragg. I'll tell him what I did. I'll convince him that Joshua knew I'd copied the plans and was getting them back."

"No! Copying the plans was an act of espionage. Do you want to be shot as well?"

"I don't care!"

Sir James shook her until her teeth rattled. "Stop it! You've got to listen to me, little girl, if not for your own sake, then for the sake of your precious Yankee."

She caught her bottom lip between her teeth and looked at her father through tearful eyes. Perhaps, in spite of his anger, he'd thought of a way to save Joshua. He was an attorney, and wasn't pulling people out of impossible spots the only honorable justification for a barrister's existence?

Sir James took her hand. "Bragg hasn't any proof that young Enright, er, Langdon, killed Humes. Unless he finds those originals, he'll have to accept that part of Langdon's story. Langdon will probably be able to talk his way out of the charge of espionage as well."

"He's not going to try to talk his way out of it, Papa! He's covering for me, can't you see that? He warned me what would happen if I were caught— you and I could be shot!"

"That's right. So keep quiet and let him do what he needs to do."

"You expect me to sit by while he goes to the firing squad?"

"If you open your mouth, you'll prove him a Yankee spy. Don't you see, no matter what you say to Bragg, he'll look guilty. He's no suicidal maniac—I'm sure he's got a plan to save himself."

She jumped to her feet and walked to the French doors to stare out at the dawn. "I'll be silent for as long as I can," she said, turning to look at him. "But somehow, someway, I'll get him free."

"Why? Are you in love with him?"

She looked away. "I owe him my life."

"You didn't answer my question."

"He's a married man."

"So? I'm your father, and you obviously didn't feel loyal enough to me to tell me what was going on. Why should it matter to you if he's got a wife?"

"It matters," she said, bowing her head. "I've got to get him free. After that, I'll never see him again. You have my word on it."

"That's not good enough. You'll return to New Orleans with Thomas in the morning. You can stay at Jasmine Cottage until I finish here."

"I won't leave!"

"I'll have you bound and trundled into the wagon, if I have to." He grimaced and clutched his chest. Damn it! His digitalis was in his room.

Arienne set her fists on her hips. "Do that, Papa, and I'll tell the soldiers that I copied those blueprints to lure Cyrus Enright into my bed."

He stared at her in helpless rage. "I thought I knew you."

"We became strangers when Mama died, don't you remember?"

He couldn't speak. Shaking his head in defeat, he left the room.

Arienne walked out onto the balcony and leaned on the railing. The fort lay black and silent on the bluffs. Somewhere in that dark bastion Joshua was chained. It should have been her.

"I don't care what you've done," she whispered. "I'm going to get you out of there."

14

"You used to come up with crazy plans, gal, but this 'un's the craziest one yet."

Thomas drew his old wagon to a halt in the alley behind Seville House. He glanced at the flowers in the garden, still wet with morning dew, then at Arienne sitting quietly beside him. Despite the warm morning, she wore a high-necked blue dress. He could barely see her face through the heavy black veil dangling from her oversized hat. "Sir James'll skin me alive when he hears I brung you to a who'house."

"I'm just here to talk to somebody, Thomas, you old woman." She climbed off the seat before he could come around to help her.

She had paced her balcony until dawn, concocting a plan, and Thomas wasn't going to talk her out of it! Especially after the news she'd heard at breakfast: Joshua was to be executed the day after tomorrow.

"Just stay here and act casual," she said to Thomas.

"Casual? Behind a who'house?"

"Smell the flowers or something. I'll only be gone a few minutes!" She pushed open the iron garden gate and entered the veranda.

She paused to adjust her heavy veil, her heart pounding thunderously in her ears. Piano music tinkled in the front room. She could hear a deep rumble of voices punctuated by feminine giggles. Wiping her sticky palms on her skirt, she walked down a long hallway to the barroom.

Then she stopped, taken aback by the crystal chandeliers, the kaleidoscopic image of dancers in the mirrors over the bar, the men holding half-dressed girls on their laps. For a moment it seemed that Bragg's entire force was being entertained.

"Ya ain't gonna get yourself a man wearing widow's weeds, honey," said a sugary voice at her elbow. Arienne turned and found herself staring at the biggest, barest pair of breasts she'd ever seen in her life. There was no mistaking the girl in the tight, low-cut red gown. She was one of the sluts Joshua had fondled on the sidewalk the other day.

Misunderstanding Arienne's angry silence, the blonde giggled and gestured around the room with a glass of whiskey she held in her red-tipped fingers. "Don't feel bad, honey, we cater to all kinds here. There's men that likes to refresh the newly widowed, y'know?"

"You're drunk!"

"Hey, where ya goin, honey? Rita didn't mean ya no harm, y'know. If you're needin' a job, I'll take ya to Miz Walsh. I got to take a breather, anyhow, y'know?"

Arienne's eyes glittered through her veil. "All right. You lead."

Two minutes later Arienne found herself in a charming whitewashed bedsitter that opened onto the loggia. A round little woman rose from behind a littered desk to shake her hand. "Hello, my dear. I'm Mrs. Walsh."

"She knows who ya are. I already told her I was bringing her to see ya. She needs a job."

"Go on back to work, Rita." Mrs. Walsh waved Arienne to a seat. "Take off your hat so I can see your face. Uh-huh, you're a looker, all right. So you need work?"

"No. I need help."

"This isn't a charity ward. What do you want?"

"I want to save a captured Union spy from the firing squad," she said with more calm than she felt. "I think you know the man."

"I don't know any spies, Yankee or otherwise."

"That's not what I heard."

"Well, even if I did, what makes you think I'd be willing to help one?"

"You're a Yankee, aren't you? Boston?"

"I make my living in the South. Where I hail from is immaterial."

Arienne hesitated. What would it take to sway the woman? "I'll pay you handsomely."

"And how would I spend it, if Bragg locks me up for aiding and abetting a condemned man?"

Arienne leaned forward in her chair. "I don't have an answer for that, but if you had any sense at all, you'd gladly accept a chance to tip St. Peter's balance book a little your way, *Madam* Walsh!"

Mrs. Walsh was silent for a moment. "Who is this Union spy?" she asked.

"Major Joshua Langdon. He was using the name Cyrus Enright."

The woman's eyes brightened in recognition. "I knew there was something dashing and daring about that man! All the girls were wild to have him, but I knew there was more to him than mere animal appeal." Arienne flushed, and Mrs. Walsh noticed. "Jealous, eh? Are you his wife?"

"No. He's already got one. I'm a . . . friend."

"Ah, yes. A man like him must have plenty of those."

"Are you going to help me or not?" Arienne leaped to her feet.

"Sit down and control yourself, young woman," Mrs. Walsh said. "Of course I'll help you. The Union has my sympathy. I've done a good bit of spying myself. I know a few tricks."

Arienne sank back in relief.

"Now then, what do you propose we do to help the beleaguered Major Langdon?"

"I need a cloth-headed girl with the body of a Venus de Milo," Arienne said.

A shrill giggle came through the window. The women looked out to see Rita prancing down the street on the arms of two soldiers. Arienne met Mrs. Walsh's gaze. Slowly they both smiled.

*   *   *

Thomas pushed himself away from the wall of a carriage house and hurried to open the back gate for Arienne. She was veiled once more and carrying a large sack. He helped her into the wagon, whipped up the horse, and caromed down the alley.

"How'd it go, gal?"

"I'll tell you once we're out of town."

After a while the stuccoed houses gave way to a long stretch of trees lining the sandy road. "They're going to help us," she said. "I knew they would!"

"Then you knows whores better'n I does."

Arienne cast him a sidewise look through her veil, but he sat hunched over the reins, gazing over the roan's ears.

"You still want me to get you a boat?" Thomas asked.

"Yes. He'll have to go straight to Fort Pickens after he escapes."

"How he gonna get out of jail?"

"He's going to blast his way out. Go to the fort this afternoon and give him this sack. He'll know what to do with it."

Thomas looked at the bag on her lap. "They ain't gonna let me give him no guns, Arienne."

"There aren't any guns in there, or anything that'll get you in trouble. You can let them examine the contents to their hearts' content."

"Then what in the sack?"

"White flour, rock candy, and a bottle of whiskey."

"He gonna eat his way out? You got a touch of sun, gal."

"Tell him to look for a note."

"A note? Supposing I gets caught carrying it?"

"You won't. It's a secret message. I wrote it with milk, just like Napoleon Bonaparte's spies used to do."

The blacksmith rolled his eyes. "You sure is one crazy gal!"

"You'll be talking out of the other side of your mouth after you see how smoothly this operation goes."

"Something bound to go wrong. You jest give up this crazy idea before it happen to you. Your pappy'll have kittens if you gets hurt."

"I won't get hurt, and Papa won't know a thing about it. I'll be safe in bed by the time he hears Joshua has escaped. Don't worry."

"Don't worry." He shook his head. "Last time I heard that, you was jumping off the smithy roof with Miz Sara's ostrich fans tied to your arms."

"I've got more sense than that now."

"Mmph." He slouched over the reins. "Ain't nobody got sense when they in love."

Arienne blushed scarlet. She didn't speak again until the wagon rumbled up the hill to the post. Thomas halted by the officers' quarters.

"I wonder who that coach belongs to?" the girl said, shading her eyes with her hand. A battered rental coach was standing before the doors. The passengers had apparently gone inside, leaving piles of expensive leather luggage for the driver to haul in by himself. He came out just then, shouldered a heavy steamer trunk, and trudged back up the steps.

"Probably somebody visiting the gen'ral," Thomas said. "You go on and lay down awhile. Gimme time to put up the hoss, then I'll mosey over to the fort see if I can get in."

"You've got to see him!"

"I'll do it, gal, just gimme time."

Arienne squeezed his hand. "You'll make a wonderful spy."

"I just don't wanta make a dead one."

Arienne jumped down from the wagon and ran up the front steps. She pushed opened the heavy door and stepped inside. The mess hall was cool and dark, a welcome relief after the warm ride from Pensacola. She took off her black hat and flung it in the corner, and then turned to adjust her hair in an ornate mirror next to a window.

Suddenly she whirled with a small cry.

"You're as lovely as ever, Arienne Dauphina," said Lord Wendell Stuart Lloyd III, rising from the depths of an armchair.

"You!" He couldn't have chosen a worse time to pop back into her life.

"In the flesh."

"I thought you were in England, you conniving old scoundrel!"

"Tut tut, my dear," he said, walking toward her, his cane rapping the floor with each footfall. He was, if anything, fatter and uglier than ever. "Is that any way to welcome a doting uncle who's come all this way to see you?"

"Leave her alone, Wendell," Sir James said, coming into the room with a decanter of brandy and a tumbler. He set the tray on the sideboard. "Come and get that damned drink you wanted." It was obvious he didn't plan to drink with his brother.

"Papa, what's he doing here?"

"Go ahead, tell her," Wendell Stuart said with a laugh. He flopped into the armchair and poured himself a drink. "Tell her that I couldn't trust you to get a simple job done, so I've come to do it myself."

"You surprise me, Uncle," Arienne said before her father could reply. "I thought the British ambassador to the United States couldn't afford to be seen consorting with the enemy."

Lloyd laughed again. "I haven't been seen, my pet. I entered Charleston Harbor on a well-paid blockade runner, then came straight here in a closed coach. When I've finished my business, I'll wave my diplomatic pass and breeze into Washington to take up my duties."

"Why don't you go today? You should never have gotten my father into this mess!"

"He could have refused the assignment."

Footsteps sounded on the front porch, cutting off Arienne's retort. The door opened, and General Bragg and his adjutant came in, slapping dust from their jackets. The adjutant was red-faced and sweating.

Bragg had not known the ambassador was coming until his presence had been announced ten minutes ago, but his aspect was calm and unruffled. He bowed to his distinguished visitor. "Lord Lloyd, I'm pleased to meet you at last," he said. "DeCoeur has done some splendid work for us. I trust your brother has told you that not only has he developed the torpedo to our satisfaction, but reworked the propulsion system for our submarine?"

"Aye, he's told me all that."

"The South owes you her eternal thanks."

"Thanks, be damned," Wendell said. "Let's have the blueprints."

Joshua Langdon gripped the iron bars of his cell, an empty ten-by-ten-foot powder magazine in the counterscarp gallery in Fort Barrancas. Arched brickwork held back thousands of tons of earth above and behind him. A worn straw mattress lay on the sandy floor. A tin slop bucket with a wooden lid doubled as a chair, and a tallow candle guttered feebly on the wall.

He'd been tried and found guilty. It made no difference that he hadn't been present at his own trial. The evidence was against him, and that was that. Bragg had given him two days to make peace with his Maker, but Langdon had no intention of doing so. The Almighty promised a man threescore and ten, and he intended to take his full allotment.

Footsteps scrunched in the gallery. Private Doug Barnes appeared a moment later with a carbine over his shoulder. His youthful face looked excited. As Doug's first damned Yankee spy, Langdon was the object of envy and admiration.

"Brung somebody to see ya, Major Enright, sir," Barnes said. He beckoned to someone down the gallery. "Come on, boy."

A tall black man stopped in front of the cell, and his brown eyes slowly took measure of Langdon. Joshua remembered seeing him around the post.

"Cap'n Buchanan says ya kin have five minutes with yer vis'tor, sir, but I'll give ya ten."

Langdon nodded his head. "That's right neighborly of you, Doug," he said, accentuating his drawl. He liked the Alabamian. The kid was an innocent, despite his rough life in the army. It was too damned bad he'd have to use him to break out of jail.

"Miz Arienne ast me to bring you some stores." Thomas pushed a sack between the bars.

Langdon hid his surprise. "Thanks."

"Ain't nothin' but flour, Major," Barnes told him. "And a bottle o' whiskey. That gal must like you some."

"She just wants to anesthetize me so I don't feel the bullets, I reckon."

"She want you fat when you goes, too," Thomas said, reaching into his shirt for a small brown parcel tied with string. "Here."

"Wait jest a dang minute!" Doug intercepted the package. "I ain't checked that!" He untied the string and opened the paper. Rock-candy crystals glinted like quartz in the dim light. "Guess it ain't nothing but candy," he said, helping himself to a piece before handing over the parcel. "Thought she mighta sent a gun or chisel or something."

"Be hard to break out with rock candy and old paper," Thomas said. He gave Langdon a slow wink. "I got to go. Wisht that gal'd sent you some milk to go with that candy."

Langdon waited until Thomas and Doug had disappeared down the counterscarp gallery before sitting down on the mattress to examine the brown paper. Nothing. He scratched the bristles on his chin, wondering at the trick. Milk. Of course! He got up and held the paper close to the candle. Soon dark brown letters began to appear on the lighter paper.

MAKE BOMB, NOT BISCUITS. DISTRACTION TOMORROW 8:00 P.M. GUARANTEED TO GET RID OF GUARDS. MEET YOU IN TREES.

Great. Arienne was going into the spy business now, and liable to get herself killed. Langdon held the paper in the candle flame until it blackened to ash. He ground the bits under his heel. Then he took a swallow of whiskey and hid the bottle with the sack of flour under his mattress.

Arienne Lloyd was awakened from a much-needed nap by a knock on the door. She opened it to find a messenger shifting from foot to foot on the mat with a card in his hand. "Gen'ral ast me to give you this, ma'am."

"Thank you." She turned her back and quickly scanned the note, which requested her presence at dinner that night. She would have liked to send her regrets, along with instructions on where Bragg could stick his invitation, but when she looked at the messenger, her face was composed. "Tell him I'll be very glad to take dinner with him this evening," she said.

If there was anything further to be learned about Joshua's fate, tonight would be the time to find out. She would be at her charming best, she decided. But had an onlooker glimpsed her expression just then, he would have seriously doubted her ability to be civil, much less charming.

To play up her dark beauty, Arienne selected the white gown her father had bought her. She doused herself liberally with rosewater and then coiled her raven hair, leaving a few ringlets cascading to her shoulders. The maid had left a spray of primroses on the washstand, and these she entwined in her coiffure. Next she applied a thin line of lampblack to her lids and very lightly rouged her lips and cheeks. With her sapphire eyes burning almost feverishly, she went down to dinner.

Bragg's staff had seen the lovely girl many times, but tonight they could only stare in dumbfounded admiration as she swept regally into the hall and curtsied. Several young men overturned their chairs as they sprang up to assist her to the seat next to Bragg's.

Sir James was seated to her left, and Wendell Stuart across from her, in the chair Joshua had usurped after playing *The Marriage of Figaro*. She had to struggle to keep her eyes off the silent piano. That night seemed like a hundred years ago.

"We're pleased you could join us, Miss Lloyd,"

General Bragg said. As he kissed her hand his deep eyes held her gaze for a beat too long to be gentlemanly.

"I'm happy to be here," Arienne said with an ingenuous smile. The general seemed relaxed tonight, his face young and smooth in the candlelight. She wondered how he could look so well after sentencing a man to death, but she knew she mustn't reveal her feelings. Bragg must be made to think she had forgotten the major.

"A toast to my niece," Wendell Stuart said after everyone had been seated and the waiters had begun serving dinner. He raised his glass and licked his thick lips. "May she forever embody the qualities of innocence, virtue, and everlasting chastity."

Arienne blushed. The men, who had heard of Cyrus Enright's attempt on her virtue last night, answered the toast with warrior zeal touched lightly with embarrassment. Sir James glowered at his elder brother and did not drink.

"May she always be protected by soldiers brave and true," said a captain, offering a second toast.

"Thank you, gentlemen," Arienne said before another could be raised, "but the honors are yours." She raised her glass. "May you ably defend the South, and may God grant you victory."

"There's no need for prayer, mademoiselle," Louis DeCoeur said from the foot of the table. Arienne had not noticed him before, but now she couldn't hide her expression of distaste. "The thing's sewn up now that DeCoeur's given them a torpedo boat."

"You discount the hand of God in the cause,

Mr. DeCoeur?" asked the chaplain from his seat halfway down the table.

The Frenchman put a finger beside his nose and gazed at the ceiling. "He put bauxite on earth, sir, and told young Adam that it was for man's use. After that, He went off to take a nap, leaving Man to fight his own battles."

DeCoeur's blasphemy prompted an outraged gasp around the table. Wendell Stuart burst out laughing. "Adam didn't have the foggiest idea how to put bauxite to use, DeCoeur. That's why God made you."

"The Almighty uses simple men to accomplish his work," Bragg said. "You'd do well to remember that, DeCoeur."

"Simple men, sir?" he said. "And do you think a simple man could have set up an aluminum-rendering operation in so short a time, and developed an engine using the stuff for power?"

"I didn't mean it quite that way, DeCoeur. Your operation is a work of genius."

"And when do you hand over the blueprints, as well as the payment for the torpedoes DeCoeur built, General?" Wendell Stuart asked.

"We'll discuss that after dinner, Lord Wendell. Miss Lloyd, may I refill your glass?"

"Please," Arienne said. Her uncle was looking at her strangely. Feeling his foot groping about under the table, she quickly tucked her feet under her chair. She looked at Bragg, determined to lead into the subject of Joshua Langdon without seeming to. "The work you're doing in the navy yard amazes me, sir. However have you kept it a secret from the enemy?"

Bragg gave her a long look, but her expression indicated only polite interest. "I fear it's not a secret anymore, Miss Lloyd. The attack on the yard wasn't mere harassment. They intended to burn the dry dock and destroy the sub, I think."

"Why, how terrible!"

"When do you shoot the spy that masterminded all that?" Wendell Stuart said.

Arienne fingered her wineglass, her agitation revealed only by a slight tightening of the corners of her mouth.

"Day after tomorrow," Bragg said.

She still had time, then. Arienne had feared the execution date might have been pushed up.

"I'd like to witness it," Wendell Stuart said.

"We ordinarily don't allow civilians to watch executions," Bragg said as he began to cut the shark steak on his plate.

"Afraid I won't have the stomach for it?" Wendell Stuart pushed a knife load of meat into his mouth. "Hell, I'll pull the trigger myself and feed the bastard's remains to the sharks."

Arienne dropped her fork on the floor and bent down to retrieve it, hiding her sudden pallor from Bragg. How was she going to get through this ghastly meal without revealing herself? Surely her intentions were stamped on her forehead for all to read!

"I'll thank you to shut your mouth, sir," said an officer sitting close to Lloyd. "I'll not abide such talk in the company of a lady, and the rest of us would prefer a lighter topic at dinner."

Arienne surfaced with the fork and gave the officer a small smile of gratitude. With an effort, she began to speak to Bragg of other things. She knew that she was drinking too much wine, but it seemed the only way to get through dinner. She was uncomfortably aware of Wendell Stuart's pale eyes on her. Realizing that there was nothing of use to be learned, she excused herself as soon as she could, leaving her food untouched.

Bragg watched her go with an unreadable expression in his eyes. She had handled herself well despite her uncle's uncouthness, but what were her feelings for Major Enright? Had she given up her romantic notion that he was an innocent Confederate officer caught in a conspiracy?

Women were flighty creatures. They could love you one day and hate you the next, or vice versa. No doubt she had finally recognized that he, Bragg, had saved her from rape last night. If she were still angry at him over Enright's arrest, she wouldn't have troubled to doll herself up for dinner tonight.

The general smiled and lit a cigar. The waiters were pouring brandy now, the steak had filled the corners of his belly nicely, and the men were free to engage in masculine conversation without the confinement of a woman's presence. There was nothing to do but sit back in an alcoholic haze and enjoy the evening.

An hour later Wendell Stuart excused himself from the table. "I'm too bleeding drunk to sit up a moment longer. Nay, nay, James, you don't need to help me. I've got double vision, but I can find at least one of the staircases to my room!"

Sir James fumbled in his waistcoat for the lovely briar pipe Arienne had bought him in Pensacola that morning. She'd bought it as a sort of peace offering, and he was itching to break it in. Somebody went over to plink out a few tunes on the piano. The playing was nothing like Langdon's masterful interpretations, but it was good enough for a late-night smoke and a drink. He closed his eyes and leaned back in his chair, puffing his pipe.

Upstairs, Wendell Stuart shed his drunkenness and walked as quietly as he could down the dark hallway to Arienne's room. Then he put his hand on the porcelain knob and slowly began to turn it.

15

Arienne had wearily gone into her room and pushed the door shut behind her. She was damp with perspiration and felt sick inside, and she couldn't stop the palsied shaking of her hands. Dear God, how horrible it had been to hear her uncle gloating over Joshua's execution!

With trembling fingers she unbuttoned her dress and stepped out of it, then dropped her hoops and petticoats to the floor, leaving on her pantaloons and camisole. Her nervousness made undoing her coiffure impossible, so she left her hair up and stepped out of her stifling room onto the balcony.

Through the trees she could make out the dragonlike bulk of Fort Barrancas. The thought of Joshua locked in its cold bowels nearly made her retch. "Please God," she whispered fervently, clutching the balcony rail until her knuckles whitened with the pressure, "help him escape the fort tomorrow night. Please help him blast his way out!"

But could he make a bomb out of the crude materials she'd sent? Mrs. Walsh had assured her that he could, but Arienne had her doubts. And what if he managed to make a bomb only to have it blow up in his face?

She didn't get a chance to dwell on the macabre image, for at that moment she heard someone behind her. She whirled around. Her uncle was standing in the balcony doorway. "Uncle Wendell! What do you want?"

"Don't you know?"

She remembered his foot searching for hers under the table, the way he had looked at her. She stepped back against the railing. "Get away from me before I start screaming."

"No need to scream, Arienne. Your mother didn't."

"What are you saying?"

"I'm saying that you look exactly like Sara."

"So what?"

He stepped onto the balcony. "I miss her."

"We all miss her. Now go away." She edged toward the trellis.

"No one misses her as badly as I. She died bearing my son."

"*Your* son?"

He chuckled softly, a wave of sound that flooded her with apprehension. "Your father went to London on business. I took care of her while he was gone. We kept it our little secret."

"That's a lie! She loved my father!"

"Your father is a weak little toad. She loved me!"

Arienne went for his face with her nails. He snatched her against his chest and clapped his hand over her mouth before she could scream, then dragged her into the room and shut the French doors.

"Sara tried to scratch me, too, the bitch," he said in her ear as he dragged her toward the cot, "but I had my way with her anyhow. Just like I will with you."

Arienne tried to knee him in the groin, but he bore her down on the cot and crushed her beneath his weight. "Stop trying to fight me!" he said. "You know you want it, just like she did. By the Powers, you're exactly like her!"

Arienne bucked against him. It was like trying to unseat an elephant.

"Maybe I'll get you pregnant, too."

She couldn't bear it a second longer. She wrenched her head to dislodge his hand and screamed.

"Quiet!" He locked his hand around her throat, cutting off her screams, and rose up until he was kneeling over her hips. He ripped her camisole open and looked at her breasts. "Yes—you're exactly like her!"

She couldn't breathe. As the seconds ticked by her strength ebbed until she couldn't struggle anymore. Blood roared in her ears. Her chest ached as though a draft horse were standing on her chest.

Bang!

In the small room the pistol report was deafening. Wendell Stuart lost his grip on her throat. He lurched sideways off the cot and stumbled against the wall, staring down at a red bloom on his shirtfront. Slowly he turned to face the man who had shot him.

Sir James Lloyd was standing in the doorway holding a smoking Colt revolver. "You're never going to hurt us again, Wendell."

"I'll see you in hell!" Wendell Stuart raised his hand and staggered toward his brother. Five feet away, he dropped to the floor, stone dead.

Private Doug Barnes gave Joshua Langdon a sketchy account of the shooting early the next morning. He didn't know about the attack on Arienne. All he could say was that Sir James had shot his own brother in the back and then had taken to his bed in a state of shock. His nigger friend was tending him. No, Doug didn't know why Sir James had shot the ambassador.

Joshua wondered if it had something to do with Wendell Stuart's coercing him into the submarine project. Arienne had sworn her father wanted nothing to do with it, that the ambassador had blackmailed him. And blackmailers, Joshua knew, often didn't live long enough to die of old age.

But the scenario didn't seem to fit the image of the gentle Sir James Lloyd. Had there been a deeper motive? He'd let himself be blackmailed in order to protect Arienne. Had he killed in order to protect her?

And how was Arienne taking this new shock? From what she had told him on the *Scarlet Lady*, there hadn't been much love lost between her and her uncle, but her father was a different story.

He was sure she wouldn't rendezvous with him in the woods that night, no matter what her note had said. She had already gone through too much. There was no sense in her risking her life. He fervently hoped she would stay home and tend her father.

But the desire to hold her in his arms was overwhelming. As he lived and breathed, he craved her! Kissing her on her bedroom floor the other night had been more than an attempt to quiet her.

"Am I in love?" His hoarse whisper echoed back at him from the brick walls of his prison. He sighed and rubbed his chin, raising his gray eyes to the bars of his cell. He suddenly crashed his fist into his thigh and stood up. He'd get out of here, by God, if he had to fight off the whole Confederate army to do it!

He brought out the parcel of rock candy, pried a loose brick from the masonry, and ground the candy to sugar. Next he opened the sack of flour and discarded all but a pound of it under his mattress. He mixed the sugar into the remaining flour, poured in an ounce or two of whiskey, and shook the sack vigorously. Tearing a long strip from his shirt, he stuck it into the flour and tied the sack closed, leaving a two-foot tail protruding from the top.

Powder of any sort, from gunpowder to flour, has a common property. When introduced to a spark, it explodes.

Just after six o'clock in the evening, Arienne borrowed Joshua's black hunter from the post livery stable. She rode aimlessly for a while and then, when she was certain no one was following, went to a prearranged spot in the woods.

Within the shelter of the trees she pulled a black dress over her white linen shift and smeared lampblack on her face with a rag she'd hidden in the saddlebag.

Her preparations done, she opened her pocket watch. Seven o'clock. Where were they? She snapped the case shut and tried to force herself to relax. She felt as tight as a piano wire inside. Since the horrible scene last night, she hadn't closed her eyes.

All day she had watched her father for signs of heart trouble, fearing that the shooting would put him in the grave as well. He had demanded the whole story from her, weeping when she'd revealed that Wendell Stuart had raped his beloved Sara. He'd gradually calmed, and finally asked Thomas to take her place at his bedside.

Arienne patted the hunter's neck as he tossed his head and stamped his hooves. Had Thomas managed to get a skiff to the beach? Would Joshua get out of the fort? She couldn't do anything to help him until he got outside. Maybe her idea was too stupid to work.

"Please, God, help him. I'll never ask for another thing as long as I live if You'll just get him out of there!"

Sara used to say that the Lord helped those who helped themselves. There were a number of ways to do that. Even at this late hour, she wondered if it might not be better to go to Bragg as she had originally intended. She could tell him that Joshua had lied about the blueprints to protect her. Surely Bragg wouldn't shoot *her*. Yet he would probably still blame Joshua for the murder of old Wilford Humes, since the original blueprints hadn't turned up in anyone else's possession. Who had them? Who had done the killing?

Lost in thought, she was startled when Mrs. Walsh and Rita came jouncing along the path on hired nags with a spare horse trotting behind them. Rita was no horsewoman, and she punctuated each fleeting contact with the saddle with a curse.

"Girls! Over here!" Arienne whispered.

Mrs. Walsh turned her mare into the clearing. "Good Lord, child, you're a mess! Look at that filthy face!"

"I was hoping to be sort of invisible."

"I'd wanna be invisible, too, if I looked thataway." Rita shifted uncomfortably in her tight red dress. The front was open to her navel, displaying an impressive expanse of creamy, quivering flesh.

"You couldn't be invisible if you tried," Arienne said, marveling once more at Rita's development. It was as if nature had planned to make two girls and then thrown all the breasts onto one.

Rita giggled and gazed down at herself admiringly. If she couldn't shake that good-looking Yankee free of Fort Barrancas, no one could!

Arienne gestured at the women to follow her out of the clearing into the twilit woods. She guided her horse carefully, alert for sentries, sometimes raising herself up in the stirrups to scan the undergrowth. When she caught sight of Fort Barrancas through the trees, she swung down from the saddle and gathered the reins of the four horses.

Mrs. Walsh dismounted easily, and Rita managed to disengage herself from the sidesaddle after a minute or two of contortions. She arrived on the ground flushed, disheveled, and in bad humor.

"This damned dress'll be ruint before the night's out!"

"I'll buy you seven new ones," Arienne said. "Now for Pete's sake, be quiet!"

The hands of her pocket watch stood at 7:45. The sun sinking into Pensacola Bay turned it to brass while plunging the rear of the fort into violet shadow. From her vantage point she could look down on the fort and see most of the soldiers on the parade ground. There seemed to be hundreds of them, and how many more down in the casemates? Suddenly her flour-bomb idea seemed childishly stupid.

"Hurry up, Rita, the mosquitoes are biting," Mrs. Walsh said.

"Just lemme finish primping, will ya?" Rita freed her long blond mane from a hair net and flipped it over her shoulder, then studied herself in a small looking glass.

"They won't be looking at your face, anyway," Mrs. Walsh said. With her measurements, Rita didn't have to worry about cosmetic beauty, although she was prettier than most.

"All right, Rita, do your stuff before it gets too dark for the men to see you," Arienne said.

"Make it the best goldarned show of your life, girl, and you'll get next week off, with pay."

Rita gave her boss a smile. Then she walked out of the woods and picked her way down the hill toward the beach. She waved gaily as masculine heads surfaced above the parapets. They whistled and cheered.

"Do you think it'll work?" Arienne gripped the horses' reins in white-knuckled fists.

"It'll work, honey. I know men."

"Uh-oh, she's having problems. She's gotten into cockleburs, I think."

Halfway to the beach, Rita had stopped to jerk at her skirt. Arienne could hear her unladylike remarks even at a distance. The men clapped and hollered, urging her on.

The dress tore with an audible ripping sound, and Rita was free, her skirts split to the knee. More heads appeared on the parapets.

Rita fixated on a small seashell on the beach. Her dress was too tight to let her stoop down. A determined girl, she tugged her dress to her hips and bent over, shaking her behind. The men bellowed and threw their kepis into the air.

Seashell in hand, Rita kicked off her slippers and stepped into the gently lapping waves. She wiggled her toes. The movement set her fanny jiggling.

"Just listen to those men shout!" Mrs. Walsh said, immensely gratified. She mounted one of the horses and took the reins of Rita's mount. "I'll give her another minute or two, then cut through the woods to meet her."

"Don't delay too long. They'll eat her alive if they catch her."

"They can go stuff and eat themselves, she's my best girl."

The parade ground was quickly filling with soldiers from the galleries below. On the drawbridge behind the fort, two young sentries looked at each other, then disappeared inside. The drawbridge was winched shut with a bang.

"Hell, he won't be able to get out that way," said Mrs. Walsh. "Hope he can find another door." Turning the horses' heads, she trotted off the way they had come.

Arienne didn't watch her go. She was gaping at Rita.

The girl was as naked as a newborn chick. Giggling merrily, she capered about in the water, her breasts joggling in time to her dancing feet. Waving at the howling men, she lost her balance and disappeared underwater, surfacing almost immediately. Sleek, wet, sexy, she glowed in the sunset like liquid flame.

The soldiers went wild. Hundreds of bellowing men left their posts to pour across the lower terreplein into the ditch. Scrambling up the other side, they dashed down the hill toward Rita, who went running down the beach on winged feet.

"Ohhh, I'm dying!" The words echoed hollowly down the long, empty gallery. Private Doug Barnes, the only soldier who had remained at his post, came alive with a start. His prisoner was dying? What the hell . . . ?

Barnes shot off his chair like a minié ball and ran down the gallery, sand flying from his bare feet. He caught one of the bars of the powder magazine and skidded to a halt, horrified.

The major was lying on the ground deathly still, his face as white as flour. The sand was all churned up around him as if he'd gone into convulsions. A wave of superstitious terror swept over Doug. What should he do? There was no one left to call.

So the boy from Alabama did the bravest thing of his life: he rammed the point of his bayonet into the lock and twisted with all his might. The bayonet shattered as the lock broke open. Doug threw his useless gun aside and stumbled forward to bend over the body.

The very next instant the body rose from the dead and delivered a healthy blow to Doug's chin. The young Confederate's eyes turned up in his head. Langdon caught him as he keeled over and laid him on the straw mattress.

"Sorry, son." Langdon quickly checked him for damage. He was out cold, but his jaw was intact. If the kid managed to stay out of hostile fire for the remainder of the war, he'd live to see Ma Barnes again.

Langdon wiped off the flour he'd used on his face. He almost left his homemade bomb under the mattress, since he'd managed to open the cell without it, then decided to take it with him, after all.

Stuffing the crude bomb into his shirtfront, he stooped to pick up Doug's musket. The barrel was hopelessly bent and the bayonet broken. He removed the flint and steel and put them in his pocket.

Drawing a deep, steadying breath, he tiptoed into the gallery and shut the cell door behind him. Then, with his hair prickling at the expectation of a bullet in the back, he sprinted fifty yards to a subterranean tunnel leading to the main works. The darkness closed over him like a blanket.

Stealing to a low-ceilinged stairwell, he paused to listen. He could hear faint shouts from outside the fort, but nothing stirring in the passageway above, so he ran up the first short flight of steps and stopped at the dogleg landing. From there he could peer cautiously around the corner to the top of the stairwell.

The passageway was shaped like a cross, with the drawbridge at the top and the main works of the fort at the bottom. The stairwell formed the right arm, the scarp-gallery anteroom the left.

Joshua had just decided it was safe to go upstairs when a burly sergeant stepped out of the anteroom and crossed the passageway to the stairwell, his long Enfield rifle with its gleaming bayonet at the ready.

Langdon drew back into the shadows, praying for invisibility.

The sergeant stood glaring into the darkness below, muttering under his breath. "Lazy hounds. Blasted whore. Gotta guard the whole damned fort by myself."

The sergeant spat, then turned on his heel and reentered the anteroom. Joshua launched himself up the steps, hoping against hope to find the drawbridge down.

Instead, he found himself face-to-face with the sergeant, who had changed his mind about the scarp gallery. For one heart-stopping second they gaped at each other, then the sergeant brought up the rifle, tightening his finger on the trigger even as the bayonet raked Joshua's shirt.

Langdon's reflexes saved him. He sidestepped and grabbed the barrel, yanking the sergeant face-first into his raised knee. Already unconscious, the man tumbled down the staircase to the landing. Langdon tossed the rifle aside and leaped down after him to relieve him of his sidearm. Scarcely taking time to breathe, he sped back up the stairs, took one look at the closed drawbridge, and slipped into the anteroom.

A small wooden door was open on the right. Joshua pushed his head and shoulders through the opening and found himself near the fulcrum of the drawbridge. A strong evening wind rushed through the thirty-five-foot-deep dry moat. Darkness was falling.

Langdon could hear shouts from the beach, but not a soul stirred at the rear of the fort. Whatever

Arienne's distraction, it certainly had cleared the garrison.

"Now to make life a little more tough on the Rebs." He removed the flour sack from his shirt, checked its rag fuse, and crammed it into the fulcrum. Then he rummaged in his pocket for the salvaged flint and steel and struck a spark to the fuse. On the fourth strike the rag began to smolder.

His legs pumping like pistons, Joshua galloped out of the anteroom and skidded around the corner to the drawbridge. He jumped to the winch and began to crank like a madman. A rectangle of dark sky appeared, growing larger with every crank.

"Hey! What the devil are you doin'?"

Langdon glanced over his shoulder. Seven or eight soldiers had appeared in the passage some distance behind him. They couldn't see him very well in the dim light.

"Gen'ral Bragg wants in," Joshua drawled, cranking faster. He had the drawbridge more than halfway down now.

"The hell! It's that damned Yankee!"

"Balls!" Langdon shouted. He reached into his belt for the sergeant's pistol and blindly squeezed off a couple of rounds while working the winch one-handed.

A hail of minié balls slammed into the bricks and zinged off the ironwork, flattening into lead pancakes against the heavy timbers of the door. Joshua dropped to one knee and emptied his pistol at the mob.

"I've got a bomb! Get out of the way before I blow you to glory!"

"Cut him down, boys!" They fired at Joshua's head.

Langdon wasn't there anymore. Like a mountain goat he had sprung up the half-open drawbridge. Teetering at the summit, he launched himself into space. The ground rushed by far below, then he struck the counterscarp glacis and rolled like a wounded leopard away from the brink.

An instant later the flour bomb blew up with a terrific report, unseating the drawbridge. Yawing crazily, the huge door hurtled flaming into the moat. How many Confederates went with it Joshua didn't take time to count. He jumped up and sprinted for the black woods on his right.

A pair of horses leaped out of the trees and nearly ran him down. Joshua veered left, throwing up his arms defensively.

"Here, catch!" A rider dressed in black flung him the reins of a riderless mount.

Langdon vaulted into the saddle as the horse thundered by. Digging his heels into the animal's heaving flanks, he followed his rescuer into the woods. Bullets smacked into the trees all around them. Angry shouts echoed from the terreplein.

"There's a skiff beached a mile from here, Joshua! Head for the road!"

"Oh, God, Arienne, it *is* you! Damn it to hell!"

"I thought you'd be glad to see me, you no-good Yankee!" She ducked under a thick branch. A bullet tugged at her sleeve, but she felt no pain. Jumping a fallen log, she risked a glance over her shoulder. His face was invisible in the gloom. His next words sent a chill of horror up her spine.

"I can't go off in any damned skiff. There's something I gotta do first."

"No! They'll be down on you like 'gators on a duck! They'll kill you this time! Let me take you to the skiff!"

"Uh-uh. You go to Pensacola and check into a hotel."

"I won't leave you!"

"Yes, you will! Now get the hell away from me before you're caught and hanged, Arienne. That's an order!" He suddenly turned his horse's head and crashed off through the trees.

"Not that way, Joshua! The officers' quarters are over there!"

But her warning fell on deaf ears. Joshua was gone, headed straight for the enemy camp.

16

Joshua Langdon climbed the rose trellis to General Bragg's balcony, wincing at the sharp bite of thorns. No light showed in the bedroom, so he jimmied the door and walked in.

A band of moonlight showed him a candle and matches on the washstand. He struck a match and made a quick visual sweep of the room, his gray eyes stopping at a landscape painting hanging slightly askew on one wall.

"Joshua! Are you out of your mind to come here?"

He swung around in time to see Arienne climb over the railing and drop lightly onto the balcony. Then he swore and dropped the match, rubbing his burned fingers on his trouser leg. "I told you to go to a hotel!"

"You're not my commanding officer!" she said in a hoarse whisper, edging around the bed.

Joshua struck a second match on the sole of his

boot and glowered down at her. She was scarcely recognizable under the smears of lampblack on her face. The ludicrous sight made him want to laugh, but he forced himself to scowl even more fiercely. "All right, since you're here, you can slip down the hall to your own room and go to bed."

"I'm not going to bed until I see you into that skiff and on your way to Fort Pickens!"

"You're a stubborn little chit."

"And you're a stubborn big one. Have I mentioned that I hate your mustache?"

"I don't give a da—ouch!" he said as the second match burned him. "Here, make yourself useful and bring me that candle over there."

She retrieved a candle and held it for him while he struck another match. When he started to take the candle, she said, "I'll hold it, you hurry up and do whatever it is you've come to do."

"Come here, then." He walked over and yanked the landscape painting off the wall, throwing it carelessly on the bed.

"Good heavens, be careful, Joshua! That's a Jean-François Millet! It's probably worth a hundred pounds."

"Which is more than my life will be worth if you don't stop interrupting me. Well, well, what have we here?" he said, looking at a wall safe he'd uncovered.

"Why are you risking your life to burgle a safe?"

"That's what I love about you. You never shut up." He grabbed her to him and forced her mouth open in a hard kiss. He didn't seem to care about her filthy face or the candle in her hand.

Arienne pushed against his chest with one hand, a muddled array of emotions swamping her consciousness. Uppermost was fear for his life, though anger and desire also struggled for dominance. Before she could break free, he snatched the candle out of her hand and shoved the base into the mouth of an empty wine bottle on the washstand. Then he scooped her up, carried her to the bed, and dropped her beside the painting.

"What do you think you're doing?"

"Answering your questions in the most succinct way I know how." He straightened and returned to the safe, taking the candle with him. "Now will you please be quiet while I steal those blueprints you copied?"

Arienne sat up slowly, feeling like a fool. The wild kiss had been meant solely to get her out of the way. She rested her elbows on her knees, her sooty chin on her cupped hands, and stared morosely at his broad back. Outside she could hear shouts and occasional pistol shots. The idiots must be shooting at each other in the dark.

Langdon pressed his ear to the safe and turned the brass dial slowly to the right until he heard a dull click. He turned the dial left, then right, then left, grasped the handle and pulled down. The door swung open.

"Jumping saints, look at that money!" Arienne said, her eyes bulging at the sight of two stacks of greenbacks half a foot thick.

Joshua turned in some irritation to find her at his elbow. "Do you want another kiss?"

She faded back a few steps and folded her arms across her breasts, giving him a lofty look, but Langdon only snorted and began grabbing handfuls of greenbacks. He tossed the money into the empty fireplace, opened the damper, and dropped the candle on the money.

"There'll be a lot of disappointed soldier boys come payday," he said as the bills caught fire. Then he returned to the safe. "Maybe they'll desert to Mr. Lincoln's army. Ah, these are what I want." He reached into the safe for the blueprints.

Suddenly they heard the echo of booted footfalls in the hallway. By the light of the burning money, they exchanged a startled glance. With one thought they turned and grabbed an armchair and pushed it beneath the doorknob.

A key scraped in the lock. The interlopers ran on soundless feet out to the balcony and climbed over the railing. "You first," Joshua murmured, helping her onto the trellis. The door rattled, and someone in the hall began to shout.

When Arienne's feet touched the sandy earth fifteen seconds later, Joshua was right behind her. Seeing torches bobbing in the woods, they crouched down to reconnoiter, but at that moment they heard the sounds of splintering wood and angry shouts from Bragg's room. In another moment the soldiers would espy them from the balcony.

"This way! Run!" Langdon pulled her into a sprint

across the dark yard into the trees. Once he located the black hunter Arienne had ridden, he boosted her into the saddle.

"Gotcha, ya dirty Yankee pup!" A pistol gouged him viciously in the kidney.

Joshua reacted instantaneously. Pivoting on his heel, he smashed his cocked right elbow into his ambusher's face. The gun went off and Langdon felt the bullet whistle by his cheek, then the soldier crashed against the horse's flank and fell to the ground.

Frightened, the horse launched itself straight into the air, hooves together, and came down with a terrific jolt. Arienne's forehead struck its bony neck. Dizzily she clung to the bucking animal, unable to bring it under control.

Shots rang out, and torches began to converge. Joshua leaped at the horse and caught its mane. He vaulted into the saddle behind Arienne. The horse shot off through the trees.

Arienne bent low to give Joshua room to guide the horse around trees and over logs. Branches lashed her face and tore her skirts. At any moment the horse could go down. If they weren't killed by the fall, the furious soldiers would surely shoot them.

Someone appeared out of nowhere and plunged a torch into the horse's face. The animal screamed and reared. Flame spat from a pistol and the horse flinched convulsively before bolting like a jackrabbit.

Behind them the pistol barked again and again.

Joshua kneed the horse in and out of the trees. From the south a strong breeze carried an ocean scent. He headed into the wind.

Five minutes later they broke from cover and raced up the narrow beach full tilt, the horse's big hooves kicking up buckets of sand and water.

"The skiff is just up there," Arienne cried after they had run half a mile. The sound of pursuit had died in the distance. "Thomas said he would hide it in the brush near that big oak tree."

Joshua reined in by the oak and flung himself off the mount. He snatched Arienne down, then smacked the horse solidly on the rump, sending it into the woods. He tore away the brush concealing a small skiff. Arienne helped him drag the boat into the warm salt water. She jumped into the bow and Joshua began to row rapidly away from the beach.

They were a hundred yards from shore when the first Rebels broke out of the woods. No one saw the boat on the black bay. The soldiers continued down the beach toward Pensacola.

Joshua chuckled under his breath and released the oars, turning around to squeeze Arienne's knee. "Damned good show, girl! If the North had more brainy little hellcats like you on her side, she'd win the war in six months."

"Hmmph. Idle flattery." She began to scrub the lampblack off her face with the hem of her wet skirt. She hated to be reminded that she had just rescued a Union soldier.

Joshua seized the oars and rowed for a while, then

let the boat drift with the current. Above the bay hung a broad band of stars. As he watched, two or three broke loose to blaze a trail down the black satin horizon.

"You wouldn't know there was a war on, it's so peaceful out here," Arienne said. The excitement over, she was becoming sleepy and a little cold.

Langdon remembered what Doug Barnes had told him this morning. He twisted around to look at her. "What happened last night between your father and uncle?"

"How did you hear about that?"

"The story was all over the fort."

"Then you know my uncle was a very sick man."

"I've never heard someone shot to death referred to as 'sick.'"

"You didn't hear the whole story, then."

His brows drew together in sudden worry. "Did something happen to you?"

She told him, and then she began to cry.

What a strong woman she was, to have endured so much, yet still have managed to rescue him from his death sentence! He reached for her hand. "Ssh. It's over now. Your father did the right thing."

"I know he did. I'm worried about his health, though. He's very ill, and I'm sure he'll never forgive me for helping you steal those plans."

"Will he care about that, now that Wendell Stuart is dead? I thought he had no taste for this business."

This was a new thought. Maybe the question of the blueprints was moot. What was to stop him now from returning to England? With Wendell Stuart dead, he owned Lloyd on the Downs and the rest of his brother's estate. "I have to go back and see him."

"Tomorrow, I promise. Tell me, why did you rescue me?"

"I . . . don't know."

"You took your life in your hands and you don't know why?"

"Maybe I just couldn't stand to see an innocent man shot. Isn't that reason enough?" She lifted her chin defiantly and pulled her hand away.

Joshua's breath left him as if he'd been punched in the stomach. She was so beautiful, her eyes like fallen sapphire stars. God, what she had risked for him! He ached to take her in his arms, to show her by word and gesture how much she had come to mean to him.

The intensity of his gaze electrified her. She wanted to reach for him, to pour out her feelings. She remembered a night not so long ago when he had sheltered her in the bottom of a boat like this one, when anger and mistrust had washed over her like an ocean tide. Those emotions had, for the most part, been replaced by something much more uncomfortable. She didn't want to love him.

Her beautiful eyes clouded over, and she turned her face away. She had asked the Almighty to help her free this man, promising that she would ask nothing more. He'd kept His end of the bargain; now she had to keep hers.

But it wasn't fair. If her plan had worked out the

way it should have, she wouldn't be here with him now, knowing a painful leave-taking was in store. Every second in his company was torture. Please God, let this night end quickly!

"Whatever your reasons, I'm beholden to you, Arienne."

It was all she could do not to weep as she said, "We'd best get on to Fort Pickens and deliver those plans."

Joshua reached for her hand again, but she drew away from him and refused to meet his glance. What had set her off this time? He had thought he'd seen a flicker of affection in her eyes. Were they forever destined to draw close only to veer away at the last instant?

Scowling, he bent his mighty back to the oars, sending the boat over the swells toward the looming blackness of Fort Pickens.

"No, I sure as hell won't send another force against the navy yard!" Colonel Harvey Brown bellowed into Joshua's face some three hours later. The two men were seated on opposite sides of Brown's big desk in his quarters within the fort's massive walls. "I had enough boys shot up after that last fiasco you and Nance engineered."

"So you propose to just sit here, sir, with two thousand men at your command, while the Rebs launch a war machine that will cripple the navy?" Langdon propped his fists on the desk and leaned into the commandant's face.

Brown twisted one end of his thick mustache. "How do I know the South even has such a machine?"

"I brought you the damned blueprints to prove it!" Langdon stabbed a forefinger at the plans spread out on the desk. "And Miss Lloyd has seen it with her own eyes!"

Brown pulled the other end of his mustache, his mind drifting to the lady. She was asleep in his room next door. It would hardly be proper to awaken her. Besides, she was just a girl. What did women know of machines? She might easily have seen something else in the dry dock and been convinced by Langdon that it was a submarine. As to the plans, they seemed far too complicated to actually work. No, the whole thing was preposterous.

"I'll take the matter under advisement, Major," he said, rolling up the blueprints and tossing them into a drawer. "You are dismissed."

Langdon straightened slowly, yearning to knock the colonel through the wall. He snapped a salute, then turned on his heel and strode from the office onto the parade ground. His boots crunched across the oyster-shell fill. Avoiding the closely packed tents of the troops, he climbed the steps to the forty-foot-high parapet.

There he sat down with his back to the wall, his gaze sweeping the inside of the pentagon-shaped fort. The fortification commanded the western pinnacle of narrow Santa Rosa Island. On one side stretched the Gulf of Mexico, on the other Pensacola Bay. To the east lay a long stretch of scrubby wasteland inhabited by deer and alligators. Joshua had only been on the island for a few hours and already he was thoroughly sick of it.

Dawn touched the eastern sky with gold-pink fingers. Langdon couldn't help but marvel as the stunted, twisted island foliage came into focus. He might have been set down on Mars, so foreign did the landscape appear.

Unfolding his long legs, he got to his feet and stared across the bay at Fort Barrancas. The dry dock looked like an ungainly whale. He pictured Louis DeCoeur inside, mounting torpedoes on his infernal machine, filling its tanks with his aluminum mixture.

You're going to lose this one, DeCoeur, he silently vowed, even if I have to go back and finish the job alone. That damned sub won't make it out of dry dock, I swear.

He paced the parapets for a long time. Finally he went below to inspect the cannon in the casemates. The gun crews looked at him curiously, but his brooding manner didn't encourage much in the way of conversation. At last he curled up in a dark corner for a few hours' sleep.

He awoke feeling better. He jogged down to the beach to bathe, since the fort's scanty supply of fresh water in the cistern was strictly off limits. Later someone lent him a patched shirt and a razor. He divested himself of his heavy growth of beard. Remembering what Arienne had said, he shaved off his mustache. His upper lip was pale against his tanned skin, but a few hours in the sun would fix that. With a renewed feeling of confidence, he mounted the steps to the parapet and squinted at Fort Barrancas.

"How will you prevent them from launching it, Major Langdon?"

He turned to find Arienne standing near him, quite at home on the high wall. She was wearing the white shift she had worn under her black dress last night. Her ebony hair was loose, a dark silken cloud blowing around her face.

"How did you manage to slip up on me like that, Arienne?"

"You were a million miles away—a herd of elephants could have managed it. Now, how are you going to stop DeCoeur?"

"I haven't worked it out yet. Brown refuses to release any troops for a second attempt on the yard."

"Does he know what will happen if Louis DeCoeur succeeds?"

"He doesn't believe the sub exists. The torpedoes he could believe, but not the sub."

"He displays an extraordinary lack of imagination. That's a Yankee for you."

"The army trains imagination out of a man."

"You didn't take well to your training, Major." She suddenly noticed he'd shaved his mustache. Had he done it for her? "My father was quite taken with your ideas on Euripides and I . . . well, I enjoyed your piano playing." Her cheeks flushed a little and she gazed steadfastly at the bay.

"You're beautiful with your cheeks on fire like that."

"You shouldn't say that to me."

"Why not? It's true. You might as well know how I feel about you."

"Stop it! Why do you torment me so?"

"Torment you? Is it painful to be told how beautiful you are?" He caught her arm before she could run down the stairs and spun her toward him. "By heaven, you're ravishing!"

"Let go of me!"

"Why? I saved your life, you saved mine. Surely that entitles us to a certain measure of affection."

"We're entitled to nothing!" She shouted so loudly that soldiers on the parade ground stopped to stare curiously up at them.

"What are you afraid of?" He cupped her chin in his hand.

She slapped his hand away, tears flooding her eyes. "I'm afraid of loving you, if you must know!"

"Why should you fear that?"

"Because you're a married man, for God's sake! I'm not one of your whores downtown, you philandering Yankee!"

"Married? Whores? What's this?"

"Don't act like you don't know! I saw you outside Seville House, and you know it."

"I went there to meet Captain Nance. The whores were window dressing. I didn't touch them."

"What about your wife?"

"I'm not married. Where did you hear a thing like that?"

"Thomas told me. Her name is Rachel Markwardt, as if you didn't know!"

Joshua smiled. "Oh, her."

"*Oh, her.* Did you forget about her?"

"I had. She's Cyrus Enright's widow, part of my cover."

"What? You mean I've been crying my eyes out over a marriage that doesn't exist?"

"You have?"

"Yes, I have, you wretch!"

Langdon unleashed a roar of laughter, relieved that this misunderstanding between them had been cleared up. Arienne, feeling overwrought and foolish, thought he was mocking her. Enraged, she let fly a left hook to his jaw, her whole weight behind it.

She miscalculated. Langdon instinctively moved his head, the blow failed to connect, and her own momentum carried her headfirst over the high wall.

17

Langdon reacted the instant he saw Arienne lose her balance. Hurling himself forward, he landed on his belly near the edge of the precipice and snagged the hem of her skirt with one hand. Holding on to the masonry with his other hand, he exercised his considerable strength to begin hauling her up.

Hanging upside down, the parade ground forty feet below her face, Arienne unleashed a terrified scream. The sentries on the walls were already making a beeline toward them, but there was no one near enough yet to give Joshua a hand. Her skirt tore, and Joshua lunged to capture her ankle. He found himself sliding off the wall. Arienne screamed piercingly.

"Hold on, Arienne!" He jammed his toes into a crack in the masonry. Inch by inch, he wormed away from the precipice. At last he was able to seize her wrist and drag her to the top of the wall. They lay side by side, too shaken to speak.

At last Arienne felt recovered enough to sit up. She glared at the major, who was grinning at her boyishly. "This was your fault!"

"I figured it would be, once everything was sorted out and the guilt assigned," he said, getting up.

Arienne stood up and swayed a little. She gathered her torn skirts in her hands. "I'll thank you never to force your presence on me again, Major Langdon," she said. "I never want to speak to you again as long as I live!"

"As you wish, m'lady," he said, bowing.

"It's exactly as I wish!" She hurried down the stairs and across the parade ground, her steps dogged by grinning Yankees. Had every last man in the fort witnessed her farcical plunge? Her cheeks burned ever brighter under their scrutiny, and she walked faster and faster until at last, reaching the quarters assigned her, she slammed the heavy arched door behind her.

Her reaction set in as she groped her way across the room. Illuminated only by weak shreds of light filtered through ventilation ports high in the walls, the dark quarters seemed to exacerbate her terror. She was trembling by the time she dropped down on her cot.

Curling herself into a ball, she relived the moment when she'd stepped off the wall into space. If Joshua had been a tad slower, she would be dead right now.

She thought of Joshua—his incredibly handsome

face, the devilish, teasing light in his eyes. She felt again his powerful hands rescuing her from the peril she had brought on herself. Another image thrust itself on her awareness: Joshua's strong arm pulling her from the sea the night she had nearly drowned.

Soothed by her memories, she slowly relaxed. Gradually the sensation of falling was dispelled by the sweet memory of being held in his arms.

"Miss Lloyd, time for you to get up and eat. You gotta wake up, ma'am."

"Go away." She dragged the pillow over her head.

"Colonel Brown says for you to come on and eat with him, ma'am."

Arienne pushed the pillow off her face and glared at a corporal standing in the connecting doorway, nervously twisting his blue kepi around and around in his hands. Arienne glimpsed a brass-bugle insignia just over the abbreviated brim of his cap.

"Tell him to give me ten minutes." She sighed as she rolled off the cot. Lighting a short, fat candle on the washstand, she bolted the door after the corporal, then stripped off her torn dress, washed quickly, and donned the black gown she had arrived in. She finger-combed the tangles from her dark hair and twisted it into a long braid, then went through the door to Brown's office. The corporal snapped to attention as she entered.

"My dear, how pleasant to see you looking so well this afternoon." The colonel rose behind his desk. He came around and bowed gallantly over her hand, his brown hair gleaming in the light coming through a narrow window behind him. He wore a full Federal uniform of heavy wool and an elegant dress sword. His face shone with perspiration.

She had been too exhausted last night to pay much attention to him. She'd had an impression of a rather short, glowering man hurriedly tucking his nightshirt into a pair of blue pants just before she'd stumbled off to a cot in the next room. It dawned on her now that she'd slept in his bed.

"You've rested well, I hope?"

She wondered if he'd read her mind. "Yes, very well. Thank you for your hospitality, Colonel."

Brown gave her a penetrating look and smiled. "Good. Come and sit down. We've got simple fare, as usual, but I'm sure you'll find it satisfactory."

At his gesture, Arienne preceded him to the desk where dinner had been laid. Platefuls of smoked Spanish mackerel, boiled clams, fried crab legs, and corn bread vied for position with stacks of government paperwork. Arienne pushed aside a partition of supply requisition forms and began to serve the food onto two delicate china plates. She handed one to Brown.

"I'm surprised to find good china out here in the wilds, Colonel," she said as the young corporal began to pour them cups of chicory.

Brown laughed. "We like to preserve a bit of civilization, even on a godforsaken army post like this one."

Arienne picked up a crab leg. "I should imagine that's a difficult task, given the overcrowding I've seen."

"It's a nearly impossible one, Miss Lloyd. We've two thousand men assigned here, and only enough quarters for the officers and the sick. The men have to sleep on the parade ground."

"Yes, I saw them folding up the tents this morning."

Brown hoped she hadn't seen them naked. Despite his orders, most of the soldiers slept in the nude as a concession to the fearsome heat. "It's an unholy mess. We're packed in here like ship rats."

"Except for that Irish regiment from New York. I understand they've taken to sleeping in the woods."

The colonel's fork froze halfway to his mouth. "And how did you get onto a piece of military intelligence like that?"

"You needn't think I've been spying, Colonel. I took a walk this morning and happened to meet some of them. When they learned I'm half-Irish, they became quite forthcoming about their activities."

Brown threw his hands up in exasperation. "Good heavens! I suppose they told you about their drinking and carousing? I'm not surprised they're proud of it. I couldn't do anything with 'em—they fight all day and distill whiskey from their corn ration—so I finally assigned them to the woods. Let 'em get their fill of snakes and mosquitoes, that'll teach 'em."

Arienne smiled widely, remembering the lilting Irish pipes she'd heard. The troops were first- and second-generation Americans, and in them she'd recognized the humor and unquenchable spirit that

had made her mother such a delight. She wasn't
surprised that Brown had been unable to impose
strict military discipline upon them. She wouldn't
tell the commandant how much they were enjoying
their punishment. She would have preferred the
woods herself to living inside the fort on a hot,
sharp bed of oyster shells.

"I heard about your falling off the wall," Brown
said, conveying a fork load of clams to his mouth.
"You shouldn't have been up there."

"You're right." Her face burned with anger as she
remembered Joshua's smirk of amusement.

"Good thing Langdon was there."

"I wouldn't have fallen in the first place if he
hadn't been there!"

"Oh? Was he forward with you, Miss Lloyd? If so,
I'll have him locked up." He looked as though the
idea gave him pleasure.

"That won't be necessary." She sipped her chicory,
trying to get her emotions under control. "He has an
irritating way about him, that's all."

Brown twirled one end of his mustache. He stirred
the crab legs on his plate with his forefinger before
selecting one. "He's a scoundrel, all right."

Arienne opened her mouth to argue with him,
then snapped it shut. Why should she defend
Joshua?

"Speaking of Major Langdon has reminded me of a
few things I'd like to discuss with you, if you don't
mind, Miss Lloyd."

"As you wish." She watched him guardedly across
the littered desk.

"Major Langdon informed me that the Rebs are building a submarine in the navy yard. Is this true?"

Would she get her father into trouble if she backed Langdon's statement? What if Brown attacked the yard again and her father was there? He often visited the dry dock.

"If it is true, what then?" she asked.

Brown steepled his fingers under his nose and stared hard at her. "I suppose we'd have to destroy it, and capture or kill the engineers and anyone else involved in the building."

Arienne went white. "Perhaps the machine won't work. It's complicated, you know. There's a good chance it will submerge and never come up again."

"Whose side are you on, Miss Lloyd?"

Arienne cast about for an answer. "I . . . don't know what to tell you. I'm a British subject, but I hate to see this war tearing the States apart."

"She certainly will be torn apart if this submarine works!" Brown crashed the front legs of his chair down on the floor. He yanked open his desk drawer and seized the blueprints. "Langdon said you copied these. Why?"

"Does it matter?"

"It might, depending on your answer." Brown's eyes were hard and cold. Arienne had the distinct impression he would extract an answer from her one way or another. She didn't fear for herself, but what might happen to her father? Could she ensure his safety by telling the truth?

"I was trying to get my father a detailed set of plans." Her voice gained strength. "He was being blackmailed by my uncle, who headed a shipping cartel in Liverpool. Wendell Stuart was also the British ambassador to the U.S., until my father shot him two nights ago."

Brown straightened. "He shot his own brother?"

"Yes. The cartel won't be getting any blueprints, after all." She folded her arms across her chest, shuddering as she remembered her uncle's attempt on her life, and his violent death.

"Can your father reproduce the blueprints for his cartel?"

"My father is a lawyer. He hasn't the vaguest notion of mechanics or chemistry. It took a mad scientist to invent that contraption. A frail little attorney with heart trouble couldn't reproduce it in a thousand years!"

"What about you?"

"I'm an artist, not a chemist. Even if I could draw the basic structure from memory—which I doubt—I couldn't possibly remember the chemical formulas involved in the propulsion device."

Brown stared at her silently for half a minute, then he barked at the corporal, "Fetch me Major Langdon on the double."

"Yes, sir!"

"I must return to Fort Barrancas, Colonel," Arienne said as the corporal dashed out the door to the parade ground. "I'm terribly worried about my father. He doesn't know what's happened to me, and his health is very bad."

"You'll stay here."

"But at least allow me to send him a message telling him I'm all right!"

"No message. You've proven yourself a capable observer, Miss Lloyd. We'll have no messages signaling our intentions to Bragg."

"I won't tell him a thing!"

Brown's sardonic smile answered her. "You certainly won't."

Before Arienne could retort, Langdon walked in. He saluted the commandant, but his eyes were on Arienne's distraught face. A muscle twitched in his jaw. "You wanted to see me, Colonel?"

"Indeed. It seems Miss Lloyd has borne out your story."

Langdon shot her a grateful look and received a glare in reply. "You intend to attack the navy yard then, sir?"

"I do not. I haven't changed my mind on that score one iota. We haven't sufficient manpower to launch an attack. The best I can do, Major, is to send a message to Washington notifying them of the gravity of the situ—"

"A message to Washington! By the time a message reaches Washington and gets kicked around in committee meetings and shunted off to some third-rate undersecretary, the Rebs will have launched a dozen subs and blasted the navy to kingdom come!"

"Nevertheless it's the best I can do, Major." A dull red flush had crept into Brown's cheeks. "The only power that can help you is the Gulf blockading squadron. Perhaps they'll send in a frigate."

"May God help any poor fool sailing against that iron monster—they'll be blasted to kindling. Maybe we can pick up the flotsam and jetsam for firewood—"

"You are dismissed, Major Langdon," Brown said with barely controlled fury, his mustache quivering. "Out!"

"Yes, sir!" Joshua looked at Arienne and then left the office without saluting.

Arienne hastily thanked the colonel for the meal and went after Joshua. But when she stepped into the late-afternoon heat, he was nowhere in sight. She peered into the shadowy casemates, but only the grins of strangers greeted her. It was just as well she couldn't find him, she supposed. There wasn't much he could do to get a message to her father, anyway. He was almost as much a prisoner here as she.

Lost in thought, she walked across the parade ground and out the southern sallyport. No one challenged her as she followed a sandy path between tall white dunes. A rattlesnake sounded a staccato warning in the bushes, but she paid it no attention. The tangy scent of the Gulf filled her nostrils.

Like giant straw feathers, sea oats waved on the dunes. Scrub oaks of deepest green hugged the white ground. The vegetation ended a hundred feet from the water, leaving a sugary expanse of beach.

Like an excited schoolgirl, she hopped from one foot to the other to remove her shoes. She tossed them away carelessly and raced into the water, lifting her skirts to her thighs.

The water was warm, bubbling, and so clear that she could see bottom for yards around. Crabs darted here and there, and schools of bright fish swam around her legs. Waves washed in to slap the beach and then rushed back into the sea. The current sucked holes in the sand under her bare feet.

She waded across a sandbar and stepped into deeper water on the other side, surprising a small shark. The creature sped away with rhythmic side-to-side motions of its broad head. Arienne was looking after it when she sensed a presence behind her. She turned quickly, ready to dash out of the water.

Joshua Langdon was reclining on the top of a high sand dune, looking like a sheikh out of the *Arabian Nights.* Propped on his elbows, his long legs comfortably stretched in front of him, he lay watching her with amusement.

Arienne dropped her skirts into the water and set her fists on her hips. She wanted to be angry at him for spying, but there was no stopping the wave of giddy excitement she felt. "Are you just going to lie there like a beached mackerel, Major Langdon, or are you going to join me?"

"Beached mackerel, is it?" He jumped up. "I'll get you, little girl!" But as he began to run down the dune the treacherous sand slid away from his feet. "Whoa!"

Arienne watched in delighted horror as he plunged wildly downward, his strides growing longer and longer, his arms whirling like windmills. With twenty feet to go he lost all control and went over headfirst, tumbling down the white slope like a boulder in an avalanche. He finished face-first at the bottom. Sand trickled gently down on top of him.

"My, such coordination!" She waded out of the water to laugh at him from close range. "Are all Yankees as clumsy as you, or is this a special talent you've developed?"

Her laughter changed to a shriek of alarm when he vaulted to his feet and charged after her. She spun around and splashed into the surf to escape, but he plunged in, boots and all, and made a grab for her.

Arienne twisted like a sea snake. Clutching empty air, he plummeted headfirst into the waves. He surfaced a second later, spitting salt water, and pursued her again. Laughing helplessly, she splashed away, her last-minute evasions causing him many accidental dives.

He went down for the fourth time and stayed down. Arienne leaned over cautiously to see where he'd gone. Surely he couldn't have disappeared in such clear water! She remembered the shark. Oh no, surely not!

"Joshua!" Anxiously scanning the waves for a black fin, she took a step forward only to have her ankles seized by something of great strength.

"No!" she screamed an instant before Joshua yanked her legs out from under her. She hit the water with a splash and went under. Then she shot out of the water and glared at him, water streaming from her eyes. He guffawed. She seized him by the forelock and jerked him underwater in mid-chuckle.

Langdon surfaced a moment later to see her wading to shore, wringing out her hair, her black dress clinging to her like a second skin. He floated on his back and smiled his approval.

"You don't look bad for a drowned sea rat," he said.

Arienne stuck out her tongue. "I wish I could say the same for you, but I've never seen you look more hideous. Your hair looks exactly like a clump of decayed seaweed."

Langdon got up and slogged through the water to shore. Arienne caught her breath as she glimpsed his hairy chest through his soaked white shirt. His build could destroy many a strong man's self-confidence.

Ignoring her rapt expression, he sat down on the beach, removed his boots, and emptied a large quantity of seawater from each. "I hadn't intended to swim this evening," he said in a voice that sent a shiver down her spine, "but now that I have, I can imagine only one activity I'd find more stimulating."

"You should be ashamed of yourself."

"Why? For appreciating the most ravishing woman on Santa Rosa Island?"

"I'm probably the *only* woman on Santa Rosa Island."

"Well, there it is. No contest."

Arienne smiled down at him and touched his wet hair. "You're such a clown sometimes. I don't know why I trouble myself with you."

"Perhaps you find me irresistible?" He pulled on his boots.

"Don't flatter yourself."

"Despite the cruel words, do I detect a softening in

the maiden's manner? Only hours ago she made me promise never to force myself on her again."

"I was angry and, well, frightened out of my wits. And you needn't assume that saintly expression. You know perfectly well that I wouldn't have fallen off the wall if you hadn't made me mad!"

Joshua stood up to sweep her a bow. "My humblest apologies, m'lady. What can this knavish oaf do to earn your forgiveness?"

Arienne regarded him seriously. "You can get a message to my father telling him where I am."

"Begosh and begorra!" he said in a murderous attempt at an Irish brogue. "And how will I do that, m'lady?"

"You're the spy—you figure it out!"

Langdon heaved a sigh and strode down the beach toward the setting sun, and Arienne scampered to keep up. "I suppose I can go back in the skiff," he said.

"And be shot the instant you set foot on land?"

"There's always that."

Arienne grabbed his arm in a surprisingly strong grip and stopped him in his tracks. "You really are the most maddening person I've ever met! Can't you be serious?"

"Only as a last resort." Fire kindled in his gray eyes, and the clefts in his cheeks deepened.

Arienne stared at him, mesmerized. She wanted to touch his warm copper face and the dark, damp hair ruffling in the sea breeze. There was an energy about him, a primal force that burned her from the inside out. Try as she might, she couldn't take her eyes off him.

Joshua held her in his spell until her knees began to shake and she was convinced she would fall at his feet. Then he took her arm in a masterful grip and led her to the path through the dunes.

"Where are we going?"

His grip tightened on her arm. "Back to the fort."

"Already?"

"It's not a moment too soon, I assure you."

"I don't understand."

Langdon looked down at her sternly. "I promised not to force myself on you again. I don't break promises. Now do you understand?"

Arienne looked down at the sand brushing past her feet. She'd forgotten her shoes on the beach. She'd be very sorry about that when she reached the parade ground, but right now it didn't seem to matter. Nothing mattered but the familiar ache in her breast, the ache she'd carried since she realized she'd fallen in love with the tall, determined man leading her through the dunes.

18

Arienne passed a fretful night on her borrowed cot. She had only to close her eyes to see Joshua Langdon's amused face, his tantalizing smile, the ivory teeth that flashed like lodestones in his dark face.

By heaven, she loved him! But what hope was there that he would ever return her feelings? He was a man possessed by an idea, by a mission that brooked no interference by what he obviously considered an idle emotion. That he desired her he had made clear, but whether desire could blossom into love she would never know, as long as he was bent on destroying the Confederacy's dream. He would succeed in that dark undertaking, she believed, and in so doing, destroy her dream as well.

Exhausted, yet despairing of sleep, she rose and lit a candle. The hands of her pocket watch stood at three o'clock. She might as well occupy herself in some useful activity.

She unfolded the white dress that had been torn in her fall from the parapet and retrieved from the washstand a needle and thread she had borrowed earlier from the corporal. She sat down on the cot and began to join the fragile material together with tiny stitches.

A sudden blast from a bugle made her jump and poke her thumb with the needle. Gunshots and masculine bellows drowned out her cry of surprise.

Seconds later the *cannons en barbette* roared. The ground quaked. A second fusillade knocked plaster from the walls and ceiling. The candle went out. Convinced that her quarters were caving in, Arienne crawled on hands and knees to the door, opened it, and stumbled into hell.

Like ants under attack, the soldiers on the parade ground were pouring out of their tents, many of them naked. Others leaped into their trousers as they ran, juggling loaded carbines and pistols. Hundreds scurried up the walls and behind the east terreplein, while hundreds more manned the casemates bearing on the bay and gulf sides of the fort.

Arienne flattened herself against the brickwork, waited until the parade ground was emptied of all but trampled tents, and then sprinted to the east wall. Heedless of the dizzying drop to the parade ground, she ran up the steps to the parapet three at a time.

"Get down, you crazy female!" A young soldier kneeling behind the skirting wall fired into the moonlit woods below. "You're going to get killed!"

"I've got to find Major Langdon!" She whirled away from the hand he shot out to restrain her.

"The hell you've got to!" He hurled himself at her back, succeeding in catching her ankle. She fell on her stomach. With a vicious snarl she twisted around and kicked his hands away. She was getting up to run when a ten-inch columbiad nearby fired. Its deafening boom knocked her flat.

She stuffed her skirts in her ears and writhed on the ground, convinced she'd been shot in the head. The cannon belched fire again, but this time the noise wasn't nearly as terrible. The pain in her head lessened.

"I've probably gone deaf," she said to the soldier, but when she unstopped her ears, she could hear the thin, high-pitched wail of Irish pipes. The sound brought her to her knees.

She strained her eyes at the grassy terreplein sloping down to the woods. Red-and-gold gunfire streaked the slash pines at the bottom of the hill. The pipes wailed defiantly.

"Are the Irish pinned down?"

"That's what they say," the soldier yelled. "Bragg tried sneaking up on us from the island side—wait a minute!" He interrupted himself to shoot at a figure dodging up the slope. "Damn, missed! He's jumping like a hot frog's leg." He reloaded quickly and squeezed off another round. "Got him!"

The boy reloaded his rifle calmly and continued speaking as though he hadn't just killed a man. "The Irish was bivouacked in the woods. The Rebs

didn't know they was in there—I reckon the boys
had finally passed out and got quiet—until they
were right in amongst them. That's when all hell
broke loose, from what I hear. If you ever want to
piss an Irishman, just try stepping on his head in
the dark."

"Or knocking it off with a cannonball! Why are
you fellows shooting at your own men?"

"We ain't. We're aiming over their heads, trying to
cut off the Rebels' retreat. It'll be over in a minute, I
reckon."

Arienne flinched as a minié ball hit the bricks by
her head. "Where do you think I can find Major
Langdon?"

"Dunno." No Rebels were stirring, so he leaned
his rifle against the wall and fumbled in his pocket
for tobacco. "He might be in the detachment that
took off a while ago to flank the Johnnies."

"He's in the woods?"

"Could be. Said I dunno."

Before the boy could stop her, Arienne grabbed
his rifle, scrambled over the wall, and careened down
the glacis like a runaway filly. She plunged into the
pines. How she expected to find Joshua in the dark,
unfamiliar landscape she didn't know, but she
couldn't have stayed behind the walls of the fort if
her life had depended upon it.

Around her the ghostly sand dunes rose from
collars of stunted, twisted trees. Cockleburs raked
and stabbed her bare feet. Thorns caught at her
hair like invisible hands. She brushed sweat from
her eyes and raised her stolen rifle to high port,

feeling very much alone. Even the cannons had fallen silent.

"Joshua?" Except for the wind in the scraggly tree-tops there was no sound. Had the Rebels retreated, then? Rounding a sand dune, she nearly collided with a dark figure.

It was only a slash pine, but she was so startled that she tripped over a root and fell. She lost the rifle in the undergrowth. Scrambling to her feet, she groped around in the bushes looking for it.

Suddenly the dry ground disappeared and she sank to her hips in dark, sucking mud. Her desperate struggles to get free only dragged her deeper. Soon it was up to her waist.

No one came, though she screamed until she was hoarse. The mud reached her chest, and still her feet had not touched bottom. Realizing she was hastening death by struggling, she forced herself to be still and think. Then, moving with infinite care, she stretched her arm toward a branch hanging over the pool. She sank into the muck another two inches before her straining fingertips brushed the limb.

Two red eyes leaped suddenly into focus barely a yard from her hand. Swinging its great scaly head, a bull alligator fully fifteen feet long unhinged its monstrous jaws and roared into her face.

Arienne reached new heights of terror. Like a madwoman she fought the quicksand, screaming until her voice gave out and she could only gasp.

Not to be cheated out of its prey, the alligator lashed its powerful tail and lurched toward her.

Arienne tensed to plunge her head under the suffocating mud, preferring quick death to the monster's yellow fangs.

A pistol cracked loudly. The alligator bellowed and crashed its teeth together. A second bullet bored into its head and exploded. The luminous red eyes blinked once and went out.

"Hold on, angel, I'm coming!"

Up to her chin in quicksand, Arienne saw Joshua leap onto the alligator's broad back. The dead reptile began to sink.

"Don't move a muscle, Arienne," he said, kneeling on the creature's huge head. He reached down into the mud and grasped her under the armpits. Leaning back, he began to pull with all his might.

At first she stuck fast, then, with a hideous sucking sound, the quicksand released her. Arienne shrieked with horror as Joshua dragged her across the scaly bridge to dry ground. The alligator sank out of sight.

Plastered with muck and shuddering uncontrollably, Arienne clung to him with all her remaining strength. He held her close, rocking her like a baby, crooning in her ear. Feeling her calm somewhat, he said, "You little idiot. You need a guardian angel."

"I have one." She tightened her hold on his neck. "His name is Joshua Langdon. He hovers over me night and day."

"Then for propriety's sake, my accident-prone little hooligan," he whispered, kissing her muddy brow, "you'd best marry him."

* * *

It took Arienne half the morning and three wash-tubs full of hot, soapy water to rid her hair and skin of filth, but at last she was clean and could begin to prepare for her wedding. In spite of the danger of another Rebel assault on the fort, Joshua had insisted they be married that very evening. Arienne was too happy to argue.

The quartermaster took her torn white dress away to be cleaned and mended. Returning the garment to her sometime later, he surprised her with a wreath of braided sea oats and red oleander flowers, and a nosegay of the same.

The only cloud on her dreamy horizon was her father. She had always pictured him giving her away, but now he wouldn't even know she was getting married until the deed was already done! He had felt betrayed by her before. What would his reaction be to the news that she'd married the spy?

Late that afternoon she arrayed herself in white. Her frock was rather plain, with capped sleeves, a low neckline, and no hoops, but the proportions were right and she looked well in it. Having no proper shoes, she decided to leave her feet bare. On an inspiration she cut satin ribbons from her sash and tied a bow around each ankle. It was unorthodox, but she told herself she wasn't getting married in a cathedral anyway.

She brushed her hair until it shone like black lacquer and left it hanging down her back. Then she placed the wreath of red flowers on her brow and picked up her nosegay. Her preparations complete, and her heart beginning to thud, she opened the connecting door to Colonel Brown's office.

The colonel rose from behind his cluttered desk, his eyes lighting with admiration. "Perhaps I shouldn't allow this wedding, after all. What's that scoundrel done to merit such a beautiful bride?"

Arienne's flaming cheeks matched the bright blooms in her hair. She was still irritated by his refusal to let her communicate with her father. She smiled stiffly. "The question is more properly, what has *she* done to merit *him?*"

Brown shook his head and then, remembering his manners, bowed from the waist. "I still say he's an undeserving devil." He came around to offer her his arm.

Outside, on the parade ground, two long lines of uniformed soldiers stood at attention while a private led a huge, saddleless white horse down the avenue between them. The animal's mane and tail were decked with red oleander.

"Your mount, ma'am," Colonel Brown said, bowing gallantly.

Arienne's eyes sparkled. "He's beautiful. Yours?"

"U.S. government issue. Yours, for the time being."

"I'm delighted." Requiring little assistance, she took a demure sideways seat on the horse's back. With her white skirts draped over her mount's left flank and the setting sun washing her complexion deep rose and honey, she was a breathtaking sight. The soldiers murmured appreciatively.

"If you're ready, we'll go meet the rascal," Colonel Brown said. Then he winked. "Unless, of course, I can persuade you to change your mind and marry me instead."

Arienne laughed softly. "I'll keep your gallant offer in mind, should we fail to find my bridegroom when we arrive at the beach."

"Good enough!" Brown said with a laugh. He caught the horse's bridle and led him through the ranks.

"Present arms!" yelled a sergeant. Scores of sabers rang from their sheaths in a brilliant salute to the bride as the garrison commander led her to the sally-port. An honor guard fell in behind them, and the gates closed on the fort.

Brown led the small procession down the same path that Arienne had taken last evening on her way to the Gulf. The sunset was a magnificent portrait of red, violet, and fiery gold framed with purple clouds. The sugary beach carried out the panorama in softer tones of lavender and amethyst, while a jeweled carpet of waves rushed in and out. Pure white sea gulls rolled along the wind, their wings flashing comets.

A group of officers and enlisted men were standing at the base of the dune Joshua had tumbled from the evening before. The face of the sandy hill still sported shallow impressions made by his body. The memory made Arienne smile. Then her heart skipped a beat.

Wearing a Federal uniform, a gold oak leaf on each

red shoulder bar, his hat brim pulled low over his eyes, Major Joshua Langdon stood watching her with a thin little priest at his side. The groom was as tall and straight as a granite statue. Sunlight danced upon the silver saber he wore at his side and upon the crossed cannon insignia on his hat. He made no move toward her but stood waiting with barely controlled impatience.

Brown walked the horse to within twenty feet of the group and stopped. Her attention riveted on Langdon, Arienne hardly felt the colonel lift her down. Even at this distance, she swayed under the hot spell of her bridegroom's eyes.

"Are you all right, Miss Lloyd?" Brown gripped her elbow.

"I've never been more all right in my life, Colonel!"

Brown grinned down at her, enchanted. "Does this mean that I'm too late to talk you out of it?"

"You'd grow blue and short-winded if you tried it, sir."

"Hmmm. And what if I were to tell you that Father O'Reilly is to perform the service? That's him in the red hair and purple nose next to Langdon." He pointed at the little priest. Wearing a black cassock and stole over his ragged uniform, he was barefoot, and had a big black Bible tucked under his left arm.

Arienne's brow quirked. "I met him yesterday morning. He said he was drunk and intended to stay that way. Can he manage, do you think?"

"Of course. I've had him locked in the guardhouse most of the day."

"What for?"

"To dry him out. He's as sober now as he'll ever be."

Arienne shook her head. "All right, then. I suppose if he falls flat on his face, we can stand him back up again without much trouble. He's not very big."

"Colonel Brown, is the maid ready?" Father O'Reilly asked in a gentle, lilting voice.

Arienne took a deep breath. Her knees were quivering, and happy tears pricked her eyes. She smiled nervously at Joshua. He smiled back and reached up to pluck the hat off his head. His black hair caught red highlights from the sunset.

"I'm ready," Arienne said.

Brown placed her right forearm on top of his left. A short, fat corporal inflated his lungs and began a lively rendition of the wedding march on the Irish pipes.

Arienne started down the sandy aisle at a much faster walk than was customary in weddings. Brown's homely face split in a wide grin. "No need to rush, girl, you'll be married a long time."

"The sooner I start, the better." Joshua was smiling at her, his teeth ice-white in his tanned face. She couldn't get to him fast enough.

Chuckling softly, Brown handed her to Langdon and retired into the background. Arienne smiled up at the tall soldier, her knees trembling so violently that she was sure she'd fall. Joshua tucked her hand under his arm and gazed down at her with a world of love and devotion in his eyes.

"Major Langdon, would ye like me to begin, sir?"

the priest asked. Joshua dragged his eyes away from Arienne and nodded.

Father O'Reilly crossed himself and began the Latin service. Except for occasional hiccups and a tendency to sway, he did very well. At last he broke into English. "Do ye, Arienne Dauphina Lloyd, take this man to be your lawfully wedded husband, promising to obey him in all things, to be a helpmeet unto him, and to bring forth children to be raised in righteousness before God?"

"Yes, I do!"

"And do ye, Joshua Tobias Langdon, take this woman to be your lawfully wedded wife, to have and to hold, to protect and to love, all the days of your life, promising to cherish the children of your blessed union?"

"Yes, I do."

"Have ye a ring, lad?"

"Yes." With some difficulty Joshua worked a thin band of white gold from his little finger. He slid the band onto Arienne's ring finger. "It was my grandmother's," he said.

"By the authority vested in me, I pronounce the two of ye man and wife," Father O'Reilly said, bringing the ceremony to a close. "Go on and kiss the maid."

Joshua had already snatched her off the ground to kiss her deeply. The wedding guests cheered and threw their hats into the air. Father O'Reilly beamed and slid a bottle of homemade whiskey out of his sleeve, took a swig, and handed it to Brown. The commander grinned and drank.

•

"Hand her over for kissing, Major!" someone shouted. The men queued up.

"Killjoys," Langdon said to his bride with good-natured gruffness.

She laughed and stepped away, allowing each man to kiss her cheek. Then she caught Father O'Reilly by the shoulders and kissed him on the forehead. "Thanks, you old dear. I'm sorry they locked you up today."

He focused on her with difficulty. Patting the whiskey bottle, he said, "I'll soon make up for the drought, me dear."

Colonel Brown bowed over her hand, then said, "Oh, what the hell," and kissed her quickly on the cheek. He shot Joshua a stern look. "Langdon, you unworthy young whelp, if I get wind that you don't daily worship the ground this girl walks on, I'll take her away from you and idolize her myself. Let that be a warning to you!"

Joshua chuckled and saluted. "The warning's well taken, sir. This unworthy whelp will forever be Mrs. Langdon's most devoted acolyte."

Arienne smiled at hearing herself called "Mrs. Langdon." Rising on her toes, she kissed her husband lingeringly on the mouth. His arms tightened around her shoulders and waist.

"Well then," Brown said, belatedly returning Langdon's salute, "now that we've got you legal, Cook's baked a cake and acquired a barrel of whiskey. Reception in my office. Fall out!"

Yelling wildly, the wedding guests dispersed up the path to the fort. Brown pulled the flowers off his horse and swung up onto its broad back, saluting the couple. Then he rode after his men.

Joshua scooped Arienne into his arms and started up the darkening path. The sun had gone, leaving a twilit glow on the silent dunes. A yellow moon was rising out of the sea.

"Where are you carrying me?"

"To the reception, and then to bed. My girl needs her rest," Joshua said with a wicked grin.

"She hasn't slept in two days—why start now?" Growling like a playful cat, she began to nibble his ear. Joshua groaned and stumbled slightly, his grip tightening on her body. Surprised and gratified by his response, she flicked her warm tongue into the hollow behind his jaw and down his neck. "I don't feel very sleepy."

"Point taken, Mrs. Langdon." The major pivoted abruptly on his heel and marched back down the path. Arienne smiled and renewed her assault on his throat, kissing and tasting until his breath came hard and he looked down at her with burning eyes. "You are going to get it, girl."

"Get what, my prince?"

In answer, Joshua carried her into the shadows between two dunes. The glittering Gulf was before them. He gently laid her down on the cool sand and smoothed her hair away from her cheeks. Ever so softly he began to kiss her, his hard fingers cupping her cheek, one bent leg trapping her thighs.

He was drunk on the sensation of her, the pure wonder of holding this fountainhead of love in his arms and knowing that no power on earth could stop him from slaking his deep thirst. Of man and war he had no recollection. Of duty there was none but the sweet duty of worshiping this trembling flower who had given herself to him with vows of fidelity and love.

The sea pounded the beach in rhythm with his heart, and the moon smiled a benediction from the velvety black sky. With the white sands as pure and clean as the maid beneath him, this place became for Joshua an ancient kiva, a holy temple for two.

"Thou art beautiful, my love," he said huskily, his eyes sparkling silver.

"Not so beautiful as thee, my sweet Joshua." She stroked the chiseled lines of his face. Slowly she began to undo the brass buttons down the front of his jacket.

Joshua shivered deep within himself. Over his countenance stole an expression of such love that tears sprang to Arienne's eyes. She smiled at him tremulously as her fingers failed at their task.

"I cherish you," Joshua said in a low voice, unbuttoning and laying aside his jacket and shirt. His chest shone like molten copper in the moonlight, the muscles undulating as he pulled the flowers from his bride's hair.

She reached for him as he lowered his mouth to her throat, but he caught her wrists in one hand and pulled her arms over her head, gently pinning her to the sand. Not being able to touch him as he suckled at her throat brought exquisite torture and a wet pulsing fire between her thighs. She moaned and writhed, unable to keep still.

After untold minutes, he dragged his lips down the slender column until he reached the valley between her breasts. Through the thin fabric of her gown he took her left nipple gently between his teeth and began to tease her.

Arienne strained against him, feeling the hot length of his manhood against her thigh. As he moved to her right breast to continue his ministrations she began to pant for breath. She was burning with a fever that made her shake in every limb.

Just when she thought she couldn't bear it another moment, that she would die of longing or explode into a million pieces, he released her wrists and began to undress her as lovingly as a husbandman stripping a rose to reveal her innermost nectar. He slid her gown off her shoulders, then down over her hips and legs, finally laying it aside. Moments later he had divested her of her pantaloons and she lay naked save for the white satin ribbons she had tied at her ankles in place of shoes.

Joshua reached to untie the bows and then decided to leave them in place. Looking down at her with blazing eyes, he lifted her right foot to his mouth and tongued her from toes to ankle.

The sensation was shockingly erotic. Arienne clenched her hands in the sand by her sides and stared up at him, gasping as he slowly licked and tasted her naked feet and nibbled at the ribbons binding her ankles. He untied them with his teeth.

The slow play was almost too much for Joshua to

endure. She was so beautiful, so young and innocent. And she was so very much his. He could do anything he wanted with her, yet the knowledge of his power filled him not with the desire to dominate but to serve her a full measure of joy.

He spread her ankles apart and stared down at the dark, soft curls between her thighs. How many nights had he awakened in a cold sweat, his body rock-hard, having dreamed of looking at her just like this?

His eyes burning brightly with sexual hunger, he licked his way up her calves to the inside of her knees, taking joy in her untamed response. She arched her spine, at the same time reaching blindly for his head, entwining his black hair in both hands.

With excruciating slowness he favored both of her firm, silken thighs with his mouth, turning her to make concentric circles all the way to her taut cheeks, then around her hips to the front. There he stopped, a mere inch from her sweet, naked womanhood, warming her already hot flesh with breaths of air.

"Don't, oh please, don't, Joshua!" If he touched her there, she knew she could no longer hold back and she wanted this to last and last and last. . . .

His tongue found her and she arched almost violently against him, but with tender control he grasped her and held her steady, persuading her to accept that most intimate lover's kiss.

"I can't stop it, Joshua!" she cried, her lithe muscles tensing as hard as steel.

"Then let it go, baby," he said hoarsely before his tongue took her again in a hot, probing kiss.

Arienne screamed in a voice she scarcely recognized as her own. Tremors seized her, rocking her on a tide of emotion as savage as a storm's. Still he did not stop, but continued thrusting, draining every drop of the torrent that swept her, cleansing her with fire.

And then she lay gasping, her ebony hair spread across the sand in a silken veil. Tears welled from the sapphire depths of her eyes. She could find no words, but feverishly clutched him to her body, unwilling ever to let him go.

After several minutes Joshua tenderly untwined her fingers from his hair and pulled her beneath him, the rough fabric of his trousers jolting her femininity with fresh shock waves of desire. He looked down into her streaming eyes and kissed her once, twice, on the lips.

"A long time I wandered in the wilderness of solitude," he said in a deep voice that shook slightly, "and then, my beloved one, you came and with one smile beckoned me out of the wasteland into your soul. I lay my heart and my sword at your feet."

He raised himself to his knees above her, unbelted his saber, and laid it at her feet. Then, silhouetted by moonlight, he unbuttoned his trousers, slid them down, and lowered himself on top of her.

Joshua's face burned with loving passion as she enclosed him in her slender fingers and guided him into her. Her hot wetness gloved him tightly, and she screamed, first in pain and then in joy.

"The world has never borne one so lovely as thee," he said. And then passion swept him away and he could say no more.

The night winds blew, the waves beat upon the island sands, and the lovers bent and swayed like sea grass on the timeless dunes in the consummation of their vows of love.

At last they were spent, and Arienne fell into deep slumber in her husband's arms, her dreams sweet and untroubled, woven of magic and peace. Joshua lay motionless, his lips buried in her dark hair, his nostrils filled with her fragrance. He was too happy to sleep, too happy to care about anything but his precious Arienne.

She slept until the moon marked its zenith, casting a sorcerer's glow over the pristine sands. A night hawk wheeled over the beach. Small nocturnal creatures rustled in the scrub oak behind the dunes. Shivering in the cool wind, she snuggled more closely against his naked chest.

"Ah, the princess awakens from the spell," he said, turning her in his arms to kiss her. "Do you have any idea how gorgeous you are asleep?"

"I've never looked at myself asleep to find out." She kissed his nose. "Perhaps we should get a mirror."

"There are uses, and then there are uses for a mirror," he said, a devilish gleam in his eyes. "We'll get three, and a fourth for the ceiling."

"Why, Major Langdon," Arienne said in a coquettish

Creole accent, "I do believe you're entertaining thoughts of a carnal nature."

"You do believe right, my intoxicating young temptress," he said. He lowered his mouth to her breasts, tracing the dark areolas with his tongue until her nipples hardened and she groaned with excitement. He slipped his thumb down to her rigid little button of flesh. "How do you like my way of thinking?"

Arienne arched against his hand, purring like a cat. She ran her fingers through his dark hair, then down over his hard chest and belly to the fiery flesh pressed against her thigh. She grasped the heavy thickness in both hands, caressing him ardently, his groans of pleasure heightening her excitement.

"Kiss me," he said, pulling her face to his until their bodies were clasped firmly together, lying side by side on the sand. "Give me your tongue."

His tongue flicked against hers, and then he was inside her mouth. The sensation made her hunger for other things, and she broke off the kiss after a moment. "My turn."

She began to nibble her way down his chest to his belly. As he reached to stroke her cheek she caught his forefinger in her mouth and sucked it lingeringly. He gasped in shocked delight, his manhood surging with fresh blood. Giving a throaty chuckle, Arienne released his finger and brushed his crisp, manly curls with her lips, her cheek rubbing his rigid flesh. Then she clasped her arms around his narrow waist and took him in her mouth, kissing him up and down in a rhythm that made him cry out hoarsely and imprison her head in his hands.

Arienne's nipples tightened agonizingly with desire, and a whirling maelstrom of passion gripped her as she kissed him. She had no recollection that there had ever existed for her a world without this mighty man whose touch robbed her of reason and whipped her into a frenzied animal that cried not for surcease but for perpetual beginnings.

When she could wait no longer, she climbed on top of him and pulled him inside her. A climax of swirling lights and colors burst upon her, carrying her to mountain heights, plunging her to the depths of a boiling sea. She was drowning, yet she needed no air, seemingly bounded no more by earthly imperatives. That she possessed a body at this point she had reason to doubt. The sensations were too exquisite to be corporeal.

Down through coral mists she drifted to the tactile world. Gradually she became aware of the deliciously soft sand beneath her, the air sliding over her skin like delicate wings, the touch of her lover's hands.

Tenderly Joshua stroked her hair. He pulled her closer and held her tightly. "Welcome back, Princess."

His heart beat solidly, reassuringly against her cheek. There was no measuring the love she felt for him. There were years ahead to share love songs, and time stretched before them like a high, white road, alight with marvels unforeseen yet certain.

"Come," Joshua said, pulling her to her feet, "let's bathe in the sea."

Hand in hand they ran down the beach and into

the dark water, until the sea tripped them and they fell into its arms. Underwater they touched fingertips, then lips, rising to the surface in a swirling cloud of bubbles.

It seemed to Arienne the most natural thing in the world to lock her legs around Joshua's strong back, to press herself fully down upon his warmth until he became hard again and filled her with that most fervent expression of love. He exalted her, filled her soul with unquenchable fire. She yearned toward him, her untutored young body arousing him to fresh heights of passion.

"I love you, Joshua Langdon," she said.

"And I love you, Arienne." He bent his head to kiss her, his arms supporting the weight of her body easily in the water as he led her through the dance. They laughed, tumbled to and fro by the waves and their own frantic convolutions.

At last they broke apart and Joshua comically wiped his brow. "I need a swim to rejuvenate this tired old body."

Arienne laughed and flipped onto her back, butting his chest with her toes. "I'll race you out to sea, if you think your ancient skeleton can float that far."

Joshua made a grab at her ankle, but she ducked through a wave. Surfacing on the other side, she struck out for deep water, her arms and buttocks flashing in the moonlight. Joshua plunged after her, and soon they were swimming side by side, more like dolphins than humans.

One hundred yards from shore they stopped to tread water. Arienne's eyes gleamed like moonbeams on the waves. "Tired yet, my venerable one?"

"Extremely. Carry me back to shore?"

"I had hoped you'd carry me. I like the feel of your arms."

"You'll feel them—and other things—soon enough, you pretty young sea witch. Let's look at the stars awhile."

With their fingers touching, they floated effortlessly on their backs, the salt water buoying them up. A diamond mantle of stars shimmered overhead, and a meteor spun from the sky and disappeared far out to sea.

"The Choctaws in New Orleans used to say the lights in the heavens were the spirits of warriors watching over their families," Arienne said as a gentle rolling wave lifted her body. "A falling star is a brave returning to battle."

"Do you believe those old legends?" Joshua moved his head closer to hers.

"Have you not fallen from the sky, beloved?"

"I'm only flesh and blood."

"But you've battled before. I've seen your limp, and the scar on your thigh."

"Which proves I'm a mortal man, and a damned clumsy one at times."

"Tell me how you came to be hurt."

Joshua was silent, disturbed by his memories. Finally he said, "I was shot at Bull Run, trying to rescue my commander. He was pinned beneath his horse."

"Did you save him?"

"I carried him back to our lines. Can we talk about

something else now, like how gorgeous you are with your hair spreading out around your naked body like seaweed?"

Arienne made a face. "That sounds rather revolting, and you still haven't finished the tale. Did you get a medal?"

"Yeah, I got a medal. I got to keep the ball in my femur, too. The surgeon couldn't get it out, though he sure as hell tried hard enough. He rooted around in there for the better part of an hour—I timed him."

"You were awake?"

"Who could've slept through that?" Joshua said in a feeble attempt at humor. "Besides, if I'd been asleep, he would have sawed my leg off to save time. I had to pull rank on him to get him to let me keep it."

"That's terrible!"

"It didn't turn out so badly. If I hadn't been shot, I wouldn't have come to the attention of the secret service, got drafted to catch Louis DeCoeur, and found you."

Arienne shivered at the Frenchman's name, fearing that Joshua would voice his desire to go after him again. She had almost convinced herself that the rest of the world no longer existed. The sea suddenly lost its magic and became a carpet of blackness, alive with invisible horrors.

"Let's swim back, Joshua," she said, rolling over. "Something's nibbling my toes." She disappeared with a kick and a splash and surfaced after a few seconds on a course for the beach.

Joshua swam after the dark little head with the

flashing white arms. The tide made the return trip easier, and soon the pair staggered from the water, far down the beach from the point where they'd left their clothing. They stopped to kiss, and Arienne immediately felt better.

"Let's get you dried off before you catch pneumonia," Joshua said. He picked her up and walked up the beach.

"I hope we don't run into anyone," she said with a nervous giggle.

"If we do, we'll bury him to his neck and set the sand fleas on him. That'll learn the varmint."

"I might have known you'd take direct action, you bloodthirsty pirate."

"Of course. I can't let callow eyes feast on my lovely prisoner." He leered at her breasts.

Arienne laughed. "You're the one who's lovely, Major Langdon. You're a hungry young lion prowling in the moonlight. You must let me paint you sometime."

"My fees are high."

"But I have just the method of payment," she said, kissing his jaw. She dropped her head onto his shoulder and closed her eyes, letting him carry her up the beach.

When they arrived at their private dune, Joshua discovered she had fallen asleep. He laid her on his jacket and covered her with her white gown, making a pillow of his shirt. Then he lay down beside her and slept.

19

Arienne didn't awaken the next morning until the sun had risen high enough to peep over the sand dunes. She stirred, rubbed her eyes, and sat up. Where had Joshua gone?

"Hello, you're finally awake. I was beginning to worry."

She looked up to find him sitting on the sand dune about ten feet above her, smiling his devastating boyish smile. He was wearing his blue trousers and red suspenders, which made his torso look even more tantalizing.

Arienne stood up and began to brush the sand off her naked body, pretending not to notice his appreciative stare. "I shouldn't have slept so late."

Joshua slid down the dune on his backside and took her into his arms. Standing toe to toe with her, he looked down into her eyes. "We can easily turn back the clock."

"How do you propose we do that? Have you a magic wand?"

Langdon grinned and pinched her buttock. "As a matter of fact, I do. Want me to grant your favorite wish?"

"You've a terribly naughty mind for a wizard, sir."

"Thank you, it's one of my more admirable qualities." He expanded his muscular chest until his suspenders threatened to pop.

"Ranking second only to your deep sense of humility."

"That's been said of me before."

She took his left suspender between her thumb and forefinger and slid her hand down to his waist, remembering how he had looked last night as he slipped off his suspenders and opened his trousers. "You really are magical, Major Langdon," she said in a throaty whisper. "The mind boggles."

"As it often does in my presence."

"Oh, you!" She stepped beside him with one leg behind his knee and pushed hard against his chest, knocking him down. She followed him to the ground and began to kiss him. As his powerful arms tightened around her she said, "Boggle my mind again, Joshua."

An hour later they went down to the Gulf for one last swim. The sun was well up, causing Arienne some concern, but Joshua had no intention of denying himself the pleasure of holding her wet body against his. If anyone was spying, well, look and be damned!

Afterward they ran back to the shelter of the dune and dressed and then, hand in hand, took the path back to the fort. As Arienne started through the sallyport Joshua said, "Just a minute, gorgeous."

He swept her off her feet. The entire garrison cheered as he carried her through the portal and across the parade ground. Reaching her quarters, he kicked open the door and carried her across the threshold. He kissed her gently before setting her down.

"So, you two finally made it home," Colonel Brown said through the open connecting door. He got up from his desk and came through to shake hands with Langdon. "I was about to send out a search party."

Arienne stifled a giggle, imagining Joshua burying a dozen soldiers to the neck. Joshua chuckled, reading her mind. "Thank goodness you didn't, sir," he said.

Brown covered an ungentlemanly guffaw with a cough. "Join me for breakfast, Major and Mrs. Langdon."

"You go ahead, Joshua," Arienne said. "I'll be there in a minute."

The two men went out, closing the door. Arienne sat down to brush the sand from her hair. She then braided it into a thick rope down her back, using a scrap of white ribbon to tie the tail.

Feathering the tip of a green stick, she dipped it into

a jar of bicarbonate of soda she found on the wash-stand and cleaned her teeth. Feeling as presentable as she was likely to get considering the rude toiletry items and clothing at her disposal, she went into Brown's office.

The two men were seated at the desk, drinking hot chicory and arguing in low voices. They broke off when she entered the room and stood up. Joshua pulled out an extra chair and gestured at a plateful of bacon and biscuits. "Have some breakfast, my pet."

But Arienne had stopped just inside the doorway, an icy premonition clutching her heart. Forcing herself to speak lightly, she said, "I know what you gentlemen are up to."

"We're up to our necks in breakfast, that's all. Join us, darling."

Arienne wasn't fooled. "You're trying to talk Colonel Brown into helping you attack the navy yard again, isn't that it?"

The two men exchanged looks. "She's brilliant as well as beautiful," Brown said.

"That's why I married her, sir."

"Don't patronize me!" She caught her husband's sleeve in her trembling hand and glared up at him through angry, frightened eyes.

His jaw tensed as he looked down at her. "This is one battle you're going to have to stay out of, Arienne."

"No!"

Langdon pushed her gently yet firmly into the chair. Brown sat down and began to munch a biscuit, studying them.

"I've never wavered in my intentions, Arienne. That damned sub has got to be destroyed," Joshua said.

"What makes you think you can destroy it when the last attempt succeeded only in getting some of Colonel Brown's men killed?"

Brown nodded and took another biscuit. "My point exactly, Mrs. Langdon, but I've agreed to let your major chance it on his own tonight, anyway."

Arienne rose slowly from the chair, staring in shock from Brown to her husband.

"The risk to myself is minimal, Arienne," Joshua said, resting his fingertips on her arm. "I'll slip into the navy yard tonight. Colonel Brown has consented to give me the supplies I need to do the job."

"To get yourself killed, you mean!"

"She's got a point, Langdon."

"Would you kindly shut up, sir?"

Brown retreated to his cup of chicory and watched Arienne over the rim. He'd never seen a woman so much in love with a man. Her fear for him was palpable. He ought to have Langdon locked in the guardhouse for his own protection.

On the other hand, if Langdon could get through, then he, Brown, would look damned good. He might possibly cobble together a nomination for president on his war record.

He lifted a note written in Langdon's bold script from his desk. "Let's run through that list of supplies you wanted one more time, shall we? You want a depth chart of the bay and the channel, a skiff with a black sail, two hundred and fifty pounds of black powder divided among several kegs, a hundred feet of fuse wire, two revolvers, two rifles, and—what's this on the bottom of the page?"

"Chloroform, sir, on cotton balls packed into a jar."

"Of course. Is there anything else you need? Maybe a little gold bouillon, or President Lincoln's job?"

"No, sir. That will be all."

"Fine. Then if you'll excuse me?" Brown stalked out of the office.

"I'm sorry, Arienne."

"No, you're not." Even as she spoke she realized she was being unfair, but she couldn't dam the bitter words. "You've lived for this day. Nothing is more important than that submarine. Nothing and nobody."

"You know that's not true." He paced to the window and stared across the sunlit bay to Fort Barrancas. "I've got a job to do, and I'm going to do it."

"Because of your honor?"

Major Langdon turned around slowly, his eyes as gray and bleak as a winter's day. "Yes, Arienne, because of my blasted honor. I don't have a choice."

Her sapphire gaze burned through him. "Then, my fallen-star warrior, I will come with you."

"The hell you will!" He was on her before she saw him move, gripping her savagely by the upper arms until her feet dangled inches above the floor.

"You'll stay here in the fort and wait for me to get back!"

"I won't! You're mad if you think I'll let you go to your death alone!"

"Would it make my death any easier to bear if you died with me?"

"It would be easier for me!"

Joshua cursed long and loudly and pushed her into the chair. "You'll stay here, if I have to lock you in your quarters and swallow the key. I'll not let you endanger yourself."

"You didn't say that when I rescued you from Fort Barrancas!"

Joshua's glare was as black as a thundercloud. His voice dropped an octave. "Why do you have to be so goldarned stubborn?"

Arienne sensed victory at hand. "Because it keeps you coming back for more."

He slowly began to shake his head in defeat. A chuckle burst from his lips. "Seventeen years old, and you've already got me figured out. Have you any idea how humbling that is to an older man?"

"You're not so old, *mon père*," she said with a laugh. "You will let me go with you tonight?"

"God help me, yes." Then his tone hardened. "But you're to do exactly as I say, do you understand?"

"Yes, sir!" Arienne said, snapping him a salute. "Do I get a gun?"

"Do you know how to shoot?"

"Of course! I grew up in Louisiana, you know."

"Where you spent all your time prowling the swamps for possums and bears, no doubt."

"When I wasn't spending my time on Lake Pontchartrain."

Joshua started. "That's right—you've sailed small boats." He bent down to kiss her forehead. "I hate to admit it, but you might come in handy, after all."

"I don't know whether to take that as a compliment or not, Major."

Langdon didn't answer but swept the plates aside and scrounged in Bragg's desk for paper and quill. "Pull your chair up and listen carefully." He dipped the quill into the inkwell and began to draw. "I'm going to show you exactly what you're to do tonight."

By midafternoon, a bank of black clouds had marched across the Gulf of Mexico and descended on the island. Lightning jagged across the sky, splitting open the potbellied clouds. The torrential rain turned the parade ground into a vast swimming hole. Outside the fort, trees lashed violently in the high wind, their limbs cracking like rifle shots, and huge breakers slammed against the Gulf beach.

Alone in a dim casemate, Joshua leaned against a cannon and watched the storm, his thoughts as turbulent as the wind-tossed waves. Would the damned storm blow itself out by midnight? And even if it did, would the bay be too wild to cross? Perhaps he should delay. But what if the sub were ready for launching? It would be a shame if he missed it by one night.

"Hell," he said. "What's to be done?"

"Proceed full speed ahead, I think," Arienne said softly, stealing up behind him. She wrapped her arms around his waist and rested her head against his broad back. A cold wind drove spray through the casemate window, wetting them both. "Did Brown give you everything you asked for?"

"Aye, we're set."

"Then we won't let this little storm stop us."

"Little storm, Arienne? Winds like that could snap off our mast and capsize us before we got ten feet from shore."

"They'll drop. Trust me."

Joshua shifted around to encircle her in his arms. As he kissed her his tension began to ebb. "You're a reassuring little sailor."

"It's my job, sir. We'll get to Barrancas, all right. You watch and see."

Langdon returned his attention to the bay. Fort Barrancas was impossible to make out through the driving rain. He balled his fist and thumped the brass barrel of the cannon. "I don't see any sign of this typhoon letting up."

"And you won't, as long as you stand staring at it like a cook watching a pot, you magnificent worrier, you."

"I'm not worried."

"Yes, you are. You need to think about something else for a while."

Joshua's dark eyes narrowed, and one corner of his mouth twitched upward. His raffish good looks started a pulse throbbing in Arienne's throat. "I've just thought of something else," he said.

"Funny, I just thought of that same thing."

He lowered his face to kiss her, sliding his hands down over her hips. "You've got the most excellent little behind, temptress."

He turned her to face the cannon. The long barrel was cold, wet with the mists of rain blowing through the casemate, but she hardly noticed it as his mouth dropped to the juncture of her shoulder and neck. His manhood surged against her taut buttocks.

"You make my head swim, Arienne."

"I'm feeling rather dizzy myself," she said, and she meant it.

Joshua's breath was coming in ragged gasps as though he'd run a long distance. Impatiently he slid her skirts up over her long legs, then unfastened her pantaloons and slid them down, his hands lingering over her hips. He began to stroke her, his skillful fingers fanning the exquisite flames of desire. Raising her gown to her shoulders, he ran his tongue along her spine, down and down.

His intimate ministrations transcended all he had previously done to her. She clung to the smooth cannon, her feverish cries drowned by the bass roll of thunder on the bay. Lightning seemed to course through her being and electrify her senses, burning her skin and transforming her to liquid flame. She was convinced she would die in his arms. He was too good, too impossibly, wonderfully, marvelously good!

As the words tumbled unwittingly from her lips Joshua slowly began to rub his hardness up and down the backs of her thighs. He loosened her hair and buried his hands in the silken mass, her sensuality catapulting him into new worlds of awareness. He was drunken with desire, hungry for satiation.

And then he was inside her, sheathed in a hot moistness that stole his last vestige of self-control. He gripped her hips and began to stroke her none too gently while she responded to him with a savagery that matched his own.

Together they climbed a wave as high as a mountain, hovered at the peak, then spun over the edge into swirling oblivion. Through the roaring in Joshua's ears he heard her throaty cries. Eyes closed, he breathed in her delicate scent and traced her neck and cheeks with his lips.

"You are love, Arienne," he said, his heart thudding mightily in his chest. "I have never in my life experienced anyone like you."

He turned her to face him, dropping her skirts over her legs. She looked up at him with wide eyes and smiled. Joshua's heart melted.

"By the wind spirits, I love you!" he declared.

"And I adore you," she said, belatedly looking around to see if they'd been observed.

Joshua laughed at her tardy caution. "No, angel, the soldiers have had the sense to stay away from the newly wedded couple. I've made sure of that."

"Ah-ha! You threatened to bury them to their

necks, I suppose." She patted her flaming cheeks with the hem of her skirt, still shaken by the experience.

"I threatened them with worse than that."

"Ugh. Worms down their backs? Snakes in their bedrolls?"

"You lived in Louisiana too long, little swamp bunny." He looked out at the bay. "Do my eyes betray me, or is the storm abating?"

Arienne narrowed her eyes against the mist. "I'm not sure."

"More wishful thinking on my part, I guess," he said. He picked her up and set her on the cannon, then rested his arms on her lap. "What's your father likely to say when he hears we're married?"

She looked away for a moment, lips tightening. What would he say? Perhaps he wouldn't be too upset. Hadn't he been wishing for grandchildren? She smoothed a damp lock of hair off her husband's forehead and smiled a little.

"He might pat you on the back and say, 'Dashed good, my boy,' or something equally lordly."

"Or he might be mad as hell."

She sighed. "That's what I'm afraid of. I just hope he doesn't work himself into a fit or something."

Joshua patted her knee, alarm bells jangling in his mind. Sir James would have more than a fit if something happened to Arienne tonight, and so would he. "Look, darling, I'm really sorry about all this, but—"

"But you've changed your mind about taking me, is that it?"

He was silent.

"You're afraid I'll become a hysterical female and get in your way, aren't you? Well, I won't!"

"How do you know what you'll do? You've been through an extremely difficult time lately—"

"And you think I'm ready to crack under the strain! I can tell you, Major Langdon, that I've never felt more competent in my life. I am going to help you get that sub."

Their eyes clashed in a contest of wills. Joshua briefly considered locking her up for the night, but then wondered what sort of married life he'd have after caging his proud wife. Besides, he'd given his word that she could accompany him. His only hope was to keep her as far out of the line of fire as he could.

"All right. But you are to obey me to the letter, understood?"

She tried to keep the triumph out of her eyes as she said, "Clearly. By the way, the rain's beginning to slacken."

Langdon looked through the window. "So it is. Still, those waves are mountainous. I hope you haven't lost your sea legs."

"Don't worry about me," she said. "I grew up in a sailboat, remember? When all is said and done, you'll wonder how you could ever have considered attacking the Rebels without me."

Joshua grinned and lifted her off the cannon. "Let's go get a few hours of rest. And this time, my temptress, we really are going to sleep."

"All right, but let's not make a habit of it, darling."

"Small chance of that," he said lightly, but the backward look he cast at the foaming black caldron of sea was sober. He'd have to pray for their safety. He hoped he remembered how.

20

At 10:45 P.M., Joshua and Arienne Langdon walked out of the fort and down to the bay with Colonel Brown and a small group of officers. It was still raining, and the winds were brisk, but at least the lightning had moved inland. Langdon's gaze fell upon a small, deep-keeled sailboat moored in the shallows. He picked Arienne up, waded through the breakers to the boat, and deposited her in the stern.

He still had deep misgivings about taking her along, but she had remained adamant. She intended to skipper the boat for him, and that was that. He tried not to dwell on the consequences if the storm were to swing around and catch them on the open bay. Loaded with two hundred and fifty pounds of gunpowder, its lightning rod of a mast reaching for the sky, the ungainly craft was little more than a floating bomb.

"I'd still like to talk you out of this fool stunt, Langdon!" Colonel Brown shouted.

Langdon shrugged off his oilskin and tossed it onto the beach. He was clad in black and, like Arienne, had smeared lampblack on his face. "I appreciate your concern, sir."

Brown snorted loudly enough to be heard over the wind and rain. "I'm more concerned for Mrs. Langdon. A woman's got no business sailing on a night like this."

"I'll hold the boom while you raise the sail, Joshua," Arienne said. She pushed the hood of her slicker back from her sooty face, grasped the end of the boom in steady hands, and nodded at him.

Joshua's heart swelled with pride. She was a headstrong, courageous little woman, and he was damned glad of it. Suddenly it didn't matter what dangers they faced, as long as they faced them together. The Confederates were in for a night they'd never forget.

Grinning broadly, he raised the black Bermuda rig sail and cast the mooring line to one of the soldiers. The boat began to drift away from the beach. Arienne took the tiller.

Brown tried one more time. "Tell your wife to leave men's work to men, Major Langdon!"

"Your men were too scared to volunteer, sir." He hauled in the sheet and brought the boat about. "I'd rather have Mrs. Langdon for this bit of work than any twelve of your so-called men."

The stormy night swallowed Brown's reply. Arienne

chuckled and said, "If you'll sit down next to me, Major, we'll get under way."

Joshua settled down next to her, holding the main sheet in his hands. Arienne began to tack back and forth to get the feel of the boat. She soon discovered that besides being heavily laden with powder kegs, the boat's strong weather helm necessitated constant rudder action to keep her on a broad reach. A heavy following sea increased the danger of their being swamped.

"All right, let's get to the navy yard," she said after the brief shakedown. With Joshua's assistance on the sheets, she set the boat flying along on a starboard tack, the black sail bulging like the belly of a whale. It began to rain harder.

"You're a dang good sailor, Arienne," Joshua said after several minutes. "Dang good."

"Don't sound so surprised, Major Langdon." She tried to avert her face from the rain.

"I can't help it. Your talents amaze me. The list grows longer by the day."

"Flattery will win you many favors, my troubadour." She leaned back on the tiller, fighting the boat's efforts to founder. Away from the slight protection of Santa Rosa Island, the swells were heavy, shining walls of black water rising higher than the boat. It was impossible to see where they were going. Arienne had to rely on her innate sense of direction, lest the constantly shifting winds throw them off course and land them far down-bay.

"Is that a light ahead?" Joshua asked after a quarter of an hour.

Arienne could see nothing through the driving rain. The boat was bucking like a wild horse, and the tiller was fighting her every inch of the way. "Harden the sheet—we're luffing."

Joshua made the correction, still squinting through the gloom. "I think there's a torch burning in the navy yard, or perhaps in the fort itself."

"Oh, really? And have they laid out a welcome mat as well?" She instantly regretted her sarcasm. She was more frightened than she wanted to admit.

Joshua looked at her closely. Her eyes were great hollows in her face, her lips a tight line. He could see the tension in her throat and arms as she battled with the tiller. "There *is* a light ahead. You're a good navigator."

"I'm just lucky."

"And tired. Come on, hand over the tiller. Take a rest."

"Not a bit. Stand by to jibe."

Joshua almost took the helm over her protests. He might have known she wouldn't spare herself. "Aye aye, Cap'n," he said, hauling in the main sheet while she eased the tiller away from the sail. They shifted their weight and ducked as the boom swung over their heads. Arienne brought the boat back on course while he let out the sheet.

"Not bad, my little sea witch. One might almost believe you had done this before."

Arienne smiled thinly, debating whether or not to tell him this was her first time skippering a sailboat at night in bad weather.

Before she could speak, a fusillade of thunder

boomed directly overhead. The wind veered, luffing the sail. Barely an instant later the following sea rushed under the stern, causing the boat to yaw and the bow to burrow into the waves. Within a second, the boom jibed viciously through a one-hundred-and-eighty-degree arc, striking Joshua in the side of the head and knocking him overboard.

"Joshua!" Arienne screamed, searching the maelstrom into which he'd been thrown. He was gone. She immediately hauled in the main sheet and pushed the tiller hard alee. The swamped boat teetered on the brink of capsizing.

Crisscrossing the boat's wake, she frantically bailed water with one cupped hand, not daring to release the tiller from the other for an instant. Small hailstones began to pock the witch's brew around the boat and sting her face. Lightning streaked out of the sky, turning the boat's black sail to ghostly blue.

She was tacking away to starboard when she heard a faint cry. Praying that her ears had not deceived her, she came about. The waterlogged boat heeled dangerously. "Are you there? Joshua, answer me!"

"Over here! No, no—steer to port!"

"I'm coming! Keep calling!" She sweated through five more bad minutes before a brilliant flash of lightning showed him struggling up the steep side of a wave. Before she could get to him, he disappeared into the trough, only to reappear at the top of the next swell.

Arienne let the boat go in irons and tossed him a

line. He seized the rope and began to pull himself in hand over hand while she hauled away at the other end.

"Are you all right?" Nearly blinded by the rain, she didn't realize she was weeping.

"I've got a hell of a headache, but I'll live." Gasping, he seized the gunwale. "You've got to bail out the boat before I climb in. Use the bucket under the bench."

She bailed water like a madwoman. "That's good enough. Climb in!"

"Did we lose the powder?"

"Does it matter?" She grabbed him by his collar to help him aboard.

Joshua dropped into the bottom of the boat, his great chest rising and falling. The parts of his face where the water had washed away the lampblack were chalk white, and there was a gash and a tremendous lump above his left cheekbone. He felt as though someone had dropped an anvil on his head and then proceeded to pound on it with hammer and tongs.

"Did we lose the powder?" He pushed himself to one elbow to scan the bow. Instead of one bow, he saw two.

"The kegs are there. Lie still!" Arienne dabbed at his cut with her skirt. By the Great Bear, she'd almost lost him!

Joshua pushed her hands away and struggled to his knees, his vision gradually clearing. "Never mind that. Let's get under way before one of these lightning bolts flirts with the powder. I should've known that damned storm would double back on us!"

The wind had indeed switched around to blow mightily off the port bow. Hailstones the size of marbles were falling, bouncing off the gunwales and striking their heads and backs. Joshua studied the sky uneasily, certain that a waterspout had spawned the ice.

The boat reached across the wind on a port tack, and the sailors crouched behind the slim protection of the sail. Swells raced by the hull at a terrifying speed.

"You were right—there's a light ahead!" Arienne said. It could only be coming from the navy yard. Then she heard a sound like a locomotive immediately behind them.

The waterspout was a vast, black monster. The top of its malevolent head was shrouded with a cloud and lit by lightning. Its long, solitary toe churned the water to boiling foam. It was scarcely a mile away.

Arienne was too terrified to scream. She had never seen anything like it in all the time she'd spent on the water. She wanted to jump overboard, dive for the bottom of the sea, and hide under a rock—anything to shut away the sight and sound of the behemoth whirling down on their tiny boat.

"Don't look at it!" Joshua shouted in her ear. His hard palm came down on top of her hand, holding the tiller steady, helping her to remember what she was about. "Keep your eyes on that light ahead. Sail like you've never sailed before!"

Strength radiated out of his hand into her fingers

and wrist and up her arm. Her whole being pervaded by a sense of confidence, she almost forgot the shrieking, sucking beast bearing down on them. Even when the monster hurled a lethal projectile of ice through the sail, she felt nothing but strength flowing from her husband's hand, a strength that imbued her with uncanny seamanship.

How long they ran ahead of the waterspout she didn't know, but finally the shrieking and roaring stopped, and she became aware of the ominous creaking of the mast. Realizing it was at breaking point, she luffed the sail to spill wind, releasing the strain. She looked over her shoulder.

"It's gone, baby, out to sea," Langdon said hoarsely. "God, I didn't know you could sail like that. I don't think we touched the water once."

"Then that . . . thing must have been holding us in its fist," she said, suddenly too weak to ply the tiller. She fell against her husband's chest, leaving the sailing to him.

Joshua pushed her hood back and looked into her face, his mind only half on his sailing. "I'm sorry I brought you out here."

"I'm not. We got away from that thing."

"The night is young. I can still get you killed."

Arienne sat up and looked him in the eye. She was still trembling, but her eyes glinted like steel. "I'd rather you didn't, Major Langdon. I want to have nine children and grow old with you."

"You'll never grow old. I, on the other hand, have aged ten years in the last hour. Our children will have an ancient stick for a father."

"It happens that I favor older men, darling. Here, give me the tiller. I can handle it now."

The rain had nearly stopped by the time they spotted the mainland. A thunderbolt briefly lit up the bluffs and the bulky floating dry dock. A torch was burning in one of the casemates at the fort.

"We'll just keep heading to leeward to get well clear of the navy yard," Joshua said. "It would be a damn shame to have come all this way only to get spotted by some kid passing water off the dock."

"I know."

"Keep a hundred yards from shore, then." He raised his shirt and checked a strip of gauze wrapped around his waist.

"Is that the bottle of chloroform?"

"Yep," he said. He reached into a compartment for an oilskin-wrapped pistol and shoved it into his belt. "Remember to count off twenty minutes from the time you drop me, then sail into the lee of the dock. Understood?"

"Certainly," she whispered. How she managed to hold the tiller steady despite her growing fear for Joshua she didn't know. If only he would chuck this foolhardy plan!

As if reading her mind, he clasped her against him for a hard kiss. "You know I have to do this, Arienne. Once done, we'll get on with our lives."

"I believe you."

"And I believe in you," he said.

Then he slipped over the stern and was gone.

* * *

Joshua covered the distance to the floating dry dock underwater, coming up to get his bearings and snatch a breath of air every thirty seconds or so. The bay was as black as pitch. At any second he expected to confront some long slimy monster with teeth. He'd heard the mako sharks in the bay had a taste for humans.

He was fighting off an image of himself seized in a powerful set of jaws when he rammed headfirst into something hard and slimy. Surfacing immediately, holding his head in silent agony, he glared wildly at a thick piling heavily coated with moss.

He'd arrived at the dry dock, all right, and despite the danger, he wanted with all his heart to curse at the top of his lungs. Bad language was just the anesthetic his abused skull needed, but in Rebel territory it could get him anesthesia of the permanent type.

Gritting his teeth, he pulled himself up to peer over the edge of the dock. Not a soul in sight. "Hallelujah," he whispered, and climbed aboard.

The floating dry dock was a long, low structure with a warehouse in the middle. Gates could be opened to allow a ship to float inside, then closed, and the water pumped out to leave the vessel on shorings.

Running across the dock on noiseless bare feet, Joshua stopped under the eaves of the warehouse. He reached into his belt for the gun. It was gone.

He'd probably lost it when he crashed into the piling. Heaving a soft sigh, he stole around the corner of the warehouse and nearly cannoned into a guard.

There was a tense moment when the two men stared at each other. Then the guard brought his rifle off his shoulder and opened his mouth to shout.

Joshua rammed his fist into the Confederate's solar plexus, packing every ounce of strength into the blow. The guard doubled over, gasping. Joshua chopped him on the back of the neck and caught him before he hit the dock.

He almost left the Rebel there but then changed his mind and dragged him into the shadow of the warehouse. He yanked off his own wet clothes and pushed them through a crack in the dock, then stripped the unconscious soldier naked. It was the work of a moment to dress in the Confederate uniform, though the jacket didn't quite join across his broad chest and the trousers were too short.

He bound and gagged the soldier with his own stockings and neckerchief, then unstoppered the glass bottle strapped to his waist and removed a chloroform-soaked cotton wad. He applied it to the soldier's face long enough for him to inhale a few breaths. Then he slipped away.

Stationed on the windward side of the dock, the second guard never knew what hit him. One moment he was hunkering miserably against the rain, the next he was being jerked off his feet from behind, and a cold, evil-smelling cotton was clapped over his nose and mouth. He inhaled reflexively and was out two seconds later. Langdon propped him up against a barrel.

Guard number three had just finished a leisurely beat around the perimeter when he saw his companion napping. Chuckling, he approached the sleeper to rap him over the head with his rifle barrel. Joshua rose behind him and, clapping the cotton over his face, lowered him to the dock.

Joshua melted into the shadows and reappeared a few feet in front of a soldier seated on a pile of canvas, guarding the warehouse doors. The soldier's rifle was parked against the wall, out of his reach.

"That you, Glenn?" the guard asked, squinting up into the drizzling rain.

"Nope," said Joshua Langdon as he captured the rifle. He jammed the bayonet under the guard's chin and urged him to his feet. "How many of you on duty tonight?"

"F-five."

"Someone's in the warehouse with the submarine?"

"Y-yeah. You ain't gonna stab me, are you?"

"Not if you cooperate and hand over the key."

"I ain't got one!"

"Is that so? Turn around!" Joshua pressed the point of the bayonet against his spine. "Your buddy's going to open the door for us, nice and easy."

"You ain't gonna stick that in my backbone, are you?"

"I don't aim to, but I'm mighty nervous right now.

One false move out of you and I might skewer you like a jack mackerel."

"Oh Gawd!"

"There's no reason to swear. Just tell your buddy to open the door, and don't tell him I'm here."

"Gen'ral Bragg'll kill me!"

Joshua's soft, malevolent chuckle stirred the hairs on the back of his prisoner's neck. "Oh, I don't think the general would kill a poor old cripple like you're going to be."

"Wait a minute!" The soldier pounded on the door. "Charlie, open up! Charlie!"

"What the hell for, Bill?"

"Gen'ral wants to see you in his quarters on the double."

"Why?"

Bill rolled his eyes in fright as Langdon probed him lightly with the bayonet. "It's—it's about your pay."

A key scraped in the lock. Before Bill could move or shout, Joshua dropped the rifle and slammed a dripping wad of cotton over his face. The guard struggled for a few seconds before slumping to the ground wearing a silly grin.

But Joshua hadn't reckoned on the wind blowing chloroform into his own face. He reeled like a drunken man just as Charlie flung open the door.

The Confederate uniform fooled Charlie for only a second. Seeing Bill snoring on the planks, he launched himself out the door, his bayonet catching Langdon's belt before raking a bloody swath across his ribs. His thick finger tightened on the trigger of his rifle.

Langdon recovered his wits long enough to hurl himself over backward, pulling his attacker down with him. The rifle skittered across the dock and teetered on the edge. Charlie followed moments later, his head ramming into a piling. He lay still.

Joshua staggered to his feet. His side was bleeding profusely, though he felt no pain—yet. He tore off his borrowed jacket and, appropriating Bill's shirt, bound his wound tightly. Then he began to pile the unconscious guards neatly on the leeward side of the dock.

Five minutes later Arienne sailed up alongside the dock and dropped the sail. She made fast to a cleat, her eyes on Joshua's bandage as he sank to his haunches to peer down at her.

"What happened?" She wished with all her heart for a belaying pin. How she would have liked to bonk him over the head and sail away with him!

"I got grazed. Let's unload."

"I'll hand them up to you," she said, moving into the bow. She hefted a fifty-pound keg of powder.

Joshua jumped down into the boat beside her and seized the keg, setting it up on the dock. "I'll have none of that. You watch those boys to see that none of them moves. If they do, give 'em a breath of chloroform. Here, take the bottle."

Arienne reluctantly climbed out of the boat and squatted near the sleeping guards, watching Joshua out of the corner of her eye. She watched his great muscles cord and stretch as he lifted the heavy kegs. She wondered and worried about his "graze." Was it her imagination, or was blood beginning to seep through the makeshift dressing?

When he had finished unloading, Joshua scrambled onto the dock and trussed up the soldiers with a rope. Then he lowered each one into the boat.

"All right, Arienne, do just what we planned. Sail down the bay toward Pensacola. Find someplace to beach the boat, then hightail it to Mrs. Walsh's and stay there until I come for you."

Arienne gripped his wrist. "You *will* come, Joshua?"

"Of course." He kissed her forehead.

Arienne grabbed his arm before he could stand up. "You're just going to blow up the dock and come straightaway, aren't you? Nothing else?"

Joshua looked into her huge sapphire eyes. "Nothing else."

She slowly relaxed her grip on his arm, though her face remained tense and frightened. He was up to something, she could feel it in her bones. "I can't leave you, Joshua."

"You bloody well *will* leave, and leave *now!*"

Though the drizzle had stopped, lightning still flashed across the black vault of the sky, like fire in the forge of Vulcan. Langdon stood to his full height to tower over the girl.

Arienne stood up, raising her chin in defiance. "I'll drop these guards somewhere, and then I'll come back to get you, Joshua. I will not leave you."

Langdon seized her by the shoulders and shook her hard, the lightning throwing his features into harsh relief. "Get the hell out of here, girl, and don't come back." Over her struggles, he pushed her down into the stern and cast off the mooring line. "On peril of your life, do not come back. This dock is going to light up the night."

Arienne dared not scream at him. She looked from him to the black bulk of Fort Barrancas on the bluffs, then at the helpless men in her boat. When she looked back, he was gone.

With an agonized prayer in her heart, she hoisted the sail and pointed the small boat into the wind.

21

Louis DeCoeur couldn't sleep. His beautiful submarine was nearly finished. All that remained was to fit the torpedoes and launch her in the morning. The tanks had been filled early this evening with a suspension of aluminum, and Wilford Humes's air-filtration system seemed to be in perfect working order.

Thinking of Wilford Humes made him smile. With the chief engineer dead, he could take full credit for every aspect of the sub's development. He had not redrawn the stolen blueprints, and without them there was no documentation that Humes had ever made any worthwhile contributions. The other engineers were dimwits to a man. They'd soon forget Humes in the face of DeCoeur's achievement.

DeCoeur's smile deepened as he considered that achievement. After his sub wreaked destruction on the United States, she would rend the British empire. France would then own the world, and for all practical purposes, DeCoeur would own France.

The candlelight cast a glow over his face as he consulted the platinum pocket watch he had lifted from Wendell Stuart Lloyd's dead body. One o'clock in the morning. Hell, he was wasting time in bed. He wanted to see his creation, to slide his hands over her polished iron skin and into her chambers.

DeCoeur climbed out of bed and silently crept downstairs and out into the stormy night. He rejoiced in the lightning, feeling its particles invade his being to become part of him. Exulting in his dominion over the very elements, he stalked through the wind-ravaged woods toward the navy yard.

DeCoeur wasn't the only restless one on the post that night. Thomas, lying on the cot in Arienne's vacated chambers so as to be near Sir James, had been tossing fretfully for hours. The storm was contributing to his sleeplessness, of course, but the mental turmoil in which he found himself was the greater burden.

Since Wendell Stuart's death and Arienne's flight across the bay with Joshua Langdon, Sir James had been thrown into such a bad state that Thomas was afraid to leave him. If the girl didn't send word to him soon, he intended to talk Bragg

out of a boat and go see for himself if she was alive
or not. Damn it, he had to. If he hadn't stolen the
skiff and hidden it on the beach, Arienne wouldn't
have disappeared.

He sat up on the side of the cot and dropped his
head to his hands. He shouldn't have let her talk him
into helping Langdon, but she had been desperate to
save the spy. She had acted so much like a woman in
love that despite his conflicting loyalty to Sir James,
he had agreed to do whatever he could to help Langdon
flee to Fort Pickens.

Sighing, Thomas rose from the cot and went out
onto the balcony. It had been a wild storm. Tree
limbs were scattered all over the yard, and he
could hear waves pounding the beach, even from
this distance. Bolts of lightning chased one another
across the sky like mischievous ghosts. He'd have
to put off his trip to the island if the weather
didn't clear.

He stared through the gloom at Fort Barrancas,
remembering what Arienne had told him about the
submersible ironclad. According to her, the strange
ship could cause the Union to lose the war.

Shivering in the chilly wind, he climbed over the
railing and down the trellis and crept along the path
toward the navy yard. He wanted to see for himself
what a submarine looked like. Maybe he could even
think of a way to sink her.

Joshua set a keg of powder at each of the outside
corners of the warehouse and strung them together

with fuse wire. Then he backed through the door into the warehouse, unreeling wire as he went, and connected the fuse to a fifth powder keg, which he'd placed next to a stack of torpedoes.

The bombs set, he turned for his first good look at the submarine. She was down in a rectangular dry lock below sea level, resting on her shoring props like a patient whale. Her iron skin and brass fittings gleamed in the lantern light, and the glass faceplate on her conning tower stared sightlessly forward.

What a boon to the Union she would prove, Joshua thought, scrambling down a wooden ladder into the lock. The damp planks rocked gently beneath his feet. He quickly climbed a brass ladder to the conning tower and opened the hatch.

It was as black as night down there. Taking a deep breath, he dropped through the hole and peered through the conning port. Visibility was surprisingly good, though the thick round glass distorted shapes.

He began to grope around the metal bulkheads and, after striking his head a half-dozen times, discovered a lamp. One turn of a thin lever started water dripping onto the carbide rocks in the base of the lamp. He struck the steel, and a flame burst into life.

The dim light revealed a console full of brass levers, switches, and glass-faced gauges with red needles. Joshua dropped onto a high stool mounted on a pedestal and began to read the engraved brass plates beneath each gadget, mentally comparing them to the blueprints he had memorized. Bless Arienne's soul, she had done a fine job copying the plans. Everything matched exactly.

There was a set of rudder pedals beneath the console and a brass control stick jutting from the deck. Joshua spent several minutes familiarizing himself with the controls, feeling the almost imperceptible vibrations of the moving fins. Then he climbed out of the submarine.

"Keep your fingers crossed, Langdon," he muttered to himself as he mounted the wooden ladder to the warehouse deck. "Here's to speed, timing, and the grace of God. . . ."

He unbolted the huge doors bearing on the bay and let the wind swing them inward. A flash of lightning reached down into the sea like a crone's finger. Had Arienne beached the boat safely? She should be cutting through the woods to Pensacola by now, he fervently hoped. Please God, don't let her be out in the electrical storm!

How would she feel when she learned he'd lied to her? Had she really believed he intended to blow up the sub? It was a hell of a way to begin married life. He rubbed his head where he'd struck it on the piling. When he brought his hand away, he saw that it was sticky with blood.

Exclaiming impatiently, he wiped his hand on his trouser leg. Then he grabbed the handles of a great wooden winch set into the floor and pushed. The wheel, designed to be turned by two or three men, refused to budge. Digging into the dock with his feet, he strained with all his might. The sea gates opened a crack, and a thin stream of water gushed into the lock below.

Joshua forced the gates open inch by agonizing inch. Seawater cascaded into the lock and swirled up to the submarine's belly. Encouraged by his progress, Joshua leaned into the winch like Samson against the temple pillars.

The submarine shuddered and floated off her props as the sea swept in. Soon all that could be seen of her was the conning tower and her upper deck. Out of trim, she listed heavily to port, bumping the dock.

Bowed over the huge winch, Joshua gasped for breath, sweat pouring down his naked torso. The bayonet wound in his side burned with white heat, and his soaked bandage had long ago ceased to stanch the flow of blood.

He stared down at the ship hovering like an iron coffin over a black pit. His brain and his spirit rebelled against going down into what might prove to be his grave, yet honor compelled him to do just that.

Straightening to his full height, he pivoted on his heel and marched with military precision through the backdoor into the night. He lit the long fuse to the first powder keg and stepped back, his gaze traveling to the dark fort on the bluffs. At his feet the special fuse wire burned slowly and almost invisibly, impervious to wind and rain. He had twelve minutes until the explosion.

He dashed back into the warehouse. The stack of torpedoes near the last powder keg arrested his attention. By the Eternal, he'd forgotten to load them! Calculating that thirty seconds had passed since lighting the fuse, he hefted one of the seventy-five-pound torpedoes over his shoulder and climbed the brass ladder to the conning tower.

The carbide lamp was still burning, he saw when he looked through the hatch. He was just shifting his weight to ease the torpedo into the hold when the submarine rocked heavily to starboard and the hatch groaned on its hinges.

Instinctively Langdon flung himself off the ladder and landed on his back on the dock, the torpedo skidding away from him. The hatch slammed shut with unstoppable force.

Louis DeCoeur launched himself off the hull, his feet aimed at his victim's chest, the bowie knife in his hand slashing downward. Langdon twisted sideways and rolled to his feet.

"You've been screwing my lady," DeCoeur said, his lips drawn back in a snarl. "Come take what you've got coming, Yankee." He waved his knife in the air.

Langdon said nothing, his eyes on his opponent, his mind ticking off the seconds. He visualized the fuse burning nearer and nearer the first powder keg.

DeCoeur lunged, but Joshua nimbly avoided his thrust. The Frenchman smiled. "You're a fun one to toy with, Federal man, but I'll be playing a tune on your throat pipes in a minute or two."

"In the meantime," Joshua said, "perhaps I'll amuse you with a description of how I deflowered your lady's little brass gauges. She's not a virgin anymore."

DeCoeur's smile melted like candlewax. He thrust his blade at the insolent face but found his forearm seized in an iron two-handed grip. His knife skittered into the narrow space between the dock and the submarine and disappeared into the water. A second later Joshua kicked him in the breastbone with killing force. The huge man reeled under the impact but came at him again.

Before DeCoeur's hands could find his throat, Langdon spun like a top, arcing his right foot across his enemy's face to break his jaw. Surely the man wouldn't come at him again after such a terrible blow!

He had underestimated the inventor. Shaking his head like a wounded grizzly, his jaw hanging at a horrible angle, DeCoeur dropped his gaze to his opponent's bloody bandage. Adrenaline coursed through his monstrous limbs. Snarling hideously, he hurled himself at Joshua, slamming his fist into the bloody wound again and again.

Langdon staggered back and hit his head on the conning tower. Half-unconscious, he fell across the curved upper deck of the submarine, defenseless under the Frenchman's ferocious assault. If he was going to die, a part of his brain told him, at least he would have the satisfaction of taking the sub's inventor with him when the powder blew, making him a victim of the same sort of death he would have inflicted on others. The irony nearly made him laugh.

Then, suddenly, Louis DeCoeur's vast weight lifted

off him. Through pain-blurred eyes he saw the black man who had visited him in prison lift the Frenchman into the air, one muscular hand on his collar and the other hooked in his belt. Then the blacksmith whirled around on the balls of his feet, swinging DeCoeur in a tight circle. After two more turns, he flung him headfirst into the torpedoes. DeCoeur lay silent and still, lines of black blood trickling from his ears.

Joshua struggled off the hull, his skull throbbing, blood streaming from his side. His useless bandage fell away. Clamping his hand over the wound, he gasped, "Get the hell out of here, the damned place is going to blow at any second!"

"Miz Arienne'll have a fit if I leaves you here to die," Thomas said, reaching for his arm. "You got to come on with me!"

Langdon shook him off. "I can't! I've got to try to get the sub out." He moved toward the ladder but missed the bottom rung and fell heavily against the side.

"You needs help." Thomas lifted him in one powerful hand and dragged him up the ladder. He opened the hatch and pushed him inside, then crawled in after him and secured the hatch.

Joshua fell weakly onto the pilot's seat. He had two minutes to get under way, if that long. Scarcely able to see for the pain in his head, he ran his finger along the instruments until he found the air intake lever. He jammed it open. The red needle on the pressure gauge trembled for a second, then flicked over to the right.

A loud hissing noise filled the cockpit as air from the tanks mixed with the liquid aluminum. Froth surged from the exhaust port, and the submarine shook and began to drift toward the open gates.

"Guide me into the bay!" Langdon shouted hoarsely, juggling the controls. "Tell me left or right." The submarine shuddered so violently that he thought the powder had gone off.

"You done hit the damn dock, Major," Thomas said, his eyes glued to the conning port. "Go right!"

Joshua stamped on the starboard rudder pedal. The submarine responded sluggishly. Again the ship hit the planks, bouncing the men about like corks.

"You gotta do better than this or we be dead!"

"Gimme a minute to get the hang of it." Joshua wondered if he had a minute.

The sub hit the dock harder than before, ripping off a six-foot section of planks. Thomas began to pray.

Ramming the dock every few seconds, Joshua wrestled the submarine through the sea gates. Her tail was just sliding into the bay when the first keg of powder exploded, disintegrating the rear of the warehouse.

Joshua jammed a second air intake lever open. The machine shot forward like a racehorse just as the remaining bombs exploded and the dry dock erupted in a volcanic explosion. Flaming wreckage rained down on the hull.

"We swinging toward land, Major," Thomas said,

sweat pouring down his face. "Oh Lawd, they firing at us, too!"

Joshua raised his eyes to the conning port. The howitzers in the fort had opened up, belching fiery tongues and red-hot balls. He applied hard right rudder, but the submarine refused to respond, listing in the swells at a thirty-degree angle.

"Ain't this thing supposed to go underwater?"

"Yeah, but I'm not sure how to do it," Langdon said, his face taut, his hands and feet frantically moving over the controls. He yanked a handle, and gallons of water poured out of the port ballast tanks into the sea. The submarine rolled to starboard, then back again, finally settling on a ten-degree tilt to port. She began to plunge through the waves like an ungainly whale.

Joshua opened the air tanks fully, increasing the sub's speed to five knots, but the violent chemical reaction rapidly turned the hold into an oven. Already the thermometer stood at one hundred and fifteen degrees. Both men were gasping for air.

Joshua slowed the reaction. The sub's speed fell off and the temperature inside dropped two or three degrees. Then a cannonball glanced off the hull. It was like being inside a great bell. Thomas fell to his knees, moaning and holding his ears.

"They've got the range," Langdon said. Water was jetting through one of the seams in the port bulkhead. "Better keep praying—we've got to dive."

22

A monstrous bolt of lightning cleaved the water near Arienne's boat, rolled itself into a ball, and skipped like a stone to shore where it blasted a pine tree to kindling.

Frightened half out of her wits, Arienne immediately turned shoreward. She intended to dump the unconscious Confederates just as Joshua had ordered, but from there his plan would undergo a marked divergence. She was going to sail back to the navy yard.

The only problem was that the men were too heavy for her to lift out of the boat. She could think of only one solution. The snag was that it could get them all killed.

Mentally crossing her fingers for luck, she reached the boat across the wind and, grabbing the halyard, hiked over the leeward side. She hit the water hard. The mast just missed her head as the boat rolled over. Struggling to her feet in knee-deep water, she

slogged over to grab the Confederates tumbling in
the breakers.

Five minutes later she had them in a peacefully
slumbering row on the beach, the waves lapping their
ankles. In another five minutes she had righted the
boat and was sailing back the way she had come.

He's going to try to steal the sub, she thought
suddenly. He never intended to blow it up—he just
wanted me out of the way!

She hardened the sheets and beat to windward,
sailing as fast as she knew how. Lightning cracked
and rolled, the wind screamed, the mast groaned
under the fearful stress, but for Arienne nothing
mattered but getting to Joshua before it was too late.
Even so, her heart told her she would never see him
in this life again.

She was rounding the point when the dry dock
exploded. The roof of the warehouse was torn off and
hurled into the air like a flaming sheet of parchment.
Debris rained down for hundreds of yards. There
were other explosions, then a wall of intense heat
rolled across the bay and struck the sailboat, driving it
back.

Arienne was thrown into the bottom of the boat.
Beam on to the waves, with the sail luffing and the tiller
swinging back and forth, the boat wallowed helplessly.
Water poured over the port gunwale like Niagara.

"No!" She dragged herself up to stare in horror at
the flaming devastation. Blood streamed into her eyes
from a jagged cut in her scalp, but she could think of
nothing but Joshua.

"I'm coming!" She grabbed the tiller and turned

the boat into the wind. Mechanically she trimmed sail and set a course for the inferno, irrationally believing she would find him there.

She probably would have sailed straight to her death had she not chanced to look to windward at that moment. Out of a sea of molten gold, a long shape slid, its iron skin the burnished color of old copper. The submarine was seventy-five yards away, heading out to sea.

Wild joy filled her. Screaming her husband's name, she stood up in the boat and waved her arms in triumph. He was a magician, a wizard. Surely God smiled on him.

But in Arienne's moment of jubilation Fort Barrancas opened fire on the escaping vessel. Geysers reared twenty feet high around her flanks, cannonballs pursuing her like wolves after a deer.

"No!" Arienne screamed. "I won't let you kill him!" She dropped the sail and flung herself to her knees, yanking a Sharps rifle out of a compartment. She slammed a ball into the breech and fired at the fort. Again and again she loaded and shot, but the cannon fire continued unabated.

She looked around. The submarine was wallowing in the waves, its nose angled downward. He was going to submerge her! Slowly the iron silhouette began to disappear.

Arienne stood in the rocking boat, the rifle dangling forgotten from her hand, her eyes shining sapphires in a golden face. "He's going to make it," she whispered like an incantation. "Please God, let him make it."

Out of the corner of her eye she saw a flash from

the Spanish water battery. A fraction of a second later the submarine was blasted out of the water, split in half, and plunged into the deep.

Arienne's mouth opened to scream, but no sound came out, because the next cannon salvo found the sailboat and burst it timber from nail. She fell into a black void.

The explosion in the navy yard knocked Sir James Lloyd out of bed. He knew immediately that the dry dock had exploded. He also knew with sudden certainty that Arienne was down there.

Struggling into his dressing gown, he joined the soldiers stampeding for the yard. He ran as fast as his skinny legs could carry him, afraid that if he fell, the crowd would crush him to death. He could hear Bragg's angry bellow from the rear, and then the general swept by on a big white horse.

Someone struck James on the shoulder. He went down hard. Instantly he scrambled to his hands and knees and fought his way into the woods. Free of the crush, he climbed to his feet and ran through the trees, a curious red glow illuminating the way.

He burst out of the woods on an empty stretch of beach some way from the fort. The dock was on fire, turning the water to brass. A dark shape tumbled helplessly in the combers.

Sir James immediately rushed into the water, knowing without question that the figure he'd seen was Arienne. Over the heavy swells he paddled, his head turning right and left, his heart beating steadily and painlessly. Never had he felt so strong.

And there she was, facedown in the ruddy water, her black hair streaming around. Seizing her head, the old man turned her over. The blood trickling from her scalp assured him she still lived.

"Wake up, Arienne!" He began to kick desperately for shore. His strength was leaving him. Too soon! Too soon!

"Joshua?"

"It's your papa, darling." He gasped for breath. "Can you swim?"

"Something's . . . holding my legs." She closed her eyes.

"Oh God! Help us!"

A wave closed over their heads, tumbling them about like rag dolls, yet Sir James clung to his daughter and kicked with all the strength remaining in him. Through his raging desperation he remembered the words of Jonah. *The depth closed me round about, the weeds were wrapped about my head. I went down to the bottoms of the mountains; the earth with her bars was about me forever: yet thou hast brought up my life from corruption, O Lord my God. . . .*

The words became his earnest prayer, and into his trembling muscles came a strength beyond any he had ever known, propelling him up through the darkness to the shore. There he laid his daughter upon the white sand and fell down, spent.

For a long time Arienne lay there senseless, icy rain stabbing her face. There were no dreams, no memories, nothing but a black chill holding her down.

It was the cold that finally brought her back. Raising

herself to one elbow, choking on the smoke hanging over the beach, she stared at the bay in confusion. Then she remembered Joshua.

The sea was black and gold—and empty. The submarine was gone, sucked into the abyss. With horrifying clarity her mind replayed the final scenes, the roar of cannons, the rending screech of metal as the sub was torn apart and its precious human cargo destroyed.

No! He couldn't be dead, not Joshua. Not the man who had held her in his arms and loved her so well just a few short hours ago. He was alive, of course he was alive! She'd find him and prove it.

She climbed to her feet and tried to walk, but her knees were too weak to obey her, and she fell sprawling on the sand. Dry-eyed and determined, she began to drag herself toward the water. Then she caught sight of her father.

He was lying on his back at the water's edge, staring at the stormy sky, his hair plastered to his waxen face. One frail, blue-veined hand lay upon his chest. His legs danced mannequinlike each time a wave rushed upon the shore.

"Papa!" Arienne crawled to him.

He couldn't be dead. She wouldn't let him be dead. If she admitted that he was dead, then she would have to admit that Joshua was, too. She put out a tentative hand and then drew back. As long as she didn't touch him, he would still be alive. Joshua would be alive, too.

For a long time she huddled by her father while the waves bathed her feet, and her shell-shocked mind cradled its fragile illusion. Blood dripped onto her hands from the laceration on her scalp, but she didn't notice.

In a little while her father would get up, and then she would tell him about Joshua and how much she loved him. And he would be happy and proud that she was married. Of course he would. She would explain it all very carefully, and he would understand.

Get up, Papa. Wake up. I want to tell you something.

She was still sitting by her dead father when General Bragg found her at daybreak. She gazed up at him wordlessly, with no trace of recognition on her lovely face.

"Are you telling me that the girl will never be right in her mind again, doctor?"

The post surgeon got up from the long table in the officers' mess to look at the glowering General Bragg and then back down the room at the girl sitting quietly at the grand piano, staring at the keys. He put a leatherbound notebook into his black bag and closed it. "That's exactly what I'm saying, sir. I believe the strain of seeing her father die was too much for her."

General Bragg had his own theories. That traitorous bastard, Cyrus Enright, had abducted her to Fort Pickens, probably to extract information on the project. No doubt he had used the intelligence to destroy the dry dock and, ultimately, the submarine. Why he had forced her to come to the navy yard with him last night would forever remain a mystery, since, if Bragg's theory was correct, he'd gone to the bottom of Pensacola Bay in the sub. And if the surgeon was right, Miss Lloyd would never recover sufficiently from the shock to tell the story.

Bragg paced slowly down the room to Arienne. He squatted beside the piano stool and looked into her face. She looked back at him with the guilelessness of a very young child, though the shadowy pain in her eyes robbed her of innocence.

"Do you want to go home, Miss Lloyd?"

Her face might have been carved of marble. She said nothing.

Bragg sighed and addressed the surgeon. "We found her father's will among his effects—it was dated the morning after he shot his brother. It said that in the event of his death, Miss Lloyd would inherit the family's estate, the controlling interest in her uncle's London trust company, houses in town, and something on the order of half a million pounds sterling. She is quite a wealthy young woman."

The surgeon's fingers left his black bag to form a steeple under his chin. Gazing at Arienne, he said, "It's unlikely she'll ever be well enough to know she's an heiress, much less spend the fortune. Still, you'd best send her back. Her solicitor will appoint her a guardian. English law is quite clear on that point, I've been told."

Bragg sighed. "You're right, of course. What a damned miserable mess this business has turned out to be! May Enright rot in hell!"

The doctor picked up his bag and started for the door. He paused with his hand on the china knob.

"You didn't find the major's body, did you?"

"Ha! The ironclad exploded all over the bay. He's nothing but fish food, the traitor!"

"Most likely." He looked at Arienne. She hadn't stirred. "I wouldn't delay sending her home, sir. The post is no place for a woman in her condition."

"I know, I know. I'll line up a coach to take her to Mobile tomorrow. They can put her on a blockade runner there."

"Fine, then. I'll check on her later this afternoon." He went out and closed the door behind him.

Squatting in front of Arienne again, the soldier looked for the last time into the saddest pair of eyes he'd ever seen. For the rest of his life, a sun-washed sapphire sky would conjure memories almost too painful to bear.

23

During the voyage across the Atlantic, Arienne spoke scarcely a word but spent long hours on deck, gazing into the cold gray water. Sometimes her gaze fell upon the ring of white gold on her finger, and then her eyes would grow as cloudy as the early-November skies.

Grieving hurt too much. It was far easier for her to lock her memory into a quiet corner of her mind, to push aside all emotions, all thought. She could not speak to anyone of the lonely game she played. To do so would have allowed memories to come flooding back. Still, with every mile of ocean crossed, the stirrings of her soul were more difficult to shut out, the need for self-deception more desperate.

She suffered terrible anguish when the voyage ended and she was driven in an open carriage through the English countryside to Lloyd on the

Downs. There was no place for memory to hide in the familiar surroundings of the old house.

She saw again her dear papa seated in his favorite chair, and a young version of Wendell Stuart stared down at her from a portrait on the drawing-room wall. She could no longer deny that her fragmented dreams had been reality—that she had indeed gone to the Southern United States and there fallen in love with a steely-eyed Union officer, only to lose him and then lose her papa immediately afterward. . . .

But even when memory had reasserted itself, she could not cry. She was too empty for tears. Her body, thin from much fasting, seemed to belong to another woman. She seemed to be all eyes looking out of a soul that would not heal. How she wished she could have remained in the twilight!

The servants hoped that time would lessen their mistress's grief, but as the weeks passed she grew even more withdrawn. A procession of well-to-do neighbors and former business associates of Wendell Stuart and her father assured her that an heiress as rich as she ought to be enormously happy. That wealth meant nothing to her without a loved one with whom to share it seemed to them a ridiculously romantic notion. After a while they stopped paying social calls. Arienne scarcely noticed, or cared.

Even her old, familiar passions seemed to have died. She did not visit the stables or pick up a paint-brush. She spent most days sitting in the library, struggling against the haunting memories of the men she had loved. She grew ever thinner, her insides paining her so badly that it became nearly impossible to keep food down. Fearing for Arienne's life, her personal maid summoned the doctor. Arienne sent him away.

And then one morning she awakened to cerulean-blue skies and pale sunshine. Snow had fallen during the night, mantling the earth with a thick white coverlet. Drawn by the pristine beauty of the scene, she shuffled barefoot across the cold floor to the window.

Upon the lawn, winter-shorn trees thrust darkly through the snow, spreading their branches to the sun. Swaying on a cold wind, they seemed devoid of life, incapable of resurrecting themselves to green vitality, as though their icy solitude had stripped away all promise of strength.

And yet as she studied the trees she became aware that the naked boughs were reaching heavenward, basking in the golden rays of the sun, which would eventually bring them to leaf.

"Could you renew your beauty year after year without the dark prison of winter?" Arienne whispered to the trees, her husky voice almost a stranger to her ears. After a moment the answer stole quietly into her mind: there is no joy without sorrow.

A pang went through her heart. Resting her forehead against the frosty windowpane, she squeezed her eyes shut. She summoned Joshua's image, and immediately the terrible, familiar yearning pierced her soul. She had been robbed of that which mattered most to her in life. How could joy follow such pain?

As she contemplated the question the weight of a mountain seemed to descend upon her shoulders. All at once she began to cry, her body racked by the sobs she had withheld for so long. Joshua's image faded from her mind, replaced by memories of her childish joys and sorrows, the happy times she had known before her mother's death. She felt again her father's strong arms, and then, slowly, their diminishing strength.

Arienne nearly writhed in agony, great mountains of grief crashing down upon her. She saw Joshua and relived each moment with him. She almost could feel his breath on her cheek, the light caress of his fingertips across her naked flesh, the heat and splendor of him as he laid her down in the soft sand and claimed her. And then in her mind she watched him die.

She screamed her anguish, beat her fists on the floor, tore her hair like a woman possessed. How could joy displace such sorrow? The notion was foolish, impossible.

After many hours the terrible weight began to lift, until she was able to sit up, to look out again upon the trees bending in the wind. Where before there had been no life in the branches, she now saw doves.

As she watched them a calmness stole over her senses—not the numbing paralysis she had endured over the last months, but a tranquillity that brought with it the will to live.

Venting her grief had unlocked her spirit from its shackles. There was a grievous ache in her heart still, yet deep down there was growing a quiet conviction that having passed out of the shadow, she need never go down into it again.

Like one awakened from a trance, Arienne rose to her feet and plunged her hands into the icy water in the washbasin. She washed herself from head to toe, ate a biscuit from the tray at her bedside, then donned a gown of sapphire taffeta and a sable cape. She pulled on a pair of black eelskin shoes and buttoned them haphazardly, thrust her hands into a wolfskin muff, and walked shakily down the long staircase to the foyer. There was no one around, so she opened the heavy door and went outside.

The sun seemed dazzling after her long confinement in the house, and her muscles were weak and shaky. The snow stretched away toward the woods in a smooth unbroken blanket, offering her a challenge. She set off for the trees.

The snow squeaked and crunched beneath her feet as she followed the familiar but invisible path into the woods. She had no specific destination in mind, just a desire to see her lands through unclouded eyes. She burrowed her hands into her muff and gently caressed her wedding ring, remembering the moment when Joshua had placed it upon her finger. Blinking away tears, she pushed through a snowdrift and kept walking, her breath freezing on her fur collar.

Finally she reached the Thames. Tired from the

unaccustomed exertion in her weakened state, she sank down on her knees to watch the dark, icy water slide by. Boats moved sluggishly in the current, their sails crackling in the cold air. The sight aroused memories of Joshua's face framed by canvas, his muscular arms hauling in the sheets. She would never again see a boat without remembering him.

She closed her eyes and choked back a sob. Coming to the river had been a mistake. It was too much, too soon. She had all her life to remember Joshua, to relive their brief moments together. She had done enough weeping for one day. Drawing a deep breath, she stood and turned her back on the river.

The wind had picked up, whipping snow from the hemlock boughs into her path. Slitting her lids against the icy darts, she drew her cape more tightly around her.

She had gone no more than a few steps when her knees buckled, and she staggered and fell into a snowbank. She closed her eyes and let it hold her in its cold white arms, listening to sparrows chirruping in the trees.

Then she heard the crunch of a boot in the snow. Her eyes snapped open.

Joshua Langdon was standing between two snow-bowed hemlocks, his blue uniform tunic and shirt open, his mighty chest rising and falling as if he had been running very fast. Great clouds of steam wreathed his head and frosted his hair. Tears sparkled in his eyes, and he was smiling at her.

"I'm dreaming again," Arienne said in a husky voice filled with pain. "You're not there."

"Arienne," he said very quietly, "I'm alive and I intend to prove it." He stepped forward and swept her out of the snowbank into his arms, crushing her against his chest. Before she could speak, his mouth swooped down on hers in a kiss of desperate joy. "Thank God I've found you!" he said, and kissed her again.

Arienne nearly fainted. Tears poured down her cheeks. She clutched at his uniform desperately, afraid he would disappear, leaving her holding nothing but thin air. "The submarine—I saw it go down!"

"It went down, all right, but without Thomas and me," Joshua said. He continued to hold her tightly. "We were thrown into the bay when she broke apart."

"Thomas? He was with you?"

"Yes. He's back in New Orleans now with his wife, and a fat reward from Mr. Lincoln for his help."

Tears trickled down Arienne's thin cheeks. "I thought you were dead, Joshua. I could scarcely go on living."

"And I nearly went mad trying to find you. Sometime I'll have to tell you about it, but for now it will suffice to say that I'll never, never leave you again, my beautiful sea witch."

They kissed again and again. Snow showered down from the branches overhead, crowning them with silvery white tiaras.

The lost one had returned. Arienne smiled at him,

a shining sapphire promise of forever in her eyes, as they walked the shadowy path into the bright light of a winter's morning.

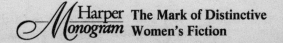

COMING NEXT MONTH

RAIN LILY by Candace Camp

Maggie Whitcomb's life changed when her shell-shocked husband returned from the Civil War. She nursed him back to physical health, but his mind was shattered. Maggie's marriage vows were forever, but then she met Reid Prescott, a drifter who took refuge on her farm and captured her heart. A heartwarming story of impossible love from bestselling author Candace Camp.

CASTLES IN THE AIR by Christina Dodd

The long-awaited, powerful sequel to the award-winning *Candle in the Window*. Lady Juliana of Moncestus swore that she would never again be forced under a man's power. So when the king promised her in marriage to Raymond of Avrache, Juliana was determined to resist. But had she met her match?

RAVEN IN AMBER by Patricia Simpson

A haunting contemporary love story by the author of *Whisper of Midnight*. Camille Avery arrives at the Nakalt Indian Reservation to visit a friend, only to find her missing. With the aid of handsome Kit Makinna, Camille becomes immersed in Nakalt life and discovers the shocking secret behind her friend's disappearance.

RETURNING by Susan Bowden

A provocative story of love and lies. From the Bohemian '60s to the staid '90s, *Returning* is an emotional roller-coaster ride of a story about a woman whose past comes back to haunt her when she must confront the daughter she gave up for adoption.

JOURNEY HOME by Susan Kay Law

Winner of the 1992 Golden Heart Award. Feisty Jessamyn Johnston was the only woman on the 1853 California wagon train who didn't respond to the charms of Tony Winchester. But as they battled the dangers of their journey, they learned how to trust each other and how to love.

KENTUCKY THUNDER by Clara Wimberly

Amidst the tumult of the Civil War and the rigid confines of a Shaker village, a Southern belle fought her own battle against a dashing Yankee—and against herself as she fell in love with him.

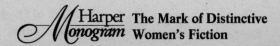 **Harper Monogram** **The Mark of Distinctive Women's Fiction**

SEVEN IRRESISTIBLE HISTORICAL ROMANCES BY BESTSELLING AUTHOR

CANDACE CAMP

HEIRLOOM

Juliet Drake, a golden-haired beauty who yearned for a true home, went to the Morgan farm to help Amos Morgan care for his ailing sister. There she found the home she sought, but still she wanted more—the ruggedly handsome Amos.

BITTERLEAF

Purchased on the auction block, betrayed British nobleman, Jeremy Devlin, vowed to seduce his new owner, Meredith Whitney, the beautiful mistress of the Bitterleaf plantation. But his scheme of revenge ignited a passion that threatened to consume them both.

ANALISE

Analise Caldwell was the reigning belle of New Orleans. Disguised as a Confederate soldier, Union major Mark Schaeffer captured the Rebel beauty's heart as part of his mission. Stunned by his deception, Analise swore never to yield to the caresses of this Yankee spy...until he delivered an ultimatum.

ROSEWOOD

Millicent Hayes had lived all her life amid the lush woodland of Emmetsville, Texas. Bound by her duty to her crippled brother, the dark-haired innocent had never known desire...until a handsome stranger moved in next door.

BONDS OF LOVE

Katherine Devereaux was a willful, defiant beauty who had yet to meet her match in any man—until the winds of war swept the Union innocent into the arms of Confederate Captain Matthew Hampton.

LIGHT AND SHADOW

The day nobleman Jason Somerville broke into her rooms and swept her away to his ancestral estate, Carolyn Mabry began living a dangerous charade. Posing as her twin sister, Jason's wife, Carolyn thought she was helping her gentle twin. Instead she found herself drawn to the man she had so seductively deceived.

CRYSTAL HEART

A seductive beauty, Lady Lettice Kenton swore never to give her heart to any man—until she met the rugged American rebel Charles Murdock. Together on a ship bound for America, they shared a perfect passion, but danger awaited them on the shores of Boston Harbor.